DEADLY
DECEIT

ALEXA WHITEWOLF

Deadly Deceit
A *Lost Royals of Transylvania* novel

by Alexa Whitewolf
Copyright ©2021 Alexa Whitewolf

Cover design by Y. Nikolova at **Ammonia Book Covers**
Editing and formatting by Luna Imprints Author Services

ISBN: 978-1-989384-19-0

This is a work of fiction.

10 9 8 7 6 5 4 3 2

ROGUES EXTENDED UNIVERSE—READING ORDER

Moonlight Rogues
Flaming Rogues
Immortal Rogues
Lost Royals of Transylvania
Vârcolac Legacy (coming 2022)

ACKNOWLEDGEMENTS

Well, here we are. Book 3 in what's going to be a longer series than I'd intended, with much more fun to follow! And boy, this one was hard to write. The next one will be harder, but it sure didn't help that 2021 was the year of all kinds of trials in both my personal and professional life.

I want to give a huge, huge thanks as always to my family for their support – to my husband for all his patience (and unwilling inspiration!), to my mom for feeding me when I forget to feed myself and finding me never-ending Netflix series to keep my brain from fizzing out. Thanks to both my mom and my uncle for their help with the Dacian research, and to my doggos for reminding me I need to see the sun (or moon!) every now and again.

This book took nearly six months to finish, my longest to date. And the last months were HARD. I wouldn't have gotten through any of them, let alone finished, without Siobhan – you seriously deserve all the thanks in the world, my friend!

Huge thanks also to the editing (Annemarie and Milica, thanks!) and formatting team (Eldon, your work is always awesome!!!) at LIAS. This book would lack the polishing it has without you guys.

Another fantastic cover done by Y. Nikolova at Ammonia Book Covers – there's a reason I keep going back!! Your work is always out-of-the-ballpark-amazing.

And last but not least, my readers, I'm sorry this took so long to land in your hands. I'm sorry for pushing the release date a few times, but I thank you so much for sticking by me! Hope you enjoy.

Happy readings,

Alexa

GLOSSARY

Vampir/vampiri—vampire/vampires

Inima mea—my heart (an endearment among lovers)

Da / nu—yes/no

Nu iară—not again

Buni—short for bunică which means grandma (endearment)

Sigur—of course

Idiotule—idiot

Frate—brother

Sorella/fratello—not exactly Romanian, but an endearment used by Silviana and her brother; it's Italian and means sister/brother.

Nu, nimic—no, nothing

Ce avem aici—what do we have here

Parcul Tineretului—Youth Park

Da, sigur—yes, of course

Ștefan/Brașov—phonetically, the ș is said as sh

Târgoviște—the princely court for the voivode of Wallachia

Scuze—Sorry

Nu, e bine—no, it's fine

Bine—fine

Iubito—also an endearment; darling

Țuică—a fantastic Romanian vodka-like drink :D

Bine ati venit la Castelul Bran—welcome to Bran Castle (aka the castle everyone knows as Dracula's Castle)

Creatures

Vârcolac/ Vârcolaci—werewolf/werewolves; in this book, it refers to Dominic's wolves.

Pricolic/pricolici—a smaller type of wolf, possessed by dark magic, at the mercy of Dacians.

Voivode—an old title given to the lord of a region; similar to king.

Cavaleri Serafim—Serafim Knights; in this universe, they're knights who have become vengeful against supernaturals.

A note on dates

You'll notice, for a certain journal, that the dates were written in Day/Month/Year format (e.g., 1 July 1456), contrary to what's usually used in North America. This is because back home, in Romania, the dates are written this way and I was trying to stay true to it. It's not a typo :D

To Siobhan
You know why.

Chapter 1

Vlad

The smell—the taste—of blood brings me back. The fog my mind was buried in lifts, as easily as the sun rises. A copper tinge fills the air, metallic. It's a taste I stay away from. A taste I've tried to ration for myself...and failed.

At least, judging by the dead human at my feet.

Nu, nu iară. Not again!

My feet shuffle backward, eyes widening in horror. Shaky hands run over my face, come back wet—with blood. The light from lampposts is faint here, practically nonexistent as with most back alleys, but the smell of the dead body at my feet makes it impossible to ignore it. Or is the stink of garbage nearby?

How? How did this happen again?

I stare at him for what feels like an eternity. Jogging pants, hoodie, a backpack lying a few feet away, water bottle at his feet. He must've been coming back from some fitness establishment—a gym?—when I grabbed him.

"Fuck."

I reach into my jeans pocket, feeling for my cellphone, my thumb already seeking the keypad to dial for help...

And then I stop. What would I tell my siblings? *Hey guys, about that thing that used to land me into trouble non-stop? The itty bitty darkness-fueled bloodlust Father warned me to learn to control? Yeah, about that... I've fallen off the wagon.*

Sure. That would go over so damn well. Especially with Nicolae and Mirabela, the heads of the family. Alexandru and Elizabeta might understand—they have *no* control when it comes to humans. But then again, they also don't pretend like they do. Unlike me. For centuries, all I've done is preach abstinence from killing humans.

I drop my phone back in my pocket, and run a hand through my hair again.

And then my ears register something so faint, I feel like I'm hallucinating. But...No. It's definitely there. A heartbeat!

For a moment, all I can do is stare. Then I snap to and rush to the human, kneeling next to him, checking for a sign of life. A relieved breath escapes me. There's a pulse; barely, but there's one!

I pick him up like a baby. He must easily weigh two hundred pounds, but in my arms? He's a lightweight. I use the shadows, calling them forth to hide me. A little trick Father taught us long ago. *Darkness begets darkness.* And we, well, we're as dark as they come.

Centuries ago, we were able to master a lot more than parlor tricks. But with Father's death came...many letdowns, not the least of which were our dwindling powers.

And now this damned curse. I shove the thought away, intent on the task at hand.

Soon, what used to be single shadows from lamp posts extend through the alleyway. They don't exactly coat me, but they change the fabric of air itself, obscuring me to any human eyes. After all, if humans were to find out vampiri exist, well, it wouldn't end well. Especially since we're the last heirs of someone who, in parts of this country, is hailed a hero, and in others, a complete tyrant.

Once my presence is fully camouflaged, I dart out into the street, knowing no traffic cameras will catch sight of me. And it's just as well. Quick glances around, while I run fast as lightning, show me glimpses of the city I've landed in—Bucureşti, the capital.

At least now I know where to take him.

It's not my first time in our infamous hub of modernity, but it is my first time in a few decades... What the hell could've brought me here, nearly 500km away from home?

With each passing second, my mind whirls. Stumbling in a city far away from home is one thing. But to actually feed, and not remember it? How did this happen?

I know how, though. I was careful. *Too* careful.

Father's voice comes to mind. *Whatever your weakness, learn to keep it in control. Always. Otherwise, others will use it against you.*

I've done everything in my power to keep myself calm. Cool. Collected. To not give in to my weakness. As a human, I'd had no control over my younger self. As a newborn vampir centuries ago, I'd been worse. Yet, with Father's careful teachings and patience from my new siblings, I learned. And I was well...at least until recently.

This latest development tells me I'm nowhere as in control as I'd thought. And given everything else that's going on right now, I can't afford slip ups. *None of us can.*

The Royal Hospital comes in sight. I automatically chose it for its proximity to Parcul Tineretului—the Youth Park—where I can easily disappear and get lost.

Mirrored windows catch my eye, reflecting my haggard look. Disheveled dark hair, intent blue eyes, stubble around my jawline. One would think I've walked out of a club after a night of drinking.

The man in my arms is breathing still, but barely. The pulse I'd felt is even weaker. If there's a chance to save him, this is it.

I quickly assess the cameras at the hospital's entrance and drop him on the side, out of sight of their angles. Then I rush out, and find someone in the parking lot. The nurse scrubs indicate it's an employee—hopefully the long hours she works will make her quickly forget me.

"There's a man, hurt, by the entrance. Go find help."

Unlike what I'd expected, she doesn't move immediately. Instead, she stares at me, glances over my shoulder, hesitating. I groan internally, but already my focus has changed. My voice lowers as I set my intention toward her next actions.

"Look at me."

She does as I bid, and her eyes widen—then glaze over. Glamour is a powerful tool, when used properly. Unlike Alex and Liza, I prefer it as a last resort... And this is one.

My intent vibrates in the air between us, affecting her own brain waves ever so softly. "There is a man. Hurt. Go find help and make sure he lives. And...you've never seen me. You'll forget my face the moment you walk away."

She blinks, then passes by me as if I'm not even there. Never to remember me again.

I allow myself a moment, a single second, to breathe. To regain some energy. The feed rejuvenated me, but using the shadows, and the glamour, leaves me feeling weaker than usual. I think back to Violeta, my other sister, and the recent development that's claimed her health. *Could I be next?*

And then I shove that thought aside as well, and I'm running away. Through Parcul Tineretului, allowing myself to get lost in there for a bit. Some teenagers are gathered around a garbage bin, playing with a lighter. The faint cloud and unmistakable smell of pot reaches my nostrils—Violeta used to love that shit. Until...she didn't.

I shake my head, and allow the park to swallow me whole, disappearing in the darkness. Then I run, and run, and run...

Away from the streets of our capital, and back home.

"Where were you?"

I make a show of closing the thick oak door behind me, if only to hide the trembling of my hands. The hour it took me to get back home, when most humans would've taken days of walking—or at least six hours of driving—exhausted me. As did using magic, even if it was only glimmers of it. We aren't all-powerful, us vampiri. My siblings, either. Though we sure try to act like it.

I turn to face my sister. Elizabeta's in her nightgown. Long, auburn hair cascades down her shoulders. Blue eyes meet mine with a faint trace of suspicion, and something else I can't quite grasp.

Judging by her attire, I must've either woken her up, or she was up waiting for me. Neither are good options.

"Out for...air."

"Air?" She snorts. "I can smell the blood on you. Don't know why you bother hiding it."

She walks away to the living room, and I get the sense she wants me to follow. So I do.

Soon as I'm there, she continues, "Only Violeta cares enough about them not to use them as food. As for me, I prefer them fresh."

The faint blaze from a dying fire illuminates her features, carved in stone. When she turns to me, the scar on her left cheek catches the light, stark against the whiteness of her skin.

I grab the wine glass she passes me and taste it. Red wine, a specialty around this region. I lift it to her in a silent *salut* and drink some. It's a show. Enough to give me a moment to think, to catch my breath, to figure out what to say. Something that'll take the attention away from my recent feeding.

"Violeta isn't wrong."

"Sure." Liza chugs more of her drink. "Then again, she's now off being actually *happy*, unlike the rest of us poor suckers." She swirls the drink, never meeting my gaze. "What do you make of it all?"

Ah.

Now I get it.

Relief seeps out of me and I try not to show it. She's not trying to interrogate me. Rather, she knows that out of the rest of our siblings, I'm the one most likely to sit down and talk it out with her. *It* being the curse standing over our heads. A curse that, like it or not, will dictate the rest of our existence—and how short it'll be—if we're not careful.

"Liza, if you mean the curse—"

"Of course I mean the curse!" she snaps.

I throw her a look. Liza's volatile and always on the brink of some snapping or another. The last thing I want right now is to get pulled into her drama, when I've got other things to think of. Many, many things.

Elizabeta gives me a nod to continue and buries herself in a couch to listen. I sigh and follow, sitting across from her.

"I think it makes sense," I finally say.

"Why? What makes you think the wolves wouldn't just come up with this crap?"

I roll my eyes. Her and Alex haven't stopped harping on about the potential danger of the vârcolaci that entered our territory, when the real threat is the vampiri clans gunning for our blood. And the hunters who've come out of the woodwork, gunning for our heads again.

"Because Violeta confirmed it."

"She gets her knowledge from the wolves, though."

I lean back in the chair. "What motive would they have to lie, hmm?" I know it's Alex's own suspicions she's voicing, and I'm not in the mood for it. They're thick as thieves, those two, and most days they amuse me. Tonight...I just want the quiet of my bedroom, and sleep to forget.

Liza slams her glass on the table. Somehow, it doesn't break. "They want the same as everyone else. To hurt us."

"It doesn't fit. Knowing about the curse is, on the contrary, helping us out because we can actually fight it. Save Violeta. And I'm sure Father's journal is equally filled with information that vouches for the same things."

"Da, sigur, if Nico would fucking let us have a look."

I narrow my eyes. "He has his reasons. Tassa's the only one who can match whatever's in there with potential remedies."

Liza falls silent. I know she's struggling with us having a human in our midst, especially one like Tassa. My sister might be all volatile and bigmouthed, but underneath it, she's as vulnerable and insecure as the rest of us. She just learned to hide it better.

I tap my fingers on the leather of the armchair. "I think the best thing we can do, either of us, is to take this curse seriously and keep an open mind. If it'll save Violeta, and the rest of us, it's worth it, no?"

She stares into the fire, grimacing. I know what she's thinking, even if she doesn't voice it. What kind of chance do we have against a god, when we're already being hunted and cornered by our own kin *and* the hunters who'd sooner eradicate us? And the sad thing is, I have no answer to give her.

"I guess..."

I take her grumbling as my cue to leave and get up.

Liza looks up, surprised. "Going to sleep already?"

"I—yeah. Got some thinking to do."

She nods and I leave, relief spreading through me. Until I'm back in my room, faced only by the quiet of it, and remembering the taste of the blood on my lips. And how it wasn't revulsion I'd first been met with, but satisfaction.

You've fought me long enough. Now it's time to let me feed.

A shudder runs through me. The voice is me—the other me. The bad me. And I know that no matter what happens next, I can't let him come to the surface. Ever. If I do, our entire existence could be put into jeopardy once more.

Silviana

Breathe in. And out. In…and out.

I open my eyes, letting the quietude envelop me. The forest helps. Here, hidden in the woods, away from my duties, from my people, I can think. Analyze. Remember what it's like to have an individuality, and not just exist for the purpose of serving others.

A low sigh escapes me. My eyes track a squirrel as it forages in the leaves, and then scurries up a tree. A simple life. Freedom.

If only I had that.

The thought is unfair, but I can't keep it at bay. Not anymore. I've been dedicated enough to the cause, but nothing I do is ever enough. And now, when I'd finally given up, determined that my brother—my twin—Ștefan is the only one worthy of their interest, they've come and given me a mission.

It'll be simple, they said. *Infiltration and extraction only.*

Problem is, it's not a regular human household I'm going into. Against them, my magic is potent, easy to resort to. Most times, I don't even have to. Between the self-defense I was taught and my looks, people are quick to underestimate me. Until they learn, the hard way.

But this time, I'm going against vampiri. Not just any, but the six most feared, for the skills their maker imparted on them—the House of Dracul.

For centuries, they were thought lost to time. Most people who were aware of their existence assumed they'd lost the fight over their territory, and packed up and left. Only my people kept watching, knowing that their return would coincide with more victims. And now…it turns out they were right.

I can close my eyes and see the newspaper articles they'd shown me. They didn't have to draw me a map...vampir was written all over the killings. And the latest message the Draculs sent, after savagely killing off the leader of one of the local vampir clans, the Ardeleans? It was loud and clear.

I care nothing for their politics and games. But their new reentry into local politics is a concern, one my people are eager to eliminate. And it seems they've found the perfect weakness.

Another sigh escapes me. This time, I get to my feet. From my standpoint, I can see my city. Brașov, in all its gorgeousness. Ringed by the Carpathian Mountains, surrounded by medieval Saxon walls and bastions and with Gothic-style churches and buildings, it's everything I've ever called home. At least, since my *real* home was brutally eradicated.

And now, I'm meant to leave it behind.

I glance at my hand, at the cut in my palm that's healing. The last time I'd practiced magic, it took more blood than usual. Such is the curse of my people. A curse that, supposedly, the House of Dracul has the key to, written in a journal that's long since been thought lost.

"Well, no point delaying it any further," I mutter and start walking back to town. "It's showtime."

Nearly four hours later, I've changed into jeans and a lavender off-the-shoulders top. And instead of getting ready to order food in and watch some Netflix in my cushy apartment—provided for by the Grand Master himself—I'm exiting a dark SUV and taking in the unfamiliar woods opening up in front of me.

"You understand the stakes, I hope?"

I look at the man exiting from the driver's side. His dark suit, crisp and shiny, has no place in these woods. I could've driven myself here, but they're not likely to let me go without some warning shots. After all, I'm only a woman to them.

I keep my expression as cool as I can make it. "Da, I do. You have nothing to fear."

Now that I'm here, excitement and adrenaline fill me, alongside nervousness. This is my first solo mission, my chance to prove I'm more than just a woman in their midst. A chance to gain more freedom, and not be forever relegated to the monotonous tasks of creating potions and elixirs while spending 99.9% of my days in my apartment or around downtown Brașov, selling fake card readings to tourists.

It's time. A chance to prove their investment in us was worth it. That I've learned, and I'm more than capable of taking on more.

"We take a big risk trusting a woman to carry this out for us."

A bitter laugh escapes me at his surly words. "You have no other choice. I'm the perfect bait, the one he won't see coming."

He nods, his features twisted as if he's sucking on an extremely sour lemon. "Very well. If things get out of control, you know how to call upon us."

He passes me a small brown sachet. When I tug on the little string keeping it closed, a talisman the size of a raspberry falls out. On one side, it has an image of a wolf. On the other, it's blank.

I look up at the man. "What is this? Can't I get a regular cellphone?"

"No, you cannot. If you get caught, they'll be able to trace it back to us. This is old magic. Simply burn it when you have the journal, and the Grand Master will feel it. It's spelled, linked directly to him."

"Okay... And how long will it take from when I burn it, for me to get picked up?"

"A few hours. Find somewhere to lie low, and we'll find you."

I could point out a few flaws in their plan, but whatever. The important thing is I'm being given a chance.

I touch the back pocket of my jeans, sensing the small athame blade hidden there. It might sound like an odd weapon, but my people believe in blessed—and cursed—artefacts for their hidden powers. And I'll take any additional help when it comes to magic.

I add the talisman to the small backpack on my back, then readjust the straps on my shoulders. "Thank you."

The man slides back inside the car without a word. A moment later, the passenger door opens, and another man exits. Sun glints off his shaved head, but the dark brown beard bordering on Neanderthal gives him an almost Viking look. To anyone else, he'd be a scary giant. To me, he's my big brother—by a few minutes.

My heart constricts. "Fane."

Ştefan, as he prefers to anyone else but me, comes to a stop half a foot away. His eyes, once filled with laughter, now stare at me blankly, but without seeing me. He has turned his blindness into strength, this dear brother of mine. And it's his strength that inspires me to be so much more, to carry myself without fear. To take on this mission, and succeed. For both of us.

With surprising accuracy, he reaches for my hand and clasps it in his. "Be careful."

"I will be."

He tugs on my hand, and I give in to his wordless plea, hugging him.

In my ear, he adds, "The Dacians aren't fooling around. We're one and the same, but you and I know there is no coming back from this. These vampiri don't fuck around."

"I realize that, brother. And I won't let you down."

When I pull back, I blink back tears and hold my head high. Then, I tap the hood of the car, signaling the first guy. "I'm ready."

He leads me into the woods, deep within, until I'm on the path toward the castle. It looms in the distance, an old relic of the past—of a time of war and famine, but also honor and... Things I sometimes wish still existed.

"You understand your mission?" he asks.

"Da. You don't have to keep checking."

"It was not my preference that you be chosen for this task."

"Why, because I'm a woman?"

He scowls. "No. Because the risk—"

I shrug. "Is no more than any other I have taken. The Grand Master trusts me to do this. And I *can* do this, if you'll let me."

He nods and starts backtracking. Once he's far enough, he looks at me. "I'm sorry."

The moment after, he lifts his hand up in the air. I only get a half-second to notice the beads of blood he casts about. Then, dark tendrils of magic release from the tree's roots. They wrap around my ankles, my wrists, and finally, my waist. And they start tightening—and burning.

I open my mouth and scream.

Chapter 2

Vlad

That scream...

I pivot, my eyes checking the surroundings and trying to figure out what's going on. I'd been unable to sleep. Unsurprising, given my body's full of human blood. So I snuck out the back, unwilling to run into Liza—or any of my siblings—again, and ended in the woods.

The sun's rising, barely lighting the sky. I'd been enjoying the rare moment of peace, thinking back on my conversation with Liza, when the scream broke the quiet of the woods.

I don't move. Frozen, immobile, I try to figure out if it was all in my head.

And then it comes again.

Ravens fly out of the trees, and something scurries on the frozen ground, among broken leaves and half a coat of snow.

This time, I don't hesitate. I run, already heading toward whatever it is—it sounds like a female.

You should keep your distance, a wise voice admonishes at the back of my head.

But I can't. Especially after last night, after coming so close to taking a life. Guilt suffuses my being, and I resolve not to be the cause of another's suffering. Not when I can help them.

Even as the trees blur past me, ideas of what the threat could be jostle me. Hunters attacking an innocent. One of the larger carnivores, defending its territory. Or...the new wolves in town. Maybe Alex's right, and we've been giving them too much credit. After all, it wouldn't be the first time vârcolaci do as they wish.

But then I emerge into a meadow to find someone—a woman— held captive by...

I sniff the air, the odd mix of sulfur, copper and lightning.

Magic. What in all hells...?

I haven't run into its like since Father. Matter of fact, the scent in the air is very much the same as what I'd encounter on the days Vlad Țepeș himself chose to use that particular skill of his. Which, toward the end, was less and less.

Without thinking, I rush toward her. A head full of strawberry-blonde hair lifts. Long locks of hair cover a heart-shaped face, with full lips that part in surprise at seeing me. Dark gray eyes meet mine and she screams, "No, wait!"

I'm already touching the darkened tendrils around her wrists. They feel like electric snakes against my skin, sizzling and scorching. I pull back, hissing. My fangs are already on display, an intuitive reaction, but she doesn't seem scared. If anything, she seems annoyed.

"It's magic, *idiotule*! Your hands are of no use against it!"

I grit my teeth. It's been a while since I've been called an idiot, least of all by the opposite sex. But her admonishment is on point, given the stinging in my palms. Thanks to my earlier feeding, it's already healing fast.

My glare settles on the tendrils, which seem to have attached themselves to her wrists and ankles even tighter. Despite her words, the woman's grimace of pain tells me I don't have long to undo this before irreparable harm is done.

And then I'll figure out why she's not worried to run into a vampir.

"How do I free you, then?"

"Blood. It only answers to blood."

My glance moves from her to the tendrils. The tighter they go, the darker they become. *Feeding.*

Gulping, I bring my palm to my mouth, letting the fangs tear into it. Blood gushes and sprinkles all over the dark tendrils—and the woman's shoulder-baring top, her jeans, her creamy skin.

Averting my eyes, I once again try to loosen the crap holding her captive. This time, the tendrils unravel as easily as petals in the sun.

The woman shrugs out a hand that had been trapped and blasts the remaining restraints with magic. Its bright, blue-tinged blaze is too strong for my eyes, causing me to avert my gaze.

By the time I look back at her, she's crawling away, coughing.

I rush to her side, holding out a hand and helping her up.

"What did I just stumble into?"

"T-thank you," she whispers. "I was... fighting with a mage. I thought I could…handle him."

I look her up and down. She's tiny, almost as tiny as Liza. Her long hair is braided, tossed over one shoulder, and manages to look both messy and sexy at the same time with locks framing her face. And those gray eyes are settled on me, unwavering.

"Why would you even attempt that?"

She glares at me, taking offense—rightly—at my words. I never said banter came easily to me.

"My bite is worse than my bark, believe me."

I hold up my palms. "Scuze. I wasn't thinking. I… suppose I'm still processing."

She's glancing down at herself, patting her clothes and muttering under her breath as she wipes some of the blood off her. My eyes linger on her waist, the flare of her hips. My idiotic male brain is getting ideas, so I try to shake them off before I act on them.

"You didn't even seem fazed."

She scoffs, still intent on dusting herself off. To my surprise, she doesn't try to heal whatever wounds are hidden by her clothes. Perhaps because of her indifference, her words come out with an even stronger bite than I'd expected. "At what, exactly? Your inability to put two and two together?"

It's my turn to scowl. "No. I was thinking more along the lines of meeting a vampir."

She meets my gaze again. Unreadable. Her facial expression, too. *Damn, she's probably a killer poker player.*

"I'm a witch, smart-ass," she finally says. "Of course I know about vampiri, and werewolves, and all manners of supernatural creatures. And like I said, *my bite is worse than my bark.* I wouldn't recommend trying to feed on me any time soon."

I jerk back at her words. "I wouldn't dream of it." Memories of last night, the hospital, are much too fresh in my mind. I clear my throat. "That being said, do you need help? Medical, I mean. There's a village not too far off."

"No, I..." She looks away. "I'll be fine."

She runs her hands over her sweater, wincing. Ignoring her protests, I grab her hand and lift the sweater sleeve. She jumps at my touch, trying to squirm away. I let her go, but I've seen enough—the skin underneath is burned in patches.

"How did they get through?"

"The tendrils, they feed off blood, they—" She shrugs. "It doesn't matter. I'll be fine. No human doctor can help."

"Maybe. But, if you're willing to trust me, I know someone who can."

She looks me up and down, then checks the surroundings. With a deep breath, she nods and picks up a backpack a few feet away. "I don't suppose I have a choice."

We walk back to the castle in silence. The entire time, I'm sneaking furtive glances at her. Magic, of all things. Especially now? It seems odd that of all times, *now* is when a witch would land in our midst, right after a pack of vârcolaci settled nearby. I've never been a big believer in coincidences...

"By the way, I didn't introduce myself. My name is Vlad."

A corner of her mouth quirks up. "Not the Third?"

"Sadly, no." No point in admitting my entire family history to her, until I know I can trust her. If this is all a ruse by another clan, well, at least I won't be divulging anything important. "It's been a while since I've seen a witch," I say, hoping to draw out more information from her.

"I'm not just a witch," she mutters.

My eyes narrow. "Then who *are* you?"

She stands up straighter. "My name is Silviana Dragoş. My parents, and their parents before them, have been keepers of the purest of witch lines. There are not many of us left."

"No, I dare say not."

She tilts her head to the side. "You know, then?"

"I know enough about persecution to understand where you're going with it." A long pause.

"Come, we're almost there."

I push forward, trying to keep the tumult off my face. Witches, much like us, went into hiding. Especially after the trials back in the medieval times, they didn't have much choice. Nowadays, they hide in plain sight. My recent research into the remaining vampiri clans showed some of them work with witches. And others with less...savory characters.

Needless to say, I'm not taking Silviana's appearance lightly. And if she's here for anything other than chance, well, it's best to keep her close. Surely.

Keep your friends close, and your enemies closer. Another one of dear old Dad's favorite sayings.

"That was blood magic, then? What I helped you recover from."

"Da."

So I was right. Father used to practice the same kind, except he never needed to sacrifice blood to do so. As far as I know, only one order of witches were known to use that method. And last I heard, they were extinct. But if they're not…what in hell would Dacians want with someone like Silviana? Why attack her?

"You don't seem fazed. And yet, if memory serves me correctly, it's only certain witches who are able to do such magic." I pause, slowing my pace. "*Dark* magic."

Silviana doesn't slow down or have any kind of reaction to my words. "Your memory serves you correctly, indeed. Now, where's this magical doctor you mentioned?"

Another half an hour later, we reach the castle. Silviana whistles low under her breath, but says nothing other than, "Nice home."

The moment we enter through the doors of the castle, I know we're in for a fight. One I should've anticipated, given how half of us reacted to Tassa's presence.

Alex walks to me, eyes narrowed on the woman by my side. "First Nico, now you with the human strays?"

I grit my teeth. "She's not a stray."

Silviana clears her throat and steps forward, extending her hand. "My name is Silviana Dragoș, and your brother saved my life."

"Of course he did." Alex sneers at her offered hand and walks away without a word. The dirty look he sends me is enough.

I run a hand over my face. The previous night's events, plus my sleepless night and now this early morning drama are taking their toll.

"I apologize for my brother's rudeness. That's Alexandru and he's not used to, err, humans."

Silviana tears her gaze from Alex's retreating back and smirks. "You mean he hates us."

There's no diplomatic way to answer that, so I don't. Instead, I gesture for her to follow me and head into the living room. Once she's seated, I bring her a glass of wine.

"I could get you something stronger, if you want. Or some food?"

Her eyes seem to dance as she meets my gaze. Interestingly, her earlier snark seems to have cooled off. "You guys carry human food around here?"

"A recent development."

"Hmm." She takes a sip of the wine, closes her eyes. Her pink tongue comes out as she licks her lips, and makes a humming sound—not unlike a cat. "This is some *good* shit." Her eyes fly open. "Sorry. It's just...really, really good."

"A wine afficionado, *and* a witch? You sure are full of surprises."

Silviana lowers her lashes and glances around. "Where's that doctor you mentioned?"

"I'll go get her. Just...wait here."

Leaving her behind—and hoping no one else pops in with questions and snarky remarks—I run up the stairs to Nico's bedroom. A few quick knocks, and he opens the door, leaning against it. One hand ruffles his hair, the other stifles a yawn.

"Can this wait?"

"Not really." I push past him into the room, and quickly avert my eyes as Tassa pulls up the bedsheets to her chest. Clearly, I interrupted something. "Sorry! Shit. I didn't—"

Nico grabs me by the shoulder and tosses me back outside. "No, you didn't. What the hell is so urgent?"

"Human. Downstairs. Witch. Need Tassa's healing."

Some of my words must've carried into the room, as I hear Tassa scrambling off the bed and yelling, "Coming! Just give me a minute."

Nico glares at me, then walks back inside and slams the door in my face. I try not to listen—we all do, though our sensitive hearing is almost impossible to ignore—but his sweet cajoling is so unlike the brother I've known for the last centuries that I find myself completely eavesdropping.

"Iubito, come back to bed. His drama can wait."

My jaw drops at his using the endearment *my love*. Wow. Talk about a total one-eighty switch from an indifferent jackass to a complete sap.

There's a giggle, then Tassa says, "Later! You're completely insatiable and I adore you, but you know I can't just sit by if I can help."

He groans—loudly—and something creaks. Probably the bed he plopped back onto. "And you're as stubborn as they come."

"It's why you love me."

The door opens then and Tassa walks out in leggings and a knee-length sweater dress. She pulls her long brown hair up in a ponytail and gestures for me to lead the way.

Nico's curses follow us down the stairs. By the time we get there, he's also joined in, wearing clothes this time. "Next time you decide to barge into my bedroom—"

He stops, and a second later I realize why. I leave him behind and enter the living room. Alex is back, leaning over Silviana's chair, his face too close to hers. The wine glass is lying, spilled, on the floor, and he looks ready to lose control.

"I'll ask again, who—"

I jump him, tackling him away from Silviana and into the wall.

Though it's reinforced brick, it still cracks under our weight, but thankfully doesn't crumble.

"Enough," Nico says.

I glare at Alex. He's holding onto my shoulder, his body tense and ready to strike back. His own glare moves from me to Nico, then he shrugs me off him.

"She's a *guest* here, dammit. And injured!" I walk to Silviana. She curls more into the armchair, but I kneel next to it, softening my tone. "It's all right. I'm sorry, I shouldn't have left you alone. Tassa here is human, and she's the doctor I've been talking about."

Tassa clears her throat and waves, etching a smile. "Not a doctor, per se. My father was one. But I'm pretty good with healing remedies. Can I see one of the injuries?"

Silviana hesitates, her gray eyes darkened with worry. Eventually, after a few seconds, she slowly pulls up the sleeve of her sweater. The blistered, red skin comes into view.

Tassa leans over it, whistling low. "Wow. That's one hell of a burn."

"Magical," Silviana says in a small voice.

I hate that my brother reduced her to this. Oddly, I find myself wanting back that spark and fire from before, the easy demeanor. Not this fearful, glancing-all-around-as-if-she's-today's-meal look.

"Could you really not control yourself, Alex? She's obviously traumatized."

"You think everyone and their pet dog is traumatized, Nico. And I simply happen to believe our brother's not asking the right questions. That's all. I was trying to help out."

I scowl at Alex. "And what should I be asking, according to you?"

He turns to Silviana. "How about why did his blood, specifically, help release you?"

"How do you even know about that?" I ask.

He jerks his chin toward the armchair. "Because I asked her details about how you met. And, clearly, you're too stupid to take in the small details. *Ask her.*"

Silviana gulps, her eyes widening between us.

Tassa takes a step forward, kneeling by the chair and touching her hand. "No one will hurt you, but this family does demand the truth. Believe me, it's best you come clean."

Silviana licks her lips, and her gaze settles on me. "I... It worked because of your blood. Your lineage. All of your lineage, I guess. I know who gave Vlad —your father—his powers. The god of death...Zalmoxis. Anyone who carries his power can control darkness."

Chapter 3

Vlad

To say I freeze would be an understatement. I take in Silviana's serious tone, even as her words register a little later.

It worked because of your blood. Your lineage. All of your lineage, I guess. I know who gave Vlad —your father—his powers. The god of death...Zalmoxis.

Alexandru was right. He saw past the innocent act, her coincidental arrival, and the big doe eyes. He read her like a book, in a way I wasn't able to.

I know who gave Vlad —your father—his powers. The god of death...Zalmoxis.

Meanwhile, I was too damned busy putting us all in danger. All to mollify my own guilt over my inability to control my bloodlust. I *didn't* ask the right questions, at all.

The god of death...Zalmoxis.

But I will now.

I move away from Alex and toward Silviana, towering over her seated form. She tilts her head back, her gaze steady on mine. I notice there's no more fear in her expression, not like before. Had she been playing me, even with that wary reaction to Alex?

"So you knew who I was the minute I stepped into the meadow."

"I did."

Her honesty surprises me. And annoys me. That I'd have fallen so quickly for it, so...stupidly.

"And why does it matter, who my father got his powers from?"

"Because it's not just a coincidence I'm here."

"Could've fucking told you so," Alex interjects.

I don't give him the satisfaction of turning to him. Instead, I keep my gaze just as steady on Silviana as she does with me.

"Then why?" I ask simply.

Her expression falters, for a second. It's enough to see the fear again. The apprehension. She's in a room with three vampiri, all three of them males. She'd be a fool if she wasn't thinking about running away.

Did I misread her, or is she still playing me?

"I... My parents." She clears her throat, and the second time around, her voice comes out stronger. "I told you they're from a rare lineage of witches. I wasn't lying about that. But they were killed and I was the only survivor. I was on my way to finding another coven, for protection, when I ran into the mage."

"What mage?" Nico asks.

"She's fucking toying with you all!" Alex clenches and un-clenches his fingers, as if he'd like nothing more than to wrap them around her neck and wring the truth out of her.

"A...Dacian."

A loud silence falls as I share a glance with my siblings.

"She's not lying about that," I mutter. "I smelled the blood magic—same as Father used to use."

Tassa glances at our stormy faces. "What does that mean, Dacian?"

Nico pulls her to her feet, away from Silviana. "The story goes that Zalmoxis didn't just give our father his powers. According to legend, he had a coven of very eager witches who wished to serve at his altar. They would convert regular humans to his religion—the religion of death. In exchange for their loyalty, these witches were given more magic. The downside was, they had to use blood in order to create spells."

"It was meant to control the amount of power they could use," I add. "So they wouldn't rise against him." I search Silviana's eyes. "The Dacians are meant to be dead. Extinct."

Something flickers in her gaze, but she soon lowers it before I can read her. "They're not. In fact, they're actively working against your legacy, by allying with other clans. It's why I was crossing through this territory. I could've gone to a coven directly, but my parents would've wanted me to warn you. It's why the Dacian mage tried to stop me."

Alex snorts. I'm tempted to not believe her, too, but—

"Why should I trust you?"

She shrugs. "Why should I trust *you*? At the end of the day, I'm the one taking a risk. Either one of you could feed on me and dump my body in a ravine. No one would be the wiser. I have no family to search for me. And I have no magic, at the time being, to protect myself. That mage exhausted me." She looks directly at me. "That last burst of magic you saw is all I had left, until my body recovers. And it will take days." A shake of the head follows at my silence. "I have everything to lose by being here. But if I don't warn you, more witches will pay the price at the Dacians' hands... They're eager to kill you all. Only you can keep the balance."

A snort resounds behind me, then silence. That's all the reaction my siblings show.

That's when Liza walks in, head tilted back, sniffing the air. "Why in all hells do I smell another human?" She comes to a dead stop when she notices Silviana. Her eyes narrow. "...the fuck?"

Nico sighs. "It's a long story."

"Not that long." Alex smirks. "Just another brother falling for a pretty head. As if we don't know how that ended before."

Silviana stands, pulling my attention. "I realize this is bad timing, now. I shouldn't have come, and you don't have to feel obligated to help me out. The important thing is I delivered the warning; the rest is up to you all."

I stop her before she leaves, my fingers tightening on her elbow. A zing of electricity runs through my arm, and her eyes widen—did she feel it, too?

"No, you don't get off that easily."

She hisses and winces at my tight hold on her arm, and I'm reminded she was hurt. Still is.

"Tassa can help you with the wounds, and then you and I will talk. I have more questions, questions to which you will provide an answer."

She clenches her jaw and nods, once, then follows Tassa out of the room. Alex pulls Liza away, already rattling off his own version of the story. Only Nico remains in the room.

He waits until everyone's gone, then steps closer to me. "Do you trust her?"

"Not one word that comes out of those lips."

"Then why play this game?"

"Because it could help us gain more information to stop Violeta's disease, and ours. She clearly doesn't know about the curse, but she knows about the god who's responsible for it. And someone wielding magic from that same god attacked her... I think we can use it to our advantage. And if I can also get more information about the clans and their plans? Even better."

"You think she has it?"

"I think, as a witch, she would've been privy to more information than us. Different circles, and all. Whether those Dacians are only offering their services to the highest bidder or actively preparing to go against us, we need to know."

Nico glances at the doors Silviana and his consort disappeared through, and nods, clapping my back. "Just be careful."

Silviana

I follow Tassa docilely through the castle, trying to hold back the shudders wrecking my body. I'd been warned the House of Dracul were monsters, but when the one named Alexandru came into the room, and his eyes settled on me...my life flashed before my eyes.

Things were easy—the duplicity, a small parlor trick masquerading as blue-tinged magic, getting Vlad to help me, my arrival at the castle. I stupidly thought I'd be in and out. His blue eyes had sold the story that he could help. But now? Now, I'm not so sure.

I have more questions, questions to which you will provide an answer.

The prospect of being interrogated isn't very appealing, but it's not like I'll have a choice. Feeding them some bullshit story about my family being dead and Dacians working against them wasn't all lies. We *are* working to bring the House of Dracul down. And my family is dead, except for Fane. But will I be able to maintain the lies when I'm alone with Vlad again?

Best thing I can do is bide my time. I palm the small athame knife in the back pocket of my jeans, reassured by its presence. One cut, a drop of blood, and I'll be able to find my way out. If they don't jump me first...

"Through here."

I glance from the worn carpet I'd been staring at to the door Tassa has opened. It leads into a small room, with all kinds of remedies and notebooks strewn around. Opposite it, I notice an office that looks like a man's, with dark wood and an energy I wouldn't want to piss off.

"That's Nico's office," Tassa says. Wryly, she adds, "He didn't want me wandering too far off while I do my research."

I enter her room, and take a seat on the armchair she gestures to. "Research?"

Tassa pauses, enough to make me wonder what the big secret is.

"Like I said before, I'm not a doctor, per se. I studied architecture, originally. But I worked alongside my dad for years while he treated the local village, so I know a little bit about remedies."

It doesn't escape my notice that she hasn't answered my question.

I watch her as she moves around the room, picking up things here and there—a bowl, some hydrogen peroxide, and a tub of some cream. She pulls a stool over and nods toward my top.

"I'll need to see what I'm dealing with."

I hesitate, then pull the sleeves a little, and then further. The burn marks around my wrists are garish, blistering and reddening like the ugliest welts I've ever seen. I turn my gaze away, even as I lean over and pull the top up to expose my abdomen, and then pull the top of my jeans up, as well.

Tassa makes a grimace at the mess. "What the hell did this? It doesn't look like any burn I've ever seen."

I swallow. "Black magic."

Her eyes widen, finally landing on mine.

"I wasn't lying about the attack. It did happen."

"I believe you." She focuses her attention on the bowl, pouring the hydrogen peroxide in it and submerging the clean cloth. She then takes it out, hesitates. "This'll sting."

I nod, but I'm not prepared for the unbearable pain that hits me the moment the cloth touches my skin. I grit my teeth against it, but still, a whimper escapes my lips. Tassa glances up, an apology in her eyes.

"It's fine. Just...get it over with. Walk me through it, it'll take my mind off it."

"Ok, well... I'm cleaning the wound right now to prevent infection. A hospital would be able to do a better job of this—are you sure you don't want to go to one?" I shake my head. "Right. Well, after, I'm going to put a balm on the skin. You'll have to reapply it a few times, at least until your magic is strong enough so you can heal the rest of it."

"What's in the balm?"

"Dandelion extract."

I frown. "Isn't that a weed?"

Tassa chuckles. "It is. It's also one of the most versatile plants ever. It can help with regulating period pains, cleansing the liver, and, unsurprisingly, healing any kind of wounds. Especially burn wounds. It's also an antiseptic and will keep any infections at bay."

"Huh. I didn't know that."

"Not a lot of people do." She takes the tub of cream and starts lathering it on my skin, keeping her movements light and airy. "I'm also going to give you a syrup to drink a few times a day. Since I don't have antibiotics and I'm not sure whether the fact you're a witch prevents infection, the syrup will work to boost your immune system."

My jaw hurts from clenching it while Tassa moves to my waist and finishes cleaning me up. She waits a few moments, then starts lathering the balm on my wrists, waist and ankle. It doesn't smell like much—a faint floral smell, if that.

What I wouldn't give to use my magic right now. But unless I want the vampiri to sense it, and my blood, I'd best play the good little patient.

Tassa pulls some gauze to wrap my wounds. When the first bit touches my newly pained skin, I hiss and let out a small scream. The door opens in that moment, and Vlad bursts in.

His eyes scan the area, as if looking for a threat, then settle on me. He takes in my somewhat undressed state—I cringe, but try to keep my face otherwise neutral—and then, to my dismay, he steps closer. "I can do that."

Tassa sends him an amused glare. "We're good."

He clears his throat. "I insist. Nico wants to talk to you."

Tassa hesitates, her hand tight on the bandage. Finally, she relents and stands. "Just don't tighten it too much. Light, just enough to cover the wounds."

He nods, and she leaves. It's just him and me now.

"May I?"

"Don't see how I have much of a choice."

A faint smile tugs at his lips, and I look away. I don't want to see the way his eyes sparkle with amusement, or how insanely normal he looks right now. I need to remember he's a vampir. Probably worse than Alex. The quiet ones always are.

Instead of sitting on the stool Tassa vacated, he kneels by my side and picks up the gauze. With one hand, he lifts my wrist, checking that it was coated on both sides. The gesture strikes me as odd—why the hell would he care? Then he slowly starts wrapping the gauze around.

When he moves to my other wrist, he has to lean over my body, and I tense. His gaze flickers to mine, then to my mouth, and then back to my wrist. His body seems just as tense now, but his movements are quick, lightweight, and soon he has my other wrist wrapped up.

He pulls back, letting out a breath. He gestures to my abdomen. "You may need to stand, for this."

I hesitate, then do as he asks. The movement puts his head level with my stomach. He grabs a bigger strip of gauze, and starts wrapping it around my waist. This time, his movements are even slower, almost deliberate. His fingers graze my unharmed skin, and a shiver runs through me. Problem is, it's not the kind that's sending me signals to run away. Rather, it feels...sensuous. Sparking a desire deep in the pit of my stomach.

It's just my hormones going haywire. Not even that calms my mind. Little electric sparks hit my skin every time he touches it. And much as I want to feel repulsed by his touch, by his kindness, I'm...not.

By the time Vlad is done, my knees are so weak, I'm glad to be sitting back down.

At least until he lifts one calf in his hand, pushes my jeans up, and traces the skin of my ankle. "You have beautiful skin."

"It's an odd thing for a vampire to say."

He grins, meeting my gaze. "Were you expecting me to comment on how good you smell?" He takes an exaggerated whiff of the air. "Because you do. Smell good, that is."

I force a laugh.

Vlad finishes wrapping my ankle, and moves on to the last one. The moment the gauze touches my skin, he says, "So, which is it?"

"I'm sorry?"

"Are you here to warn us about Dacians, or because one of them attacked you on your way to another coven?" He looks up, his gaze no longer amused. "You can't have it both ways."

I try to pull my ankle out of his grip, feeling weirdly vulnerable, but Vlad doesn't let go. His grip on my calf is strong. His other hand stills with the gauze.

"It's a simple question."

I glare at him. "I wasn't lying. These wounds are proof of it."

"Then why are you so defensive?"

His words cut through my annoyance, and I deflate. I can't let him see how worked up I get. The point is for me to stay here, to gain access to the journal. I can't do that if I'm kept away.

"You're right. I'm sorry. I can only imagine how it looks to you guys, who are already dealing with vampiri attacking you, when I conveniently land in your midst."

His blue eyes narrow on me. "How did you know we're being attacked?"

"Alex mentioned it, when he was..."

"Being a dick. Da, I get it."

I take a deep breath. "To answer your question, it's both. My family *was* attacked, and I *was* on my way to find another coven. But in the village before this one, I was in a pub, and I heard some men talking. They...weren't being careful. Probably on account of being drunk." I shrug, the lie coming easier now. "I'm a woman, so they assumed I wasn't listening. They were more interested in leering and grabbing at me as I passed them."

Vlad's grip tightens on my leg, giving me pause. I don't know what to make of it. Is he mad that some strangers acted inappropriately with me?

"I heard them talking about the House of Dracul. My parents told me stories... So, I lingered. I didn't hear specifics. Not names or alliances. Just enough to know they were working together. And then one of the men went outside and I saw him use blood magic. That's when I realized he was Dacian. My parents taught me everything about our history, including the dark parts. I knew enough to recognize the magic."

Vlad purses his lips, and starts back on my ankle. Part of me thinks he doesn't want me seeing his expression as he keeps bandaging me. "How did you know where to find us?"

"From them. They mentioned your location."

"And the mage caught up with you in the woods?"

I nod. "I'd felt I was being followed for a few hours, but I wasn't taking precautions."

He drops my ankle to the floor. And then he puts both his arms on either side of me, caging me into the armchair as he leans a bit closer. My heart kicks up its dance, but not in fear. Not like with Alex. This is more of that stupid, weird giddiness and desire from before.

Vlad watches me for a few long moments. Then, as abruptly as he leaned over, he pulls back and stands, holding out his hand. "Come. I'll get you settled in a spare room."

Bemused, I follow him out of Tassa's remedy room and up some stairs, until we get to a wide room. It's modest and simple, with a view out onto the grounds, and furnished with a bed, a mirror, and a dresser. Not that I'll need it.

Vlad points to my bag, on the bed. "I brought this here."

I'd left it in the living room area, knowing it would seem even more suspicious if I tried to hide my belongings. Part of me wonders if Vlad looked through it. If he did, he couldn't have found anything incriminating. Even the talisman I was given would be incomprehensible to anyone not of my kin.

"I'll let you sleep. My siblings shouldn't bother you, but if they do... I'm just down the hall."

Weirdly, that reassures me.

Vlad

I can't fall asleep. Over and over, I replay the day's events. The prior night's events. But every time I want to focus on the guilt I feel over that feed, something else fills my mind. Silviana. Those gray eyes. Those pouty lips. The strength she showed, even when faced with my anger.

Restlessness seems to be my de-facto mode nowadays. I leave my room, thinking that I will go for a walk. Nothing like some fresh air to clear my mind, and cool off my spirit. After all, just because we have a curse looming over us that's meant to force mates—consorts—upon us doesn't mean *she* is the one for me. There are plenty of other reasons why I can't get her image out of my mind. And one of them is that I need to get laid. But...not by her.

Down the corridor I go, my footsteps barely touching the ground in my haste. But then I pass by a corner and that ache in my head starts.

Not again.

I pause, leaning against the wall. Focusing my attention on my fingers touching the rough wall, the curtains nearby, the seal of the House of Dracul emblazoned everywhere.

Still, the darkness in me rises. If it takes over, if I lose control again... I think of the man I'd drank from last, and how I never bothered to check at the hospital if he was all right. And then the image morphs into Silviana, her throat slashed.

Enough.

I force myself to move, to get out of the castle.

As I pass by the living room, I hear noises. Shuffling, drawers being opened and closed, impatient sighs and an erratic heartbeat.

A faint flicker of uneasiness crawls up my spine as I poke my head around the door and... And find Silviana, rifling through one of the cabinets.

"What do you think you're doing?"

She whirls around to face me, her eyes wide.

A couple of things pass my mind in equally fast succession. I'd believed her, earlier. It was much too easy, when she was making so much sense. And I did my duty by relaying all the information she gave me to Nico. We both agreed to keep an eye on her. Now I'm wondering if maybe we should've been keeping her under lock and key.

Obviously, she's here looking for something. But it also seems clear that she doesn't know what or where to find it. Is this a game to her, then? Are my siblings correct and her woe-is-me act is just that—an act?

"It's not what you think."

I take a step forward. "Really? Then tell me. What is it that I'm thinking?"

Rather than step backward, she tosses her braid over her shoulder and meets my gaze head on. "You're thinking that I'm here for nefarious reasons. That I'll hurt your family. When, in fact, I'm actually here to help you."

That's a new one. "Really? How so?"

"You saved my life, it's only fair I help you in return."

A scoff escapes me. "I would thank you, but what makes you think you have what it takes to help out a clan of vampiri as old as us?"

Lightning flashes in her gaze. "I was trying to find good spots to set up spells, later on. When my magic's replenished. *To protect you all.*" At my disbelieving expression, she adds, "Don't forget my family comes from an old lineage."

While plausible, her excuse sounds weak to my ears. And her heart is beating a little too fast for me to believe her. "Maybe do that some other time. My siblings wouldn't take kindly to seeing you snoop around the place. Just...go back to sleep, Silviana."

She's silent as I walk away, though if I'm to be honest, I'm taking my sweet time. Hoping she'll say something—anything else.

"What if I said I know what's afflicting you?"

I pause. Turn to her, slowly. "I already know what's afflicting us."

"Not 'you,' plural. I mean *you,* Vlad."

That freezes all my muscles. How can this stranger have figured out what I've been painstakingly hiding from my siblings?

Silviana

I don't know what possesses me to poke him. I have no idea what afflicts him, at best I'm guessing. But it makes him turn toward me, those blue eyes—so similar to his siblings— focused on me.

"What, exactly, do you think you know?"

I gulp. No backing away now. Whether I know what he thinks I do or not, I gotta say something convincing. Something that'll pass for a good enough bluff.

Chapter 4

Silviana

"I..."

Shit. Why did I have to bait him? Why didn't I just let him get the hell out of the room, so I could keep snooping? Why, why, *why*, dammit! I've been trained better than this. You don't engage your target until you're prepared.

And I'm anything but prepared. Something about Vlad unnerves me. Maybe it's because he seems so human, so unlike everyone else... It drives me crazy. Vampiri aren't meant to understand. They're not supposed to look at you like...like...like he is. Like I'm a woman in his eyes, and he has some manly needs.

The memory of his touch on my bare skin is enough to send shivers running up my spine again. I ignore them, straightening up instead.

"I know. About what it is you're dealing with."

He tilts his head to the side and takes a step closer. "So you said."

I reach behind me. My knife is still in the pocket of my jeans. All it takes is one swipe of my finger on it, a prick of the knife, and blood seeps. Vlad's nostrils flare.

"Did you cut yourself?"

"It's nothing." I show him my finger, watching him closely for any sign of losing control. I wouldn't trust these beasts as far as I can throw them. "Just a paper cut."

"Paper cut? From snooping around?"

I scowl. "I wasn't snooping, per se. I told you, I was looking for good spots to set up spells. Hidden spells, so anyone who comes here can't find them and undo them. And, I wanted… What I felt in you. I was trying to find an explanation." I reach for the hint of magic within me, letting it wash over me like a gentle wave. Enough so I can see his aura. Enough so I can see past it, find a clue. Enough so—I pull back, trying to hide my shock. "And I found it…"

He's in front of me in a flash, his hand on my elbow. It's a gentle hold, but firm. I feel his grip through my sweater, and I'm insanely aware of how easily he could snap my elbow to get his answers. And yet, he doesn't.

"Found what?" he asks through gritted teeth. "I don't have all night."

"I thought vampiri don't sleep."

"Older ones like us, do. We use the time to quiet our minds, to recover." He frowns, and his grip tightens. "Come off it, Silviana. Speak."

I swallow past the knot in my throat and give him the answer he wants. "I see the darkness in you." And it's true. I'd seen it, clear as day. "You hide it from your siblings, but it's there, just under the surface. All that...guilt. Shame. Why?"

His grip on my elbow grows slack. My words were pure conjecture, a mere guess at what I saw. I'd learned psychological games from the coven, but I didn't think it'd be so easy to use them.

I lift my hand to his cheek, touching it gently. "Vlad?"

His nostrils flare again, and he takes a deep whiff. It's only then I realize the finger I'd cut is the one touching his face. He's sniffing my blood. The thought should repulse me, but the way he stares at me, his blue eyes darkening, only makes something else tighten inside me. Just like earlier today. It's a sensation unlike any I've experienced before.

And then he closes the last of the distance between us, leaning toward me. His mouth inches closer, mere millimeters between us. I hold my breath, waiting for him to stop, yet not knowing what I'll do if it he doesn't.

At the last possible moment, Vlad freezes. "You should leave now. While you can. It's not smart to bait a vampir, even less so when it's one of the House of Dracul."

I jerk away from him, my heart beating a staccato against my ribcage. And then I run out of the room, up the stairs, and to my own chambers. And the entire time, one panicked realization hits me. It's not just that he almost kissed me.

It's that I *wanted* him to.

Vlad

I watch in stunned resignation as Silviana walks out of the room. How could she, a complete stranger, know about what it is I'm dealing with? How could she even think to—

Ah. It's a ploy. It has to be. What else could it be?

I caught her looking around, and she knew she'd been busted. Which brings my brain back from wanting to shag her and more into... wanting something else. Like answers.

I need to give Alex more credit, after all.

An odd sense of disappointment settles into my chest. Don't know why, since I've only known her for half a day. But something about her... I wanted her to be here for a real reason, nothing that had to do with backstabbing us. After all, we have enough of those enemies coming after us.

Rubbing my chin, I make my way up the stairs to my floor. Wondering, not for the first time, if it was wise to place her in a room near mine. Because this odd burning in me... is it bloodlust or something else?

Do I even want to find out?

No. What I do want to know, without a doubt, is whether she's here on behalf of one of the clans, or whether she's a honeybee meant to trap me for someone else.

I'm in the midst of such thinking, when I trip over the last stair and go slamming into the nearest wall. Normally, such a stupid move would've dented it but instead, an odd, sharp pain ratches up my shoulder.

I step back and stare at the offending wall, with its fading paint. There's not a mark on it. My shoulder, on the other hand?

My hand moves up, rubbing it absentmindedly. I try to set it to the back of my mind, but the sharpness of my vision becomes blurry.

I have the hardest time crossing the last of the steps to my room... And when I finally enter, panting and losing my mind, it's only to crawl to the bed.

What the hell's going on?

Part of me wants to cry for help. The other part...says to suck it up. I'm immortal, after all. What's a little weakness of limb and loss of perception?

It'll go away in the morning.

But something tells me it might not.

That in fact, it's something much, much worse, and asking for help will soon be the least of my problems.

Morning finds me feeling almost hungover.

Yet I know I need to talk to Silviana, to either get more information out of her or...get her out of the way. So after a shower and getting dressed, I head downstairs. Thankfully, it seems my momentary lapse was just that—a lapse.

I'm halfway down, passing the same wall I hit last night, and I slow down. Rubbing my shoulder now, it feels fine. But for how long? Zalmoxis' curse was clear. We either find our mates, or die. And once the curse has started, we cannot stop it. Nico's escaped it for now, because Tassa's with him. Violeta's curse has abated ever since she accepted Marcus as her consort. But the rest of us? We're fair game.

Shaking my head, I move away from the wall and start back down the stairs. A buzzing in my pocket interrupts me. I grin as I hit answer. "Vi!"

Violeta chuckles on the other end. "Other V! How are you, frate? Everything okay?"

"Mmm. One can say."

"You don't sound too convinced."

"Nu, e bine. Please don't worry. How are *you*?"

"Don't think I don't notice you changing the subject." She pauses. "But I'm good. We're...good. Excellent." I can hear the smile in her voice. "Marcus is out cutting wood, and I guess you can say we've settled in nicely."

"Good. That's really good."

"Has Nico heard anything from the Ardelean clan?"

"You mean the vampiri he glamoured and sent off into the sunset to spread our message? Nope. Nothing as of yet."

Her silence tells me there's more to this call.

"What is it, Violeta? What's going on?"

"Nothing. I mean, it could be nothing. One of the kids, the orphans Marcus helps and keeps hidden? Well, they're integrating more into villages now that the threat of the Ardelean clan is gone. And...one of them came for a visit the other day."

I frown at the wall. "You should be careful. They could lead someone to you."

"The kids are careful. And, anyway, it's not me I'm worried about."

It dawns on me. "He brought you news of other vampiri?"

"Something like that. Said he's seen new people in town, people he's not used to seeing. People who smell weird—his words, not mine."

"They could just be travelers."

"Not likely. They don't go out in the sunlight much."

"Ah. Newbies, then."

"Da. And...he saw a tattoo, on one of them. Of a mountain."

I rub my chin, thinking back to my research. "You think they're from the Munteanu clan?"

"I mean, Munteanu does mean *mountain*, so is that so far-fetched?"

"Not really, no. I guess you have a point." I let out a long exhale. "I'll tell Nico. And everyone else. Mirabela was planning to leave to find us a new castle, so it's best we're all in the loop."

Speaking of, I wonder if anyone bothered telling my older sister about our new guest... Hmm.

"Good." Violeta's sharp tone brings me back to attention. "Now, what is it you're not telling me?"

I think back to last night. To the weakness. To the night before that. The darkness. The blood on my hands.

Shutting my eyes, I let out a low groan. "I'm in shit, Vi. So much shit."

Her voice softens. "You can tell me. I may be far away, but that doesn't mean I can't handle it. Or that I can't help."

I push out another breath, then admit, "That weakness you felt? How it all started? I'm starting to feel it too."

"Shit." A beat later, she adds, "How bad is it? Are you having any...weird...cravings?"

"Not yet, no. I hope it won't come anytime soon." I pause. Nico discussed with us Violeta's cravings for vampir blood, in the later stages of her experience with the curse. To think that's what may be in store for me...

"Tell Tassa to give you some of what she gave me. The concoction with muroni blood, I mean. I know she's having a hard time making more of it, what with most of them having gone into hiding after we killed Dmitri but it should be enough temporarily. It helped....for a bit. If I'd had it earlier on, it might've helped more. Maybe postponed all the rest of the changes."

I lean my head against the wall, suddenly drained. "It's not just that. There's a woman...a witch. I saved her yesterday."

Quickly, I summarize Silviana's situation for Violeta, including last night's debacle and almost-kiss. When I'm done, she's quiet for a long time.

"That's...quite a web you're weaving, Vlad."

"Yeah, tell me about it. Not to mention it's made all the more complicated by Liza and Alex's behavior."

Violeta sighs. "They mean well. I'm sure all the revelations around the curse didn't help. We all thought we were in control of our fates and now, well..." A beat later, she adds, "Besides, you're our little brother, and they're worried."

"Da, because I was turned last *and* away from you all."

Violeta goes quiet for long enough that I check the phone to make sure we didn't lose connection. Finally, she says, "I always thought Father had a good reason for you."

"You mean, a reason similar to why he let you and Nico disappear on him for nearly half a century?"

The silence is more pronounced. I can almost feel her hurt trickling down through the phone, and I wince.

"Scuze, Vi. I heard Alex muttering about it..." Though I try to keep the petulance out of my tone, it's still there when I ask, "How come you never told me? All these years?"

"I had my reasons. When Father brought you, I think we all envied you. After the destruction of our home at Târgoviște—you would have loved it, Vlad, the old charm that palace had! Anyway, when you came, we were all taken aback. We thought Father was done creating vampiri, and here he brought home one who was almost…emulating his own perfection."

I cringe. "It wasn't an easy transition. Father helped me through it, and I felt I owed him my life."

"Of course. In a way, we all do. And we all felt the same. But suffice it to say, we each had our own relationship with him, and struggles. And when I was turned, it was nowhere near easy. You know how bad the bloodlust got for me, but you can't grasp the magnitude. Nico was there, and he blamed himself for suggesting my turning to Father. Father blamed himself for having done something wrong, in as far as he saw it, that made me act out. But he was also grieving his first wife's death, he was…" She lets out another sigh. "He was broken. And the Ottoman War that followed in those years—"

"The Ottoman War? But that was… Father was involved in that in 1460! He was captured soon after."

"Da. And that's when Nico used Father's inattention, his focus on something else, to take me away."

"You *left* Father? To deal with the war all alone?" It's too late to pull back the accusation in my tone, but I still try. "Violeta, I'm so sorry. I know how it came out—"

"It's fine. Like I said, I struggled with my change. Being away is how Nico thought he was helping me. At least until he realized he couldn't do it alone and, decades later, went crawling back to Father to beg for help."

I think of my brother, who up until recently was insufferable, and finally understand him better. "It's why you guys are so close. Why it took your sickness to snap him out of his…detachment."

"Da… My sickness, and meeting Tassa." She waits a beat, then adds, "But, Vlad, that doesn't mean I love you any less. Or that any of them, regardless of their alliances, love you less. We're all in this together, and if Liza and Alex are being rude, it's only because they care, deep down."

"Right... except the curse is hitting *me* now, not Mira, or them. So, it's not going in order of who was turned when."

"That would be far too easy," she mutters.

We're both silent for a beat; me, trying to get my head back on track; her, probably lost in other thoughts.

Eventually, Violeta says, "Okay, you don't need me yapping in your ear about the past. Regarding Silviana, my advice is simple: try getting her away from the family, see where her head's at. Pay attention to what she says, but also what she doesn't."

"Huh?"

"Women, Vlad. We speak with our body language, as well as our lips. Pay attention to *all* aspects of her, not just what's in your face."

"In other words, don't be a man."

"Pretty much."

Another sigh escapes me. "Great. Thanks."

"Keep me posted!"

I murmur a goodbye and hang up, trying to ignore the excited undertones to her voice. Violeta shouldn't be happy about another woman being tossed into this mix. Even if she *is* a witch who could be useful.

More wearily than before, I continue down the stairs. On the next level, I get stopped by someone calling out my name.

I pop my head in Mirabela's room. "You called?"

She meets my gaze in the mirror of her vanity, and sets aside the brush she'd been using for her hair. With practiced, graceful movements, she twists the mass of black locks into a bun that some-how looks like she's paid a professional to do so.

When she's done, she turns to me. "Saw you passing by. Eve-rything okay?"

I roll my eyes. "You mean you heard Violeta's voice on the phone. Yes, she's fine. Enjoying herself, by the sounds of it."

"At least one of us is."

I shrug. "I was just about to grab Silviana and head into town so if there's nothing else?"

"Ah, yes. The new witch." She arches a dark eyebrow, her blue eyes cool as steel. "Are you planning to bed her, same as Nico did Tassa?"

While I'm busy picking my jaw up off the floor, Mirabela rolls her eyes. "Please. You two are so predictable. Just try not to antag-onize Liza and Alex. While I'm gone, they're all you have left."

"Gone?"

It's only then I take in the suitcase packed by the bed.

Mirabela notices my gaze and gives a delicate, one-shouldered shrug. "We need new headquarters, and I've been looking into some properties. Planning to go visit a few, so I'll be gone for a few days."

"Oh. I thought... I mean, I knew it was coming, but I didn't re-alize you'd be leaving so soon."

"Don't tell me you're going to miss me?" She laughs at my ex-pression, then kisses my cheek. "Are you sure you want to head into town? Given how the villagers are acting with Nico..."

I shrug. "Nico's the enemy. They don't know my face enough."

"And we don't know if there are hunters in the area."

"I'm more than capable of handling myself. And protecting one human. But if it makes you feel better, I'll grab Liza."

Mirabela purses her lips, then nods. "Bine. And while you're there, would you please arrange for a new supply of wine? Oh, and a new laptop. Alex broke the last one."

"What do we need a laptop for?"

She rolls her eyes. "How else am I to set up the last details for visiting the properties I was looking into? Besides, I'd say if we're all going to fall in love, we'll need not just another home, but a *bigger* castle."

"Huh."

This is the first inclination she's given of being even remotely open to the possibility. I hide a grin. Now if only it was this easy to convince Alex and Liza.

"Laptop, got it. Any preferences?"

She taps her chin, deep in thought for a few moments. "Nothing with too many bells and whistles."

I stifle a laugh and nod, then head out of her room and downstairs. Liza's nowhere in the castle, so I head out the back in the mini courtyard. Sure enough, she's busy playing with an old-school crossbow. After watching her struggle a bit, I clear my throat.

"I know you're there," she mutters. "What do you want?"

"Someone's in a mood."

She grumbles something but it's only when she turns that I notice her tired expression. Given we're immortal and it takes a lot to mar this perfect complexion, it's enough to bring any thought of joking to an end. "What's going on, Liza?"

She meets my gaze for the briefest of seconds, scowling. "None of your business. Just like your midnight wanderings aren't mine. Right?"

"...Right."

Her defensive tone tells me now may not be the best time to have her around a human, so I quickly backtrack. "Never mind. What I wanted can wait."

I move back inside the castle, wondering if I'll ever truly understand my mercurial sisters.

Silviana

I don't know what to think. Last night, I could've sworn I'd blown my cover in a stupid, idiotic way that's not worthy of the training I've had. This morning...Vlad acts like none of it happened. Matter of fact, he doesn't even try to bring it up. No. Instead, he knocks on my door and offers me shopping, of all things.

"Umm... Sorry, what?"

"Shopping. You must need new clothes, and I'm heading into town to run some errands."

I glance behind me at my meagre belongings. To be fair, he has a point, but—

"I don't have any money."

"Did I ask? Consider it a token of our appreciation for the warning you delivered."

Bemused, I have no choice but to follow him. Down the stairs we go, and he patiently walks side by side with me instead of speeding past me and waiting downstairs. He's equally patient once we're out of the castle—holding the door open for me—and as we walk toward the woods.

Once we're in the woods, he turns to me. "May I?"

I stare at him in naked confusion.

A smile tugs at his lips. "We can either walk forty-five minutes to town while you're in shoes that are ill-fitting...or I can carry you. You know my true nature, so it shouldn't be a hardship."

Is that a jab at what happened last night?

I choose to ignore it. If he wants to play games, fine. I can play them better than him.

"Go on."

He picks me up and in so doing ends up yanking on my braid. With an ow and a muffled cry of pain, I tug it back and glare at him.

"Scuze." He grins, and it looks too damn good on him. "A downside of your female charms."

He thinks I have charms?

Before I can say anything, he takes off.

And I'm reminded of all the reasons why I should be hating him. *Vampiri are ruthless and they don't care who they hurt and who they don't. They're a menace to society, human and Dacian. Hell, they're a menace to all supernaturals, period. And with the most recent in-fighting, it won't be long before they try to force another war.*

But then everything else I've seen so far about Vlad completely contradicts that. He's caring to a fault, and he's too damned patient with his siblings—most of whom seriously weren't spanked enough as kids, judging by their attitudes. And yet, Vlad is completely different.

But he's still a vampir. And a dangerous one. For all I know, this is just another façade, a game he's playing until he has me under his thumb. After all, he's everything I should hate.

I should hate his blue eyes. I should hate his smile. I should hate everything about him. Including his touch. And the way he's zooming past the trees, fast enough to make me nauseous.

Instead, all I can focus on is the little zing of electricity I feel wherever his hands touch me. And the way air seems to stop entering my lungs as it should, replaced instead by an odd feeling in the pit of my stomach.

I could call it nausea, sure. I could call it hate, definitely.

But am I lying to myself?

Vampiri killed our parents. They left us orphans. Fane's voice is so loud in my mind, it's as if he's standing right next to me. It takes everything in me not to jump out of Vlad's arms, to demand that he puts me down.

My idiotic brain melt is gone, replaced instead by what should've been there all along.

Get your head in the game. I can't let him know how I despise him, or how I despise most of his type. He cannot know. If he does, there's no more mission. And I'll need him, if I'm to accomplish my goal.

Chapter 5

Silviana

I wait until we're on the edge of the woods and Vlad sets me down on my feet to broach the conversation. "So...how were you turned?" Maybe if I get him talking, he'll let something slip—like the location of his vampir sire's journal.

Vlad shoots me a side-glance, then faces the throng of people we'll be approaching. "I'll tell you, but try to keep your voice low."

"Why?"

"When Tassa and Nico got together, the villagers weren't too happy. He's not accepted, and neither are the rest of us. The one upside is not all villagers are familiar with how we look."

I take in his sweater, the hoodie pulled up over his head, the flash of his startling blue eyes, and the mop of hair emerging out of the hood. My hand reaches for it before I realize what I'm doing, and I smooth it down, until some locks fall into his eyes, casting them in shadows.

Vlad freezes at my touch, and I slowly pull back. That stupid jolt of electricity is there again. *It's cold outside. I'm warm, his skin is icy. It's just regular static.*

I clear my throat. "Just keep your eyes lowered to the ground. I'm sure the startling blueness of your eyes isn't something that can be ignored, and it'll hint at who you are faster than a flash of your fangs."

He smirks—said fangs on full display, until he retracts them. "You think my eyes are startling?"

I roll my eyes. "It wasn't... Never mind." I grab his sleeve and tug him forward. "So, my answer?"

He sighs. "Do you really want to know?"

I toss him a glare he ignores. "You're about to pay for my clothes. The least I could do is make conversation, no? A little friendship never hurt anyone."

A chuckle escapes him. "Friendship, huh? All right." He clears his throat and ducks his head as we enter the full throng of people. He waits until we're back walking down the cobblestone paths before he speaks again, and his tone is a whisper I have to strain to hear. "Father found me when I was in a dark spot. I was lost, you could say. He'd already turned them all by then—Nico first, then Violeta, Mirabela, Alex and Liza. You haven't met Violeta yet, as she's away, but she sends her regards."

So that's where the sixth sibling is. I make a non-committal sound and point to the inside of a store. From the outside, it looks like it sells jeans and regular clothes. Vlad nods and follows me inside.

"Good to hear. So, Țepeș found you and...?"

"Offered me a choice."

At my surprised look, he chuckles again. The sales lady throws a look our way and Vlad makes sure to keep his back—and blue eyes— away from her.

"Surprising to most, I'm sure," he says. "He wasn't exactly famous for his mercy."

I think of the bloody history lessons—of the thousands Țepeș was rumored to have killed, whose heads decorated the pikes around his castle until time ravaged them and only bones were left. "You could say that."

Vlad chuckles. "Believe it or not, he saved me from making the worst choice of my life. See, up until I met Father, I'd been a killer."

"Seriously?" I'd been given a file on each siblings with what their life was like before they were turned, so this isn't news. Still, I infuse enough surprise into my voice and widen my eyes in response to his admission. If anything, what really surprises me is the fact he did admit. And that he sounds repentant.

"Da, seriously. Țepeș saved me, in more ways than one." My expression must communicate my doubt, because he adds, "I know what you've heard. What a lot of people know. But the man they talk about, the monster from the history books..." Vlad touches a shirt hanging on a rack, and shakes his head. "He's not the one I know." A beat later, he corrects himself, "Knew."

"You miss him?"

His eyes meet mine. Wordlessly, he nods. His jaw clenches, and he looks away, this time fully avoiding my gaze. The action is so raw, so...human...that it leaves me mute.

Vlad gestures vaguely to the clothes. "Choose a few things. Take your time to try them out, if you want."

Startled by his abrupt change in demeanor, I do as he bids. My gaze turns to the t-shirts, sweaters and jeans laid out. I pick two of each, not wanting to be greedy—also fully aware that I won't be around longer than it takes me to wear them.

"The shirts should fit me fine," I mutter to Vlad. "But I'll go try on the jeans."

He nods, still not meeting my gaze. I head to the sales lady and she points me in the direction of the fitting room. It's small, and I'm alone. Looks like there aren't many people around at this time. Maybe because it's early, who knows?

Slowly, I remove my current tattered jeans and sneakers and pull on one of the new pairs. The movement rubs up against the gauze, and I'm surprised to feel less of the ache than I did last night. *I guess Tassa knows her stuff.*

As for the jeans? They fit like a second skin, but my attention is not so much on them, as it is on the man outside.

Vampir. He's not a man. Get your head on straight, Silviana.

But then, why's he emitting every sign of grief? And I should know them well, given I'd seen them all in the mirror when looking at my reflection, and also seen them in Fane.

Thoughts of my brother make me miss him even more. He'd know what to tell me. He'd be able, with one conversation, to tell whether Vlad is truly someone I can trust or whether he's as duplicitous as I've been told.

But without Fane around, all I can rely on is myself, and my own instinct.

Movement outside has me on high alert. I hear Vlad speaking to the sales lady, then he comes in the back. A second later, a knock sounds on the fitting room door.

"Silviana, we need to go."

"Why, what's wrong?"

There's a pause, then, "Open the door."

Something in his voice broaches no tone for argument, so I do as he says. Vlad pushes the door open the rest of the way and slides inside. My heart start slamming into my ribcage, even as I move backward, until my back hits the wall.

"I—"

Vlad stops talking when his eyes land on me. I'd been about to try one of the other sweaters on—just in case—and he caught me midway through undressing. My tank top barely hides the red material of my bra, thin enough that he can surely see *everything*.

The blueness I'd mentioned earlier turns a dark hue, and a muscle ticks in his jaw. In that moment, staring at me so intently, seeing right through me, he steals my breath. And yes, it's because he's a vampir, and we're alone, and my heart is thundering. But it's because he's a *man*, too. And the naked desire on his features is something that's never been aimed at me.

I've had casual sex before, sure. But it was mutual, and more like a checklist, no real passion. The men looked at me with desire, but Vlad...it's like he wants to eat me up.

And I might just let him try.

I draw in another jagged breath, and he seems to catch himself. Shakes his head, as though snapping himself out of whatever thought held him captive, and turns his back to me.

"I won't hurt you, try to calm your heartbeat down. I'm sorry for bursting in, but we have a problem. You mentioned you knew about the perils we faced? Well, it seems one of the vampiri clans around the area has men here. And I've just spotted one outside this store."

With shaking hands, I pull on my regular sweater and take off the store jeans, before pulling on my own. I fold everything in a pile, taking a moment to collect my thoughts.

"Okay, I'm decent. You can turn around now."

He does, his eyes sad. "Please don't be afraid of me."

"I'm not." When he frowns, I lift my chin defiantly. "Try me. Come closer, and see if I scare."

What the hell are you doing? A voice at the back of my head warns. But I'm too far gone to care.

When Vlad doesn't move, I do. I grab two handfuls of his sweater and pull him toward me. He comes all too willingly, and we crash into the wall.

Vlad

I brace my hands on the wall so I don't crush Silviana, not that she seems to mind. She stares up at me, her gray eyes full of fire, her lips pursed—and goddamn, all I want to do is kiss her.

The image of her half-naked body is imprinted in my mind, and some very real manly desires course through my body. I glance down at her, trapped between me and the wall. "What game are you playing?"

The glare she gives me sharpens. "None. Other than to show you I'm not afraid."

"Your heart would say otherwise."

"There are other reasons why my heart would beat fast. Fear isn't the only one."

Arousal. Excitement.

I ignore the tiny voice at the back of my head. Instead, I move off Silviana, shaking my head. "The man outside. We need to hurry."

She picks up her clothes without a word and heads back outside. We go to the cashier, whom I'd had to glamour so I could gain entry at the back. She looks solely at Silviana as she rings the items, even when I hand over a wad of cash to pay for everything.

When she's bagged everything, I grab Silviana's hand and tug her after me, ignoring the way it feels in mine. Fragile. Warm. If I move my finger just so, I can feel the strength of her pulse beating. And the blood flowing underneath it.

Dammit.

Outside the store, there's no sign of the man I saw. We head into a computer store a few blocks down, where I quickly purchase a laptop for Mirabela, and get that bagged as well. Once we're outside again, I smell him.

"Keep walking," I tell Silviana. I haven't let go of her hand since we bought the clothes, and she doesn't seem to be inclined to get rid of me.

But no amount of walking fast will save us.

The man following behind us says one word. "Dracul."

I stop. We're close to a crowd of people. The last thing I want is to cause trouble for them, or have them realize who I am. So I turn to the man, handing Silviana the bag with the laptop. "You see that small restaurant with the patio?"

She looks over my shoulder and nods.

"Go grab us a table and wait for me there."

"But—"

"Go."

She scowls, but after a beat and a glance at the man, listens to me. I wait until she's out of earshot, before taking a step closer to him. He's a few inches shorter than me, but bulkier. His tattooed arms are on full display in a short-sleeved shirt. Equally on display are his fangs.

"Are you insane?" I hiss. "Humans could see you."

He shrugs. "And?"

I glance around—no one's watching. Good.

The moment after, I've got him by the throat, slammed into the wall. If anyone looks, they'll assume it's a usual fight and ignore us. What I need them *not* to see is our fangs and my eyes.

"*And* I'll remind you that the royal decree says we're to hide our presence from humans."

"Ain't no royals around to enforce the decree."

My grip on his throat tightens. My nails lengthen, digging into his skin. He gulps, his eyes widening.

"You clearly haven't seen the message in the Ardelean compound, have you?"

He tries to swallow, but can't. My grip is too tight.

"What clan do you belong to?"

"Fuck you."

I tighten my grip on him. Let some glamour slip into my eyes—it's no easy feat to glamour a vampir, but when they're weaker than us? I feel the link nearly slip into place, his mind opening to me—

"Stop!" He lifts a hand to his forehead, breaking eye contact. "Fuck. Just...stop. I'll tell you what you want to know."

"Now we're getting somewhere." I don't remove my hand off his throat. Only glance over my shoulder at the other approaching vampiri, enough to glamour them. "Don't you fucking move against me." When they're frozen, I turn back to the guy. "You were saying?"

"Hatmanu. I'm with the Hatmanu clan."

He still won't look at me, which is just as well. I'm trying to fight off the surprise in my expression. The Hatmanu clan is settled in the northern part of the Carpathian Mountains, *far* away from our current location.

"Aren't you a little far away from your territory, vampir?"

He stares at the ground, saying nothing.

"You can either make me use glamour—and we both know it'll be painful if you resist me—or you can willingly tell me what I want to know."

"What was all that about?" Silviana asks when I finally join her at the table.

I wipe my hand—and the vampir's blood—off my dark jeans, and take a seat opposite her. "More problems. Vampir politics."

The waiter comes then and we order some food. I wait until he's gone.

"Maybe it would help if you talked it out?"

I meet Silviana's gaze. It's direct, no ounce of guile in it. What I really need to do is talk to my siblings and warn them. Instead, I pull out my cell and shoot a quick text to Violeta: *You were right. They're hunting us. Tell Marcus to be careful.*

Her answer pings less than a few seconds later. *You, too.*

Sighing, I set the phone away and look up at Silviana. "What do you know about the set-up of the vampir world?"

If she's surprised at my opening, she doesn't show it. "I know the House of Dracul was meant to be the top dog. The royals, above all clans. Their edict was to be followed by every vampir. But...my parents heard rumors that this wasn't the case, in the end."

"Da, you could say that."

The waiter returns with a salad for Silviana and a glass of red wine for me. She glances at the drink, then at me when I sip it.

I grin. "Wine. It's refreshing."

"Right." She takes a bite of her salad, then gestures for me to continue. "You were saying?"

I take another sip of wine. The darkness of the liquid feels too damn good, quieting my bloodlust somewhat. "Originally, Romania had thirteen vampiri clans. While we were in self-imposed exile, those thirteen clans amalgamated to six: Ardelean in the territory bordered by the Carpathian Mountains, Cazacu in the northeast, Eder in the southeast, Lazarescu in the southwest, and two clans *in* the Carpathian Mountains themselves—as in, the inverted L-shaped string of mountains—Munteanu and Hatmanu." I swirl the wine in the glass, then drink again. "While that should be good news for us, it's the exact opposite."

"Because it means more power against you?"

"Something like that."

"And then there's the vampir hunters."

I frown at her. "How do you know about that?"

"My parents."

Her explanations are shorter than mine, and that alone should set me on edge. But I'm so damned tired of seeing enemies everywhere.

"Well, they're right. So yes, we have six unruly clans and who knows how many hunters after us. And, according to you, dark witches who should've been extinct." *Not to mention a deadly curse.* "And our only hope of keeping some kind of calm is by retaking our place among the vampiri."

"To rule them."

I incline my head and take another sip. And another. And a third.

"What if there's a simpler way?"

"What do you mean?"

"Well…" She swallows her last bite of salad, and it takes me a moment longer to tear my eyes from her lips. "I know it's what I said originally, and I stand by it. It's what I thought, when I came here, too—that the only way you could win is by coming out of the shadows and ruling, and therefore keeping the balance among the supernaturals. But what if the witches could help? If you send some of your siblings to scout for more…"

"We don't want to split up. It's bad enough Violeta is away from us. Our only strength right now lies in numbers."

That, and if we split up, none of us will know whether the curse is hitting the others.

Silviana surprises me by reaching over the table, touching my hand. "I'm sorry. For everything you're going through. If there's anything I can do, please… I already owe you, so I'd like to help."

I nod, flipping my palm to touch hers. "Thank you."

A bolt of electricity shoots me when she rakes her nails in my palm. And then the damned waiter comes with our main meal, and I want to strangle him when his arrival makes Silviana pull her hand away and lean back in her seat.

To say I'm elated by the time we return would be an understatement. My bloodlust is under control, replaced instead by another type of lust—something even more primal. As I pass through the trees like lightning, I can't help tightening my hold on Silviana. Her hair tickles my chin, the tidy braid once more undone. A faint whiff of jasmine hits my nose, soon gone. And then we're at the castle. Regretfully, I let her go, and force my hands back by my side.

Silviana looks up. "Thank you. For today. It was nice to be normal, for a change."

I nod, already filing away her comment for a later time. Violeta told me to pay attention to everything she says and does... Yet at the end of a day spent with her, all I can say is Silviana is a mystery wrapped in seduction. Does she have any malice toward us? Nothing she said hinted at it, but I don't know if that's because it's what I want to believe, or whether it's the actual truth.

The minute we step into the castle, it's to another argument. *For fuck's sake, can't they behave just once? Is that so impossible to ask for?*

Groaning, I pass Silviana and enter the living room—just in time for Liza to send something flying my way. I duck and shield Silviana as whatever it is crashes against the wall. Silviana's gasp is muffled against my throat, her pulse beating wildly.

"Relax," I say, pulling back and offering a smile. "It's not a war. Just my siblings being crazy."

Behind me, Liza erupts. "It's one thing hearing her in the house, Nico, but can you fucking keep the PDA to a minimum?"

"Says the one who spreads her legs for anything that moves."

A screech follows his less-than-tactful delivery, and I groan again. Even more so when Liza turns blazing red eyes to me and Silviana.

"And *you*! Where the fuck were you?"

Mirabela stands and sets her drink on the table loudly. "Getting me a new laptop."

"So now we're errand boys?"

"Enough, Elizabeta. Need I remind you, dear sister, we are still precariously on the edge with the vampir community and the sooner I can find us a new castle to operate from, the better?"

"About that." All eyes turn to me. "I had an interesting encounter with a member of the Hatmanu clan. And Violeta told me one of Marcus' kids has seen other weird people in a town near them."

"They're looking for us," Nico says.

I nod. "They heard the message about the Ardelean clan, loud and clear. Now it seems they're eager to take us on before anyone else can do anything."

"And you don't think it's weird all this comes about when *she* arrives here?" Liza snarls, pointing at Silviana.

"No, I don't," I say. "Now, can we sit down and enjoy some dinner so I can fill you all in?"

With grumbles and more than one dark glare, we all move into the dining room. And all throughout, I keep my eye on Alex, quiet in a corner. When *he's* quiet, I know things are about to get messy.

Silviana

Having dinner with a table full of vampiri was not something I'd ever thought I'd experience. But...here I am. And despite my best efforts to keep my heartbeat under control, I can sense Alex's glare on me. It hasn't left me since I arrived.

I'm not fooling him. And I know when I should stay away, and when I shouldn't. Alex is the type of dangerous I want nothing to do with. The way he follows my every move is enough to make my skin crawl. His predatory intent is clear—to kill. Exactly what I'd expect from a vampir.

"They're not so bad."

I nearly spill my drink on myself when Tassa leans in to me. I'm not an idiot—they placed the human next to me at dinner, intending to make me feel comfortable. Safe. As if I ever would in a den full of vampiri.

I don't let any of my revulsion show. Especially not to her.

When I turn to her, there's a biting remark on my lips. Something I intended to sound offhanded. Yet I meet her open gaze, her vulnerable expression, and that remark stalls on my lips.

Instead, what comes out is, "How so?"

"Well." She gives me a small smile, as if pleased at my answer. "Take Mirabela, for one."

I look at the statuesque beauty, the way her head is leaning toward Nico.

"She seems..."

Tassa chuckles. "I know. She's scary as hell, but really, she's just protective of everyone else. Being the eldest female and all."

Without looking at us, Mirabela raises her voice. "Careful you don't make me sound like a teddy bear, Tassa."

"Never," she shoots back. There's a glimmer of amusement in her eyes when she turns to me and winks. "Want to go for a walk?"

"Erm—"

Before I can say yay or nay, she's got my hand in hers and pulling me after her.

Nico calls out behind us. "Not past the woods, inima mea."

She blows him a kiss over her shoulder but never stops dragging me. Once we're out of the castle, the night sky above us, the stars shining brightly, the moon hidden behind a single cloud… it's easy to get lost in the fairytale.

"It's beautiful, isn't it?"

I take in the small courtyard we're in, where once upon a time stables might've been prepped for guests, page boys and knights might've run around… and I nod. "Very."

She grins. "You know, when I came here, I was a mess. That's why I'm probably the best suited for you to talk to."

Wariness fills me, though I try not to show it. Is she here to draw more information out of me? They think because she's human, I'll be able to connect or something?

It won't work. I've been trained better than that, and I can keep a cool head around them. So I say nothing, waiting to see what her next move will be.

"I know vampiri have the worst reputation."

"Especially the House of Dracul."

She chuckles. "See, you have an advantage. When I came here, I didn't even know about them, let alone their existence. And lo and behold, I'm now entangled with one of the heirs." She shakes her read ruefully. "Life is full of surprises."

I'm not convinced, but I nod to placate her.

To my surprise, she adds, "I'm not here to convince you to like them. Only you know what your experiences were that led you here and what filters you're using to judge them. But, tough as they may appear, they're also...not. If you allow it, you can find out for yourself."

I say nothing again, and the moon hides underneath another cloud, hiding Tassa's expression. A shiver runs down my spine.

She turns to leave, and I find myself not wanting her to. "Wait. I... Thank you, I guess. I'm not quite sure what to make of it yet. But, how did you land in all of this? I mean, to hook up with a vampir... Weren't you afraid?"

"My father was killed," she says softly.

The revelation leaves me stunned. "I—I'm sorry to hear that."

"It's okay. I... Time helps. But what I meant to say is, I could have also been killed then."

"Why?"

"Because my father was assassinated, murdered by some creatures. He was a doctor and he helped both humans and vampiri."

I barely restrain my jaw from dropping.

"Nico was there. I fought off some assailants but if he hadn't come, they would've burned the house down, and me with it. So, no, fear doesn't really come into play."

"And what makes you think he wasn't involved?" It's a cruel question, but one that needs to be asked.

She meets my gaze unreservedly. "I thought so, too, for a while. But these guys? They're really not as bad as you think. Give them a chance. At least...the less murderous ones."

With a wink, she's gone.

And then I become aware of another presence—a distinctly less friendly one.

"I wouldn't listen to the human, if I were you," Alex warns.

I whirl on him, trying to remember my breathing exercises so I can keep my heartbeat under control. "What do you want?"

He snorts, pushing off the wall he was leaning against. His blue eyes are cold, impenetrable—shards of ice. "Cute. You really think you can hide your fear from me?"

I take a step back, then stop. Tilt my chin upward. "I'm not afraid."

"Keep lying to yourself. But I bet your blood tastes so, so sweet."

My heartbeat thuds faster, and this time, I can't stop it.

Alex's smirk widens. "Watch your back, witch. You never know when the next corner you turn might be your last."

A beat later, he's gone. It takes me a lot longer to calm down.

After running into Alex, I return to the dinner. He follows shortly after, acting completely unruffled. *Psychopath.*

Tassa keeps my attention the rest of the dinner, and walks me to my door when we're done. Something I'm inherently thankful for, given I'm wary of Alex ripping my throat out before anyone can intervene.

"You okay?"

I look up from the ground, into Tassa's worried expression. "Yes, sorry. I was just lost in thought."

She tilts her head to the side, frowning. "Did Alex say something to you?"

"What? No, he—no."

Tassa's eyes widen, then she scowls. "That prejudiced idiot. I know he's got a thing against humans—God knows why, since he was a doctor in his past life—but this is getting out of control. I'll talk to Nico and—"

"No!" I grab her arm before I can stop myself, then release it just as fast. "I mean, please, Tassa, just don't say anything. Alex is... I get it. I get him. I'd be worried if someone popped up out of nowhere and threatened my family, too." *Not really, but that's beside the point. If I stir up shit between the siblings, my chances of getting that journal before I'm kicked out of here are zero.*

Tassa seems to think it over, then nods, slowly. "Okay, fine. I won't say anything, but on one condition. If he says something again, or does anything, let me know."

Relief spreads through me. "Deal."

She gestures to the door to my room—I hadn't even realized we were on my floor. "How are your wounds, by the way?"

"Good. Much, much better, thanks in large part to your magic balm."

Tassa gives me a small smile. "Nothing magic about it. But, Silviana... While you're here, I'd love your help with some herbs and maybe some potions. There's a lot I haven't been able to replicate that my dad used to do and, well, I think it'd come in handy."

I sense there's more to her request, but see no harm in agreeing. "Sure, I don't mind."

"Great! I'll leave the stuff down in the kitchen—Nico's siblings don't really go there—and some instructions, as well as more of my balm for your wounds. Sound good?"

I nod and watch her go, wondering if she's heading to Nico's room, or back to the village. And then I realize it doesn't matter, and it's not my business anyway. She's not my friend. She's just a way in.

The next morning finds me bright and early in the kitchen, after a quick shower in the closest bathroom I could find. As promised, Tassa left some herbs in jars—labelled—and some instructions for what she needs done. A small container holds more of the calendula balm, and I reapply it to my wrists, ankles and waist. The burns are almost gone already, which is both insane and humbling. Mother Nature sure takes care of us.

Thankfully, Tassa's writing is easy enough to decipher. Most of what she needs are creams, which I'm able to quickly whip up, with the help of a little bit of magic. The last two, however, seem a little more complicated.

A few hours later, I'm still trying to figure out why they're bugging me, when Mirabela waltzes in. She leans against a wall and arches an eyebrow toward me.

"You're still here, then?"

I steel my spine and face her. "Tassa mentioned she needed help with healing potions. I can speed some processes along."

"Ah. Well, if *Tassa* said so, then I suppose we'll all fall in line."

I turn my gaze away, focusing on what I'm doing.

"Didn't you spin my brother some tale about your magic being depleted? It seems fine to me."

Gritting my teeth, I hiss, "Small spells are easy, and require very little focus."

"Interesting. And yet your focus already seems shot to hell, if you're cutting yourself instead of the herbs."

Shit. She smelled the blood.

I don't get enough time to worry about that, or the connections Mirabela might make. The second after she speaks, she's by my side, breathing down my neck. I jump and lose control of the fire, incinerating the herbs in the process.

"Hmm. Looks like you won't be that helpful, right?"

I scowl at her. "If you're trying to intimidate me—"

Maybe Tassa's words the night before gave me false hope where she's concerned. But suddenly I can see how she's just as intimidating as her crazier sister.

Especially when she pushes in my face until we're almost nose to nose, her fangs on display. "Intimidate? I must've lost my touch. I want you *gone*. Tonight. If you know what's good for you."

"Tassa—"

"—is but a human. In *my* house."

"Vlad—"

"—can't see past your deceit. But I can. And I'm not fooled by your doe-eyed pleas for help in the least." She moves her lips to my ear. "If you really are the witch you say you are, then a coven should be expecting you. Run along."

"Mirabela."

She freezes at Vlad's tone, but doesn't move away. Instead, she mouths to me, *Tonight. Gone. Or else.*

The moment after, she turns and disappears down the hall. I fall back against the counter, my hands shaking.

"I'm sorry about her," Vlad starts. He says something else, but I don't hear it.

My thoughts are churning into a mess. That's a few too many times I've gotten threatened, and the only thing that's saved me is Vlad. But what if he's not around? What if I find myself alone? I was so petrified earlier, I didn't even think to use my magic. And let's face it, Mirabela would've cut my throat before I could even get enough blood to cast a spell.

Fane said not to take any chances. But our Grand Master, and everyone else, expects me to find that damned journal. And while I haven't had a single chance to look for it, that's no excuse—the clock is ticking. The two arguing sides war against each other in my mind, and only one has the right answer.

Without looking at Vlad, I walk away.

Shaking, I make my way to the room to collect what few belongings I have. I'll just have to find another way to infiltrate them. The Grand Master gave me two weeks until the new moon, and I'm only in the first few days of the mission. But I have to play it smart, lest they see through my disguise. And if I end up dead ahead of time, the mission will be a failure anyway.

A voice at the back of my head warns me that getting attacked would be stupid—I'm anything but stupid. Today was nice with Vlad but while I might have forgotten his family's history for a bit, I never once forgot what he is. And I don't want to become food—especially given the way he's been gazing my way a few times.

Done packing, I open the door, only to find Vlad on the threshold. "You don't have to go."

His blue eyes are sad, contrition radiating off every bone in his body. Not even that is enough to get me to stay.

"But I do. I don't want to come between you and your family, and add to what's already a complicated relationship." I grip my bag tighter. "I'll be fine."

He searches my features, seems about to say something, stops. Then recovers, "Where will you go that's safe?"

"An inn in town, for a bit. Then move on and make my way to a coven." *With your dad's journal. One way or another.*

"I see." He rubs the back of his neck. "Let me at least bring you to the village. It's getting dark."

With Vlad carrying me, my backpack and the bag of clothes we'd bought the previous day, the trees blur past. Night is full on, the moon barely casting a glow. The stars are insanely bright.

Too soon, he sets me on my feet. His hand lingers on mine, loosely holding my fingers. "Are you sure about this?"

I nod. "I'll be fine."

He glances over my shoulder, nodding toward a dark brown building. "That inn is good. At least according to Tassa, she's helped them a lot. You should be safe there." He slips a piece of paper and some cash in my hand. "My phone number. If you need me."

"Thank you." Without thinking much about it, I hug him.

His hands come around my waist, squeezing me as though he doesn't want to hurt me. When I pull back, we're close. So damn close.

Move away, a voice at the back of my head says.

Kiss him, says another.

I choose the second option, allowing my lips to graze his. Vlad inhales sharply, and then his hand is on the back of my neck, deepening the kiss. My toes curl, my knees weakening with each swipe of his tongue against mine.

I've had kisses, before. Same as I've had sex. So why the hell does *his* kiss feel so—so—

Forbidden. Sensual. Addictive.

I shove the thoughts away, swept away as I am by his lips moving against mine, his body covering mine. Making me feel safe. Secure. Protected.

Breathless, I pull away from him. Vlad searches my eyes, trying to figure out what I'm thinking. I don't give him a chance to figure it out, before walking off.

I did it for the mission. Because the kiss will keep him wanting. He may be a vampir, but he's also a man. And if he wants me, I'll see him again. I'll have another chance to get the journal. That's all. That's the only reason why I did it.

Still, it's in a daze that I check into the inn, get a room, and go up to it. Without even bothering to get undressed, I go back down to the bar and purchase a bottle of wine—the same deep red Vlad drank the previous day—and head back to my room.

I open the bottle of wine and am halfway through enjoying a well-earned glass when there's a knock on the door. *Could be a drunkard.* Something tells me it's not.

Setting the glass aside, I get up and open the door. The minute my eyes land on the newcomer, they open wide and I pull him inside the room.

Then, I face the familiar man from the coven.

"What's the meaning of this, Valeriu?"

"Your brother sent me."

Fane hates his guts. He's seen him sniffing around me way too often to trust him.

"I doubt that."

"Fine, the Grand Master sent me, but Fane also sent a message."

He hands me a letter. I set it aside to read later, in peace and alone.

"What does the Grand Master want?"

"A report."

"Isn't it a bit early to ask for one? I've just been kicked out of the castle!"

He doesn't appear impressed by my diatribe. "The news, Lana. Now."

"Don't call me that. Only Fane does."

He shrugs and waits. Reluctantly, I explain the situation. His scowl worsens.

"I'll inform the Grand Master and make sure the room is taken care of."

"Don't. Unless you want them to find out."

He taps his chin. "How did they seem?"

Complicated. Aloud, I say, "Aloof. But I seem to have caught one's attention. I plan to capitalize on it."

"You do that. No matter what the cost, the mission comes first."

The nausea doesn't go away when he leaves, so I finish the bottle and give in to sleep.

Chapter 6

Silviana

The lumpy bed doesn't make for a good night of sleep, not that I could really sleep, given Valeriu's appearance. It left me feeling oddly off-balance. And angry, if I'm truly honest. I guess I'd thought the fact they were finally letting me in on a mission meant they trusted me. That I'd be allowed to carry out the mission as I saw fit, in so far as I got results. And yet, that's not what I'm gathering based on last night.

Are they keeping an eye on me, then? And what if I screw up?

Fane's letter was a short one-liner, dictated via his computer and printed, as is his fashion—warning me to watch out again. Watch out for the vampiri, or for our people? I can't say it makes much sense.

And I desperately wish I had his counsel to rely on right now, given the instructions I'm getting.

I watch the sun rise past my window, enjoying the somewhat peaceful morning—even if it's not so in my head. Recalling breakfast is at seven, I drag my butt downstairs, pile some food mindlessly on my plate, and force myself to eat. A family of tourists speaks in English in another corner of the dining room area, but luckily I'm seated as far away from them as possible. The food tastes like ash on my tongue, but I force it down, knowing my body needs the fuel.

I'm halfway through the plate when a hand waves in front of my face and I jerk. Tassa quickly pulls it back, giving me a weak smile.

"Sorry! Sorry. I saw you through the window and barged in before I could think twice."

"Oh."

I don't know why I'm so surprised by her appearance. I know, based on the last few days that she spends half her time in the village, half of it at the castle. And Vlad alluded to how the villagers don't necessarily like that latter bit.

My eyes scan the area out of habit. The old lady who'd served me my breakfast has her narrowed gaze on Tassa's back. If she's aware of it, she doesn't show signs of it.

Instead, Tassa seems to take my monosyllabic response as an invitation to sit. "I heard what happened from Nico."

Instead of answering her this time, I shove food in my mouth and keep quiet.

Tassa continues, "Mirabela'll be gone soon, you know? She's preparing to go on business, out of town. Which means she won't be at the castle anymore."

"Liza and Alex will, though."

She tilts her head, her gaze sympathetic. "They gave me a hard time, too. They still do, some of them. But Vlad's a good one."

I choke on my toast, swallow some water, then speak through teary eyes. "You speak as if we're an item."

She shrugs. "I'm not trying to assume, but he's pretty keen on you."

A blush creeps up my cheeks. Especially remembering our brief kiss yesterday. The same kiss that sparked some rather carnal dreams I've been trying to forget. I don't need this cloudiness in my head.

Why are her words making me feel good? They shouldn't. At all. I should be disgusted. But the warmth in my stomach can't be ignored. I reason it as tasting success. If Vlad is keen on me, he's more likely to lobby for me to get back to the castle and therefore I'll be closer to my goal. And once I have that success under my belt, no one—not Valeriu, not the Grand Master—will be able to say I'm just a woman.

Tassa clears her throat. "Anyway, what I really came to say is tomorrow's my birthday."

"I...oh. Happy birthday."

She grins wider at my weak reply. "Thanks. Nico's taking me to one of the local pubs to celebrate. Some of his siblings will show—the ones who don't hate my guts—so you're welcome to join."

"I wouldn't want to intrude."

"You're not. I'm inviting you. Come, please. I'm sure Vlad will be happy."

A wink later, she's gone. I stare at my food, contemplating her request.

Would it be that horrible of an idea to show? Valeriu said to do whatever I need to in order to succeed. I won't be whoring myself out to a vampir, unlike what he implied, but it doesn't mean I can't use some form of seduction to turn Vlad to putty in my hand.

Of course, I could use the time to sneak into the castle and get what I need but... *Some of his siblings will show—the ones who don't hate my guts.* Something tells me that excludes Liza and Alex. And if they catch me snooping? I'm guessing they won't be as likely to let me go as Vlad was.

At the end of the day, if he's my "in," I might as well take it.

Resolved, I finish off my plate and head back to my room. Time to see if I have anything to wear...

Vlad

I set the fifth book back on the shelf in the library, and turn to the window, sighing.

"Penny for your thoughts?"

I face Nico. Too many words are on the tip of my tongue, from the truth of what happened a few nights ago, to asking if Tassa has seen Silviana. But I say nothing of the like. "Just thoughts, is all."

Nico nods and heads to the shelf, and the book I'd just set back. His eyebrows rise mockingly. "*Pride and Prejudice*? Brother, I didn't think your tastes ran so..."

I scowl at him. "Cut it out. I was randomly browsing."

"Mm." He sits on the side of the armchair. "I've *randomly browsed*, too." When I say nothing, he switches the subject. "About what you were saying. Your encounter with the Hatmanu man."

"What about him?"

"I want to show you something. Before I flap my mouth to the rest, who are less...calm...than us."

"Okay..."

Nico stands and zooms out, presumably to his office. Slower, almost at a human pace, I follow him. I could've just as easily rushed up the stairs, but that sluggishness from a few days ago feels right upon me again. And, frankly, the last thing I want is him to ask pointed questions.

Up the stairs I go, then down a maze of corridors. I finally enter his office—a smaller version of the main library, decorated in dark wood and sofas. Massive windows give onto the grounds, letting some light enter, considerably brightening the otherwise somber room.

Nico shuts the door behind me and goes behind the desk. Unfurls a long map. Curious, I step toward it.

"This is—"

"A copy of the map you created, yes. I had someone at the print store in town duplicate it in color." When he sees my look of alarm, he rolls his eyes. "Relax. I glamoured them to make sure they don't go blabbing."

He finishes rolling the map and uses some paperweights to keep it flat on the table. Then, he points to a spot roughly in the middle of the Carpathian Mountains. "This is our location, right?"

"Mhmm."

His index finger travels across the map, to the left of the country, near the border with Hungary. "And Violeta is hiding here for now."

"Right..."

"And she said it's in town that the kids saw some weird people, presumably vampiri." His finger moves a little north of Violeta's location. "So, fairly close, right?"

"Da..."

He then uses his free hand to point to the inverted L of the Carpathian Mountains. "Romania is split now in six areas, one for each of the clans. Ardelean, which now belongs to us"—he points to the inside of the L—"Cazacu"—he points to the right side of the L, between the mountains and Moldova—"Eder"—the area under the Cazacu land—"and Lazarescu"—the area to the left of that, under the mountains.

"I drew the map, remember? After all the research I compiled once Tassa told us. None of this is new to me."

"I know, brother. Bear with me." He points to the inverted L of the mountains. "Doesn't it strike you weird that instead of taking the rest of the country, there are two clans who have taken over the L of the Carpathian Mountains?"

"It did... but we figured they liked the cover of the mountains."

"Maybe."

"You're not convinced?"

"No."

I frown. "Then, why do you think they did this?"

"Because I think that similarly to the wolves we've found, there are shifters within these forests. And...hunters."

I drop into the chair, stunned. "They're forming alliances. Beyond just vampiri..."

"Yep." Nico takes a seat as well, resting his chin on his palm. "Which puts your encounter with the guy from the Hatmanu clan into a new light, right?"

"Because they're trying to warn us off, flexing muscles to show they've got alliances at the ready."

"But wouldn't it be interesting if yet another clan wanted to ally instead with us?"

My eyes widen. "You think the Munteanu clan would be willing to do that?"

Nico hesitates, then pulls out a piece of paper. "I found this jammed in Tassa's door when I went to her yesterday."

I unroll the old-school parchment and read. The message is simple, written in a manly, cursive handwriting. *We wish to meet.* Underneath it is the sigil of the Munteanu clan—a mountain shaped as an M.

"Marcus' kids, they saw men with the M tattoo in town." I run a finger down the map, tapping it randomly. "Did you show the others?"

"Not yet. I plan to."

"Because you want to take the Munteanus up on their offer?"

Nico says, "We'll see. First, we have to see how everyone feels about that."

I hand him back the paper. Right as he puts it away, the door to his office opens and Tassa walks in. She slows down when she sees me, though her grin only widens. "I can come back?"

"No, no, inima mea. Come in. We're done for now, anyway." He nods at me. "Keep it between us for now."

I incline my head and get up, kissing Tassa on both cheeks before heading out the door. As I close it behind me, I catch Nico's tone softening.

"What's got you looking like the cat who ate the canary?"

Tassa drops her voice to a whisper, but it's easy for me to catch. "I saw Silviana just now. And invited her to my birthday party."

"Nataşa…"

His mock-growl doesn't sound nearly as intimidating when it's followed by her giggle.

"I'm not meddling, I promise!"

"Aren't you? We talked about this. It has to be done in their own time."

"And it will. But...a little nudge never hurt anyone."

Words change to other sounds then, and I quickly move away from the door. Whatever Tassa's meddling in, I'm more than happy to let her if it means I'll see Silviana again.

Silviana

I thought I'd feel out of place in my dark jeans and another off-the-shoulders top, but it turns out I fit right in when I walk into the pub where Tassa's party is being held.

After spending all of the previous day in a fit of nervous energy and angry ruminations—about Valeriu and my coven's underhanded tactics—I'm more than ready to let go and have some fun. Staying uptight won't make me any friends, and this is a chance I can't lose.

My eyes scan the area, and I immediately find the Dracul clan in a corner of the bar, occupying a few booths. Nico's arm is around Tassa, whispering in her ear. As I'd expected, I can't see Alex or Liza anywhere, but there's another dark-haired woman with a tall guy sitting opposite Nico and Tassa.

Before I can observe more of them, Vlad's at my side. "You're here."

His wide eyes settle on mine, and he grins slowly. His blue irises seem to reflect the dim light around us. I take in his regular t-shirt, dark jeans, and Adidas shoes. "You look almost normal."

He chuckles, moving a step closer. "I'll take the compliment."

I can't help giving a small smile back. "Tassa invited me."

"I'm glad she did. Shall we?"

The memory of our kiss seems to linger between us like an unacknowledged entity. I don't know if that's a good thing or not, but all we do is stare at each other for a moment.

Why is it so damn easy to forget he's a vampir, and I'm here on a mission?

The deep beats of some rock & roll piece roll through the bar. I move closer—or Vlad does—and then his hand is on my lower back, sending jolts of electricity through me all over again. He steers me along to the corner his siblings are in. I shouldn't be feeling heat from his touch, but it's like suddenly I'm on fire.

Once we're close by, Tassa glances my way and extricates herself from Nico to give me a tipsy hug. "You came! I'm so glad." Lower, she adds, "Come, meet Violeta."

Before I can answer, Vlad's hand tightens on my back. He glances over his shoulder, toward the entrance, and a low growl rises from him. It's enough to have me tense. And he's not alone in his reaction. Nico stands from the table, his face a stormy mask. With nary a glance to me, him and Vlad take off.

Tassa watches them go with a perplexed frown, then shrugs. She pulls my hand, bringing me to the booth and forcing me to take Nico's seat.

"This is Violeta and her c—boyfriend, Marcus."

I don't miss the odd pause as she introduces him. He gives me a nod, while Violeta grins at me. She looks so much like Nico, it's uncanny. Same raven hair, only hers is straighter and cut just below her jawline, while his is curly; same flaming blue eyes; even the curve of their jaw is similar. There are some dark circles under her eyes, but overall she's the picture of the peppy sister. Her guy, on the other hand, is much more subdued. And his gaze, too, is stuck on the front entrance.

"About time my siblings learned to diversify," Violeta says, taking my attention of his odd behavior.

"Um...?"

She chuckles. Marcus' gaze is still glued somewhere else, but neither Violeta nor Tassa act like it's weird—what the hell is going on?

"You're a witch, right? Or so Tassa tells me."

A hint of arrogance infuses my tone. "Da, I am."

"If only you'd been around weeks ago." She chuckles. "You missed all the fun."

"Fun?"

Tassa rolls her eyes. "Never mind that! Let's get some drinks."

Three rounds of țuică shots later, I'm buzzing with energy and heat. Romanian homemade vodka will do that to you.

Vlad and Nico are still not back, so I answer Violeta's barely-veiled questions—stopping just short of an interrogation—while keeping an eye on Tassa. As the only other human between us, I want to make sure she's not too drunk by the end of the night. Especially since her boyfriend seems to have disappeared.

As if my thoughts conjured him, Nico returns to the table, followed by Vlad.

I stand to let Nico retake his spot, but he shakes his head and holds out his hand to Tassa. "Dance with me?"

She grins and nearly falls into his arms. With practiced ease, he holds onto her waist and brings her to the dance floor. They look almost...normal. A normal couple, with normal problems. But something tells me the things he's whispering in her ear aren't just sweet nothings.

"Silviana?"

I glance at Vlad, only then noticing his outstretched hand. Blushing, I take it and get to my feet. The room spins around me for a second. *Damned shots.*

Vlad chuckles, his gaze going to the table littered with empty shot glasses. "I see you girls had fun."

"It's the least we could do. Loneliness begets—well..." I tap my chin. "There was a line about that, right?"

Vlad shakes his head, shares a glance with Marcus, then drags me to the dance floor. With his hands on my hips, his body next to mine, I soon get lost in the rhythm—at least, for a moment. When's the last time I've had a night like this? When's the last time my days didn't consist of proving myself, of denying myself?

Too long.

So I let Vlad lead the dance, and my body answers his. Our hips sway in sync, and when he pulls me even closer, I don't object. That same electricity I'd felt before seems to now hum between us, its own living, breathing entity.

But I still can't stop my mind from churning.

When the song changes to a slower beat, I wrap my arms around Vlad's neck and press my mouth to his ear. "What happened, earlier?"

I feel him shivering, and my body tightens in response. I don't know why I'm reacting like this to him—like I'm actually attracted to him—but that's a question for another day.

"Just...clan business."

I pull back, meeting his gaze. Vlad's eyes drop to my lips, and for a second, I forget my train of thought. But like an annoying mosquito, it comes back.

"What kind of business?"

Shadows of doubt linger in his eyes. Am I pushing too hard? Maybe. But it's not like I'll get answers if I don't ask.

"Tassa was worried."

"She seemed pretty oblivious to me."

I frown. "That's not a nice thing to say."

He sighs, dropping his head against my shoulder. "You're right, it's not. It's just... do you remember the people out in the street, the other day?"

"Yeah, you told your siblings they were from the Hatmanu clan?"

"Right. Well, Nico thinks he saw some of their people outside here. And with Tassa... He didn't want to risk it."

A shiver runs up my spine. "So, were they?"

Vlad lifts his head, his expression tense. "Da. But they disappeared the moment they saw us."

I let him sway to the music for a bit, lost in thought, before I ask, "What does that mean, then?"

"It means things are about to get ugly."

Vlad

Having Silviana in my arms is more than I'd hoped for. When I came here, I expected to see her, talk to her, but this...is pure torture. And still I can't make myself stay away.

When I sense her tiring in my arms, I lead her to the table. Nico and Tassa are still dancing—she seems to be having a blast, which is probably what he's aiming for so she's not aware of the danger courting us.

Uneasiness still lingers with me, though, so I murmur to Silviana that I'll be back and head outside. One more look to make sure they haven't returned, that's all I want. That...and some air.

Was Silviana asking me those questions because she cares, or because there's another reason?

I want to trust her. To believe she has no ulterior motives. But Liza and Alex's accusations are hard to shake off.

Still, it's not like I can stay away. Soon enough, I can't help navigating back to Silviana. Only, she's not in the spot I left her in.

Violeta reads the question I don't voice and points to the bar. "She went to get refills."

I find her head of strawberry-blonde curls and make my way to her, then stop in the throng of people. She's not alone. The man next to her is dressed casually enough—jeans, black t-shirt—but he's leaning in her personal space. Even from afar, I can tell her back is tense. But before I can do anything, he glances up, sees me, and steps away.

Odd. Even with the distance, I should've been able to hear him.

I make my way through the rest of the people and touch Silviana's shoulder, glaring at him. "Something wrong?"

"Nothing," she says, lowering her voice. "A drunkard, is all. Don't worry about it."

A dark head of anger peeks past my cool exterior. I recognize the feel—the bloodlust—and shove it back down. "Are you sure?"

She looks up at me, lips parted, and nods. But instead of moving away, her eyes drop to my mouth. That same humming electricity from before, during our dance, is back. Stronger. More demanding. And then Silviana rises on her tiptoes and kisses me.

The soft press of her lips takes me by surprise—and then I'm kissing her back, moving my hand from her elbow to her waist, pulling her body against mine. She gasps, and I take advantage to own her mouth, a delicious victory as I finally, finally taste her the way I've been craving and ignoring.

By the time we pull apart, she seems dazed. I grin, then reach for the tray behind her. "I'll carry these to the girls."

When I reach the table, it's to hollers from Violeta and amused glances from Marcus. But Silviana...she's gone.

Chapter 7

Vlad

After searching for Silviana everywhere in the pub and stalking the women's washroom, I have to admit she's gone. Right after we kissed. Was it that bad of a kiss? Or did I scare her with what I said about the vampiri?

Or was it the guy she was talking with, whom I couldn't hear?

Doubts and nagging thoughts keep assailing me, so I keep away from my siblings while I try to get a handle on them. A glass of red wine at the bar turns into three and, soon enough, Violeta taps me on the shoulder.

I turn and she hugs me, whispering in my ear, "Just wanted to say bye before I take off." She watches me shifting from foot to foot for a bit, then tilts her head to the side. "You really like her."

It's not even a question, the way she says it.

"Do you think—"

"No." I shake my head before she's even done with the question. "It has nothing to do with the curse. It's just...her. She quiets the monster inside me."

Violeta touches my arm. "You've kept that monster at bay for a long time, frate. We're proud of you for it."

Shame fills me—if only she knew. If only they all knew.

"I—I have to go. It was good seeing you. Tell Marcus bye for me."

And then I turn tail and walk away, bursting through the doors and into the cool air. Not even that helps dampen my need for...something.

I come to, groaning as my neck cracks. Little by little, I become aware of my surroundings. A dumpster nearby—the smell enough to make me gag. Eventually, I get to my feet. And stumble back. And then some more.

Two bodies—both male. Both not breathing. My vision blurs on their exsanguinated corpses.

I can't remember what I did. I can't remember anything past... *Fuck.*

I check the bodies quickly, but it looks like I didn't leave any sign of my feeding. There's no point trying to hide them or disguising the crime. That's another two bodies on my conscience, another two lives

I snuffed out while so deep in my darkness, I can't even remember.

I walk out of the alley and into the sparse dawn traffic. Thankfully, no one notices me.

Where the fuck am I, though?

A sign in the distance tells me: *Bine aţi venit la Castelul Bran.*

Welcome to Bran Castle. For fuck's sake. Leave it to my subconscious to bring me around what all of Romania—and the world—knows as Dracula's castle.

A few hours later, I enter our castle lands again, sneak through the doors, and run to my room to bathe. I toss the rest of the clothes into the fireplace—might as well burn any evidence of bloodshed. Too bad I can't burn those men's images from my head.

Finally, I hop under the water and let it cascade down my back. I try to ignore the voices outside—Nico on the phone with Tassa, Mirabela in her room, Liza muttering to herself—but it's nearly impossible.

I try to sleep, after. If only to quiet my thoughts, and try and refresh my mind. But nothing I do helps—not music, not focusing on my breathing, and definitely not staring at the ceiling. When Liza's voice is joined by Alex, and their exchange seems to get heated, I sigh and get up.

Once dressed, I join my human-hating siblings downstairs.

"What's with all the ruckus?"

Liza stops mid-sentence and arches an eyebrow. "You look like crap."

Alex only watches me. I ignore him and head for a glass of red wine. That sense of weakness is back, dragging at my limbs, and it takes all my strength to pretend I'm okay.

"Your fighting woke me from a rather good sleep."

Liza tuts. "Not my fault. Alex here seems to think a witch—like the stray you brought home—would be useful in our midst."

"He does?"

I turn to my brother, wary. His dislike for humans is well-known.

"Of course," he says. "She can be useful in casting curses and helping us regain an advantage. Especially considering the Hatmanu clan keeps sniffing around us."

I scowl. "I should've known you only want to manipulate her."

"Well, it's not like I'm going to ask nicely. Besides, she's totally head over heels for you. Might as well use it."

"No, thanks."

Alex moves closer. "I wasn't asking."

"And I wasn't listening."

"Listen, little one." I clench my jaw at his condescending tone. "You weren't in exile for a full two centuries like the rest of us. Father dearest went easy on you, and maybe he shouldn't have. *Maybe* if he hadn't treated you as if you were made of glass, you'd understand that this isn't the time to be *nice*. It's the time to get your big boy pants on and be an adult." He sneers. "Or just let the actual adults handle it."

I take a step closer to him, my fists clenching. It takes everything in me not to punch him. "I said, *no*. We all have equal rights here, it's not a dictatorship. And you may have an issue with Father choosing me, but that's how it is. *Deal with it*. And I say Silviana is off limits."

We glare at each other until Mirabela walks in. Her hair is half-done and she's holding the laptop I got for her balanced between her hands. "We have a problem. Forget your bickering about petty humans and look at this."

She turns the screen to us. Lined side by side are three articles, all with clamoring headlines: "Murder victim found exsanguinated," "Rapist meets death—bloodsucker vigilantes," "Are vampires back from the dead? Two more bodies found." The latter being in the area I was in. From this morning. Guess it didn't take much to hit the afternoon news.

Alex whistles low. Liza snatches the laptop to scan the titles, then hands it back to Mira. "Wasn't me."

"Neither of us would be stupid enough," Mira says. "But some-one's trying to bring us out into the open and they're hunting way too close to home."

Relief spreads through me with such force, I lean against the mantle and clutch the glass of wine so I don't drop it. They don't even think it's me, they think it's the other vampiri.

And on the heels of that relief, just as quickly, comes shame. Because I should tell them. I should be honest. Now's the chance to bring everything out in the open. Except...I stay silent.

Nico walks in, eyebrows arched. "Missed something?"

"Your balls," Alex mutters.

Mirabela hands him the laptop without a word. He reads the articles, then passes it back, his jaw clenched. "We have another problem. Someone from the Munteanu clan approached Tassa. In broad daylight. Gave her a message for us."

"Is she okay?" I ask, if only because no one else does.

"Who cares?"

Nico scowls at Liza, then says, "She is. But this isn't the first message." While everyone listens, he quickly sums up what he'd told me. About his theory on the Hatmanu and Munteanu feud, and the latter wanting an alliance with us. "All that, coupled with the Hatmanus' increasingly annoying attempts to corner us... Makes me think we should take the meeting."

Mira sits on the sofa, tapping the laptop keyboard in thought. "It might be worth hearing them out. If nothing else works out, we can always kill them." Her cold smile tells me she's only too serious about it.

Nico nods. "My thoughts exactly. In the meantime, I'm going to Tassa's to convince her to come back here for the time being. If not, I'll stay with her."

"Have you considered, dear brother, that this is precisely what they want?"

"I don't care. I'm not losing her."

Mirabela sighs heavily, drawing his attention. "What's their message exactly, Nico?"

His jaw clenches. "They want to meet. Tonight, eight o'clock. Same bar we were at for Tassa's birthday."

It's my turn to arch an eyebrow. "Coincidence?" I check my phone's screen—that's only a few hours away.

"Don't be stupid. They were most definitely watching you," Alex growls. "I warned you."

"This is just great," Liza mutters.

For once, I couldn't agree more.

Not that any of our opinions deter Nico.

"Let's see what we can pull together," he says. "Alex, stay here and guard the place with Mirabela in case it's a distraction. If no one shows up, Mira, grab your bags and leave with the cover of darkness; find us a safe new home. Vlad, you and Liza can come with me." He glances at his watch. "We have another eight hours until we meet.

You two can scout the area, I'll go talk to Tassa first. If anyone finds anything, keep us posted."

And then he's gone. Liza and I share a look, and follow after him.

Silviana

A knock on the door rouses me from a deep sleep. Part of me wants to hope it's Tassa, but I already know it's not.

As I walk toward it, I pull the small athame blade and nick my index finger, waiting until a drop of blood wells to the surface. Only then do I open the door, magic at the ready.

Valeriu arches an eyebrow. "Is that how you greet a friend?"

"You're no friend." When he makes a move to enter, I shove him back and exit the room. "Out here is fine."

He glances over my shoulder. "You got a vampir stashed in there?"

"You're disgusting. And your stunt last night could've blown my cover."

"Really? Seemed you handled yourself quite fine."

I blush at his innuendo, memories of Vlad's kiss pulling at the edges of my consciousness. That's two kisses, and I didn't hate either as much as I wish I had.

"Get to the point."

A moment passes while he stares at me, licking his lips. He nods. "We received word there's to be a meeting. The Munteanu clan with the House of Dracul. To broker a peace deal. Seems the vampiri clans aren't all on the same page and the Draculs' extermination of the Ardelean clan has...sent a message."

So, I wasn't that far off when I was spinning tales to Vlad. My coven is playing politics—hard. And they're in it to win.

"And what am I supposed to do?"

"Go there. Listen. Try to sabotage, if possible. If not, make sure you drive yourself under young Vlad's skin and get him to...shall we say...feel protective toward you. We need you back in the castle looking for that journal. Your presence here isn't doing anything and the Grand Master is more and more impatient."

"Noted. Now leave."

I wait until he's gone, before heading back inside my room and locking the door with shaking hands.

There's no way I can disobey Valeriu's orders. If I do, it'll go to the Grand Master, and then I'll be pulled off this mission. And my one and only chance to prove myself will be gone.

No, I have to stick around. And it's not like I've managed much by myself so far. While I would've preferred to be away from Vlad for a little while longer—to get my head together—I can't deny that this opportunity is too good.

A few hours later, I shower and ready myself, then leave the inn. I head down the streets until I reach a store I'd been eyeing the other day. Unlike the casual clothes I'd gotten there, this one sells high-end dresses. I use the athame knife to turn some scarves into cash—a little illusion that won't last forever, but at least it'll let me borrow a dress.

Then I go into the fitting room and try it on. The moment the black silk covers my body, I know this is the dress. Whether it'll turn me into predator or prey...remains to be seen.

I'm walking up the stairs, heading to my room back at the inn, when awareness creeps onto me. I slow down, but even before I turn the corner, I know he's there.

Sure enough, Alex is leaning against the wall opposite my room, playing with a knife. He's tossing it up and down in the air, catching it, then repeating, seemingly without a care.

I force my feet to move toward him, even as my brain screams at me to stop. "What are you doing here?" At least my voice comes out annoyed, not scared.

Alex flips the knife one more time. My eyes go to it, and I freeze.

"Lose something?"

I do a quick body scan and, sure enough, the small weight I'm used to feeling in the back of my jeans is no longer there. That's *my* athame blade he's toying with. And the only time I'd taken my jeans off...was in the store.

Fury runs through me. "Were you *following* me?"

He meets my gaze, arching a mocking eyebrow. "My, my, the witch is angry."

"Give it back."

"Ask me nicely, and maybe I will."

As calmly as I can, I move to my door and hook the hanger—and the dress it's on—on the doorknob. Then I turn to Alex, leaning against the door.

"All right. Say what you've come here to say, I'm listening."

For some reason, my words seem to annoy him. He pushes off the wall and takes a step closer, the athame still in his hand. At least it's covered by its regular leather sheath... Somehow, that's not very reassuring.

"You think I take orders from a human?"

I roll my eyes. "Wow, you're some kind of thickheaded. *You* came to *me*. All I'm asking is for you to spew the bullshit you've come here for, that way I can get on with my day."

His gaze moves to the dress. "Curious. Tell me, how does a witch with no coven and barely any belongings have enough money to buy a dress from one of the most expensive stores in town?"

I arch an eyebrow at him. "You didn't strike me as the type to keep tabs on the latest in women's fashion."

A flash of anger in his eyes—almost a blaze of red—warns me I'm toeing the line. *Wow, he must really hate engaging with humans. Everything I say seems to piss him off even more.*

I hold out my hand. "May I please have my knife back?"

His nostrils flare, and he glances at said blade. Then back at me. Instead of angry, his expression is speculative. "What's a witch doing with an athame, hmm?"

"You've clearly not known many witches. We all have them."

"Funny. The witches I've met, they don't." He tilts his head to the side, sneering as his gaze rakes me up and down. "I don't know what my brother sees in you. Then again, Nico was worse." He tosses the blade at my feet. "Don't come near us again unless you plan on making yourself useful and binding yourself to us. And even then"—the sneer grows more pronounced—"something tells me you don't have much to offer."

Done with his little repartee, he turns on his heel and disappears down the hall. I wait until he's out of my sight, before bending down and picking up my athame.

What had he said? *Don't come near us again.*

I could listen to him. But then, where would be the fun in that?

Vlad

Liza taps her foot impatiently. We both scouted every entrance to the village, and nothing so far. Now, bathed in shadows, we wait opposite the bar for Nico.

"It's almost eight."

I chuckle at her annoyed tone. "Would you relax? He still has ten minutes."

Plus, I know my brother. If he's in the village, he went to see Tassa, or at least check on her. I'd do the same. Matter of fact, not for the first time, my gaze moves down the street, to the inn I know is a few minutes down around the next corner.

Is Silviana there? Has she moved on already? I want to get her out of my mind, but it's damned near impossible. Every time I close my eyes, I see her, taste her lips, and yearn for so much more.

Liza lets out another annoyed puff. "Nico wouldn't be late if it wasn't for that—"

"Elizabeta."

She shuts up at my tone. And then stands up straighter. I follow her gaze, to the entrance of the pub. And the three vampiri who are skulking inside.

"Time to see if they brought back-up," she mutters.

I nod and we take off for another check-up. By the time we're back—empty-handed—Nico's waiting for us.

"Well?"

"You have some nerve," Liza snarls at him.

He takes a step closer to her, his entire being darkening with fury. "Do you want to go in there presenting a united front, or showing them just how divided we are?"

Liza glares at him for a long time, then looks away. "United."

"Bine." He arches an eyebrow at me, as if challenging me.

I hold up my hands. "No complaints here." In the uncomfortable silence that follows, I add, "Three of the Munteanu clan are inside. No back-up that we could find."

Nico nods. "I didn't expect them to bring any. Come on."

We enter the pub, which, for eight o'clock, is fairly sparse. Must have something to do with it being the middle of the week.

Nico immediately heads to a booth in the distance. The three men are sitting there, dressed in leather jackets, and with an identical M tattoo on the sides of their necks.

"They couldn't look more conspicuous if they tried," Liza says.

I shake my head at her. They turn to us, and we approach slowly, taking our time. With our backs to the rest of the populace, we're able to let go of the rein we hold on to our emotions. And I can tell by the reflection behind the bar that the blue gaze of our lineage is even more striking for it.

Nico stops by the side of the booth. I'm not sure at first what he's doing, but then I understand. The Munteanu men share a look, then the lankier one stands and inclines his head. "Welcome, sons and daughter of Dracul."

"My, my," Liza drawls.

Nico throws her a look. He waits until the other two stand, and repeat the greeting. And even so, he waits another beat.

When a man or a prince is strong and powerful, he can make peace as he wants to; but when he is weak, a stronger one will come and do what he wants to him.

It seems, from all of us, Nico actually did pay attention to Father's teachings. Because standing next to him, I could swear I feel our father's energy coursing through him.

"You may sit," he finally says.

The men drop as if released from a spell. Slowly, Nico takes a seat opposite them, then Liza, and me.

"We didn't think you'd show," the lanky man says.

"I find that hard to believe, considering you made it clear you're not above going near my consort to get my attention."

The man's gaze widens; he stares at Nico, then us, then back at him. "A h-human? We didn't—that's not—it hasn't—"

Nico waits for his stuttering to die off. He gestures to the bartender, who comes with a glass of scotch for him, as if pre-choreographed.

"I'll have one of the same," I say.

"And me," Liza adds.

The men shake their heads. But then, on a second thought, the lanky man says, "Three shots of țuică for us."

The bartender returns with the drinks a few moments later, then leaves us alone again. But not before he shoots another look at us—and Liza's scar.

Nico takes a sip, then he sets the glass on the table. "Da, Tassa is human. Da, she is my consort. *Da,* it is not usual for a vampir to choose a human, but that is the case. And you are correct in stating that it has not happened in a while. Centuries, even. Which is why it's even more precious." He takes another sip, and his voice is deadly calm when he speaks again. "You may think me stupid for revealing this."

Then he lunges across the table, grasping the lankier man's

throat, and pulling him halfway out of his seat.

"Let's get one thing straight. I don't fuck around. Neither do my siblings. You may think we were in hiding or in exile—we had other priorities to deal with." He releases him suddenly and he plops back down, as if nothing happened. "So if this meeting is meant to scare us... rest assured, neither of you is walking out of here alive. We're not above leaving messages the rest of the vampir community can understand."

A deadly silence lingers on the table. The other two men seem intimidated, and ready to bolt. The lankier one is thoughtful. Nico still sips his drink. I reach for mine, surprised that Liza has so far remained quiet.

"We didn't come here seeking a quarrel," the man says eventually. "My name is Ludovic. You can call me Ludo. I'm the right-hand man of our leader, who asked us to feel the waters. See if the House of Dracul is open to an alliance."

"Why would the Munteanu clan be interested in such an alliance?"

"Because we don't want to stand against you."

Liza snorts in her drink. "As simple as that?"

Ludo nods. "As simple as that."

Nico finishes his drink. "We'll be in touch."

The moment after, he stands—and we do, too, and shuffle out of the bar. Once outside, Nico returns to our spot in the shadows, across the bar. And then, we wait.

The three men exit after a moment, look around, and take off. Nico pulls out his cell. "Marcus, they're coming your way, in the woods. Stay out of sight, both of you."

I stare at him. "You pulled Violeta into this?"

"We needed more bodies. I didn't trust them not to try anything."

"And do you trust them now, dear brother?" Liza asks.

"I'm not sure." He rubs his chin, then jerks it toward the bar. "Let's go back for another drink."

We head back inside, to the same booth, and Nico and Liza sit next to each other while I sit opposite them this time. They're soon deep in conversation as to whether the Munteanu clan are, or are not, trustworthy. And what Marcus or Violeta might find.

A few moments later, Nico's cell rings. He answers it and Liza and I lean closer to listen in.

"It checks out," Marcus says. Thanks to my vampir hearing, I catch each word as though it's in my own ear, and I have no doubt Liza does, too. "Their leader and four others were waiting deeper in the woods. Past anything Vlad or Elizabeta could've noticed. From the sounds of it, they're under pressure from the Hatmanus to the left and the Cazacus to the right. They—the Cazacus—want to take over the territory the Ardelean clan left behind, and the Munteanus don't...because they've realized it belongs to you."

Nico nods. "Good. Then the others will realize it eventually, or perish trying. So, Cazacu and Hatmanu are looking for a fight?"

Violeta's softer voice comes on the line. "Looks like it. You guys need to be careful."

"We will be." Nico meets my gaze. "We're going to have to approach the others, and soon. But first, we need to tell Mira and Alex what's going on."

They're still talking, and part of my attention is still on them. But the other has picked up on a laugh—one I've heard before, albeit briefly. I turn to the side and catch sight of strawberry-blonde hair, the curve of a sleek cheek, and a black silky dress that leaves nothing to the imagination.

But Silviana's not focused on me. No, the little witch's attention is completely taken by a man with gray eyes. My eyes narrow on him as she loses her balance and topples into him. Granted, I have no claim, but that's not how it feels when all I want to do is rip him apart for even steadying her on her feet.

"What's gotten into you?" Liza's irritated tone bursts through my annoyance.

"Hmm? Nothing."

"Bullshit."

My eyes track Silviana. I must be fairly obvious, as Nico also focuses on me. Liza gives off an annoyed scoff.

"Unbelievable. Excuse me while I go find myself a drink."

Somehow, I don't think she's talking about alcohol.

I, on the other hand... "I'll be back."

With a mutter and a wave, I move to the bar, conveniently near Silviana. Her jasmine scent hits my nostrils, as does the steady beat of her heart. Her nape looks all too inviting from my angle, but I try to focus on other things—only catching the end of her conversation with the guy.

"That's so interesting. I've never met an actual antique restorer. And do you melt the gold, when you to restore antiques?" she asks.

I grab my drink and turn to her, clearing my throat. The man glances at me, an eyebrow arched. Silviana takes a moment longer to focus on me, then she turns, tossing her braid over her shoulder.

"Oh, hey."

That's all the greeting I get after two kisses that rocked my world?

I grit my teeth and lift my glass toward them. "Am I interrupting something?"

"Nu, nimic."

Nothing, he says. Hmm. Somehow, I doubt it.

The man's smooth Romanian immediately rankles me. This part of town sees tourists on occasion but... "And who are you?"

"My name is Tytus."

"That's not a Romanian name."

"Vlad—" Silviana places a hand on my arm, then removes it just as fast at the burst of electricity that zaps her.

Our eyes catch and hold. For a moment, I think hers darken with emotion, but then she blinks, and it's gone. Her thudding heartbeat isn't so easy to conceal, though. Neither is Tytus'. Almost dwarfing hers, his heartbeat's thump-thump-thump is so loud, as if a bigger body's buried under the human façade.

I angle my body between him and Silviana. "What are you?"

Before he can answer, Nico's heading our way. And by the time I turn back, Tytus is gone.

I frown at Silviana. "Who was he?"

"Don't know. I was as surprised as you are."

She chugs her drink, avoiding my gaze, and drops it on the bar. Then she heads back—washroom, I suppose. I watch her go, the silk of her gown molding to her body. More than one pair of male eyes turns her way. Nico's talking behind me, and I can see Liza out of the corner of my eye, but all I can focus on is the pull—magnetism— drawing me toward...her.

"Vlad."

I snap to, barely. "What is it?"

Nico's eyes narrow, then his expression softens. He glances toward the washroom, and back at me. "Go. But be careful."

I nod, and then I'm off, knowing—hoping—he'll have my back. Already the possibility that I might lose it is at the back of my mind, replaced instead by Silviana and her hypnotic scent. Before I'm even aware of my steps, I'm by the washroom door. A woman steps out, wobbling on her feet, then another.

I can't wait anymore. I step inside.

At first, I don't see her. Panic seizes me. And then...she's there.

Braiding her hair in the mirror like she hasn't got a care in this world.

Silviana

I catch sight of something in the mirror and then freeze. My eyes hook onto Vlad's and I lose all ability to breathe. My heart thuds in my chest, threatening to rip it open.

I'd hoped to draw his attention. That my cool demeanor would infuriate him, maybe stop this pull between us. Maybe make it easier to walk away. Maybe not. Maybe I'd meant to ensnare him, as I've been ordered. And it seems it worked. Because I've brought him straight to me.

"W-what are you doing here?" I hate the shaking in my voice. I'm here on a mission. I need to keep my eyes on the prize and the prize is making him believe—until I find the journal. Only, as he prowls toward me, there's no way I can hide the shaking of my hands.

Vlad steps behind me, a hair's breadth from my neck. And then he steps closer. Closer. Until I'm trapped between the sink and him.

He inhales deeply, then moves my braid to the side and drops his nose to my neck. Nuzzling me, like I'm a fine wine he wants to sample.

And then I notice his fists, clenched by his side. I reach for one, intertwining our fingers, and bring it to my waist. His fingers clench mine and a groan—not unlike a plea for mercy—escapes him. Then the fingers release mine, digging into the flesh of my hips, pulling me closer to him. To his hardness. The pulsing sensation in my lower back, letting me know that much as I want to believe he's undead, he's very much a man—with manly desires. And I haven't been this turned on in ages.

"You—"

"Shh."

He nuzzles my neck again, and this time his hand moves up, to my breasts. Lightweight at first, then rougher, he touches one. Tracing underneath the curve of my breast, sending goosebumps up my arms, until my nipple puckers through the flimsy material. His thumb grazes it, and his eyes fly to mine, capturing them in the mirror.

"You drive me crazy." His voice is rough, filled with barely held back control.

"We can't—"

"Shh."

This time, the hand on my hip slides lower, lower still, until he's cupping me through the dress. The lacy underwear I wore under feels like it's practically nonexistent. I move my hand on top of his—to stop him? Push him lower?

Before I can decide, there's a heavy knock on the bathroom door. A second later, it bursts open and Liza walks in. She takes one good luck at us and shakes her head in disgust. "When you're *done*, deign to join us, frate. The clan's not coming back, at least not tonight. We're leaving."

She's gone, leaving the door open. Vlad's grip on me tightens for a second. Our eyes meet in the mirror. His are almost black with desire. And the intensity of my own need scares me. Then he drops his head to my neck again, grazing the skin with his teeth. I shiver in his embrace, arching against him—and he pulls away.

"Another time."

He's gone with a soft smile that goes to my gut. I drop against the counter, releasing a pent-up breath.

"Goddamn."

Then Liza's words clue in. *The clan's not coming back, at least not tonight.* I didn't stop their meeting. Tytus distracted me, and I didn't hear anything worthy of interrupting, anyway. By the sounds of it, there'll be another meeting. *That* is what I need to sabotage...and, ideally, *after* I get hold of Țepeș's journal.

I turn to the sink, drop some cold water on my face, and head back outside. My eyes scan the area. Humans are blissfully drunk, bartenders are busy pouring drinks—Tytus is nowhere to be seen, and neither are the royals.

Did Vlad really go back with them?

I pay for my drink and push through the throng of drunks. The fresh air hits me with a rush, clearing any alcohol from my system. Something tells me to head right, and I do...

But I soon regret it. The slurping sounds I hear, barely a few feet away, are that of a monster. And when I peek around the corner, into an alleyway, I see Vlad. He tears his fangs from the man's neck and looks at me—I don't recognize the cool expression on his features. His eyes, darkened with desire before, are now cool as ice. They fall on me and move right past me.

Shivering, I back away... and away. When I turn around, intending to run off, I bump straight into Liza.

She sniffs the air and something akin to surprise flashes on her features. Then she shoves me to the side, back to being bitchy. "Get out of here. I've got this."

On shaky legs, I move away.

"Wait."

She's in front of me the next moment, her blue eyes shining brightly. I try not to look at them, but already she's turning on the glamour; its intensity vibrates in the air between us. "You won't remember any of this. You had a drink, and went back home." Then she glances at Vlad, and back at me. "You stupid bitch. I could glamour him out of your head right now...but he'd never forgive me."

She shoves me away, knocking me into a wall. I keep the dazed expression on my face, even as I stumble away.

It's only once I'm safely away, tucked into the throng of people at an all-night diner, that I stop to question her words. And thank the heavens Dacians can't be compelled by any vampir, royal or not.

HOUSE OF
DRACUL

Chapter 8

Vlad

I wake up as if hungover. *What the hell happened?*

Once again, that same weakness from before fills my every limb. I stagger off the bed—how did I even get here? The last thing I remember is Silviana, the bathroom, her scent all around me...And the bloodlust. The darkness calling to me.

On weak legs, I drag myself to the bathroom and hold onto the sink. My arms shake, and even my tight grip on the has-seen-better-days marble doesn't mark it. Normally, it would crack it, or dent it. No such luck.

I stare at my hands. Then, slowly, raise my gaze to the mirror.

Dark circles mar the skin under my eyes. The blueness of my irises seems subdued. My skin, normally a hue good enough to pass for human, is now ashen.

"What did I do last night?" I ask my reflection.

But no matter how much I try to remember, all I come up with is...a blank.

After a shower that takes way too long, I drag myself back to the bed and plop on it. The entire routine can't have taken more than half an hour, but I feel drained.

Of course, the door to my bedroom opens then and Liza walks in. She takes a seat on the edge of my bed, uninvited. "Do you remember anything from last night?"

I do. Same images as before. Silviana, the bathroom, wanting desperately to sink into her heat, know what her body feels like...the meeting with the Munteanu clan. The...fog. darkness. The darkness. And now, waking up to no hunger.

"What—"

Liza taps her foot on the floor, waiting for me to finish my thought. I would if I could, but my mind is about as useful as a chocolate teapot.

When, moments later, I still haven't come up with anything, she crosses her arms and full-on scowls at me. "Are you out of your mind?"

My only answer is to drop my head back on the bed and close my eyes.

Smack.

I groan, cracking my eyes open and squinting at her. The spot she'd slapped my thigh throbs.

"Ow."

Her scowl turns to a frown. "What's wrong with you?"

"Nothing."

"Bullshit. Something's going on, else I wouldn't have caught you drinking from a human last night."

I close my eyes again, gritting my teeth. "No one saw."

"Yeah. Thanks to me. You're welcome."

Something in her tone rings alarm bells, but I'm too drowsy to string any ideas together. All I can do is watch and listen as she paces, muttering under her breath.

Eventually, Liza sighs. "I thought Nico would be our problem, but you seem to be even worse." She tosses a cell at me. "Call Violeta. She should have better words than I do. She always does." The moment after, she's gone, leaving me to my recollections.

Something's nagging at me. A flash of strawberry-blonde hair...

Shit. Did Silviana see me lose control? And if she did...where the hell is she now?

I glance at the phone. Maybe it wouldn't be the end of the world to ask for help. Unless it is. Because I'm making things worse.

Hours later, close to late afternoon, I finally open my eyes. They fall on the cellphone I'd tossed on the bed, before falling back asleep.

Sighing, I key in Violeta's number and wait for it to ring. After a few seconds, she answers. "Da?"

"It's me."

She pauses, then, "Something wrong?"

I stare at the ceiling, wondering where to start. What comes out of my mouth surprises even me.

"How did it start? The...curse. With you, I mean."

"You mean, the symptoms?"

"Da. I know you've told me before, but I want the details this time."

Another perplexed silence lingers, then she says, "Weaknesses. Blackouts. Bouts of insomnia. Cravings for weird things. And...feelings of being human. By the time I got to that point, I was too late into it." She hesitates. "Did you ask Tassa for some of the muroni concoction she gave me?"

"No."

"At least you're honest." She sighs. "Vlad, ask her. Today. And tell them, they need to know."

"I don't want to. They've...there's enough to keep us busy."

"With the clans, you mean? The Hatmanus can easily be taken over."

"I'm not so sure about that."

"Vlad. Worry about yourself first, little brother. Please."

I mutter some kind of agreement, then stand and leave the room. I can hear voices in the library, so I head there. Liza and Alex are absent, but Nico and Mira are standing staring at a map splayed on the table. It takes me a few seconds to rest my blurry gaze on it and recognize it.

"Are you going over last night's events?"

Mirabela nods, not looking at me. "Da, among other things."

"I thought you were heading out to find us that new property?"

She taps the table with her long nails, still engrossed. "I'll leave...soon. Something about all this still bothers me, and I wanted to hear how the meeting went."

I stagger to the table, and she finally looks up. And frowns.

"What's going on with you?"

I groan. "Not you, too."

Instead of dismissing me, Mira contours the table and heads to me. She lifts a hand as if to check my temperature, then lowers it. "You don't look good."

"Da, Liza pointed out something similar."

Nico leans against the table, also staring at me. "Talk to us. What is it? Is it Silviana?"

Mira's eyes flash at the name. It's a cool reminder that though she may play nice, she still hates humans.

"Nu, it's...maybe. I don't know."

"If you're worried about her, you should get her to come back and live here. We can both keep an eye on her, and potentially use her magic skills to defend us."

I scowl at him. "Alex suggested much the same."

Nico shrugs. "Nothing wrong with asking if she'd like to help. If she says no, no harm, no foul."

"Seriously?" Mira asks.

Nico throws her a look I can't interpret.

All Mira says in response is, "I still think you're wrong. And until I'm proven wrong, I stand by my words."

"Huh?"

They both ignore me. Nico takes a step closer, and my body chooses that moment to sway, nearly toppling into him. Mira rushes to me, too, and then her eyes meet mine.

"I've seen this before. It's happening again, isn't it?"

"What is?" Nico asks.

She glares at him. "If you hadn't been so detached back then, you'd recognize it. Vlad's exhibiting the same symptoms as Violeta.

The curse is striking again...fast."

Nico wraps an arm around my waist and helps me to the couch. "Well, I'm here now, and I intend to make it count." He kneels in front of me so we're eye level. "How bad is it?"

So, I tell them. It's not like I can hide it.

When I'm done, Nico nods. "I'll go ask Tassa to make some of the mix. She's grabbing some things from the village, but she should be back here soon. It should buy you some time."

"It's what Violeta said, too."

He squeezes my shoulder, then he's gone.

Mirabela stares at me, her expression both pained and pensive.

"You don't think it'll help, do you?" I ask.

"Not really, nu. But, and much as I hate to admit it, your little witch might know some spells." Her eyes flicker to the entrance, and her expression hardens to granite. "And speak of the devil."

Silviana

I tried to stay away from him. Most of the day, I forced myself to go through the images of what I'd seen the night before. Vlad, being the monster he is. Sucking someone's blood.

Not the other Vlad, in the bathroom, who ignited my body so easily.

And, as the French say, it's all *peine perdue*. A goddamned lost cause. All I know is I need to talk to him, to see him, to be around him. Even if he's not in his right mind, or whatever it is the vampiri call it.

So I do what I do best; I barge inside the castle without an invitation, all the while hoping they decide to extend me one to stay.

I enter the library, having heard voices, and I'm stricken when I see how bad Vlad looks. Circles under his eyes, ashen skin. I thought vampiri were supposed to be more alive-looking after a feeding, but he looks the opposite.

My gaze flickers to Mirabela, then him. "Can we talk?"

"We're busy," she says on a growl.

"Yeah, I got that." I keep my stare on him, undeterred. "Please?"

He tries to stand, but wobbles on his feet. Mirabela nearly tosses him back on the couch, before facing me. "You picked a damned good time to show up."

"Mira, please."

"No, Vlad. I'm tired of this."

"You just said she could help."

"I clearly lost my mind. This witch is useless to us." She sneers, her gaze on the backpack dangling by my fingers. "And the sooner she figures it out and leaves, the better for us."

I look to Vlad, hoping to hear him say I should stay. But he says nothing, instead staring at the carpet. Part of me wants to go to him, to touch him. That tantalizing pull I feel when he's near me is even more present now, insistent, demanding, craving... But, the other part of me is more than a little annoyed.

"I see." Clenching my jaw, I refuse to give either of them the satisfaction. So I turn on my heels, hoist my bag over my shoulder, and leave.

Their voices soon rise behind me. And, while I'm mad at Vlad for being so dismissive—especially when I have questions!—I know this might be my last chance to find what I need.

With them busy, I do a quick sweep of the rooms on the main floor, using my magic and hoping they won't catch the smell of blood. No sign of the journal, at least as far as I can tell. My last recourse is their individual bedrooms, but I don't have time to check them all.

I'll have to pick one.

Nico's out with Tassa... I'd seen him leave toward the village, and I'm assuming there's only one spot he'd go to. Alex and Liza don't seem to be around either, else they would've been around me already.

Guess I got my target.

I hesitate on the stair landing, every bone in my body on high alert. Then I kick off my heels and tiptoe up, and up... Down the hallway. I use the athame to prick my finger, then whisper a noise of suppression spell on the door—it makes the air denser—and step inside.

Inch by inch, I make my way through, opening drawers, rifling through them, then setting things back where they'd been. Nothing. I look under the bed, mattress...

On my way out of the room, a painting catches my eye. It's a little off balance. *Hmm.* I look closer, move it away from the wall a little and... there's the journal. It has to be, why else would it be hidden?

Hands shaking, I reach for it—dark leather covering, pages yellowed by age—and tuck it in my small backpack. I may not have gotten answers to my questions about Vlad, and this connection between us, but at least I got what I came here for.

I slide my hand back in the backpack and rifle around for the talisman they'd given me. I run to the window, open it, and place the talisman on the windowsill. With another small prick of the athame, and a muttered incantation, it bursts into flames. I use one last small spell to toss the talisman out in the air, where it can burn—safely.

There. That should give the Dacians my message, and hopefully help doesn't linger too long.

Without another look around, I make my way out of the room, and the castle.

The woods are pitch-black, the trees trunks thick and ominous. I never pegged myself for an outdoor person but this—something lurks in these woods. And it's watching me. The feeling grows and grows, until I'm no longer sure if it's paranoia or reality. Both are equally disturbing.

I keep myself moving, magic at the ready. An hour I've been dallying about, and there's no sign of my coven, no indication of anything in the air.

And then I feel the presence draw closer. I duck behind a tree and—

A hand clasps my wrist. "It's just me."

Vlad's voice is a relief.

Wait, what? A vampir, relief? After what I'd seen the previous night? I should be petrified!

"W-what are you doing here?"

"That's what I'd like to know." His blue eyes shine like jewels in the dark.

"I'm—it was a mistake coming here, and I was just leaving."

All I can think of is the journal in my backpack, and how I need to get it to my people. How much longer until they get here?

"No, not anymore, you're not. We have unfinished business."

When Vlad moves closer, my heart starts beating wildly. His proximity does something to me...something bad.

"You weren't interested in what I had to say earlier."

His blue eyes flash. "I wasn't feeling well. Now that I am, let's talk."

"I..." Words fail me. All I can do is stare in his eyes. And then I see something past his shoulder. "Vlad—"

"No, I'm not leaving until—"

"DUCK!" I yell and drag him down to the ground with me.

A second later, the tree behind me bursts into flames. Angry, dark flames, fueled by darkness. Dacian magic.

Vlad has a moment of shock, then he's on his feet. He's slow, as if he's running at half-speed, but he's still impressive. His fangs are out, the light in his eyes blazing. And then he's gone.

Moments pass, with no sounds emerging. The forest is quiet— too quiet. That sense of uneasiness grows, coupled with the feeling of being watched.

A twig snaps behind me. I whirl around, ready to summon my magic, only to remember I haven't cut myself yet. A shadow moves, and I back away...and trip over a tree root, falling on my ass.

I'm still trying to catch my breath when Vlad returns to the clearing and helps me to my feet. "Are you all right?"

I nod, trembling all over. "W-who—"

He's already shaking his head. "There was no one in the woods. I have no idea where it came from." He reaches for my cheek, wiping away my tears. "I'm sorry, Silviana."

"Sorry? What for?"

"Chances are this has everything to do with me and the enemies my family has accumulated."

I should tell him that's not true. That I'm pretty sure it's my own people coming after us...but why? Without knowing why, I can't form my story.

What the hell are they playing at?

Before I can say anything, a burst of fire flies our way from the woods. Vlad sees it and pulls me against him. The fire bursts behind us and a moment later, I feel a burn on my ankle. More black magic links around me, same as during the first attack, days ago. Luckily, I can feel a scratch on my skin. Enough blood to use... I pull at magic and free myself of the darkness, shattering the binds. Another tendril takes its place.

Vlad tenses, a growl reverberating in his chest. He turns around—two small wolves, or would-be wolves, are facing us.

At my sharp inhale, they look toward us, and I see their red eyes. I know immediately what they are.

Pricolici... Here?

A shudder runs through me. They're creatures bound to darkness, created from it, and answering to only one master. Dacians used to put their heads on pikes when heading into battle, to scare off the enemies. From afar, they looked like wolves.

But even wolves have compassion. These creatures, they have none.

And all at once, I'm shattered. Because Dacians—my coven—kept their hold over the pricolici as time went by. Which means someone, nearby, is controlling them.

"Stay here."

Vlad stands, and this time I see a darkness around him. His fury is palpable. I remember Fane telling me of vampiri of old, and the way they'd been able to use the magic we have, too. But that they lost it.

Seeing Vlad, the shadows nearing his hands, tells me that's not entirely true. The magic isn't as potent as mine, but the darkness...it's there. It *listens* to him. It slithers toward the pricolici, ensnaring them as if gluing them to the ground.

And then Vlad attacks. If before he'd been slow, now he's full-on snarling. In two swift movements, he tears one's head away. Viscous blood the color of coal soon coats the ground under where it had stood.

The other creature frees itself from the binds and heads toward me. I raise my hand to stop his jaws from clenching around my throat.

They clasp around my forearm, tearing into the skin. I scream.

And then Vlad is there, taking hold of its jaws and ripping it apart. He reaches for my hand, the blood overflowing. His eyes are red. Will he drink from me?

For a second, all I see is his nostrils flaring. Then, the red fades away, and the blue returns.

"Fuck—I'm taking you back. Right now."

And as he carries me away, I realize what the Dacians who'd set up this attack were attempting. They were trying to make him feel more protective toward me. All the better to arrange my heist.

Except...I already have my bounty. In my backpack. Which now dangles uselessly from my arm. And I'd sent them a message saying as much... Why would they choose now to attack?

And why am I burying my head in Vlad's embrace to hide my tears?

I'm shaking, trembling like a leaf by the time Vlad whisks us back into the castle. Why would my own have attacked me? This wasn't planned, I knew nothing of it. And I could have been hurt. I could have died!

Tassa's words come back to me. *If Nico hadn't come, they would've burned the house down, and me with them. So, no, fear doesn't really come into play.*

Vlad... I look at the angle of his face, all I can see from the way he's holding me. Take in the clenching of his jaw. He's...angry. With a jolt, I realize it's on my behalf. This vampir, who's usually so soft-spoken and careful, is ready to go to bat for me.

I try to ignore the warmth spreading through my chest at the thought—but it's hard.

"I—I can walk from here," I whisper.

He jerks his head, once, in denial. "Not happening."

A moment after, we're at the castle and he's storming through the doors. "Tassa!"

His bellow has me cringe, but it also brings Tassa, Nico and Mirabela running. The lovebirds must've returned not long ago, because they still have on their coats.

Tassa takes one look at the blood on my sweater and points to the kitchen. "On the island. Nico, boil me some water. Mirabela, get some clean rags. And find some țuică, would you?"

Mirabela scowls at the orders, but nonetheless disappears. Not before I notice her speculative look directed at me. Out of all of them, she, Liza and Alex are still the most suspicious.

Vlad gently places me on the old wooden table and I wince. My arm hurts like a bitch.

Then Tassa's there, opening an old-school leather bag full of tricks. She sees my glance and smiles. "Don't worry, I'll have you fixed in no time." She glances around. "We can also take you to a hospital. There's one not too far off."

Vlad looks sick at the thought.

I shake my head. "No. Last thing I need is them having a sample of my blood."

She nods and gets to work, cutting the sweater around the area.

Mirabela returns with clean rags, some dry, some soaked in hot water. Tassa uses the soaked ones to clean my wound, followed by the țuică Mirabela gives her to clean it.

She passes me half of the glass. "Drink."

I toss it in one go, feeling the burn as it travels into my stomach, starting a fiery burn.

"Good." Tassa bends over the wound with a dry rag, wiping it dry. And then she pulls a needle and thread. I gulp, and my attention wanes...to Vlad.

Nico clears his throat. "What, exactly, happened?"

"She was attacked," Vlad mutters. "Obvious, no?"

If Nico's shocked at his tone, he doesn't let it show. "I can see that. But *what* happened?"

Vlad glares at him, exasperation in his voice. "Can't this wait? Silviana's in pain."

"And Tassa's taking care of that."

Nico's voice is almost...hypnotic. I try to tune it out, focusing my senses instead on the pain caused by the needle Tassa's using to thread my flesh back together.

All I'm aware of is Vlad's voice getting louder, the pain getting worse, and then—darkness.

Chapter 9

Vlad

"Silviana!" I *feel* it when she's gone, and I panic. No amount of Nico's persuasion or would-be glamour can quiet me. I shove him aside, grasp her shoulders and try to shake her awake. Her eyes fall open, showing me only blankness—she's unconscious.

I turn to Tassa. "What did you do?"

She frowns at whatever she sees on my expression.

"You were close to her. What did you—"

"Vlad."

Mirabela's there, her lips to my ear. Her hand firmly grasps my shoulder. "Release the human. Tassa will take care of her."

"I'm not—"

And then I look down. I am. I've got Silviana cradled to my chest, holding her tightly as if the thought of being separated from her would tear me apart. Tassa, despite my earlier tone, has leaned halfway over the table, trying not to yank out all the stitches she's put in. Nico's behind her, as if getting ready to protect her.

From me.

I glance again at Silviana. The pallor in her cheeks. The lack of color in her lips. Same lips I'd kissed. Same lips I want to kiss again.

My thoughts jumble around, unfocused. The attack in the woods. She'd been leaving, but she protected me. Everything they'd said—that she could be playing me—makes no sense. It doesn't.

She's mine.

Mine.

"I—"

"Release her," my siblings say in unison.

When I don't move, Mirabela reaches for my hands. Finger by finger, she unlocks my hold on Silviana. A faint growl leaves my lips, but I don't stop her. With more gentleness than I'd ever thought her capable toward a human, Mira sets Silviana back on the table.

Then with equal gentleness and a touch of firmness, she shoves me away, until there's a few feet of distance between us. It's all I allow, and then I sink my heels into the ground, refusing to budge any farther, and becoming an immovable wall. Mira glares at me, but I ignore her. My eyes never leave Silviana's unmoving form.

What in all hells happened?

What...*was* that?

I've heard of vampiri being glamoured into doing someone else's bidding, but this wasn't it. No one can glamour us except our father, and he's long dead. Nico might've tried, earlier, but not even his status as head of this house gives him that power.

So what in all hells possessed me to act so unhinged? To go against my siblings?

I think back to the darkness in me. The one that saved us both in those woods. How it'd come into me, unbidden, at the thought of Silviana being harmed. How I was reinforced, refueled by an energy I recognized.

Even the darkest parts of me wanted to protect her.

"I think you should take some space," Mirabela says. "Clearly, something has affected your judgement." She throws a speculative glance to Silviana, then back at me. "Whatever it is, this isn't healthy."

"I'm not—" I take a deep breath. "Please don't send me away."

"We're not," Nico says as he moves around Tassa. He's frowning.

Great. I've turned my two allies against me. I can't imagine what Liza and Alex would say, if they were here to witness this.

"But something is going on here, and we had best figure it out before it gets out of control."

Mirabela watches Nico, tapping her chin a moment. Then she turns to me. "Did you drink her blood?"

"What?"

"The witch. Did you drink her blood?"

"No, of course not!"

"I don't think this has anything to do with him *drinking* the blood, Mira," Nico says. "Look at his hands."

Her eyes drop, as do mine. My hands are coated in dried blood—Silviana's blood.

"I think her blood is exacerbating his need to protect her. She's..." He looks to Silviana, then at me, his eyes strengthening in resolution. He doesn't even appear surprised. "I had that same need with Tassa. Frate, I think she's your consort."

Shock rattles my chest, cutting off my breath. I normally don't even have to work to remember to breathe, since we've spent time around humans. But this time, I forget everything I've trained myself to do to appear normal and just stare in shock.

Silviana

I'm aware, vaguely, of people around me.

No, not people. Vampiri.

To the outside, I might seem normal. But underneath the surface of my mortal body, my magic has rallied to my cause, wrapping me in a cocoon of healing. It won't be like the movies, causing me to wake up without a scar. But it'll be damn close.

Despite the cocoon, I can hear them... Yet my mind drifts away. To Fane. To the Dacians. To that attack in the woods.

Did they cause this? I'd had my suspicions, back in the woods. What I'd feared would happen, finally did. And there's a big chunk of accountability on my shoulders. After all, Valeriu warned me enough times that I was moving too slow. But...why would they do this? Why make sure Vlad protects me, when I already have what they want?

Would they really hurt one of their own?

You know they would.

The voice, clear as day, is intrusive and not my own. A male.

I flick my eyes open, but all that surrounds me is white emptiness.

This isn't normal. I'm not alone.

Nothing should interfere with my healing. Nothing—and no

one—can get past the cocoon my magic automatically draws around me. At least, no one ever has...

"Who are you?" I call out.

"Does it matter?"

"To me, yes."

He emerges from the whiteness—a gorgeous man, tall, lanky, eyes of pure silver, raven-black hair. I recognize him immediately. "You! You were at the bar. We talked about..." I rack my brain, trying to remember. It feels like an eternity ago. But then I finally re-member. "Gold! You're an antique dealer in jewelry, living in a nearby village."

He gives me a faint smile.

"Tytus is your name."

"Very well, little one."

"I don't understand. Who...? How are you here?" I frown, no longer calm. Is he another pawn my coven is using against me? "Who sent you?"

This time, I get a full-blown smile. And it's blinding. "I am on no one's payroll, fear not. You could call me an interested party."

"An interested party in what, exactly?"

"Recent events."

My frown deepens. "Are you a sorcerer?"

The gray eyes flash. "Not quite, no."

"Then what are you doing in my dreams?'

"Finally, a question I can easily answer. I am here to warn you. That your people are not who you think they are. They don't have your best interests at heart."

Despite what I'd been thinking about them, despite my doubts, I immediately sense my hackles rising. "You know nothing."

He takes a step closer, and I back away. He stops, holding up his hands as if that will make me trust him. I know better than most that weapons don't have to be visible to hurt.

"I know the sibling bond that keeps you there," Tytus says. "I have a similar one. But it does not have to be your fate. You have a chance, with the vampiri...do not squander it. Leave your silly little mission aside, and grasp this new chance at life while you can."

I reach for my magic, trying to push him out. He must be a powerful sorcerer, because I can't even muster an ounce of magic to rally against him. It's almost as if the same force that feeds me is...*afraid*...of him.

A smirk plays on his lips. "I will leave, for now. But heed my words while you still can."

He's gone the moment after, and I'm back in my mind, away from the whiteness. Thinking over what he said, hating the nagging suspicion at the back of my head now. But then I think of Fane, of his loyalty to our coven. Of how they protected us since our father was killed, and how we have a future with them.

And I know that Fane would've known about the attack. Valeriu said he's keeping a close eye on this, and everything goes through him. So if Fane's doing this, agreeing to this way forward, then it must be the right way—the right thing to do. And I must forget my doubts, for good. My brother would never do anything to hurt me.

I wake up to complete silence. When I open my eyes, I'm startled to find someone still around me. Mirabela's there, staring at a spot on the floor like it holds all the answers to the universe. Nico and Vlad are gone.

Disappointment fills me. I don't know why I'd expected Vlad to still be here when I wake up, but...I do. I need his presence nearby, in an almost irrational way.

My arm is throbbing. I inhale sharply at the pain, only resulting in Mirabela staring at me instead. Given our last few interactions, I fully expect her to yell at me, or order me gone again. Instead, she's almost speculative.

I squirm under her gaze, not liking the feeling like she's peering past my soul. The last thing I want is for a vampir to see past everything I'm hiding.

But then I glance at her, and notice she's not even attempting to use glamour on me. On the contrary, she's just watching me like I'm a puzzle she wishes she could put together.

Before I can ask her why the face of death, Liza bursts in. Her expression is furious, her knuckles white as she lunges for me. Mirabela stands up and blocks her path, but she can't stop the words being hurled at me.

"Who the fuck sent you here, hmm? Because the more and more I hear of your little exploits with my brother, the more I'm inclined to think this isn't just a coincidence."

"I haven't—"

Mirabela shoots me a look that has me shut up instantly.

But Liza's not done. Her glare lands on me, eyes nearly red with fury. "I glamoured you to forget witnessing his feeding, but I should've glamoured you to stay the fuck away from him instead."

"You did *what*?" Mirabela's tone is deadly calm.

Even Liza senses it, and cools her heels—for all of a few seconds.

When I don't reply to her vitriol, she snarls all over again. "You don't seem all that surprised." Her expression darkens, becoming even more dangerous. "Did the glamour even work on you? Or are you immune?" When all she gets is more silence from me, she hisses, "You won't even deny it, will you? I know you're lying about why you're here, you little—"

Mirabela steps between us, her attention on her sister. It's scary, seeing them face off. Though Mirabela's easily a head taller than Liza, she's calmer. A lot calmer. The redhead is nearly crazy with anger, her nails digging into her fists.

"Control yourself," Mirabela says. "What's the meaning of this latest outburst?"

"Meaning?" Liza scowls. "You know full well. This is the second time Vlad's been in danger because of her!"

"And?"

"And! He's our *brother*. And he doesn't deserve to be taken for a joyride by this witch especially given his—"

"Enough." Mirabela's voice is low, but the steel in it draws my attention.

Vlad's what? His weakness? His... something else? What is it that they're hiding?

Could it be the darkness I'd seen in the forest? The same thing I'd innocently alluded to ages ago, when he'd caught me snooping?

I don't get a chance to ponder further. Liza pretends to leave, but the moment Mirabela drops her guard, she rushes past her, toward me. I react by instinct, pushing back against the wall. Problem is, I overestimated my force, and my head bangs against the brick with a thud. I see stars...and then, nothing.

Vlad

"I still don't see why it's such a big deal," Alex mutters. He sips more of his wine, his bored expression making me want to punch him. "So our little brother can't stay away. Why doesn't he just fuck her, get her out of his system, and presto, problem solved?"

Nico scowls at him. "Because you don't get to just fuck it out of your system, Alexandru."

Our brother arches an eyebrow. "Maybe you just don't know how to."

Nico's fists clench, but to his credit, he doesn't rise to the bait. Instead, he turns to me. "I should have told you. I suspected it for a few days now, especially since every time you're around her you're less...you."

I drop into the couch. "Less me?" Thinking back to the last few times, I guess it could be seen that way. I've never been one to pick fights with them. Or act the rebellious teenager. Even now, all I can think of is shoving them out of my way so I can be by Silviana's side again. And never leave it.

"He means less of a pussy," Alex supplies. That earns him another glare.

"Where the hell were you, anyway?" Nico asks. "Absent seems to be your middle name these days."

Alex shrugs. "So what if it is?"

"You don't think it's weird that on top of the vampiri, we now have to worry about unseen forces, too?"

"Maybe, maybe not." He gets up to refill his glass, turning his back to us.

I drop my head in my hands, blocking everything. Except, with my eyesight blocked, my ears open wider, and then I hear it—Silviana's voice, Mirabela and…Liza.

"Shit." I'm off the couch and rushing down the hallway the moment after. I burst in the room just as Silviana collapses once more. The scent of her blood is in the air, Liza nearby.

I don't think, I just act. Slamming into my sister, and into the wall. She yelps under me, and soon Alex is between us, pulling us apart. "Stay the fuck away from her!"

They face off against me. Nico steps between us, while Mirabela checks on Silviana.

"Is she okay?" I ask her.

"She'll be fine."

She picks her up in her arms and moves out the door. I leave the mess behind and follow her, all the way to Silviana's old bedroom. A few seconds later, Nico brings Tassa in.

I watch quietly as she examines her. But after a few moments, an odd light starts emanating from Silviana's skin.

"What the—" I take a step closer, fearing danger, but it's the opposite. If I focus hard enough, I can almost sense this light…helping her.

"Is it bad?" Tassa asks, looking from Nico to me.

Slowly, I shake my head. "No. It's… I've never heard of this happening to a witch, but I'm guessing it's normal. It feels like it's helping her."

"I'm guessing then that it'll heal the small head wound," Tassa mutters. She meets my gaze. "Don't worry, I'm pretty sure it wasn't a hard bang."

All I can do is drop on the floor and wait.

Hours pass by, and I just watch Silviana, tethered to her side like I no longer have free will. Nico comes back in the room. For long moments, he just leans against the wall, watching me.

"You don't have to be my guardian, you know?"

"I know."

I shake my head. "I'm tempted to agree with Liza sometimes. It was better when you didn't care."

He chuckles. "Believe me, it was better for me, too."

I look from her to him. "Was it this potent for you? This"—I take a deep, shuddering breath—"consuming?"

"Yeah." He shakes his head. "Tassa broke through every wall I'd ever erected around me, anything that was keeping me away from the world. The more I was around her, the more I wanted to be burned by that flame, regardless of the consequences to me, to her...to you all."

"I can't wrap my head around it, Nico."

"It'll take some time, I won't lie. But you might as well, because this isn't going anywhere. You and I both know it."

Silviana moves then and I lean forward, waiting for her eyes to open. And then they do, and they settle upon me. I'd expected some shift, something cosmic and romanticized. But it's still the same gaze filled with wariness that meets mine.

She doesn't know about the bond, about being my consort. Of course she's still wary.

The question is, when should I tell her?

Chapter 10

Silviana

"What...what happened?"

Vlad frowns at me, something in his expression shifts, and then he leans back, giving me room to breathe.

Everything from before hits me like a torrential downpour. My wanting to leave—the journal in my backpack. The attack in the forest. The pricolici. Blood, flowing down my body. Vlad, taking me back to the castle. Tassa patching me up... And then darkness. Waking up again—Mirabela; Elizabeta. They'd been there, but the specifics escape me. And then, darkness again.

And somewhere in there, a man...whispering about me not

trusting the very people who I've given my life to. The very people who took Fane and I in, and protected us.

"How much do you remember?" Vlad asks.

I glance at Nico, far away from the bed, and back to Vlad. Why does he seem so uneasy? So...uncomfortable?

He's hiding something.

I shove the nagging voice aside, and clear my throat. Vlad reaches for a glass of water on the bedside table and hands it to me. Electricity zaps my fingers when we touch. Despite the fact I'd wanted his presence earlier, now, it's all I can do to look him in the eye.

After a sip, then another, I finally answer him. "Everything." I rub the back of my head, surprised to find it healed. My wide gaze goes on them. "It healed." Which means they saw my cocoon of healing... Shit, shit, shit. Did they figure out where it comes from?

"Da, it did," Nico says, as Vlad keeps staring at me like I'm an angel returned to Earth. "I've never quite seen a witch heal herself like that."

"You've known many, then?"

A wry smile from him is the only answer I get.

This isn't good. The more they stick around, the more questions they'll ask, and I might slip up and say something off. I need to buy myself time.

"I think I'd like to sleep some more." For emphasis, I yawn, then lean back down on the pillows.

I can almost feel Vlad itching to say more. But, with a muttered whisper to Nico, they both finally leave. And I stare at the ceiling until sleep does overtake me.

Hours later, I'm tossing and turning in bed. My arm itches, the sensation won't go away. I should try to contact my kin, to find out what it is they had planned, and why they didn't tell me. And why they didn't come, as they said they would, when I burned the talisman.

My thoughts drift to Fane. He'd been wanting to climb the ladder for so long...did he manage? Was this the last rung he had to climb, the last obstacle?

He wouldn't use me for that. He wouldn't.

Then I remember my half-dream, and the guy, Tytus. Was he real? I've been raised to believe everything supernatural, but there's a strong chance my brain just planted the guy from the bar as a distraction.

Only, it hadn't felt like one.

Your people are not who you think they are. They don't have your best interests at heart.

If he was real, and he was right, then I'm fucked. I don't have anyone else to rely on. I have nowhere to go.

A tear slides down the side of my cheek and into the pillow. I wipe it away and curl onto my side. I hate these emotions. In a way, seeing Alex and Liza, I envy their ability to not feel. Things are less easy for us humans, that's for sure.

With my right hand, I reach over to my head and mutter an incantation, hoping it'll help soothe the ache. It does, but barely. This has nothing to do with me banging my head, and more to do with my whirring thoughts.

If this was daylight, I might be tempted to seek out Tassa and get one of her remedies. As it is, I'm not about to intrude on her.

Minutes turn into more minutes, and still my mind is awake, whirring, unable to shut off. I roll over and blindly reach for my backpack. Rummaging through it, my hand wraps around the leather journal. Țepeș's journal.

I should leave. Right now. Hand it over to my coven, and forget about this mission.

But then I remember the way Vlad had stared at me, and a shudder runs through me. Not of revulsion, but something else.

I release the journal, not wanting to touch it. Wanting to forget all about it. Instead, I punch the pillow a few times, trying to let out my frustration, but only succeed in making my head ache more. At a loss, I get out of bed, pull on jeans and a sweater, and leave the room.

Wandering around a vampir-owned castle in the middle of the night is probably not a good idea. I make it a point to stay away from the area I presume their bedrooms are in, and instead I head down to the kitchen and out the back.

The courtyard is bathed in shadows. Out of habit, I gravitate to them, keeping myself hidden to eyes that might wander. Instead I focus on my breathing, on listening to the breeze, the hoot of an owl, the—

I come to a full stop, freezing. *Was that...?*

It couldn't be.

But instead of walking away from the sound, I move closer. Keeping my footsteps light as they can be until I turn a corner, to where the stables used to be. And my jaw drops.

Liza's leaning against a wall, her head tossed back, her expression full of rapture. One slender hand is buried in a man's thick hair— a human. His exotic olive skin and bulky frame, as much as I can see of it between her creamy thighs, is completely unfamiliar to me.

They're a sharp contrast; her, moaning and undulating as his mouth pleasures her; him, on his knees and servicing her like she's a queen.

Which, in many ways, she is.

I should tear myself away from the view, but I can't. There's something about it that's so powerfully alluring...

The man must be really good, as Liza's moans grow louder. She's about to come, and I know it's so wrong to keep watching, but I can feel my own body heating up, my nipples tightening under my shirt, my—

A hand covers my mouth, stifling any screams. An arm wraps around my waist. And the moment after I'm gone, no longer watching Liza. Instead, I'm back in my bedroom.

"I'll let you go now, but don't scream."

Relief spreads through me—it's Vlad.

I whirl on him the moment he releases me. "What the hell are you playing at?"

"Me?" His eyes narrow. "Do you have any idea how dangerous it is to sneak up on a vampir in the throes of passion?"

"I wasn't sneaking up on her!"

"Sure looked like you were."

I can feel my cheeks heating. "I couldn't sleep, my head was hurting and—"

"Are you okay?" His annoyance seems to deflate, replaced by contrition. "How are you feeling, after... I know you couldn't stay awake for much conversation earlier."

I wave my hand around, dismissing his concern. "I'm fine. I mean, in pain, but better. Tassa did a good job and my healing"—I bite my lip, hoping he'll believe me—"Tassa mentioned it freaked you guys out. It's normal, part of something my family's always been able to do."

"I see." He runs a hand through his hair, and that frustration rises at the surface again. "So, what? You decided to wander at night and spy on a vampir?"

"No! I was minding my own business, walking, and she was there just—just—"

Vlad's expression lightens and he chuckles. "Yeah, that's Liza. She's never been afraid to go after what she wants."

I think back to what I'd witnessed. And now, away from the shocking image, I can finally pinpoint why I'd been unable to tear myself away. I'd envied her. My few amorous pursuits were boring and lacking any kind of creativity. Yet there she was, enraptured, and *I. Envied. Her.*

The revelation is shocking, causing me to gasp.

Vlad inches nearer, touching my shoulder. His touch heats up my nerves. I'm afraid to look at him, but with his free hand he lifts my chin up with his free hand.

"Look at me."

It's a gentle command, and it's enough to break my resolve. I meet his gaze, and it darkens in response to whatever's in my expression. His hold on my shoulder tightens, just enough so I don't try to shy away.

"You liked that, didn't you?"

"I—No! I don't make a habit of spying on people."

He chuckles and moves closer. "A lie, darling. You liked it. You *want* that." His thumb moves to my lower lip, caressing it. Sparks of fire run through me at the touch. "I'm more than happy to oblige. Just say the word."

"W-what?"

My brain has stopped functioning. Less than half an hour ago, it wouldn't shut up. And now, in Vlad's presence, it's gone completely off the rails.

He moves his thumb, now tracing my upper lip, even as his head is coming closer. He kisses the corners of my mouth, then the side of my face, and then right under my earlobe.

The unfamiliar heat spreading through me is too much. I've never felt something like this, not to this extent, not—

His tongue snakes out and licks my earlobe, and a moan escapes me. When his teeth nip that same spot, the moan turns louder. And when he sucks on it, softening the suction with swipes of his tongue, my knees crumble and I drop in his arms.

Vlad doesn't miss a beat. The hand previously holding my shoulder moves to my waist, holding me tightly against him. The one to my chin arches my head to the side, baring my neck to him.

Alarm bells start ringing in my head. I'm exposed—vulnerable.

"Let me have a taste..." he whispers.

I jerk, but before I can shove him away, he's already kissing my neck, and moving lower... It's only once he's on his knees in front of me, reaching for my jeans, that I realize he doesn't mean a taste of my *blood*. He means a taste of *me*.

By the time the realization dawns on me, Vlad's got my jeans down to my ankles, and his hands are caressing my bare flesh, inching upward to my panties.

I meet his feverish gaze just as he pushes aside the fabric and licks me, once. My knees buckle. And then he does it again. I hold on to his shoulders. And again. My nails dig into his skin. And still he doesn't stop, relentless. A wave of something builds in me, a storm that'll tear me apart from the inside out. Vlad doesn't care. He's still licking, sucking, alternating.

And then he moves his hand, pushing one finger inside me, and my eyes roll in the back of my head. A noise I've never heard escapes me—something half-way between a sob and a plea for more. I don't have to worry about him not understanding, because he does, giving me exactly what I need... And more... Until I shatter, collapsing to the floor and into his arms.

I'm not sure if I pass out for a second because of the intensity of my orgasm, or if I'm simply so focused on breathing and learning anew how to draw air into my lungs that I'm unaware of anything else.

When I finally come back to, I'm aware of two things. One, Vlad's hardness against me—not just his body, either. And two, the gentle way he's rubbing my back.

He seems to sense my return to life, so to speak, as he shifts and picks me up in his arms, then stands. I wrap my arms around his neck out of pure reflex. My mind is whirring, expecting him to lead us to the bed.

Instead, he walks us to the windowsill, and picks up a blanket along the way to wrap me in. On his lap, between the blanket and the light of the moon, I feel oddly vulnerable.

What does he want from me?

"How are you feeling?" he asks softly.

I meet his gaze, silent for a long moment. Truth is, I don't know how to answer him, and that makes the situation even more awkward. What *was* that?

"I... Fine. I'm fine."

A corner of his mouth quirks in a half-smile. "Just fine?"

I roll my eyes. "Better than fine, not that I have to elaborate."

He leans closer. "I wish you would."

"W-why?"

"Not to stroke my own ego. Only, it would help me understand that wariness in your eyes."

I tear my gaze away. "There's no wariness."

"There is, and I don't get it." He reaches for my hand, tugging it out of the blanket. His thumb forms circles in my palm, making me shiver. "Your body responds to me. You feel this ache, too. So, why? Unless you're not here for the reasons you say you are."

I jerk my hand out of his and stand. "I'm tired of your accusations."

"Then tell me the truth."

"I have!"

He shakes his head and stands, too. "No, you haven't."

Vlad

I can't get her image out of my mind. The way she stared at me as I left her room, only to now find myself pacing like a lion in a cage. I need blood. And the more I ignore that need, the stronger it gets.

Much as I try to focus on the reason for my restlessness, it's no use. The hunger is there, taunting me... Before I know it, Silviana's far removed from my mind as I head out of the castle.

"Vlad!"

I stop, turning. Liza's watching me, then she smirks. "Hungry, brother?"

"Perhaps."

She laughs at my terse reply. Never mind it's her fault that I'm in this mess in the first place. We've mixed sex and bloodlust too much for me to be able to differentiate it now. Yet another effect of this life we've been thrust into.

"I am, too."

"Didn't you just feed?"

She arches an eyebrow. "And how would you know that?"

I scowl. Shit. I've played my hand and it won't be long before—

"Ah. Playing voyeur now? I wouldn't have pegged you for one."

My teeth grind hard enough that I hear it. "I don't have time for this."

I whirl around before she can stop me. And then I'm flying, drifting through the woods, scenting my prey. The village closest is tempting, but I know it would be stupid to hunt in our own backyard. And I can't go in the same spot I did last time, so I head east.

Like an annoying buzz, I'm aware of Liza's presence behind me. Of course she followed me. She's like a dog with a bone. And out of all of them, she's the last one who should know what's going on in my head.

This darkness is dangerous. It might be contagious, for all I know.

Then a bark of laughter builds in my throat. Liza's dark enough, there's no way she could do much worse. After all...

We're here.

The darkest part of me is way too eager.

I stop on the edge of the forest. A road goes in parallel, leading to a small town. A walled town. The kind I used to love, back in the day. Because it fed my darker impulses. And now, it's back to full circle.

I lick my lips and get on the road, forcing myself to walk instead of storm through. Liza appears out of nowhere, interlacing our arms.

"What are you doing?" I hiss out of the corner of my mouth.

"Helping you, brother."

"Like you helped Silviana smack her head?"

Liza rolls her eyes. "She recovered, didn't she? And unless I'm mistaken, she's the reason you're in such a state." When I say nothing to contest her words, she continues, "Besides, a lonely stranger in the middle of town will seem suspicious, especially to these dim-witted humans."

"They're not all dimwitted."

She laughs. "Just because Nico's managed to find himself a passable one, doesn't mean they're all the same."

It's my turn to arch an eyebrow. "I didn't realize you *approved*."

She scowls and tries to move away. "I don't."

I grip her arm in mine, aiming for a sweet smile. "Sure sounds like it. But, for better or worse, you're right. And your help would be much appreciated... So long as you keep this between us."

Her grin only widens. "My kind of secret."

The village is quiet. Shops are closing. Pubs are open and raucous. I instinctively move toward one, but Liza stops me with a tug. She giggles low—for show—as we pass a few people, then points toward an alleyway.

It's a dark one, I don't even know how she noticed it. *Because she's not focused on the bloodlust,* a nagging voice says at the back of my head.

"Follow my lead," she whispers in my ear. She leans against a wall and grabs my shirt, pulling me closer, a wicked gleam in her eyes.

"What are you—"

She crashes her mouth against me, moaning loudly. My brain takes a while to cue in that it's for show, too. While we're not blood related, over the centuries I have come to see her as my sister, and this feels...wrong. On so many levels.

The bloodlust has no such moral qualms. It surges through me, more demanding than ever. More expectant.

Liza's still kissing me.

And then I hear footsteps passing by...slowing down...coming closer. Two sets. Male, judging by the heaviness.

"Ce avem aici?"

Liza lets me go, smirking, and leans against the wall, pushing out her chest seductively. "Want to join, boys?"

The construction-looking men take one look at her and smirk.

One of them says, "Sure thing, darling. But maybe we'll get your man to take a hike first."

The bloodlust pounds now. I meet their gazes, settling my glamour on them. "Problem is I'm not her man. But her brother."

They have no chance to run, not when my glamour takes control over their minds. And then I'm on the first one, my fangs digging into his neck. Blood gushes out and I drink, and drink, and drink... the man goes limp against me and still I drink.

You'll kill him. Like the others.

I don't care. I tighten my grip on him.

Then slender fingers wrap around my neck, yanking me off him. I turn, crouching, whirling on Liza, ready to attack her. Her amused expression gives way to alarm, then concern.

"Vlad, what's going on?"

The man I'd been feeding off is slumped against the wall. The other, his friend, wavers on his feet.

"Vlad."

I turn my gaze to Liza once more. Whatever she sees in me, she takes charge. Turns to the humans and takes over the glamour. "Your friend got sick after a night at the pub. You're going to take him home, give him some iron pills, and be on your merry way. Forget everything about tonight."

He turns and robotically does as she asks. They disappear down the street. Soon enough, the glamour will become part of their memories and they won't recall anything.

After a beat, Liza turns to me, her expression guarded. "Want to tell me exactly what's going on?"

"Nothing."

"Nothing, my ass. You've never been this…savage. That's my job. And Alex's." A beat later, "Sometimes Mira's. Never yours." As if to emphasize her point, she adds, "*Ever.*"

I glare at her. "I get it."

"If you get it, then what's going on?" She narrows her eyes. "Don't tell me it's the curse."

"It's not it."

"Then what?"

"*Nothing.*"

She jerks back at the fury in my tone. We stare at each other for a beat, then another…and then I leave. I've had my fill of blood, there's no reason for me to stick around.

Liza catches up to me in the woods. She slams into me, jostling me into a tree. It rips apart under the force of my hit.

I shake my head. "What are you doing?"

She doesn't answer, instead moving so she's barring my way. "You have two options, frate. Tell me what's going on with you, or we're going to stay here until you do."

"You won't do it."

She arches an eyebrow. "Want to test me? Because we both know I have no limits, unlike you. Or, I thought you had."

"Why the sudden interest? You've always been happily ignorant of anything else but your bloodlust."

She scowls. "That may be so, but we're a family. One that's as dysfunctional as possible, but nonetheless... And feeding like that, recklessly—"

"It's no more than you've done. Or Alex."

"Not true. We've gone on rampages before, but always in control. You had no control tonight, Vlad. Nor did you have any the night Silviana saw you."

"She—"

Liza's eyes flash. "I glamoured her. Not that it seems to have worked, and none of you care, but that's beside the point. That little witch is not the point here."

"Then what is?"

"You are. And the fact you're losing control, more and more. The sooner you realize that, the better."

I don't want to admit she's in the right. But... isn't she?

This isn't the first time, nor will it be the last. When the bloodlust takes over, I can't—

I shake my head, my shoulders dropping. "Very well. What do you remember of your life, your human life, I mean?"

"Why should that matter?"

"Because that's the crux of my problem."

"I don't have that problem."

I sigh. "Liza, listen to me. We all do. We've lived for centuries, more than humans are meant to. We are, at our core, those humans still. The deepest part of us."

"Not me. I *like* being the apex predator."

A chuckle escapes me. "Do you think that's what we are? Not damned souls?"

"I don't care. This is an existence I'm happy with. Now, stop avoiding the question."

"I'm not." I take a deeper breath. "When I was human, a long, long time ago, I wasn't the man you see before you. I was quite the opposite. You could even say I was evil."

She scoffs. "You? Yeah, right. I know about you. Father was *so proud* of you, always."

I shake my head. "No. He acted that way, but only the others know. You and Alex, you've never been told, because... Well. Your change affected you differently."

"Differently, how?"

"Violeta and I, we both had issues. As a human she was sweet, but when she was turned, she was out of control. When you and Alexandru were turned, Father realized the same streak ran in you. Or so he said. I was...the opposite." I take a deep breath. "When I was human, I was a killer. It started with my parents, when I was young. My father beat my mother. I killed him one night, slashed his throat in his sleep. Mom tossed me out the next day. Police—guards, back then—hunted me. I ran from village to village, a criminal. And I developed a taste for blood. For hire."

"You? As if!" Liza lets out an awkward chuckle. It dies off when she sees my serious expression. "You're lying. You're practically virginal, compared to us."

"I'm not. It's why Ţepeş chose me, or at least why I think he did.

Our father saw darkness in me, and I believe he saw it as a reflection of himself. I don't know if he followed me for days, and knew me when he chose me, or if it was impulsive. I have a feeling it was the latter."

Liza arches an eyebrow. "Why do you say that? I have a hard time seeing Father being impulsive. He was always so calculated."

"Because…" I struggle with the right words, before finally admitting, "I was sent to kill a witch. That particular job, I mean. But she was…she was pregnant. By then I had become ruthless, and I would've killed her, had Father not shown up and interrupted me. I didn't know then why he was there, nor did he ever tell me. But he intervened, saving her. Then he took me by the scruff of the neck, and before I knew it, I was chained in some place. That night, he turned me. He kept me chained for days until I came out of the initial change. And even after, he never left my side. Making sure I wasn't going to lose the bloodlust. Teaching me to control it." I laugh bitterly. "You all think it was fun, being the last one turned? Vlad Țepeș had no mercy on me, or my weaknesses."

Her eyes are wide, taking me in. "I have a hard time reconciling that with the vampir you are today. You're so…soft. And I don't remember you being bloodlust-crazy when you joined us."

"That's because Father didn't allow me to until my humanity ebbed away. The more the vampir side took over, the more I reinvented myself. After the initial loss of control—which only Nico, Mira and Vi know of—I chose to let go of the darkness. Felt less. Was taught by Father to keep everything under control, tightly so. But some things have consequences."

She tilts her head to the side. "Is that why you're losing yourself now? Because of your *human* side?"

I nod. "I have no other explanation. I've kept everything in line, but this... it's more. And I'm starting to have issues controlling it."

"So let me help."

"How?"

"I'll retrain you. I'm the best at feeding and leaving no loose ends, remember?"

As far as ideas go, it's not a horrible one. And it's not like I have many options left. Either I do something, or we'll all pay for my inaction.

Hesitantly, I nod.

Chapter 11

Vlad

It's morning when Liza barges into my room, unceremoniously drags me out of bed, and out of the castle. I follow, trying to wipe sleep out of my eyes, and the heaviness out of my limbs. I had some of Tassa's tincture last night once I'd gotten back, and while it helps, I feel another attack of weakness.

Would it stop if Silviana and I get together, same as Violeta and Marcus did?

Maybe. Maybe not.

I haven't seen her since yesterday, and all I know is it'd be hard to accept anything when she can't even seem to accept being near me, or liking my touch. I know what I'd felt—her release on my tongue, her moans in my ears—and she'd enjoyed every second of it. But the moment it was done, she'd shut down.

And I can't be making any progress with her constantly shutting down and hiding things.

At least if Liza helps me with my darkness...

I bring my thoughts back to the present. "I don't see how exactly you plan to control my bloodlust. We'd need someone bleeding."

Liza glances over her shoulder and rolls her eyes. "So little trust, brother."

My gut churns as I follow her into the woods. She's not going through to the village, rather on the other side, hiding deeper in the woods, leaving the castle behind at light speed. And, like a fool, I follow.

I know Liza has no limits and what she's got planned is probably not going to be my cup of tea. But do I have a choice? I've gotten to a point where I'm putting us all in danger.

Still.

When we start ascending the mountain, I move faster and catch her by the arm. "Are we not dangerously close to the Munteanu clan lines?"

She shrugs. "Just a little farther. Don't worry, it won't create an incident. Just trust me."

I'm ashamed to say I don't. I trust her to have my back, yes. But to not get me into trouble? Not really.

But I shove that thought back down and follow in silence for another few seconds. Liza finally stops in a cluster of trees. I do, too. And then I hear it—a man's moans.

Liza grins and moves to the young man she's got tied to a tree. He's slouched over, half-dressed in some jeans and a torn shirt, barefooted. His hands are pulled behind him, tied with a thick cord around the tree. He watches my sister approaching apprehensively.

I grab her wrist. "What the hell is this, Liza?"

"You know what it is. You need to control your bloodlust. This boy toy was a great lay for one, and instead of letting him go, I decided to use him a little more. And he doesn't mind." She turns to him, and while I don't see her expression, the man's face goes slack and his eyes glaze over. A sappy smile spreads on his features. "Isn't that right, baby boy?"

"Yes, my queen."

Jesus. Is that what she does, glamouring them until she's had her fill?

Sickened, I step back. "This is wrong. Sick."

Liza whirls on me. "No, what's *sick* is being tortured for weeks to see how much I bleed. Whether parts of my body will grow back. *That* is sick."

"But he had nothing to do with that!"

"Wrong. His father lives in the village. He knows more than he says."

It takes me a moment to understand her comment. Then, it dawns on me.

"His father... He's part of the order protecting us, isn't he?" When she doesn't answer, I take a step closer. "And you think because of what Tassa found out, that some of them were working with hunters, that he was tied in to what happened to you?" I fling my arm into the air. "Liza, that was *centuries ago*. Those men are dead!"

She only glares at me, saying nothing.

"So, this is what you do? This is what you've *been doing*? Going after the sons of the men who might know what happened to you, because one of their ancestors might've had a hand in it?"

"Not might! *Did!* I tortured one of them—oh, don't give me that look!—and he admitted as much. I saw their records. And I wasn't the only one."

She glances over my shoulder, her expression thunderous. For a second, I fear Silviana somehow came here, but a quick look confirms we're alone. What the hell is Liza looking at, then?

Her attention returns to me. "Violeta herself said the hunters she and Marcus faced used muroni blood. They're not above using supernatural means to extend their powers—*and their lives*. Not that you all care, since you're so goddamned busy giving in to the words of a pack of wolves!"

I shake my head. "Liza, this curse thing is real. It's happening to me, same as with Violeta."

She stumbles back, her eyes widening. "What?"

"It's true. I wake up to weakness. I've started taking the tincture Tassa prepared for Violeta. Nico suggested I talk to Silviana, to see if the witches know anything about it. It's happening, whether we like it or not. And it won't go away."

Her scared expression is soon gone, replaced by blankness. "Alex is right, you all lost your heads."

"No, we haven't. We want to survive."

"And you think we don't?" She scowls. "You think you're so mighty? Want to explain to Nico and the others about your little excursions? I saw the articles, brother. You may think you're better but at the end of the day, the same bloodlust rises in you. The difference is that I give into mine while you repress yours. If that's not fucked up, I don't know what is."

I gulp. "But I do. This isn't any better."

I go to leave, but I hear a sharp inhale. The moment after, the scent of blood hits me. I turn back, slowly. Liza shows me the man's bleeding arm. As I watch, nostrils flaring, she moves to his other side and rakes her nails on his bicep. A thin gash, but it doesn't stop the blood from flowing freely.

"Come on. Give in."

Saliva coats my tongue, and my fangs elongate. I dig my heels into the earth, trying to focus on its musky scent, and not the coppery trail of the blood. But it's impossible.

It surrounds me, suffusing every particle of the air, until it's all I can breathe, all I can focus on. That, and the heady thrum of the pulse under the man's skin.

One bite. One drink. It won't hurt.

"No."

I force myself to take a step back. This isn't how I want to learn to control my bloodlust. Not by killing another person.

Liza tilts her head to the side. She moves her hand to the side of the man's neck, and once more, her nail digs into the flesh. Blood flows out, coating his chest.

I drop to a crouch. A snarl builds in my throat, and when I look back up, I can sense that red haze descending on me.

"There he is." Liza places herself between me and the man. "Come on, Vlad. Fight it. Focus on something real, something to bring you back."

I can only think of the blood as I run toward him. Liza comes between us time and time again, until I snap and shove her to the side. She grunts, splitting a tree open, a branch running through her gut.

I focus on the blood, kneeling next to the man. Then I sink my fangs into him, enjoying the taste. Someone restrains me, grabbing a fistful of my hair and yanking my fangs off him.

"Take a deep breath. Now try again."

No matter how I fight against her, she's got me trapped. Her free hand binds my wrists, until I'm entirely at her mercy. So I listen and take another drink.

"*Focus*, Vlad. On my voice. On his heartbeat. Hear how strong it is?" I do. "And now, it weakens. Make yourself stop. Or else you'll kill him."

She lets me go. She won't stop me. No one will. The heartbeat weakens some more.

Silviana. I think of her smile, her kiss, and I pull back so brutally, I land on my ass a few feet behind.

Liza grins. "Well, what do you know? This is a start. Next lesson is in the real world."

She turns to the man. He's unconscious, but alive.

On our way back to the castle, we're both quiet. Liza, lost in whatever thoughts that fill her head. Me, torn between gratitude and anger.

In the end, gratitude wins and I turn to her. "Thank you."

Liza meets my gaze and nods. Then she scowls at something over my shoulder.

"Silviana." Her scent gives her away. I turn to her, smiling hesitantly. "How are you feeling?"

Instead of acknowledging me, her eyes land on Liza. She's frowning, as if seeing something I'm not. "Who is he?"

Liza jerks back. "Excuse me?"

"The man next to you."

I glance at my sister—there's no one there. But Liza looks as if she's been slapped. Then she recovers. "Mind your business."

"But—"

Liza moves on her, growling. But there's a desperation in her movements, like she needs Silviana to shut up. I intervene before she loses it.

Silviana

My eyes flicker between Vlad, Liza, and the man by her side. He watches me with a wry, amused grin, his eyes glinting. For a moment, I thought he was there, as real as anything else. From a distance, it had seemed that way.

Now that I'm so close, I can tell his consistency isn't quite the same as everyone else's. For one, there's a translucent vibe around him, as though he's not quite there. In life, the eyes staring at me might've been blue, might've been gray; but I'm fairly sure he's not alive right now...

At least, if Liza's expression is anything to go by.

"Who are you?" I ask him directly.

He opens his mouth to say something, but Liza steps in front of me. Her eyes are red, her hands hard as she shoves at me.

"I told you to mind your own business!"

I hold my ground, rubbing my chest where she shoved. Ow.

"And I know what I'm seeing."

Vlad stares between us, his hand hesitating as he reaches for Liza. His expression is harder to understand. After yesterday—after the orgasm he'd given me, after the way he'd walked out—I don't know where we stand. But I would've thought he'd at least, I don't know, take my side in this.

The hesitation in him tells me that's not necessarily the case. And it hurts more than I want to allow it.

I shake my head, looking at Liza again. "You want me to think I'm crazy, but I'm not."

She takes a step closer. "Crazy? No, bitch, I think you're suicidal. Do you know what the cost is of facing off against a House of Dracul member?"

I toss my head back refusing to back down. "Probably the same as breaking up asylum law."

Surprise flashes across Liza's features. I smirk.

"What, you thought I wouldn't know? Once upon a time, the Draculs were the head hierarchy, no? And in so doing, you allowed asylum to the supernaturals who sought you out. Those who became your allies. Such bonds were sacred, never to be broken."

"You're not here under asylum."

I grin. "Aren't I? Because Vlad specifically said I'm under your protection..."

Liza snarls, moving even closer to me. The man behind her says nothing, only shaking his head. Whether it's at me, or Liza, I can't tell.

Vlad snaps out of his trance then and tugs on my arm. "Silviana—"

I try to yank myself out of his grasp, but his fingers tighten around me, pulling me away from Liza. I don't miss her smug expression.

"Please, stop."

I stare at him in shock. "You're taking her side, then?"

"It's not like that. She helped me with something, and you're antagonizing her."

"*I'm* antagonizing *her*? You've got to be kidding me!"

He leans toward me, his face near mine. "Enough. You're trying to pick fights, all so you can avoid dealing with what we both know is sparking this."

"And what's that?"

"What happened between us."

No, he's not playing this card. "Nothing happened between us."

He lets go of my arm, only so he can take hold of my chin. It's a small touch, but it freezes me, forcing me to meet his gaze. Unable to look away, I see the lust swirling in its depths, and sense my lips parting. This instant chemical reaction is *not* in my control, but that doesn't mean I have to give in.

"It was a mistake," is what I say instead.

Vlad arches an eyebrow. "Really?" And then his mouth crushes mine.

And despite all my best intentions, despite me wanting to shove him away, I do the exact opposite. I hold onto his shirt, pulling myself closer, ignoring Liza's disgusted scoff from far away.

I can feel the kiss to my toes, from the way he holds me against his body, to his tongue tracing my lips, to the way we battle for who gets to win the never-ending game of dominating the kiss.

And then I realize what I'm doing, and I pull away. Again.

"What was the point of that?"

Vlad says nothing, only stares at me.

I glance over his shoulder at Liza. She's staring off into the distance, or so it would look. But I'd bet money on the fact she's glaring at the translucent guy. Why haven't I seen him before? Who is he to her? That's a question for another day.

Slowly, I raise my gaze to Vlad's again. "You don't get to do that, not after you've taken Liza's side over mine. I'm not crazy. Ask her who the guy is, and she'll lie. She'll deny it. I guarantee it."

And then I push out of his arms and walk away.

Chapter 12

Vlad

When Silviana stomps away, Liza sticks by my side. "I don't understand it. First Nico, now you. At least Violeta had the good sense to pick a vampir."

I face her, clenching my fists. "You helped me, I don't dispute that. But your attitude is lacking, sister. And all it does is push us away."

For the second time today, she looks like I've slapped her.

"If that's how you feel, fine. Fix your own damned bloodlust."

As she takes off, I yell, "Who's the man Silviana spoke of?"

She stops, rigid. "No one. She's delusional."

Without a glance backward, she keeps moving away from me, and back into the woods. I'm not sure what to make of it. Silviana may be many things, but delusional isn't one of them.

Which begs the question, what the hell has she seen, and what does it mean for the rest of us?

A few hours later, Nico finds me sulking in my room. He walks in without a knock, probably having listened in and realized I'm alone. At least, that's what I think at first. Once I have a closer look at his expression, I straighten from my slouch in the armchair.

"Have you heard from Mirabela?" he asks.

She'd left as soon as Silviana regained consciousness. The reason she gave us was that she needed to get a move on sooner rather than later, but part of me wonders if it's so she doesn't have to deal with the fallout from my new consort and the mess of integrating her into our family.

"Not since she left, no. Why?"

He takes a seat, uninvited. "Might be nothing. Getting an odd feeling, is all."

"Mm."

He arches an eyebrow at my lack of a verbose response. "What's gotten up your ass?"

"Coming from you, that must mean I've got a shit poker face."

He only watches me, his blue gaze so disconcertingly direct, compared to before. It's enough to remind me of Violeta, and our long chats into the night. The itch to call her hits me, but I don't want to disturb her and Marcus.

And besides, what would I disturb her with? *Sister dear, I'm having issues with Silviana, and keep being tongue-tied around her.* Wait. Been there, done that. Maybe, *Oh, and Liza might potentially be haunted by a ghost, but only Silviana can see him.* Yeah, that'd go over well. Well enough to send me to the looney bin for supernaturals.

"How's Tassa?" I ask instead, in an effort to divert the conversation.

Nico throws me a look that says he knows what I'm doing. Nonetheless, he answers. "Good. No more reach outs from the Munteanu clan. Or anyone else, for that matter. It helps that she spends her nights here. Plus, I've made it a point to go everywhere with her."

I chuckle. "She must love that."

He grimaces, then says, "What about you?"

"What about me?"

"Besides the fact you're acting weird?" He leans forward. "How are you dealing with...the revelation? Of Silviana being your consort?" He frowns. "Matter of fact, how are you feeling, period? Has the curse hit you more?"

I nod. In this, at least, I can be honest. "Da, it has. Stronger than the last few days. But, I think I'm handling it."

"Tassa's concoctions?"

"They work about as well as they did for Violeta. Which is to say, not for much longer."

Nico nods, as though he'd been expecting it. "Which brings us to Silviana."

I look away.

"You can't keep avoiding it, frate."

"I'm not. It's just, things are complicated."

"How so?"

I throw him a bone, hoping he'll get off the scent. "Do you ever feel like Liza's...off? Lately, I mean."

Nico leans back in his chair, his frown more pronounced. "What do you mean?"

"Weird happenings. I... Earlier, Silviana was around us. We were coming from the woods, and she said something about a man being around Liza."

"A man?"

I tap my finger against the armchair, thinking back to the moment. "It's weird. I would've thought it was a hallucination, and Liza certainly seemed to want me to believe that. But there's more to it, somehow."

"You can't think it's the curse?" He seems alarmed now. "If she's getting sick..."

"No, I don't think it's that. At least, not yet. But we never did figure out which of us sparked it, did we?"

"Ah." Nico stands, paces to the window, then back to me. "No, we didn't, you're right. But Liza... She won't be easy to talk to. I'll try, but I can't promise anything." He tilts his head to the side, gazing at me more intently. "So, is your plan to hide in your room, hoping solutions will magically arise to your issues?"

I shrug. "What would you do, in my stead?"

"Tell Silviana. Be honest."

I arch an eyebrow. "Not the advice I expected from you, frate."

He drops back into the armchair. "You can either do that, or lie. I've learned the hard way that secrets don't...hold."

I cringe and stand, unable to sit still anymore. "Speaking of secrets."

Nico eyes me quizzically as I let out a small sigh.

"Silviana's hiding something, too."

"More than you?" When I say nothing, he continues, "I saw you with Liza."

"And?"

He sighs and leans back. "And. I'm making a move. *We* are making a move to reclaim our spot in the vampir world hierarchy. We cannot have secrets among us."

I break our gaze. "Don't know what you mean."

Nico leans forward again. "You do, brother. For weeks now, something's been bugging you. Before Silviana came along. Something more, something from the past. Is it the darkness you struggled with when you were turned?"

I pace away, running a hand through my hair. "It's not."

"Isn't it?"

"No."

His eyes glint red. "Don't lie to me."

I've forgotten. It's been easy, seeing how loved up he is with Tassa, to forget the steel behind Nico's moods. I have two choices. Either I tell him the truth, or I keep putting us all in danger with my silence.

I can't be responsible for them being in danger. Not because of me.

In the end, I bow my head. "It is the darkness. Little by little, it came back. I've had...blackouts. Waking up next to human victims, some dead, others on the verge of it. Where possible, I've tried to save them, but those are few and far between. I..." I chance a glance at him. His expression is cool, unreadable. "I'm sorry. I should have told you, before it started hitting the newspapers."

"That was you? Not the vampiri?"

I nod, dropping my head again. "It was."

Nico allows a few moments of silence, his expression going pensive, the red light gone out of his eyes. "Well."

"What does that mean?"

"I always thought you and Violeta got along so well because you both reacted to the change similarly. Seems I wasn't quite off the mark."

"What will you do now?"

"Make sure it doesn't come back to bite us." He sighs. "How much control do you have over this...bloodlust? And don't sugarcoat it."

"I used to have a handle on it. But now? Not that much."

"Since when?"

"Around the same time Violeta took off."

He rubs his chin. "Shit. It has to be the curse."

"I can't just keep blaming the curse." This time, I meet his gaze full on. "There's accountability to be had here, and it's all mine. The curse might've enhanced certain dark urges, but the feeding, the secrets, the loss of control? That's all me."

Nico's gaze sharpens on me. "Which brings us full circle. I can take care of the narrative around the deaths, and we can keep an eye on your bloodlust—" He stops, as if struck by a thought. "You and Liza were coming from the woods. What were you doing there?"

I'm already shaking my head before he's done asking the question. "Not what you think. We weren't feeding. She... She figured it out, and she was helping me." If he's surprised, he doesn't let it show. "She had a human in the woods, and she... Well, you know Liza. Her ways are not exactly innocent. Still, it worked."

His expression darkens at my admission. "She'd better have

glamoured that human. Last thing we need is someone to give credence to the newspaper articles."

I nod. "She did."

Nico sighs, dropping his head in his hands. For long moments, he stays quiet. When he finally speaks, I almost wish he hadn't. "You might as well tell her."

I know which *her* he's referring to.

"Tell her what? That she's my fated consort, because of some damned curse? Yeah, that'll go over well."

"She could help you. She's a witch."

"You mean help *us*. Regain our throne."

He shrugs. "So what if she would have multiple uses?"

I'm about to tell him where he can shove his idea, when we both hear it—a thudding heartbeat. Right outside the door. And then her scent hits me.

"Fuck me," I groan.

Silviana

Of course, it doesn't take me long to figure out I need to apologize to Vlad. He was stuck in a hard place, and I'm hardly someone he needs to give his loyalty to, especially when the choice is between me and a sister who's been by his side for centuries.

But it hurts.

I ignore the voice and make my way back to his room, knowing I need to get through to him. Just in case he wants to toss me out of his castle, I grab my backpack—with the journal.

My steps feel leaden on the way to Vlad's room, and a journey that's normally only a few feet is more than that. I stop by one of the windows, glancing out. The moon is gone. It's pitch dark everywhere.

Maybe that's why I notice them—flickering lanterns in the woods.

Must be kids out for a thrill. If only they knew.

Finally, I turn and cross the last steps, until I'm in front of Vlad's door. I raise my hand to knock, but find it shaking. And then I hear voices inside. Vlad and Nico.

"You should tell her."

My hand drops to my side. Heart thundering.

"Tell her what? That she's my fated consort, because of some damned curse? Yeah, that'll go over well."

I back away from the door, my hand still raised to knock. Vlad's words bounce around in my head. *Tell her what? That she's my fated consort, because of some damned curse?*

I stumble back from the words. They can't be true. They just can't be! The implications...

The rest of what they said hits me, slowly. *She's a witch...multiple uses...regain our throne.*

I pay no attention to where I'm heading, and a vase clatters, shattering to the floor. I'm already running, running, running... but I feel him, behind me, chasing me.

Still, I don't stop. I rush out of the castle, past the courtyard, my backpack slamming against my back.

He can't be my consort.

I know what a consort is—a vampir mate. A bond that's older than time itself. A bond forged in love and understanding and acceptance of an eternity spent together.

But that's ludicrous.

Vlad's a vampir.

He's a monster.

He's...

Sexy and sinful and thoughtful and—

No! He can't be.

But he is.

My mind is at odds, so much so I can't think. I can't breathe. I can't...move. I pause by a tree, panting, trying to get my head geared on straight.

I was sent here on a mission. I—

A nagging thought hits me. One that makes my stomach roil in confusion and revulsion. Did they send me here knowing this would happen?

Did... did my brother know?

I swallow air, multiple times, hard and fast to stop myself from hyperventilating.

And then *he's* there. The breeze hits my face, carrying with it his scent. I turn around, slowly, to face him. Vlad's expression is forlorn.

"I didn't want you to find out this way."

"Didn't...You knew? All along?"

He nods, taking a step closer. I hold up my hands as if to ward him off. But my magic won't even work against him. There's nothing in my core, nothing at all.

"Silviana—"

"No. It can't be true. It isn't."

His expression is forlorn. "I should have told you, and I'm sorry I didn't. I only found out a few days ago, when you were hurt. The curse, it's not our choice!" He takes a step forward, then stops when he sees me moving backward. "You know Zalmoxis—the god you mentioned?"

The name freezes me. I watch him, waiting.

Vlad goes on, "His daughter was Țepeș's first wife."

"That's not possible."

"It's the truth! It's why our Father was created, to keep her safe. And when she killed herself, thinking she'd lost him, Zalmoxis blamed our father. He cast a curse on his entire lineage...it's what this bond is. You and me. Violeta and Marcus. Nico and Tassa."

"You're a *liar!*"

"Why are you so against the idea? You've seen Nico and Tassa. It's not an impossible match."

I shake my head. "It is for me."

"Why?"

"Because—"

Before I can even say anything, ropes fly out. Magic. Dark tendrils, more potent than I've yet faced. They wrap around his wrists, merging them together with an audible snap. More wrap around his ankles. The moment they touch his skin, they sizzle and glow with a golden aura. It makes the darkness within the magic look even more sinister.

Vlad falls to his knees. A second later, my brethren step out of the woods, their eyes on him. Eight of them, all with bleeding hands. And then the last one steps in. The Grand Master himself.

Dressed in a dark suit and shirt, he blends in well with the darkness. His white beard and goatee are trimmed neatly, and he snaps manicured fingers to his acolytes.

His dark eyes settle on me. "Silviana. You've done well, child. We can take it from here."

Vlad stares at me, then at them. His expression is filled with agony—a lot of it because of me, and some of it because of the magic. But then he passes out, and I follow them as they lead him away from the castle.

And all throughout, something in me says I should've stopped this. That I should be running back to his siblings, telling them everything.

When I glance over my shoulder, however, it's to see smoke coming from the direction of the castle. I remember the lights I'd seen, in the woods. Was it vampiri, or more of the Dacians? I don't know, but the sight alone of the dark clouds rising is enough to tell me there are no other options.

If the vampiri survived, they're more likely to tear my head off. Or let Alex do it. And if they didn't...

Straightening my shoulders, I force myself to put one foot in front of the other, and follow my coven members blindly. Soon, we exit the woods onto a small road, near the village I'd been in. A few dark SUVs await us.

Vlad is tossed into one, and the bulk of the Dacians—all dressed in dark suits, same as the Grand Master—head in after him. Two of the remaining men join me in one of the other SUVs. The Grand Master enters the last one.

So. Even after everything I did, all the orders I followed, I'm relegated back to my old role?

All throughout the journey, I shove back the contradiction in my heart, the one in my mind, and I keep my eyes on the ground. And not on the SUV holding the imprisoned vampir, the one I've just found out is my consort. A bond that is more sacred than anything...

We cannot be fated together. Because if we are, that means everything I've believed in is a lie.

Chapter 13

Vlad

When I wake up, the bloodlust is high and potent in my veins, in my throat. It takes me a moment to recall what happened. When I do, I jerk against my bindings, only to find myself restrained in a cave. My wrists are bound with dark tendrils encompassed by light—they're constantly burning my skin, only for it to heal, and repeat. I block the pain as much as I can, focusing instead on other things.

Silviana—

No.

There's no need for me to worry.

She was part of this, all along. Liza was right, as was Alex. And not only did she fool me, but I've allowed her to put my family in danger. To use me as bait, for whatever these people plan to do.

A darker need rises inside me, one I haven't felt since I picked up the axe and killed my father. It's not bloodlust, but worse— revenge.

I don't want to give in to it. The last time I did, things didn't work out well. They wouldn't have, without my new father. But how could Silviana have done this?

She's supposed to be my consort. The most sacred of bonds, for all eternity.

Betrayal burns through me, harsher and stronger than the ache in my wrists. And all throughout, another question assails me.

Would it have stopped this, if I'd told her the truth?

I want to believe it would've made a difference, but in the end... it wouldn't have. I'd seen the revulsion in her gaze in the woods, felt the rejection like a slap against my skin. Silviana played me for a reason, with a clear goal in mind.

The question is, did she achieve it? Is that why I've been captured?

And more to the point, who's behind it? Because she didn't cook it up herself, that's for sure.

I compartmentalize that, too. Her face in my mind, her taste on my lips, her moans in my ears—none of that has a place here. This is a place of darkness and for me to get out, I'll have to dive into the worst parts of me. The ones I've been avoiding for centuries.

So be it.

I sit back on the floor, crossing my legs and taking a yogi pose. I close my eyes, ignoring the constant throbbing of my veins where the skin is shredded by the light and once more fused together. Instead, I take breaths I don't need, in an effort to focus my mind on something—anything—other than my own stupidity.

They will come to me, my captors, I have no doubt about it.

And when they do... May the heavens help them.

Silviana

I take the bottle of water I'm offered and drink greedily, though my eyes never leave the Dacian's. He's younger than me by a few years at least, but eager. The glint in his eyes says as much, as do his frequent side-glances to the woods where the others have disappeared—with Vlad.

I take in the area we've been brought to. It's near enough to the main compound, the apartments being only a few minutes away. The Grand Master specifically chose the outskirts of Braşov to set up shop. Close enough to the humans, but far enough to conduct our business without their nosiness.

I've spent my life in these apartments, and in the woods surrounding them. But *these* woods are denser, darker, and I'd detected a faint trace of a barrier as we entered. Almost as if the barrier took us from one spot, to the other.

How is the Grand Master maintaining a barrier, when it would require a constant blood supply for the blood magic to feed on?

More importantly, how does he have so much magic to tap into? I've been told my entire life that the vampiri are the source of a curse upon us, one that depletes our magic, one that must be stopped. It's why I'd volunteered for the mission, as soon as Fane told me the rumors.

Did I volunteer for a lie?

My eyes follow the Dacian's glance to the woods, again. Instead of asking what I really want to, I try for another question. "Where's my brother?"

"Wrapping up another mission."

"Ah."

I itch to go to him, but I don't want these guys to see that need. They would scoff at the emotional, feminine side of me. And I've worked too hard to distinguish myself. Clearly, the success of the mission has already spread like wildfire, because the Dacian's eyes are full of respect when they land on me.

My glance goes to the woods again, and the network of labyrinthian caves I know would exist past them. At least, I'd imagine they would. They existed in my woods, near the apartment, so surely the Grand Master would have chosen a similar spot to hold Vlad? He's nothing if not predictable, after all. Caves means multiple entry and exit points, and cover against human technology. They also make for great cellars to store supplies...and prisoners.

"Where have they taken the vampir?"

The man frowns, and I catch my misstep. I shouldn't be asking about Vlad.

"I have more information for the Grand Master, that's all."

When he keeps staring at me, I roll my eyes and reach in my backpack for the journal I'd stolen from the Dracul siblings.

The Dacian looks at it, then nods. "Follow me."

To my surprise, he takes me past some trees to a house built nearby. It looks like a cabin from the outside, but inside, it's as opulent as any palace. Persian rugs, marble floor underneath, gold-plated furniture as far as my eyes can see.

I barely hold back my gasp of surprise. I've never been allowed near the Grand Master's quarters, until the moment I'd received my mission. And even that meeting had taken place in my apartment, not his. To be surrounded by all this wealth....

"Wait here."

I take in my surroundings as he disappears around the corner. Something about this lavish display of wealth strikes me as odd. Weren't we meant to abstain from material gains and lead humble lives as hermits, more or less? Then why—

Not my place to question how the Grand Master lives.

I take the backpack off my shoulders and reach inside, pulling out the leather-bound journal. Țepeș's journal. It feels meaningful, in my hands. I've been running around and trying to outmaneuver vampiri, it's not like I took a moment to actually look through it. But now...

My curiosity is too strong. Before I can stop myself, I flip the cover open, then the first few blank pages, until I land on the first entry.

> *1 July 1456*
>
> *Cursed. I am a cursed man. I must be, because how else can such tragedy befall me?*
>
> *My dearest Ana, for years you begged me to write you letters, and for years I was consumed with keeping you safe. I'd promised your father, I made a pact with him, and he is not a man to be trifled with. He is not a man, period.*
>
> *But all those pacts, all those deals, and for what? My bloodlust only brought more raging wars at our door, and now...it has taken you away from me.*
>
> *Why didn't you wait for me, beloved? Why did you be-*

*lieve that stupid letter from the hands of an Ottoman
traitor, when I was racing to come back home to you?
Only to find your lifeless body on the rocks underneath
my fortress. Your cold skin... I'll never forget the image.
I'll never forget you, beloved. How can I? When you
took your life, you took mine with you, too.*

The page is jagged in some parts, the way old paper gets when
it's wet, then dried again. Some of the ink is smudged, enough to
make me think of tears... But would Țepeș, the feared voivode himself, be crying over a letter?

And then his words sink in. *He would've, if this was when he
lost his first wife.* My thoughts wander to Vlad, yet again. This is part
of his history. Why would the Grand Master need this journal, when
all it does is speak of the past?

Gritting my teeth, knowing I'm running out of time, I flip the
pages. More of his pain, in words that seem to fly off the pages and
embed themselves in my chest. How could a vampir, a monster like
him, feel so much, and so deeply?

On a shaky breath, I stop. I've found another entry, and a name
jumps off the page.

15 December 1459
*Have my prayers been answered? Perhaps. I may not
be destined for the rest of this cursed existence alone.
Nicolae. Ana, you would have liked him. He has fire this
boy, though he does not know it. He has a thirst to prove
himself. I have seen it over the time I have known him.
And while I feel his strength will be of use to me, he*

cannot be alone. Now that I've made this choice, I know you would not want me to turn only one, beloved.

So I will create a lineage, one everyone will fear, that will mark my heirs as unique and voivode of this land when I am gone.

Footsteps echo in the cabin. I hurry on to the next entry.

19 December 1459

Three days ago, I turned Nicolae. It was hard, harder than I would have thought. He had so much anger in him, so much loneliness. But it had to be done. I have freed him from a useless life, and perhaps, in time, he will thank me.

I tear my eyes away from the rest, just as the Grand Master's footsteps get louder. The moment I close the journal, the man himself enters the hallway.

"Ah, Silviana. You have done well." He kisses my cheeks, smiling like a patronizing jackass. "You have something for me?"

He looks down pointedly at my hands. The weight of the leather-bound journal feels more than it should, and I'm reluctant to give it away. Especially when I haven't been able to read more of it.

The Grand Master holds his hand out. I reluctantly hand the journal over, feeling like I'm missing a huge part of the puzzle. It's all I can do not to howl accusations.

He saves me the trouble. "I did not expect the trap to work as well as it has. You seem to have developed quite a deep connection with the monster."

"You knew? You sent me in there...knowing...about the bond?" I barely contain myself, and the rage boiling under my cool façade.

"Of course."

"And why wasn't I told?"

He turns away from me, setting the journal in a small golden chest by a table. "Why would you be?"

I stare back, stunned. "Because—"

"You had a purpose. Ensnare one of the princes. And you did."

"But I thought it was the journal we needed."

"The journal was a convenient excuse."

A convenient excuse? I risked my life, for days on end, for a convenient excuse?

"And the attack in the forest? Was that also a convenient excuse?"

"Indeed."

No shame. No apology. Not even an ounce of remorse.

I think back to Vlad's contrite expression when I learned about the curse, about us being fated together, and I can't help comparing. The Grand Master makes it that much easier.

"You wish to tell me something else?"

"No. Nothing. I was mistaken."

His eyes narrow on me for a split second. The air around us changes, charged with intent. But then his expression mollifies, and the Grand Master gives me a cool smile. "You did well, as I said. You may take a few days to rest, and then return to your duties."

"My dut—" I bite down on my lip, tempering my tone, before I speak again. "It was my understanding that I'd be offered a chance, after this mission. To...progress."

He arches an eyebrow. "Oh?"

It was useless. All of it. The danger I put myself in, the lines I crossed, even allowing Vlad's capture! The Grand Master had never intended to let me grow alongside the men, clearly. Which means the only thing I can expect from this life is what I've already had—a set of daily tasks, and leeching onto Fane's knowledge of magic. No relationships. No companionship.

Something in me—a last shred of hope?—shrivels and dies. And with it, so does my respect for everything I thought worthy to be believed in.

"Never mind," I mutter, turning my back on the Grand Master. Without waiting for his permission, I walk away.

Past the Dacian standing guard outside his door, back into the woods... And before I know it, I pass that odd barrier again, and find myself on the edge of Brașov. I glance behind me, but all I see is the regular woods.

Hmm. So he's definitely using magic, in large bulks, and that's some kind of entryway to another part of the country. But...where? And why would he go to such lengths? Is it to hide his own location, or Vlad's?

If it's the latter, that means he's expecting retaliation. But I'd seen the smoke at the castle...

I force myself to shake it off, and walk to my apartment. Minutes later, I'm standing on the threshold, door open, keys dangling in my hand. I picked them up from the security post downstairs, and walked up four flights of stairs instead of taking the elevator. And now, it's like I have to force myself to step inside.

So this is what I left behind.

With a sigh, I cross the threshold and enter. Toss the keys on the plain granite countertop. Take in the simplistic, if contemporary, décor. Curved pale green sofa, green bar stools, a small dining room table with a wooden table and chairs with green cushions. Past it, my small bedroom, and a bathroom. On the nightstand, my cellphone is charging, waiting for me.

It's not much, but it's home.

At least, it used to be.

And it's not like I spend much time here, anyway. I'm usually either picking fruits and herbs in the forest with the other women, or grinding them into pastes and potions in one of the larger apartments we use as sort of a mini-headquarters. And if it's not that, I'm out doing card readings for tourists, or selling our wares at the local markets.

That's really all the women are good for, in the Grand Master's eyes. I'd thought it was because he saw us as soft, and if I could show him the opposite, show him I could complete a mission and keep myself in check, that it would mean I'd be allowed to do more. Learn more magic, the type Fane's always learning.

What a foolish notion. Clearly, the only use the Grand Master has for me is as another cog in his machine.

So, was it really worth it? All the pain I've caused, especially to Vlad. I can't get the image of his distraught features out of my head. And all of it, for *nothing.*

It's fine. So I crossed a few lines, caused a little hurt. At the end of the day, he's a vampir. His kin killed my parents. Made us orphans. There's nothing to feel guilty for, when all I did was strike back. Nothing at all.

No matter how vehement my words might be, another voice, smaller, soon contradicts me.

Liar, my heart whispers.

Vlad

It doesn't take them long to come. Four men enter the darkened cave, and light bursts from the walls, illuminating them. They're each dressed in suits. I don't have to check the brand tags to notice the nice cut, the way the material drapes over their bodies. The witches I'd known were always frugal in their livings, but these... These are no ordinary witches. Their presence alone is enough to make me stand straighter, awaiting a curse.

Instead of coming any closer to me, they form a line, two on each side. A fifth man enters, dressed in a somber suit. His beard and goatee are groomed to perfection, his salt-and-pepper hair glinting in the torches' light. Eyes the color of obsidian stare at me calculatingly. A smirk stretches his thin lips.

I stare at them, waiting for someone to speak.

"Welcome, son of Dracul," says the man who seems to be the leader.

"And where, exactly, am I welcomed?"

"Kogaionon. A sacred place for my people."

Kogaionon... Why does that sound familiar? And since when do witches need a sacred mountain?

My poker face must be shit, because his smirk widens. "You may call me Grand Master Liviu."

Liviu. Why do I know that name? Sure, it's a common enough Romanian name, but I've heard it, and recently. I heard it from...

An image of Tassa talking to Nico slams into me. We're outside the caves she was being held captive in. He'd taken care of Victor, the human behind it, but Tassa was saying... *There was another man. Besides Victor. A vampir hunter, Liviu. They were working together.*

Using vampiri to experiment on. My dad found out, he tried to go against him and they turned new humans to kill him. So it couldn't be traced to them.

Without Tassa knowing, Nico searched for the guy, far and wide. He was never able to find him. None of us could...until now.

"Ah. I see you've remembered something." Liviu smiles as though I'm a child in need of encouragement. "Go on. Tell me."

I glare at him. "You're the vampir hunter who went after Tassa."

All I get is laughter. Then he points to the darkness holding my hands together. "Do you think a mere vampir hunter could do this? My, you have no idea what I mean, do you?" He turns to the man by his side, chuckling. "Silviana did an excellent job."

A snarl rises in my throat, unbidden. I shouldn't want to be defending her, but I don't like the way her name sounds coming from his lips. From any man's lips, period.

He throws me an amused glance. "Let me put you out of your misery, vampir." A few steps closer, he pulls out a knife from the inside pocket of his suit.

It's my turn to sneer. "You think a knife can kill me? Get close enough, I dare you."

He tuts, avoiding my gaze. But instead of aiming the knife my way, he turns it to his palm, and cuts into it. Dark tendrils, from the shadows, move toward him, lapping at the blood. Its scent hits my nostrils, and I recoil in horror.

When he looks up, whatever white was in his eyes is gone, replaced purely by darkness. "We are Dacians, vampir. More powerful than you. More blessed than you. By the same god who cursed you." His voice is deeper, hoarser. "And Kogaionon is our sacred mountain, so any hope you might have of escaping, you can consider it extinguished."

Now the deluge of information hits me. Kogaionon, sacred mountain of the Dacians, because Zalmoxis stayed there in a cave for three years. His people thought him dead, disappeared into the darkness of the cave. But after three years he resurrected and showed himself to them, convincing them of his holiness...

The last purposed location of the mountain was around the old Dacian capital. They used to call it Sarmizegetusa Regia, a massive fortress that could never be taken by enemies. But the mountain's actual location was never found, only theorized upon. And according to one such theory, it could put my location by the Gugu summit, near the Oraștie Mountains.

I hold back a look of surprise. They've managed to transfer me over 200 kilometers, easily half a day's drive, without waking me up nor my siblings tracking us. That is some skill.

They're not to be underestimated. But you already knew that.

When I say nothing to their admission of our location, the Grand Master—Liviu—smiles. "You can pretend to be unfazed, but surely the binds around your wrists hurt."

I say nothing.

"No? Hmm. Perhaps some....blood?" He offers his wrist and when I make no move, he takes out a dagger and cuts deeper into his palm.

Blood drips freely to the floor, drop by drop. My eyes are drawn to it. No matter how I want to keep control of myself, the bloodlust is at its peak. Too much so, almost.

I can't give in.

I move fingers just enough, to dig into my skin and keep me rooted.

I can't give in.

They've left. Thank the heavens I don't believe in.

I slouch back against the bars, my back to the entrance. My thoughts linger on the little things Liviu said. That he's the same man who masqueraded as a vampir hunter—or perhaps not, for all I know he's both a Dacian *and* a hunter—and kidnapped Tassa, nearly killed her. This means he's known about us for a lot longer than we've known about him.

What was his purpose, to taunt me with this information? To let me know exactly where I'm being held...

Maybe it's to point out that your siblings could've gotten to you already, if they'd wanted to.

I try to shove away the nagging voice, but the doubt has been planted.

What use am I to them? Aside from not letting the curse take hold, doing my part. I've nearly shown our existence to humans. I'm losing control of myself. And if the curse kills me, well, that would all be gone. If I were them, I wouldn't come for me, either.

It's not long before I hear soft tiptoes. I should've known they would use her. After all, she's the whole reason I'm in this mess.

How much did she know?

Now's my chance to find out. If I dare.

Silviana

It took some bribing and a good dose of magic to get past the two guards at the entrance. But, thankfully, they were distracted enough.

Apparently, the Grand Master had just visited the prisoner.

Once I pass them and enter the deep underground tunnel, I wait a little until I use magic to flick on the torches—and only enough so I can see where I'm going. Then I emerge into a vast cavern, where they've set a massive cage. Its steel-enforced bars glint in the faint light, which does little to show me the person they're trapping.

Vlad's back is to me. I have no words to say to turn him around. I shouldn't even want to. But something about the slope of his shoulders, the way he's so remotely turned away from me... I find myself saying them anyway.

"I'm sorry."

There's no change in his form. Nothing...at all.

Disappointment runs through me, then annoyance.

"Did you hear me?" I raise my voice. "I said I'm sorry."

A silence as long as forever extends. Two deep breaths, four, six...

"I heard you," he finally speaks. Only, his tone is devoid of its usual warmth. No longer inviting, playful and alluring. It's cold, remote, and...blank.

Though he hasn't moved, or done anything at all, I feel that to my core. I deserve it. I know I do. I never intended his capture, didn't even know it was planned. But I went in undercover, intending fully to harm him. And now, the tables are switched on not just him, but on both of us.

"And you have nothing to say?"

It's a taunt. It's a torture for me, pushing him to speak more. To hear the coolness I rightfully deserve. But, I do it anyway.

His head shifts infinitesimally to the right. He's not looking at me, but he's acknowledging me. That's something, isn't it?

That hope is dashed with his next words. "What are you seeking, my absolution?"

"I—No! I have nothing to be absolved for."

He scoffs. "You sure about that?"

I take a step closer. "I have to stand with my people."

"Sure."

"I have no choice."

"Mm."

"You would have done the same."

He tosses his head back, resting it against the bars, depriving me of his profile. "Who are you trying to convince, me or yourself?"

His words strike me harder than if he'd lashed out. Because they're true. Here I am, defending myself, defending my purpose, to the exact same type of monster who orphaned me and Fane. Here I am...unapologetically...trying to gain his forgiveness.

I step back, stunned at the realization.

And when he doesn't move, I leave. Because I can't stand being there and watching him be cold to me. And I can't stand being there and accusing him of being who he is. And more than anything, I can't stand there, expecting anything to end differently.

Vlad is right.

I may not want to admit it, or give it thought, but the truth of the matter is he called me out on my bullshit. My own hypocrisy.

I made my choice. Now I have to live with it, come hell or high water.

I leave the cellar and exit in the woods. My gaze turns to the east—
what would happen if I just turned and walked away from it all?
Refused to be part of this any longer? Could I, even?

Not without Fane.

I turn back to the Dacian headquarters and walk toward them,
refusing to let my doubts nag at me. But they do. Too much. Vlad's
words, his total acceptance. And what of the fire? When I'd left the
woods, I'd seen the sky painted red. Vlad was already out of it, and
he doesn't know, but... Was that our fault, too? Or someone else, like
the rival vampiri clans?

I need to know.

Hesitating, I head back to the rippling river. Cut my finger on a
stone and mutter an incantation. A pull within me drags the magic to
the surface, and as the blood mixes with the water, it swirls, forming
a one-way mirror. In it, I see my mind's question. The castle, burning.
Nothing left of the roof—at least the side I'm seeing. The windows
look equally shattered, leaving behind only ruins of the stone as the
fire burns into the night.

Did any of them escape? And why do I care?

The truth is, I shouldn't. But I do.

"There you are."

I turn—Fane.

I rush to my brother, embracing him. His tall frame. The safety
I've been seeking. I breathe in his woodsy sandalwood scent mixed
with lime, and hold back tears.

"They told me you were on another mission."

"Mission?" He snorts. "Hardly. Took care of lodgings for some
new recruits. Not sure why they'd have said otherwise."

His admission stuns me into even more silence. As if sensing it, he pulls back and frowns, looking vaguely toward me. He may be blind, but he's always been attuned to my emotions.

Which is why I force an easy tone as I say, "Yeah, me either." But that nagging doubt grows more and more.

Chapter 14

Silviana

I follow my brother to his room, holding on to his arm, loath to let go of him. Most people would assume Fane needs my help to be steered around, but the truth is he had a lifetime to learn how to take care of himself. And me. And he's definitely in no need of my help. So I simply soak in his proximity, enjoying the peace and quiet it offers me.

"Make yourself at home," he says.

I move to the island in his open-concept studio, knowing he's about to make us some nice coffees. To say my brother has the magic touch with food and beverages would be an understatement.

I watch him move about the kitchen, pulling cups off their

hooks, touching a few buttons on the kettle, then moving to the coffee can of instant coffee. He moves assuredly, confident in the place each thing has in his environment.

He adds two teaspoons to each cup, followed by two of sugar and some almond milk. Then he grabs a teaspoon and whisks each mix into smoothness. By the time the water finishes boiling and he adds it, the heady aroma of caffeine fills the space.

Then Fane sits opposite me and says, "So, spill. How did it go?"

"It went fine."

"Mmm, that catch in your voice says the opposite. This is me, Lana. What's going on?"

"I..." Truth is, I don't know how to explain what I'm feeling. Other than a confused mess.

So I don't bother. I let the words pour out, detailing everything— even the private moments with me and Vlad. I've never hidden anything from Fane and I'm not about to. Maybe he can make sense of it all, including how in hell I've gotten myself entangled with a vampir, and found myself to be his consort.

By the time my coffee cup is empty, he's all caught up. But all he does is sit in silence, staring somewhere above my head.

"Fane?"

He jerks back to the present as if lost from something. "That...is quite a tale."

I watch his expression for anything that would tell me he's not mad, or disgusted, by what I've said. We've both grown up hating vampiri. We've both wanted to do everything possible to get revenge for our parents' deaths. And here I am, conflicted as hell over a choice that should've been simple.

"Tell me I'm not going crazy."

"You're not... But I also feel that being around the vampiri has affected you."

"They didn't glamour me."

"They didn't have to. You got taken in by one of their own."

I look at the table, whispering, "Do the spell, then. Make sure."

"Lana, it's not necessary." His cool tone, so rational, has my emotions overflowing. "I believe you."

"But I don't believe myself! At least, not anymore."

"Vampiri can't glamour us. Their abilities come from the same magic that gives us ours; they negate each other. *You know that.*"

I keep staring at the table. "Please, Fane."

He sighs, then stands. With sure steps, he reaches for the block of knives. It's a measure of his nervousness about the spell—and what it might reveal—that his hand slips, and he loses his grip. Instead of getting frustrated, he restarts his approach, feeling each knife by the handle, until his hand rests on the smallest one. He pulls it out, makes a small cut on his index, and as the blood drips into the sink, he mutters an incantation. I close my eyes, sensing the energy swirl around me.

That's the thing with Fane. His magic, while the same as mine, is more potent. He senses things others don't, things invisible to the naked eye. He'll be able to look into my aura, and if anything is there that shouldn't be, at least we'll know. At least the emotions in me will make sense, because they aren't mine. Everything will be so much simpler, including hating Vlad for what he is.

But a few moments later, I sense Fane's magic disappear, and he takes a seat opposite me. "Nothing."

I open my eyes, shocked. "What do you mean, nothing?"

"There's nothing in your aura to indicate glamour or anyone else controlling you. Your emotions are your own, Lana."

His tone feels like a death sentence. Tears fill my eyes. "Do you hate me?"

"No!" He reaches for my hands, finds them, pries each finger off my empty cup until they're covered by his. "I never could, sorella. I'm only worried. Now that he's caught, you know what his fate will be."

I do. I'd heard as much from the others. And I don't want to imagine it.

"Do you think his siblings survived the fire and might come after him?"

"I don't know if they survived. But there's no way they'll be able to follow us here, that's for sure. The mountain is sacred for a reason. It will protect us."

"That, and the barrier."

Fane frowns. "What barrier?"

"When we came... You're saying you didn't feel it?" I'm brought back to what I'd seen around Liza, and the man she was speaking with. Could I be losing my mind?

"No, but that doesn't mean it isn't there. Where did you feel it? I haven't been allowed to exit our regular grounds for a while now."

My frown mirrors his. "But... Valeriu said you were watching attentively. He brought me a note from you, when I was with the vampiri."

Fane freezes. For a long moment, he says nothing. When he finally speaks, his voice is low, as it always is when he's angry. "Believe me, Lana, if I'd been around, I would've intervened to make sure you were never fated to a vampir, of all creatures! I don't know what game Valeriu is playing, but I sent you no notes. I had no news of you until you returned."

I can't wrap my head around the information. I should be able to, it's not rocket science, but nothing makes sense.

Luckily for me, my brother is the more rational of us. He recovers faster. "The barrier. Lana, where did you feel it?"

"Near the woods, where they took Vlad."

"Closer to the mountain, then?"

I nod, then say out loud, "Da."

"I'll have a look later tonight."

I watch his pensive expression. "What is it?"

"Nothing. I mean, it may be nothing. But… Doesn't it seem weird, the Grand Master capturing the vampir? You went there for the journal and now he has it. It seems…odd. It's not what we're about."

"So why do you think he did it?"

"Not sure, but I'll keep my ears to the ground."

"Something else bugs you."

He grins. "It's good to know you haven't lost your ability to read me."

"Never." I squeeze his hands. "Now, tell me."

Fane nods. "Bine. I also find it odd that you were told—even if it was only implied—that I had anything to do with that attack on you. I never would have agreed to such a thing."

His words shake me to my core. I remember that same resolve, the unshakeable belief he wouldn't cross that line. Then, the acceptance that if he did, I also had to accept things were as I was told.

"What…" I stop, and Fane pulls one hand back to rub his chin.

"I've been kept busy with the most asinine tasks while you were gone. Any time I asked for updates, I was told you were going above and beyond and not to worry about it. But now—" He shakes his head.

"But what does it all mean?"

"I don't know, sorella, but I'll be damned if I don't find out. Trust in me."

Vlad

A day and a night go by without movement. It makes me wonder what they're planning. Through it all, the rage inside me grows, from an ember to a full-blown blaze.

I push it aside.

The light cuffs around my wrists never let go. It makes me wonder what, exactly, powers them.

Father told us Dacians use blood magic. He also lied and said they were extinct. Who's to say anything else he told us about them is truthful?

Mid-way through the second day, Liviu returns. This time, he's carrying someone. A bound human, his scalp lacerated and bleeding.

I stand from my crouch—slowly, sluggishly. I'm acutely aware of the smell of blood, the taste of it already filling my mouth. My fangs elongate, giving away my hunger.

Liviu smiles. "Da, I thought this might pique your interest."

"And why is that?'

"Because this man serves the Hatmanu clan—the same vampiri who are after you. We brought him to you as a show of good faith."

I raise my bound wrists. "I have a better idea for a show of good faith."

He clicks his tongue. "No, I don't believe so. Those cuffs bind you to this earth, and ensure your darkness has no way to escape. We cannot remove them."

I hold back a scowl. But, in the end, he's given me some information. There has to be something in this brain of mine that'll help me break them. Centuries of knowledge can't be *that* useless, just because I'm being faced with a type of witch I'd thought to be extinct. But I can't focus on a solution until this human is away.

His bleeding increases, red rivulets coating the ground, only adding to my hunger. I find myself taking a few steps forward, then stop.

The Grand Master smiles. "Do not hold back, vampir. We wish to feed you, to ensure you are as comfortable as you can be."

"Why?"

"Because we need you in a good state of mind when the hour of the sacrifice commences. You must be in *full* vampiric capacity, not half as you are now." He tuts. "What a state you've let yourself fall into."

I can only focus on one word he said. *Sacrifice?*

Before I can ask more, Liviu tilts his head to the side. Silviana enters, accompanied by a taller man. His head is shaved, but stubble fills the lower part of his face. His eyes stare at me—unseeing. Something in the traits of his cheekbones, the way he's holding himself, tells me he's related to her.

Not that it matters. Seeing Silviana next to another male has that primal part of me going out of control but I can't afford it to. No... not now.

"You do have a connection," Liviu murmurs, almost to himself. "Interesting." He pushes the human to the bars. "Come now, drink."

I recoil from the offering. Instead, my eyes find Silviana's. She seems shaken by what's taking place—or is that just another front? Have they brought her here, knowing what we are to each other, in the hopes it'll make me change my mind? Or, worse, help me toward breaking my own rules?

"I will not."

"No?" The man sighs. "I'd hoped you would not make it so difficult."

He moves then, faster than I would have expected one of his ilk to move. And with one perfectly timed move, he slashes the man's carotid artery. I can vaguely hear Silviana's shout, but the red haze descends on me.

All I sense is blood, on my skin, entering my pores.

All I taste is the metallic taste, a whisper on my lips.

All I want is more...and more...and more...

With a growl, I launch myself at the human, pulling one of his arms through the bars and digging my fangs in him. There's no Liza to hold me back this time. No one to save me, as I give in to the trap they've designed just for me.

Silviana

"See?" The Grand Master turns to us, smirking. "I told you he was a beast."

Fane grunts something like an assent. He may not be able to see Vlad, but he hears the slurping noises as he drains the human of his blood. It aggravates me that he doesn't have the full picture. He didn't see Vlad's reticence, his aversion, his capitulation as he'd felt the hunger take over.

I had.

And I can't tear my eyes away from the picture. What I should be feeling is revulsion, seeing him in his natural state, so unhinged.

Even more so than when I'd seen him in the alley. He's almost feral, incapable of control. But instead of revulsion, I'm reminded of when those fangs had grazed my skin, and my heartbeat increases.

Everything I've been raised to feel, to think, seems to have evaporated. Instead, all that's left in my body is this odd longing, and a dose of pity. For Vlad, for what they've reduced him to, and for the man he'll soon kill.

I want...to touch him. To save him. Even though I shouldn't.

Before I can expand on the thought, the Grand Master moves to the bars and yanks the human away. He's limp—dead, probably. If not, he will be soon. No way he can survive having all his blood drained like that.

The Grand Master kicks the bar with his foot when Vlad snarls, forcing him back. Like a dog.

Something in my chest snaps, and I take a step forward.

Fane senses my movement and grabs my arm. "What are you doing?"

I turn to him. His unseeing eyes are fixated above my head, but his grip on my hand is firm. Restraining.

"I—"

"Don't."

The Grand Master's words break our little moment.

"See, *prince*? At the end of the day you're weak, just like every mortal. And now that you've had your fill, we can begin. I will see you at the next full moon."

He turns and leaves with the other man. The human's corpse floats behind them. Only Fane and I are left, alone with the snarling vampir in the cage.

Vlad's eyes connect with mine, and there's nothing left of the gentle blue in them, only an angry red. "Seen enough?"

His taunt makes that pain in my chest ache more. I take another step toward him, but Fane's hold on me tightens enough to bruise.

"Let's go, Lana," he whispers. "Now. You're not thinking straight."

I stare between him and Vlad. He makes it easy for me to follow Fane, shuffling to a corner and turning his back to me.

As soon as we're back to my apartment, Fane slams the door. "What the hell were you thinking?"

If I didn't know his anger is motivated by fear, I would've easily gotten annoyed. As it is, all I can do is ask, "Are you hungry?"

Without waiting for an answer, I move to my fridge. It's stocked, as usual—thanks to the system we have in place. The Grand Master has set up this entire compound, for lack of a better word, to have us all in one place. Housekeepers come by weekly and make a note of provisions or food preferences. Then a team of Dacians ensures supplies come on time, through various retailers in nearby towns. It saves us having to grocery shop, and ensures we can focus on the great work of, well, magic.

Behind me, Fane grunts and moves closer. "Lana, talk to me. I heard him—your vampir has no problem draining another human of his blood. And yet you wanted to go to him?"

I stay silent, but reach inside and pull out an already prepared sandwich. I sit at the island, similar to Fane's, and unwrap my sandwich, taking a bite. And then another. In seconds, I finish it off, while my brother paces back and forth like a lion in a cage.

The moment I swallow the last bite, he speaks. "Even *if* what the vampir told you about his curse is true, this doesn't add up."

"Vlad."

Fane glowers in my vague direction. "What?"

"His name is Vlad. You keep calling him *he* or *vampir*. He has a name."

"And I don't want to use it, I thought that was implied."

I look at the empty wrapper, feeling the sandwich rise up in my throat. "You said you weren't disgusted by me."

"Lana—"

He stops himself and comes closer. His hand touches the counter, then slides over it, blindly reaching for mine. When his fingers graze mine, I pull them away, childish as it might be.

"I meant what I said," he whispers. "I don't blame you for any of this, I only wish you didn't have to go through this at all. Whatever's going on, whatever the reason for his curse, I don't... There's got to be answers. I feel like you're being used."

"If I am, it's not just by the vampiri. At least they were upfront with me. But it feels like the Grand Master has his own agenda and I've been just a puppet for him."

Fane rears back as if I'd slapped him. But instead of pulling away, he holds out his hand still, waiting for me. After a few more seconds pass by, I finally set my palm in his, and he intertwines our fingers.

"I'm going to get to the bottom of this. You're my life, Lana, and nothing and no one will threaten you."

"And if the threat comes from the inside?"

"Then we'll find it and deal with it." A beat later, he adds, "But in the meantime, while I dig, I want you to stay away from the vampir. Please."

"Ok," I say, knowing full well that I don't plan to listen.

Chapter 15

Silviana

Despite Fane's warning, I can't stay away. I try, at least at first. But a need deeper than anything I can understand fills me, and I know I can't. Not anymore. So I sit in my kitchen, dripping blood into a bowl and keeping my spell going. A spell that lets me listen to sounds way beyond the thin walls surrounding me, and everyone else.

But I don't care about their secrets. I don't care about their machinations. What I *do* care for, is the moment when they all fall asleep. And once most of them do, I don a cloak and skulk through the woods, until I'm back at the underground cellar, hidden behind a tree. Two new guards are keeping an eye on it.

This time, I'd brought my athame. I cut into my palm and mutter another incantation. I watch as a nymph-like creature—illusion of my own making—walks toward them, naked. Her charms soon attract the guards, but the moment they get close to her, a whiff of her breath puts them to sleep. She disappears, cackling.

I set another illusion spell to take their place as guards, should anyone else come look. Then I cloak their bodies, and step inside. Torches light up as I walk to the cage.

Vlad seems to have dozed off, but he jerks up when he hears my footsteps. His wary eyes find me. "What are you doing here?"

"I...came to see how you're feeling."

He snorts. "And you would care, why?"

A good question.

His snort turns into a mocking expression. "What, you've come to see more of earlier? To gloat that you finally have the monster under your thumb?"

Heat—the shame of today's earlier events, what they'd made him do—fills my cheeks, and I take a step closer. "That's not why I'm here."

"Could've fooled me."

Anger, I can deal with. Just so long as it's not the resignation from earlier... This is familiar territory, for however long it'll last.

"I'm guessing you have questions."

This earns me a full-blown glare. "Are you mocking me, witch? Because I may be behind bars, but that doesn't make me any less dangerous."

"Okay, fine. Maybe you don't have questions, but I do."

"Your Grand Master already did his best."

"I'm not here for him."

"As if I'd believe that."

I take a moment before I open my mouth again. Clearly, I'm not getting anywhere with him. I don't know why I keep trying... Except, that need in my gut is too deep, too increasingly hard to ignore.

"Did you mean it?"

He runs his bound wrists over his face, then winces as the dark tendrils cut across his cheek. "I'm tired, Silviana. Did I mean what? Use your words and stop dancing around the topic."

The coolness of his tone immediately has me straighten to attention. I will my own hurt away, and something switches behind his eyes. But he looks away before I can determine what I'd seen.

"The bond... What you and Nico were talking about. What you admitted to, in the woods, before—"

"Before I was captured like a fiendish beast?" He sighs, and leans his forehead against the bars of his cell, looking anywhere but at me. "Da, I meant it. Much to my chagrin."

My feet move closer of their own accord. "That's not possible. A vampir's consort is a sacred bond."

A mock laugh escapes him. "What do you know of bonds and their sacredness? You betrayed me, betrayed your friend—I know you and Tassa became close—and who the fuck knows if your actions didn't also hurt my siblings."

I remember the burning castle, and bite my lip. Vlad seems to sense my uneasiness, as his gaze moves up to mine.

"What is it? Do you know anything about them?"

This is it. My bargaining chip. And I'll be damned if I don't use it. "I'll tell you... If you answer some questions for me."

Whatever emotion that was in his expression falls, and he looks at me with something akin to hate. "You'll deny a dying man his last request?"

I frown. "Dying?"

He shakes his head, dropping it back against the bars. "Never mind. Ask me whatever it is you wish to ask me."

"Start by explaining what you mean by dying."

"Fine. Don't say I didn't warn you." He takes a deep breath, and says, "My family and I were the top of the hierarchy. Father's the one who sent us into hiding, over two hundred years ago. While we didn't understand it at first, we trusted him, especially when he died. But we've learned, lately, that something else spurred this self-imposed exile."

When he goes quiet, I prompt him, "And what was that?"

"A curse." He raises his gaze to mine, the blue turbulent. "From a god."

"Zalmoxis."

"Brownie points for the human," he says mockingly.

"Not so much, since you told me that in the woods, before you were captured. But what was the curse, Vlad?" I take another step, fighting to keep my tone from pleading with him. "Tell me. Please."

"You already know. You have the journal, no?" At my expression, he rolls his eyes. "Of course. Your Grand Master does, doesn't he? No matter." Another sigh. "The curse was meant to punish our father, through us. Each of us would fall in love, be destined for one consort. But it would be an impossible match, one designed to make us fail—a human for Nico; a vampir for Violeta, whose disease..." He trails off. "Anyway. Clearly, you're my demise. And by extension, theirs."

I frown. "What do you mean? I can't... Why would our relationship affect your siblings?"

"Because the curse is linked. If one of us doesn't fulfill the love, doesn't consummate the relationship, accept the bond, then the others suffer. It settles like a disease, sapping our strength, our...everything. Turning us human, until we're not... We're something worse. Something feral."

He falls silent, even as I try to wrap my head around everything he's admitted to.

And then, in a broken voice, he whispers, "I've answered your questions. Please, tell me what happened to them."

"I... I don't know. When we left the clearing, I saw fire. I used a spell once I arrived here, and all I could see was a part of the castle, burning. I saw nothing of your siblings, or anyone else."

He shakes his head. Then, in a burst of fury, he slams his hands against the bars. "I was such a fucking fool! So besotted with you, taken in by your innocent act, by what was going on between us... I should've been paying attention to what was happening around us. I could've helped them, prevented it." Trembling, he drops to his knees, as though the fight's been taken out of him. "Leave me, Silviana. Just leave me."

"I can't." When he says nothing, I move closer again. "Vlad, I can't. There's this need inside me, I can't—I don't—"

"Do you think I care?" he asks in a deadly tone. And then he looks up at me, his expression stone-cold. "If they died because of you, because of anything you did, I'll make sure to hunt you down and kill you. And if your Dacians kill me first, I will come back and haunt you, believe me. You won't be rid of me so easily."

"I don't—" I don't want to be rid of him. The admission stuns me into silence.

He turns his gaze away. "Leave me. I have a death sentence to await."

"Will you not even try to escape?"

He laughs bitterly. "Why? To give them more information for their little experiment? No, thank you. I will stick to what I have been doing."

I march to the bars, wrapping my hands around them. "But you haven't *been* doing anything!"

He's on me in a flash, his hands around mine, his eyes locked on me. Feverish. Burning. Incinerating. Obliterating my defenses with the truth.

"Did you not see me kill that man? On demand, no less. Like a good little *pet*."

"Vlad, I—"

One hand reaches for my throat. I hear the sizzle of the light burning his flesh.

"I could tear your pretty throat as easily as I drank him and have my fill once more."

"But you won't."

"You really believe that?"

"I do."

He frowns at me, searching my expression as if the answers to everything are in there. I don't flinch. I should, but I don't, because he has every right to do it. And because I want him to see I'm not lying. Not this time.

The hands around mine drop and he deflates a moment later, then moves back. And back. And farther inside the cell, until shadows cover his features and only his voice reaches me. His voice, and his blue eyes.

"Go. Just go, Silviana. You shouldn't be here."

The thing is, I could listen to him. But before my mind can catch up with my body's actions, I'm reaching for the lock of the cell.

Pressing my hand against it, using the blood that's still running down my palm, I mutter an incantation, and the click echoes loudly inside as it opens. Then I move inside.

A few more steps. My heart thunders in my throat. Part of me is screaming, *What are you doing???* But another part, a deeper, darker, part, understands exactly where this is coming from.

Soon enough I'm facing Vlad, and he's staring at me like he doesn't understand what I'm doing. So I stand on my tiptoes, wrap my arms around his neck, and pull his lips to mine.

For a long moment, he does nothing. He's a complete statue against my lips.

I press closer against him. He shifts his hands away from between us, to the side, so the cuffs don't come into contact with me. And a low, primal groan rises from his throat as he kisses me back.

His lips move against me the same way they did back then, in the room. When he made me come so hard I saw stars. Our tongues clash and battle, before deciding on a sinuous dance that makes my knees weak.

Vlad's lips move from my mouth, down my jaw, my neck, and stop there. I can feel the flash of his fangs against my skin—and then he tears himself from me so fast, he slams into the wall behind him.

His eyes are blazing, with conflict and desire, much like mine must be.

"You have to go," he says. "I don't trust myself around you. Not after what they did."

"Vlad—"

"Go!"

"NO. You're not going to drink from me."

His eyes go back to my throat. "I wouldn't be so sure about that."

I clench my fists as I take another step. "And if you do, so what? It's not the end of the world."

"No. But it would be the end of you." He closes his eyes, letting out a long breath as he allows himself to slide to the ground. "Just go, Silviana. Not just away from me, but away from this wretched place. You deserve better than them. I know you think they're your people, but whatever they once stood for has been tainted by your leader. Don't let that trickle down to you."

It's the most words he's said to me since being imprisoned. And it doesn't escape my notice that he's saying them for my own good. So I can be all right.

I take another step toward him, but he's shut down again. Eyes closed, head rested against the wall, I might as well not exist to him.

Heart in my throat, I whirl on my heels and exit the cell door, locking it back behind me.

Vlad

I wait until I hear the cell door lock before letting out a loud groan and dropping to the ground. It shakes under my pounding, but the rattle of my bones, of my physical form, is nothing compared to what is in me. A darkness, a bloodlust that would've taken Silviana, if I'd allowed it.

Liza taught me how to control it. I have to.

But the tidal wave taking over me is unlike anything I've felt before. It's...ripping, tearing me apart. I drop my head to the cold stone ground, trying to stop the tension pressing down on me. But it's useless.

I felt it when Silviana came here, felt it strengthen with her heartbeat, drowning out her words. I don't know how to stop what's taking over me. This burning in me. This feeling of otherness, of a complete loss of control.

I am lost. I know I am. No father. No siblings. They haven't come for me, and if they haven't come, it's either because they don't know where I am, or because they can't.

They can't because they're dead.

Or because they know it's my weakness that brought this havoc onto them.

Darker thoughts circle me, pushing me into an oblivion of senselessness. There is nothing I can do but try to push back. But the more I do, the more the darkness rises in me, as if strengthened by an invisible hand. Relentless. Unflinching. It rises and rises, until something like a pop resounds in my head.

I hold still. *Is it gone?*

But when I raise my head, I know it's not. It's there. Waiting for its next victim. And whoever walks through those doors next, I'll be powerless to hold back.

It's what they wanted.

Yes, the Dacians were goading me into it. But I hadn't expected it to work. Even with Silviana coming here, I hadn't... I'd been angry, but I'd thought I could hold back. Now, I know I can't.

And no matter what she's done, I can't bring myself to hate her. Not when all I want to do, deep down, is whisk her away from this place and keep her safe. Love her.

A different kind of tightness reverberates in my body. *Please, Silviana, stay away. I'm not safe for you. Not anymore.*

Chapter 16

Silviana

I barely sleep that night, after my conversation with Vlad. I spend the day in my room, watching out the window as the rest of my people go about their days.

Some of the Dacian men are running fighting drills on a tennis court that's been refurbished for their needs. Others are building, farther in the distance, another set of apartments. Does this mean more Dacians are to be born? Or more witches will join us?

Long ago, either thought would've filled me with joy. It would have meant new joys, something to celebrate. The Grand Master loves throwing parties to welcome our new members...

Now, all it does is fill me with dread. *If more witches join us, even if it's not Dacians, they'll be used to fight against the House of Dracul. And the more magic they must fight against, the less chances of their survival. If they're even still alive.*

The window feels cool against my forehead. And still, my eyes linger down below.

If I wanted to, I could join the women. In the shade of a tree, they've set up baskets on a wooden picnic table and look like they're sorting through herbs. More than likely, they'll be using them to make remedies for the same Dacians who are shooting themselves up with magic now.

A knock on the door startles me. With a sigh, I head to it and open it. Valeriu stands on the threshold, a smirk plastered on his angular face.

"What do you want?"

"Now, now, is that a proper greeting?" He moves inside, throwing his arm around my shoulders. "And here I thought we'd gotten close during your mission."

I shrug him off, and shove him away for good measure. "What. Do. You. Want?"

He plops down on my sofa, uninvited, and drops his feet on my glass coffee table. "Just want to see how you're settling back in." He arches an eyebrow. "Shouldn't you be out there with the women, going about your chores?"

I scowl at him. "The Grand Master said I could take a few days to rest. Not that it's any of your business."

"How generous of him... Well, if you're feeling lonely—"

"I'm not." I point to the door. "Now, leave."

He stares back at me, insolent, for a long moment. He's gotten bolder since he was assigned to be my handler on the mission, and I think it's gone to his head. Narcissism, I can deal with. But the malice in his gaze... I hold back a shudder.

"Leave, Valeriu. I won't ask you again."

After another beat, he stands, dusts himself off, and walks to the door. I wait until it shuts behind him, before returning to the window. Moments later, he exits the back of the building and I follow his progress across the grounds, past the tennis court, and into the woods. Same woods I'd gone into.

Is he going back to the Grand Master? And if yes, to do what? Report me?

My gaze flicks back to the men who are training. Before I'd left, their efforts at spells were unfocused, almost lazy. Now, there's a new intensity to their training, almost as if they're...preparing for war.

A shudder runs through me. A moment later, a door opens on the court, and a man walks in—Fane. The trainees stop what they're doing and some look at him with respect, others, I'd bet, with jealousy. He tends to inspire one or the other.

I can't hear what he says, even when I creak my window open. But after a beat, the trainees go back to their repetitive movements. Fane stands, head tilted as if listening to the cacophony of their movements.

If it hadn't been for Fane, throughout the years, I never would've learned all the spells I know now. But even I can tell that what they're doing is beyond my level, maybe even Fane's. Which seems odd, if we're supposed to be trying to use *less* magic, not more. Yet the ground under their feet is covered with blood.

I turn my gaze back to the women. Picture myself going down the stairs, joining them. They'd welcome me with open arms, and avoid talking about my mission. They'd give me a bundle of herbs to sort through, and before long, it would be near sunset. Then we'd head to the larger eating hall—a former cafeteria—under this apartment building, and eat together. There would be merriment, and laughter...

And all of it would feel empty. Less than. Same as how I feel right now.

Hours move by. And with each passing minute, all I do is second-guess every moment of my life.

Late in the afternoon, I finally dial Fane's number. He picks up, walking away from the trainees to a corner of the court.

"Since when are you in charge of the trainees?"

A sigh echoes on the line. I can hear curses muttered behind him.

"Lana, it wasn't my choice. Orders came from the Grand Master last night."

I wait a beat, then another. "Can you come see me? When you're done, I mean."

"I will... But why do I have the feeling I won't like what you have in mind?"

"Because you know me so well."

I hang up before he can try to talk me out of it.

That same evening finds us traipsing through the woods, in search of the Grand Master's cabin—the same one I'd been in upon my return.

"This is a bad idea," Fane hisses behind me.

"I know."

We're walking slower, holding hands. I know he's using his extra hearing to catch onto each sound my feet make as they crunch over leaves, and uses that as some sort of beacon for where to put his own feet. It's how he learned to hunt, and best most of the Dacians in our coven.

"A *real* bad idea."

I ignore my brother, instead shushing him. "You said yourself this feels weird."

"Yes, but I wasn't implying we go and steal a journal from the Grand Master!"

"We're not stealing anything. Just going to take a look."

What Vlad mentioned about the journal, the way he reacted... It reminded me of how I'd felt when I'd handed it over. Like I shouldn't have. Like I was missing an important clue.

Now's my chance to find out.

Fane groans. "Why do I listen to you?"

"Because you love me."

"Yeah, you got that right."

When we move through the barrier again, I turn to Fane. "Did you feel that?"

"The shudder? Sure. What about it?"

"Since when has that been here?"

He seems to think for a moment, then says, "A few days after you left, I guess. I told you I haven't been out in this area much lately. Why?"

"Because, the woods we were just in? They're not the same as these ones. We're somewhere darker, denser... And the air feels different, too."

Fane stops moving, going fully immobile, and I follow suit. I know he's listening with all his senses, gathering information in that unique way of his.

"You're right," he says finally. "There's power, here. Hidden. In the earth itself."

I look around us, at the frosted leaves, wooden logs, moss growing on trees. "I wish I could see something that would make sense."

Fane shrugs. "A mystery for another day. Let's just keep going, before we're caught."

Moments later, we finally arrive at the Grand Master's cabin. No lights are on, only a sentry who seems like he's already falling asleep standing.

"One man," I whisper to Fane. "No lights."

He nods, takes a deep whiff, then pulls a small athame from his pocket and cuts deep into his palm. Dark magic sizzles around us.

"Go."

I do as he says. With each step, I'm surrounded by fog and shadows. Somewhere, I hear the sound of a body hitting the ground, and I know Fane put the man to sleep. Which means my way is clear.

With a slice in my palm and a quick incantation under my breath, I walk into the house. After a short moment to orient myself, I cast another spell—keeping in mind the image of the journal. A dark wooden chest to my left, covered by a woolen blanket, glows softly. I head to it, uncover it, and open the latch gently.

The journal is in it, along with a myriad of other documents. Despite my curiosity, I focus on one thing only.

I take out my cellphone and snap pictures of each page. I only get through half before something tells me to get the hell out. It's an instinct I've learned to listen to, so I place the journal back where it was, cover up the chest again, and run.

Back in Fane's room, he plugs my phone into his computer, runs the pictures through a software, and then prints them. One set is in Braille for him via his Braille embosser, and another is in regular color for me. The monotone sound of his computer repeating instructions is the only thing breaking the silence.

My gaze settles on the embosser, recalling Fane's joy when I'd gifted him the precious gadget on his birthday, a few years ago. It uses Braille translation software to turn any document into Braille cells, basically ensuring he can print anything he wants in a format that's easier for him to digest. Though he has the latest dictation software on his computer, Fane is old school, like me—we both like the feel of paper in our hands.

Once all the entries I'd taken pictures of are printed—nearly a hundred pages of a cursive script for me, and the Braille version for him—we both sit down with our individual piles and read through the first half.

Normally, having something laid out in front of me helps to make sense of it. This time, though, I find the entries confusing as hell. My eyes blur as I try to make sense of them. I start with the one right after Țepeș turned Nico.

7 April 1460

Nicolae is adapting well to this life, beloved. He has taken to his role as my heir with a natural ability I had not expected. My only regret is you are not here to enjoy these times with me.

Not a day goes by without me thinking about you, Ana.
Your scent, the softness of your skin—

My cheeks heat, and I skim over the next lines where he goes in excruciating detail over their more intimate moments. The ending of the entry catches my eye.

Your father is angry, beloved. I hear him at night, when the darkness is at its strongest. I feel my powers waning, as though he is punishing me for your death. And he has reason to. I punish myself each and every single day.
But now I have something new to live for. Nicolae...and the siblings that will follow. And the revenge they will help me enact.

Needless to say, he doesn't sound like the monster I'd pictured. Which, in and of itself, is even more confusing.

"Fane..."

My brother stops tracing the Braille letters with his fingers and tilts his head toward me.

"Nothing. Never mind."

I'm thankful enough he's helped me with this. But it's probably not the right time to start telling him that I think we were wrong, and not every vampir is a monster... Then again, I might be surprised.

I curl up on the armchair, flicking through more pages.

18 November 1460
Nicolae has chosen his next sibling, and perhaps I

should have been careful. But I was not, taken as I was by the idea of no longer being alone. And I might have made a mistake, beloved. Because the woman I changed, she has gone rogue... If my conversation to-night with her does not calm her, I may have no choice but to eliminate her. Will Nicolae forgive me?

The sibling he speaks of must be Violeta... I remember that night at the pub, and how she'd mentioned—between drinks—that she was turned a year after Nico. But I have a hard time believing she'd have lost control like that. And for Țepeș to be ready to kill her?

If they ever see this, the Dracul siblings will be shattered.

Still, I can't stop myself from reading some more.

24 December 1460

What a fool I was, beloved. To give immortality to two young simpletons, who have discarded me as easily as if I were an old shoe. And your father is having a blast at my expense, believe me. His laughter keeps me up at night. His minions hiss and mock me from the shadows. And now, my enemies are circling. Circling, circling, endlessly circling. Everyone wants a piece of me—of my power, my immortality. Well, I will show them.

Let Nicolae take his sister away. Let him deal with her bloodlust. Let him fail... And when he does, they will both be persecuted by the uncouth humans who wait in the shadows for their own moment to strike.

As it is, I have wars to fight. Plots to unfold. Only time will tell if I will come out winner, or loser...with the price being my death.

Your father sure would be happy of it, no?

It's a bit weird a vampir is thinking about dying... But, I'll bite. My eyes scan the next entry.

16 January 1462

Well. It has happened. I am finally captured, at the hands of none other than Corvinus himself. Yes, my dear, a former ally has been instrumental in my capture, and he plans to keep me now. He says the people dread my bloodlust, and cower in fear. That I am not the voivode they have chosen.

Perhaps he is correct. There must be some truth to it, as I have yet to use my glamour on him to escape. In a way, I deserve some of this. I realized soon after Nicolae and Violeta left me, that I was too unforgiving.

If I had given her a chance...not second-guessed Nicolae's choice... Ah, but time and hindsight go hand in hand, do they not?

All I can do now is wait. And wither away. They still do not know what I am, else I would be burning at the stake by sunrise.

"I don't understand," Fane says, bringing me out of my reading. "What is it?"

I watch his fingers trace the Braille over his printed copies again. First one page, then another. He shakes his head again.

"Look at the entry from 3 June 1772."

I rifle through my own pages, until I find it. He's way more ahead than me, which doesn't surprise me as he's always been a faster reader.

"Okay, I have it in front of me. So?"

"Lana... You said this is Ţepeş's journal, right?" I nod. "Then why is he writing as if to a friend? Look. He says, 'I swore to be careful, dear friend, but I might have missed something.' And then later, he adds, 'I wish I could take it back but my rage got the best of me. I know they were your kin, Dacians like you, but I was defending myself and mine. I will not let them take my new family from me.'"

We frown at each other as the realization dawns on us.

"Vlad the Impaler was *friends* with one of us?"

Fane nods. "Looks like it. The question is, who?"

"It could've been anyone. Some of the best of us have lived far longer human lives than normal." I bite my lip. "We need more of this. We need to read it top to bottom."

"We do. But in the meantime, stay away from the vampir."

If only I could.

Vlad

I wake up in agony. Pure agony. Fire burns my throat. Parches my body. I need air. Claw at my throat. Pace my cell. Tear at the cuffs of my wrists until my skin hangs, and then heals. Barely. Weakness fills me and, with it, the bloodlust grows.

Stronger and stronger, like a tsunami getting closer and closer, ready to obliterate everything in its path.

A beat starts in my head. A drum. Like a heartbeat, but not quite.

It's demanding. Curse...a curse?

I try to pace, to give myself some strength, but all I can do is drop to my wobbly knees. I can barely keep my eyes open.

My gaze lands on the puddle of blood, farther away. The puddle of blood the Dacians left for me. I lick my lips, wanting a taste—then bile rises in me, stronger than that need.

Everything in me fights, tears, demands...

I give in and pass out.

A door closing wakes me. When I blink, I hear slight footsteps. Smell jasmine.

Fuck. Silviana.

I can barely make myself go through the motions. Standing. Opening my eyes to stare at her bleakly. "What are you doing back here? I told you to stay away."

She hesitates, taking in my appearance. Smart. Perhaps she'll feel how close to the edge I am. How unlikely to survive much longer.

Alas, it is not to be. Rather than keep her distance, she moves closer. I try to keep to the shadows, but with a mutter, the light off the walls soon blinds me. I look away, but I hear her gasp.

When she undoes the lock to the cage, a low moan escapes me. "Don't."

"I need to speak with you face to face."

There is no stopping her. She walks in—again.

That drum in my head starts again. My eyes drop to her throat.

"Fane and I, we did some digging." Her heartbeat is so loud. "He's my brother, and I wouldn't trust anyone else with this. We looked into your father's journal. It seems he knew a Dacian. They were friends."

I lick my lips, trying to look anywhere but at her throat.

What did Liza say? *Focus. Ground yourself.*

Oh, she would laugh if she were here, saying I've done it to myself. Picking a human for a consort. As if I ever had a choice.

"Are you listening?"

"Da."

"Look at me."

I can't.

She moves closer. "Why aren't you looking at me?"

She keeps coming nearer. My back is to the wall. I can't avoid her touch on my skin, her strength as she forces me to meet her gaze.

She blinks. Her eyes widen. "Why are your eyes red—"

I pounce on her. One hand on her mouth, stifling her cry and tilting her head to the side. The other grabbing her wrists, holding them behind her as I push her body closer to me. Her nape, so creamy and ivory—

I part my lips. She struggles against my hold. The bloodlust rages.

My fangs sink in her neck, and I groan.

Blood floods my mouth, her taste so fucking unique. So appealing, like the finest of wines. I inhale deeply, prepared to take another drink...

And then I hear it—her heartbeat. The strong rhythm.

The realization is so sudden, I push her away, snarling.

Silviana clutches her throat, her wide eyes still on me.

I claw at the wall behind me. My voice sounds raspy when I speak. "Had enough?"

"W-why are you doing this?"

"Because I don't need you pitying me. A human. As if it mattered. Go with your tales somewhere else."

Instead of cowering away from me, or yelling at me, or doing anything else, she meets my gaze defiantly and lifts her chin. A faint trickle of blood slips down into her collarbone.

"Fine. I won't bore you anymore, I'll take my *tales* elsewhere. Maybe even to your siblings."

She's out the moment after, the cell door shutting behind her, and I slide to the ground. Head in my hands. My shoulders are tense to the point of pain, and I know there's no more fighting how far I've fallen.

All this time I thought I was flying high, but all I did was fall faster.

The cell gets cooler as night comes again, not that it has any effect on me. I'm thinking back to Liviu, to what he'd said. *Sacrifice.* If he knows everything—and I have no doubt he does—then the only thing he can be planning is to kill me. I have no regrets leaving this life. In a way, now I understand what Violeta lived through.

I do, however, regret what happened with Silviana. How this bond has complicated everything. How we'll never know what could've been. How she'll eventually forget me, once I'm dust and ashes, and find a Dacian to take care of her.

If he ever does.

I would've loved you like a queen, iubito.

Shaking my head, I drop my forehead on my knees. It takes me a long moment to hear the heartbeat in the shadows. When I do, I jerk upright, seeking—

"Finally. I was beginning to think you were dead."

It's the man, from days ago. The one with the shaved head, who'd stood by Silviana.

"Who are you?"

He snorts, looks around—only, he's not quite looking. A few moments later, I realize he's *listening*. Trying to see where I am.

I take a tentative step, louder than I would, to the side. His unseeing gaze lands on me.

Interesting.

"I was under the impression humans with disabilities tend to cower away from danger, not seek it outright."

A smirk plays on his lips at my words. "Then you clearly have not met your good share of humans. We tend to be resilient."

"Sure."

He takes a step closer, emboldened now that he knows where I am. Oddly, his heartbeat is still steady, thrumming slowly. Is he the brother Silviana meant?

"My name is Ștefan. I have your father's journal," he says simply.

I try to keep the shock off my expression, then realize it wouldn't matter, as he can't see it.

His amused chuckle soon tells me otherwise. "You're surprised. Shocked, even. Da, I'm a bit of an oddity, vampir. I turned my blindness into strength. And everything people assume I don't see, don't hear, I only sense it more. So you can try to hide, but in the end, I'll see past your machinations."

"It's your sister who did the machinations."

It's a stab in the dark, but the grin on Ștefan's face widens. "And I'm a proud brother for everything she's succeeded at."

"Succeeded at?"

He shakes his head as though he's disappointed with me. "I don't know what she sees in you, really." He takes a step closer. "Tell me, why do you think Silviana did what she did—tricking you, and all?"

"Because she was told to."

"Uh huh." Ștefan waits a beat, and when I say nothing, he adds, "And...?"

"There's an 'and'?"

This earns me another chuckle. "If you've gotten the feeling that our coven seeks to promote and support female empowerment, you'd be wrong. Women have a particular place in our society—to serve. To carry on the bloodline."

Fury fills my blood like hot lava. "Your sister is so much more than that."

"Maybe you're not so dumb, after all. Yeah, she's much more than that. A hell of a lot more. And I've protected her all my life. This mission was her chance to secure a good position within the Dacian community."

"For herself, or for you?"

Ștefan growls, moving even closer. The light shines on his hand, and the dark magic building there. Along with the blood dripping by him. Blood I hadn't smelled. Blood that even now, when I see it, I don't want to taste.

"I would never push Silviana to do anything that would gain me favor. I've worked for everything I have, as she has. Not that I'd expect you to understand, seeing as you're someone who's had everything handed to him."

"You'd be surprised."

"Spare me your sob story, little prince. It's not why I came." He takes a deep breath, as if to center himself. "I'm here to warn you, this once—my sister, for whatever idiotic reason, is taken with you. Hurt her, and I will guarantee you a death worse than anything the Grand Master can do."

I say nothing. Ștefan turns and walks away. But at the edge of the hallway, he turns around.

"Did your father ever have a Dacian friend?"

Again with this question. It's my turn to snort. "Why would he? So he could get stabbed in the back, like I've been?"

Later, after he's gone, I realize the entire conversation had been a distraction. The true reason for the man's presence was that last question—about Father.

But why would a Dacian like Ștefan be interested in our history?

Chapter 17

Silviana

The arm of the couch digs into my back, but I can't be bothered to move. To say I'm engrossed in Vlad Țepeș's journal would be an understatement. Especially considering it's the only thing that can keep my mind off how much of a dick my Vlad was.

My Vlad... When the hell did I start calling him that?

Shaking my head in silent admonishment at my own stupidity, I let my eyes linger on the pages again.

30 August 1475
I have betrayed your memory, beloved. And I can feel

*your father's anger once more, this time raging against
me. If he was not imprisoned as you told me he was, I
would expect him to strike down from the heavens and
kill me. But even the mighty Zalmoxis has limitations.
Corvinus gave me a choice. He saw he was losing, and
our beautiful region was suffering without my leading
hand. He went back on his betrayal and recognized my
sovereignty as voivode of Wallachia once more. In
exchange, I am to marry his widowed daughter.
The marriage took place today, and Corvinus, the wily
old fool, made sure it would be consummated. I felt no
joy in touching her, beloved, I swear it. I was half out of
my mind with opium, starved of blood...
All I can do is apologize and swear I will never touch
her again. You have my word on that, beloved.*

I wipe at my face, shocked to find tears. It's surprising, the
amount of emotion Țepeș's writing can pull out of me. This isn't the
first time I'm reading one of his entries, but the sheer guilt emanating
from the pages breaks my heart. And reminds me all too much of
Vlad, locked up, and in equal pain.

Gulping, I force my eyes back on the page and move past a few
shorter entries, all apologies to Ana, until I find the next lengthier
one.

*5 March 1479
I grow weary. What is the sense of this life, with no
heirs and nothing to help me? I thought I could overcome your death, beloved, and overcome everything*

we lost. Or at least get some of it back.

But that second marriage was useless. It is not enough that it entrapped me, but it also excommunicated me. Can you believe it, beloved? I married a Catholic princess for political reasons, and it became the sole reason the Orthodox Church needed to excommunicate me.

In a way, it is almost good that everyone mortal thinks me dead. Basarb and his Ottoman supporters "won." It makes me laugh. It has been two years since they thought they killed me, and still they speak my name in hushed whispers, unaware that I am still alive. Still breathing.

A cursed existence, devoid of purpose.

Oh, Ana. Only you could understand. You always did, my dearest.

Everything we could have had haunts me, day and night. But I find only darkness, everywhere I turn. It shadows my steps. It eats at my dreams.

What is this senselessness I've bought into?

Perhaps I should have died for good, and not pretended to die. That would have made your father happy. Is it not enough that I have lost everything, including Nicolae, including Violeta? Is it my life he wants as penance, on top of everything else?

Perhaps it is. Perhaps the only way out of this is death.

Again, with the talk of death. Țepeș was obsessed with it, and it almost seems to me that even years later, after losing his wife, all he wanted was to be reunited with her. It's a tragic story, in a way.

And, yes, it does make my mind wander to Vlad. Is our story any less tragic? Considering he's imprisoned, and soon to be killed—or whatever else the Grand Master has planned?

Shaking my head, I bury my nose in the next entry.

21 November 1499

Beloved, how amusing fate can be. Two years ago, when I ran into my hateful second wife, I could not forget her poison. She had a hand in my demise, I am sure of it. She despised being married to a monster, and wanted nothing more than to escape me. It started with the excommunication, then the political plotting all over again, until I was led to that fateful battle in 1776. Well, my dear widow has definitely found her escape now. Because I found her again, and I took my vengeance upon her. Her soul is long gone for the Underworld, where I hope it rots. I thought killing her would quiet the demons inside me. Quiet Zalmoxis' voice... but I can still feel his wrath.

I thought I would feel remorse, yet none came. But as I was nursing a fine glass of red wine—you remember the one you loved?—who walks in, searching for me...but Nicolae himself?

He was groveling, begging for help. Not for him, but for Violeta. In thirty years, she has not mastered her bloodlust, and he is afraid for her. For her soul. And the cursed existence they are both living.

So, I struck a bargain with him. Yes, beloved, it had to be done. If they will be my heirs, they must obey me.

And once I had Nicolae's promise that henceforth he will listen to every order I give him...I followed him to his sister.

Da, I have spoken to Violeta. Brought my family back together. Her lack of control led to the death of an innocent, and she is truly repentant. Indeed, I fear she will never feel the need to feed if she continues down this path. What a difference a few years makes, no?

Perhaps I am an idiot, speaking to you through written words, but this joy—or semblance thereof—is so new, I had to tell you and—

Fane barges into my room, startling me from my read. For a blind person, he sure finds his way around things easily.

"Lana."

I set the pages aside on the coffee table and tap the corners of the couch, knowing he'll hear me. And he does, heading toward me. Hands stretched out, he touches my features, feeling them, then kneels next to the couch.

"What happened?"

"What do you mean?"

"You've been crying. I can feel the wetness of your tears, sorella. What's wrong?"

"Nothing."

Even as I say that, more tears pour out of my eyes. And Fane feels them, his thumb trying—and failing—to wipe them away. Realizing it's not stopping, he gets up and feels his way to the couch, sitting down, and pulling me into his arms.

"Oh, Fane," I whisper and let the safety he exudes reassure me that everything will be all right, even if it won't.

Later, when I've settled and stopped crying, he picks my hand up in his and intertwines our fingers like he used to, when we were kids. Back then, it was done as encouragement. Now, I know he's also doing it to sense my pulse and state of mind.

Fane clears his throat when he senses I'm calm once more. "I have something."

"What?"

"See for yourself."

He reaches in the pocket of his coat and pulls out a worn leather-bound journal—Țepeș's. I reach for it, touching it with reverent fingers.

"I don't... Fane, how did you get it?"

"I made sure not to leave a trace. The Grand Master is dealing with some visitors in town, so we need to be quick."

"Okay. I'll read." I flick open to the middle, roughly where I'd stopped taking pictures, and begin reading.

2 January 1503

Nicolae is not happy with my new choice of a sibling for him and Violeta. But, it had to be done. Since we have been reunited, I have felt the need to solidify our alliance, to start over again. And thanks to the promise Nicolae and Violeta have both made me, I have their undying support.

The new addition's name is Mirabela, and she is the sole survivor of a brutal attack in the countryside. I found her with her children in her lap, their necks slashed. For a moment, I feared the madness—what they say women get after birthing—might have reached her, and she was responsible, but it was not her. I found footsteps...and men, farther away.

I did what I always do, beloved. I killed them all. They fought better than most humans do. Part of me thinks they had training, but I did not stop to interrogate them. Only time will tell whether I was right.

When I returned to the house with Nicolae, to give them all a proper burial, we heard Mirabela's heartbeat. She was alive, but barely. I offered her a chance to live, to get vengeance, and she took it.

Only the vengeance she'll help get will be mine.

My heart stutters. Mirabela lost her entire family to humans? No wonder she hates them so... Now, I understand better why she's so protective of her siblings.

Fane's silence draws my attention. "You okay?"

He shrugs, then leans against the couch. "I'm not sure. It's weird, hearing him talk about all of them like...like..."

"Like they're human?"

Fane hesitates, then nods. "Is that what you saw?"

I think back to my time with the Dracul siblings. "They're ruthless, I won't lie. But they're also complicated. And underneath that ruthlessness, there's a need for love, for belonging. It's not war they seek, Fane. It's a chance to live in peace, to rule as they were meant to."

He grunts, then gestures for me to keep reading.

13 April 1687
I was right. The hunters who attacked Elizabeta, they

are no regular vampir hunters. Someone is coming for me, my friend, someone powerful. And I cannot tell if it is because of who I am, because of my heirs, or because of that cursed prophecy.

"Why did you stop?"

"I—" I try to figure out how to explain it to Fane, then settle for the truth. "It's weird, but it feels like his tone shifted."

"Shifted, how?"

"Remember what you pointed out, about the friend? Well, the entries I was reading, the earlier ones, they're written as if to his dead wife. But this, 'my friend?' It definitely feels like it's to someone else. And then the mention of a prophecy..."

"Okay, so go back a couple of entries, see if we missed something."

I do, then gasp. "The pages are ripped." It's why I'd flipped over them without even realizing it.

"What?"

Fane reaches for the journal, running his fingers along the length, then over the frayed edges of the paper. "They're old, as old as the journal. This wasn't done recently, so not by the Grand Master."

"Then by who?"

Fane frowns, tilting his head down. "It must have been Țepeș himself. There was something in here he didn't want anyone to know about."

I think back to the earlier entries, detailing his life with the Dracul siblings. Then I shake it off. Whatever the reason for this secret, it's just another in a long line that died with him.

"Okay, so he tore a few pages off. And then he starts off talking as if to someone else—a friend—and his entries are focused on their enemies."

"Keep reading," Fane says.

I do as he asks, returning to the book:

I know not if they are sent by Zalmoxis, as he has pledged to hurt me. Or if they are sent by someone else... You would ask, who? Because you do not know. But the vampiri clans under me, they are growing rowdy. Rumors of rebellions abound. It seems I have misjudged the shift in attitude, and a monarch is not what they were looking for.

"That's it for that one," I say. "Then it moves on."

Fane's watch buzzes, then an automated voice says, *3 PM*. He scowls. "Keep reading, and don't stop. We have two hours before I have to return it."

I continue, going through similar entries. Țepeș putting together the pieces, something about various enemies, and the driving forces behind them. It seems the clans started rallying against him, sending threats, but that came out of the blue. And then he talks about the Dacians attacking him, and some hunters.

"It's interesting," Fane says when I stop for a sip of water, "that Țepeș didn't just behead all the Dacians."

"Yeah, I find that weird, too. We were told he was a monster. Instead, he sounds so..."

"Human," Fane finishes for me.

I sigh and start reading again. "This is from a year later."

11 November 1796
I was right, my friend. It took a year of keeping a close eye out, but I have learned why the vampiri clans are

pushing against me. And it has nothing to do with their resentment for a monarch... Nor even with the witch from 1707. For a time, I'd thought it was choosing Vlad that brought all this upon us. But, once more, I was wrong.

The darkness following us is not of my heirs' fault, but of my own. The vampiri I've interrogated, the ones I caught? They have been clear about the voices that keep whispering in their ears.

I have sent my heirs into hiding. They hate it—they hate my orders—but they will listen. It is best they are away for what will follow. At least, away from me, they will be safer.

You would ask why I bother writing this, instead of telling you face to face. Because I do not want you to be in danger, either. You have become a true friend to me, one untainted by the darkness of my daily life, and I do not wish to change that.

When you do find this, when I am dead, please re-member that, Davide.

The journal drops out of my hands. Fane inhales sharply.

"What did you just say?"

I look at him, the shocked expression on his face, then the journal lying on the floor. My heartbeat is erratic. *Davide.* It's not a common spelling. Only one man, one Dacian, ever had that name with that particular spelling—our father.

"T-that can't b-be."

Fane reaches for my head, squeezing hard to the point of pain.

"*Finish it*, Lana. We need to know."

With shaky hands, I pick up the journal, find the spot I was at, and read the next entries. There are only two.

15 November 1796

Four days since my last entry, but it feels like an eternity, my friend. You once told me that being silent is as bad as not doing anything to stop a bad thing from happening. It is advice Ana was keen to give me, as well. I miss her. So much, Davide. You have your beautiful children, your wife, I'm sure you do not understand it. I hope you never have to understand such pain. Most days, it rips me apart.

But I must be strong, for them. My six beautiful children. My darling angels—as flawed as they are. I have made them, and I will protect them.

Shivers run up my spine, but I move on to the last entry.

21 November 1796

There. It is done. My children are in hiding... They will hate every moment of it, but it will keep them safe. Because the threat they are facing is not only the vampiri. The hunters...the information you gave me was correct. They do have leaders, and they are also linked to the Dacians.

They will try to pit us against each other, Davide. We must resist. And if I die, when I die, you must promise me to protect my children the same way I would yours, if anything were to happen to you.

I will leave instructions for what to do with this journal, when you find it. When you find my body. It will not be long now. There is only one way to stop this, and it is by going to the source. Zalmoxis must hear me.

You will ask 'hear what,' and I will tell you. Your god placed a curse on my family. A curse tied to love. When it is triggered, my children must find their consorts, and accept the bond with each of them. Not doing so will result in their death...and the deaths of their consorts. The twelve touched by this cannot walk away, cannot run away.

And I know my children, Davide. They are flawed, and they have high expectations. They will never settle down. Which means I must go to Zalmoxis, and entreat his pity. And if that does not work, hand over my soul as punishment. Perhaps, if he has it, he will finally leave us alone.

When I'm done, I stare into nothingness for a long time, my brain scrambling to make sense of what I've read. "I don't understand. Dad was friends with this guy? How is that even possible? This was all taking place in the late 1700s, which would've made Dad—"

"—almost two hundred years old when he was killed."

"That's not..." My eyes widen. "Fane, *how*? He wasn't a vampir!"

Fane says nothing.

I get up, pacing, unable to control my nervous energy. "And there's another problem. If Dad was his friend, why would Țepeș—or any of his vampiri—have killed him? Yes, vampiri can be unpredictable, but after meeting his heirs, I'm pretty sure they're no more unpredictable than regular humans are."

I stop pacing long enough to stare at Fane. He's still quiet—rigid, almost.

"Fane?"

His head turns in the direction of my voice, slowly. And then I notice his magic, swirling around his hands, out of control.

"F-Fane?"

I've never seen my brother mad. Frustrated, yes. Flat out angry? Never. Yet in this moment, he looks ready to make heads roll.

And then he's on his feet. "They *lied* to us. They fucking *lied* to two young children."

"What are you—"

"Think about it, Lana. We had great magic. They weren't going to let us go. And so what if Father lost his life protecting Țepeș's secret? They didn't care." His tone is roaring now, the magic making everything shake. "They played us. Manipulated us. And now they've gone and triggered the bond between you and Vlad!"

"But that makes no sense. Why would they—"

"They could've taken you out of there at any point after you said you had the journal. But they didn't. They kept you there. Pushed you to get closer. Knowing that all along, they were condemning you to be fucking intertwined and part of this curse! A curse set upon their lineage by the same god *we* serve. The same one who gives our powers." His voice lowers. "Do you see, now? Everything they did was never for our good. It was always for their selfish gain, for their schemes. And I—" He runs a hand over his head, then delivers three quick blows to the side, as if attacking himself. "I should've realized! I should've protected you better. Lana—"

"Shhh." I pull him into my arms, resting my head on his chest. "Fane, you have nothing to feel guilty for."

He holds me tight, trembling as if he'll burst. So I take a deep breath, and let it out. And another. Before long, he lets go of me and rubs his chest as though it aches.

"I'll make this right. All the lies they told us, I will unravel them and find out the truth."

I scowl at him. "Don't go being a hero. We need cool heads about us right now. Besides, I have one more question."

"Which is?"

"Why start the consort bond with Vlad? Me, him, us being together would only *save* the Dracul siblings, not help them."

Fane stills again, his mind whirring. "It must be because of Zalmoxis. The Oracle they use, the one in that forest we hate? She's told them things before. This must be their way of making the Dracul siblings suffer. By intervening with the curse, and making sure...you *don't* end up with him."

Because they plan to kill him. Fane doesn't say the words, but they linger in the air between us, as though spoken out loud.

"But why the Dacians? Why the interest?"

He clenches his fists, looking even more immovable than before. "That, I'll find out."

Vlad

The pain hits me while I sleep. Curled on the cold ground, I'm aware of the ache in my wrists, where the magic binds me. The ache feels like it spreads, fire in my veins, in my head, until the pressure increases and increases and...finally...explodes.

I open my eyes, but what I see is not what's in front of me. It's not the damn cave, nor the metal bars keeping me hostage. No, it's not even my bound wrists.

Instead, when I look down at my clothes, I'm wearing torn pants, shoes that are split down the middle and held down with rope, and a shirt that's seen better days—and smells atrocious.

I take in my surroundings, the darkness—and then my eyes widen. Is this a hallucination?

The faint glow around everything would point that way, but hell if it makes any sense. Because where I am, it's in the past. More specifically, on the night when I met Father.

Same as I did that night, I enter a village. There's barely any smoke coming from chimneys, and there should be—it's cold outside. These stone houses will hold in the cold from outside same as in the summer months they hold the heat.

Instead of trying to break into a house for shelter, I keep my footsteps purposeful. Heading toward... The present-me struggles through the memory of that night, trying to remember the details. But in the hallucination—memory?—my steps are sure.

Soon enough, I stop in front of a shop. A woman is gathering her wares, setting them away for the night. I catch sight of jewelry, tarot cards, and a few other items. When she turns away, I notice the slight bump under her clothes.

It's enough to make me pause in my approach. She carries a child—that much I remember. Even now, the memory of that realization is enough to bring bile up my throat. I'd struggled with the decision for a lot longer than it felt, before finally unsheathing the knife at my waist and approaching.

She turns to me, the woman. A tentative smile is on her lips. She has long strawberry-blonde hair, and dark eyes. Her clothes are in a much better state than mine. That's all I get to register before I raise my hand, and the knife glints in the light.

The woman's eyes widen, then steely determination comes upon her features. She reaches for something on the table—an ivory comb with a sharp handle. I'm stunned by her choice of weapon, not realizing until too late that she's using it to cut her palm. The moment blood starts dripping, her hair flies around her face.

Then she's chanting, words I can't understand. *A witch!*

It's not enough to deter me. Or maybe, in some way, I'm hoping she'll put me out of my misery and kill me. Whatever my reason, I charge at her, knife raised—

And hit an immobile block.

The hit is so immediate, I drop onto the ground, landing on my ass. Something cracks in my backside, and a burst of pain pushes into every facet of my body. The knife flies out of my hand, landing a few meters away with a clatter.

Stunned, I look up—and freeze. I've seen pictures of this man. Portraits, followed by stories designed to scare children and adults alike. Of his vampiric abilities, his immortality. His ruthlessness.

And now he's standing in front of me, looking no older than mid-thirties. Long black hair falls past his shoulders. Piercing black eyes meet mine. Facial hair covers his jaw, but not enough to turn into a beard. Dressed all in black, with a black cloak, and towering over me, he looks almost feral.

"What is your business with the Dacian?" he snarls.

When I don't answer, he leans down, picks me up, and shakes me like a leaf.

"I asked you a question, human! Speak."

I gulp past the knot in my throat and whisper, "Kill her."

He drops me back to the ground unceremoniously, then turns to the witch. She's watching us warily, her palm still dripping with blood.

The man—I can't bring myself to say his name—takes a step in her direction, before seemingly thinking twice. "Florinela, I know of you, and I am not your enemy. I know not if this man comes for the same reason I did, but I will make sure he does not hurt you." He throws me a withering look over his shoulder, then turns back to her. "You and your child are safe."

There's a moment of silence, then, "And you think I'd believe the word of a monster like you?"

"If I was such a monster, I would have let him kill you. I will dispose of him, then return shortly. All I ask is that you answer one question, and I will be out of your life."

She looks at me, the woman—Florinela—and then at him. After another beat, she nods. "Very well."

The vampir faces me once more, grabbing me by my shirt. "Come, fool." And then he does something—all I see is everything moving fast, so fast. Seconds later, I'm in an underground cellar, chained up. That was the last night I spent as a human.

I wake up from my tortured slumber. What was the point of revisiting that memory? Now, when I'm imprisoned and there's nothing I can do? And how did Father know about Dacians, yet he never told us?

I rub a hand over the back of my neck, then my forehead. It feels hot and clammy, like I'm running a fever. Which is idiotic, considering I'm a vampir.

It's the curse. All over again.

My thoughts go back to the memory. After that night, Father came back and turned me. As I told Liza, he kept me chained for days until I came out of the initial change. And even after, he never left my side. Making sure I wasn't going to lose to the bloodlust. Teaching me to control it.

But why would that, of all my centuries of existence, come back to my mind? Is it because of the Dacians now imprisoning me? Is there some kind of link? And what burning question did Father need the woman to answer?

My head aches, as if warning me to stop thinking so hard. To make it all worse, my joints are stiff, my mouth pasty. I don't feel like myself. Instead, it's like the weakness Violeta described, all over again.

Fuck.

This, if nothing else, is proof of what I lost. Without Silviana, I'll be nothing. Soon enough, if the Dacians don't outright kill me, being away from her will.

And there's nothing I can do. There's no hope.

I need to let her go, because this bloodlust inside me? It may be weakened for now, but it's not going to stop. And next time, I won't be so lucky to stop in time—and she won't be so lucky to step away unharmed.

I have to...let it go. Let her go.

If it brings my death, so be it.

I'm sorry, my siblings. If you are still alive, and if my choice condemns you, I am sorry.

This torture is of my own making and the best thing I can do is give in to the darkness.

Silviana

I look at Fane, unsure. "Are you sure this is a good idea? What if someone comes and checks?"

"They won't. I told you, he's entertaining visitors, and we still have an hour."

"What kind of guests would keep him away from the journal?"

"I don't know."

I follow him in silence. Same as before, once we're close to the cabin, he spells the guard, and we enter under the cloak of fog and shadows.

Luckily, there's no one around inside the cabin. "How is it that we keep getting so lucky?"

Once more, my brother doesn't answer my question. Instead, he moves farther into the room, as if he's very familiar with it.

I know as a matter of fact that it takes Fane at least a few weeks to learn the layout of a room and how best to navigate it without help or bumping into things. There's no way he would know exactly where everything else is... Unless he was already familiar with it.

"Fane, what's going on?"

"I don't know what you mean."

"You know your way around. And you and I both know that doesn't happen in a day. So, you want to tell me what's really going on?"

"Now is not the time. I'll tell you after."

I close the door behind me and make sure it's locked. Then I start tapping my foot. "We're not leaving here until you tell me. And if that means we get caught, too bad."

Fane freezes. Then he slowly turns to face in the direction of my voice. "He's grooming me to be the next in line."

I frown at him. Dread builds in my stomach. "You mean..."

"To take over the Dacians, yes. Liviu says my magic is strong, stronger than he's ever seen."

I think back to what he told me. How angry he was. This explains it. He's been even more fooled than I was. "We'll make this right."

"I know. Because I know where he keeps the scrolls with the information he doesn't want us to know."

Then he turns to the old-school screen desk and taps on the drawer. It opens with a pop. It slashes into his hand, drawing blood. Fane hisses in pain, then clenches his jaw, muttering under his breath. "Give me what I seek." A moment later, the illusion disappears and something else comes out, pulled by a dark tendril—a dark tendril that answers to my brother.

When did he learn this type of magic?

All questions are pushed to the side as I realize what he's found— it's a scroll. Old, worn and dated. Fane runs his hands over it, and it becomes Braille writing, not regular writing. He then runs his fingers over the letters as he reads a story I'm nowhere prepared for.

> *I, Liviu Constantin, Grand Master of the Dacians, hereby have entered into a contract with our supreme god. In visions of the feared Oracle, Zalmoxis has spoken to me, chosen me as his direct disciple, to carry out his deeds.*
>
> *The supreme god is imprisoned, but not powerless. His*

voice is strong in my head, his intent, even more so. We are to reach out to our Serafim brethren, and entreat them to turn their ire from the zmei, to the vampiri in the region. Specifically, one family—the ruling one. Cut the head off the snake, and the body will stop wriggling. They shall become the new breed of hunters. Organized, working as a team, for one goal and one goal only—to eradicate the House of Dracul. And I, Liviu, will carry out Zalmoxis' wishes through them.

Fane hands me the scroll with one hand. With the other, he feels his way to the bottom of the page, then stabs his index at it. "The seal is all blood. As is the writing. The Grand Master was very precise."

My eyes widen. "So this means it's not only us after the vampires. The hunters, the ones the scroll speaks of, the ones from that weird faction, they're after them, too. Just like Țepeș said."

Fane nods. "I thought... Something didn't ring true, when they sent you off. Now we know why."

"But these Serafim, and the zmei? Zmei are—"

"Eradicated, I know."

I shake my head, everything jumbling in my head. All except one thought. "I need to warn Vlad."

"Not just yet, Lana."

He holds his hand out for the scroll. I glance at it, noticing it reverts back from Braille writing to legible words. I quickly take a picture of its contents before handing it to him, and he sets the scroll back in its resting place. Then he sets the journal back where I'd last seen it, and we leave.

Outside, in the woods, he faces me again. His features are blank, and a different kind of shiver runs up my spine. "Fane?"

He takes a deep breath, then says, "If you want your friend—your consort—to live, it's not enough to warn him. You need to free him."

"But..."

Fane raises his hand, stopping me. "That means leaving behind everything, me included. Are you prepared to do that?"

Chapter 18

Vlad

I don't know what day it is. What time it is. The gates of my cell door close in on me. I am alone.

You are not.

But I am. There is no escaping this darkness. The worst of what I did. All I have to do is close my eyes and hear the screams of my victims—not just since I've been turned. But when I was human. When I was a weapon.

Before Țepeș found me. Before he gave me a home. Before…

No, please don't!

I'll do anything.

I have a child/wife/ill parent to take care of.

All the pleas, and I never cared. Not. A. Single. Time.

And then Țepeș turned me, became my new guiding father, and...everything changed. Or so I thought. But when I close my eyes, I still see the new victims. The new headlines. Have I really gotten any better? Or have I just gotten better at lying to myself?

The door opens as I lie on the ground, panting. Too soon, the man comes in. I blink through bleary eyes. It's Liviu again, dressed in a fancy new suit now. He stands watching me, until I get up. Slowly. Weighed by the burden of my human past, of my recent past, and of the last day...and Silviana's gaze as she left.

"Looks like you're having fun." He takes out a cellphone and I hear a beep indicating he's filming me.

I swallow past my dry throat. "Why...?"

"What, this?" He grins. "You alone, here, has fed my wildest musings. But if I could get your siblings? Even better."

I try to push down the flicker of hope. Him admitting they're alive is more than what Silviana could give me. Which means he's watching them. If he sends them a message...they'll come, won't they?

And then that hope dies out, snuffed out by my own darkness. *There's nothing of worth for them to save.*

I try to change tactics, if only to prevent him from getting the upper hand. "How do you know so much about us?"

"How do you think?"

"Spies."

He grimaces. "Close, but not quite. No, you see, long ago, my people knew of your kind. Our maker created them all over but when he created Țepeș, well...that was something else."

"Zalmoxis, you mean?"

Why is it taking my brain so much to get things straight? If I didn't know any better, I'd swear I was drugged. But drugs don't work on vampiri.

I look at the cuffs on my wrists. Could they...?

A slow clap draws me from my musings. "Very good. I was told you were intelligent, and I'm happy not to be disappointed. Yes, our blood magic comes from our master. As for how we know about you... Well, know thy enemy." He pauses and stares at me. "Of course, we had to move in closer once it became apparent you are solidifying alliances. A smart move. One worthy of your father." He steps closer. "Too bad you're not nearly as imposing as he was."

I clench my teeth. "You haven't met my siblings yet."

"No, they're too busy fighting off an attack from a clan." He laughs at my stunned expression. "Did you really think I'd allow you to gain influence again? The world doesn't need more vampiri. Your time of shadows and games is over."

"And let me guess. Yours has begun?"

"In a manner of speaking. You see, when the curse struck your kind, it also took something from us. Luckily for us, Zalmoxis loves us enough to provide us with a...solution." His eyes glitter with malice. "A vampir's essence, when drained by one of us, recharges me with all the magic I would need. *And* as a bonus, it extends my lifetime. Quite handy, no?"

Dread fills me. So that's what he plans. I'm just a battery to him, same as would my siblings would be...if he gets them.

"You're insane."

"No, son of Dracul. I am simply ahead of my times. You will see, soon enough."

He keeps smiling at me, as if I'm missing something important and he holds the key. Then he grins and lifts his hand. I sense the blood too late—and then a zap of darkness zigzags toward me, hitting me full frontal. I scream, unprepared for the jolt of lightning in my body. I can't believe I've been so unaware, when I was taught better than this.

On the second hit, I grit my teeth and bear it. Fire nips at my wrists and ankles, but it's nothing compared to the agony burning its way through my body, through my mind.

On the verge of unconsciousness, I ask, "Why not kill me now?"

"Because *he* doesn't want you dead just yet. It has to be slow."

And then it begins again. I writhe and jerk until he leaves me a trembling mess. And all throughout, I sense a faint hint of jasmine.

Silviana, stay away...

Silviana

I've heard enough. I step back as quietly as I can from Vlad's cellar and run back up the stairs. Thankfully, the guards were too busy yapping to see me go in and they're definitely still oblivious as I sneak out. I run through the woods, to my brother. He alone can help.

I burst into his room minutes later. "Fane!"

He freezes, in the process of making himself a coffee, judging by the smell. Without further ado, I quickly fill him in on what I've seen.

His expression darkens. "You shouldn't have gone near him."

"I know, but—"

"Did you get what I asked for?"

I pull out herbs from my jacket, wrapped in paper. "Here. For the sleeping drought."

We get to work. And the entire time, my conviction sharpens. What I heard the Grand Master say... He confirmed everything we'd read, and more. I still can't get my mind around what, exactly, he hopes to achieve by Vlad's torture.

As I grind lavender and sage into a bowl, I ask Fane, "Should I reach out to his siblings? The Grand Master confirmed they're alive."

He snorts, but doesn't stop drawing the symbols with his blood on the counter. "Don't be silly. Consort or not, they'll skin you alive without him. With him, you have a chance."

"Point taken." I glance at him, touching his hand. "Fane... Thank you. For helping me with Vlad."

"As if I'd ever let you do this alone." He shrugs. "Besides, I saw past your lie, didn't I? I know you need to be with him. Hell, if you're not, it'll mean both your deaths. So it's not like there's much of a choice."

I look at the kitchen table. "But I still made it."

"You did." His tone softens. "And I understand it, Lana. This is bigger than us. Much, much bigger."

I gulp past my tears. "What will you do, though?"

"Unfinished business. There's too much we don't know, and if we're to ever find out the truth, I must stay. Leave word for the location of their new castle, all right? At the inn in town."

"I will. Thank you."

He pulls me into a hug and I try to hold back tears. Will I really have to lose him, so I can have Vlad? Can I not have both? Deep inside, I know life is about sacrifices but I don't know if I'm ready to leave my brother in the clutches of these people.

But do I even have a choice? Not really.

The moon is nowhere to be seen but the stars cast enough of a glow in the forest that I can find my path without a light. By the time I reach the cellar, the guards are asleep. Fane did well with the sleeping draught... It has the added benefit that it leaves no trace, unlike our magic. It'll simply look like they fell asleep on the job.

I move past their sleeping bodies, inside the cellar, to Vlad. I light the torches as I speed through the tunnel, until I'm back in the cavern-like room where he's being held. He's in a corner of the cage, panting. Red, bloodshot eyes meet mine.

"Vlad, it's me." I move to the cage, slowly. He watches me approaching. "I —I was wrong, so wrong. You have no idea. You guys weren't the bad guys. The Dacians are. I... Vlad?"

He looks at me, eyes glazed. "I am a bad guy."

No, no, no.

I catch sight of the burns on his wrists and open the cell door, then rush in.

He inhales sharply. "You have to leave."

"No!" I shove him against the wall and we glare at each other. Then I reach for his wrists again, cut myself with the athame, and whisper over the incantation.

Vlad whimpers. "You have to go, Silviana."

"I'm not leaving you."

"You have to. There's nothing... Don't you remember what I did, before?"

"So you drank from me. Big deal."

It takes him a second, but he meets my gaze with focus. "I attacked you, Silviana. You can't brush that under the carpet."

"I'm not! You weren't yourself. You need... *We need* to get you out of here."

He stares at me like I'm crazy. At a loss, I rise to my tiptoes and press my mouth to his. Vlad struggles to put distance between us, but the wall is at his back, and there's nowhere to go. In the end, he gives in with a groan. The kiss soon has me dizzy for lack of air, so I push against his chest.

"Silviana..."

"I know the truth. I read your father's journal, Vlad."

His glazed eyes settle on me. This time, his voice is a whisper. "You have to leave."

"No. I refuse. We either escape together, or I might as well be in here with you."

"You can't—"

I shush him with my finger on his lips, and then focus on the cuffs around his wrists. I cut my palm and whisper the words to get them off him.

Just as they fade away into nothingness, he freezes. I do, too. Feet clack on the ground, warning of someone coming. I know it's not Fane—he's a hell of a lot quieter. And it can't be the guards. Which means it's someone else—someone dangerous.

Vlad is quicker to move than me. He grabs me by the arm and tosses me out of his cell with enough force to send me into the corner. I catch myself on the wall, my palms scraping it, and look over my shoulder at him.

His eyes are wild—desperate—as he whispers harshly, "Go! I won't have you paying for this."

I scramble backward, and then into the shadows. My blood feeds them, and soon they're cloaking me, hiding me from human eyes. The spell works too fast, too soon, and it feels like I have help.

Once I'm completely hidden, I use the shadows to drift toward a tunnel hidden away. Tears streak my cheeks, making my retreat harder.

It was supposed to be easy. We were supposed to be gone.

What the hell went wrong?

Chapter 19

Vlad

The moment I know Silviana's safe, I let go of my hold on darkness, staggering against the wall. I don't know how I was able to find the strength to do what I did—call upon the shadows again—but I managed it.

At least one good deed. Now, time for the next.

I push off the wall, still staggering, and try to balance myself. My muscles won't listen, not at first. But then I think of Silviana, of needing to buy her time so she doesn't pay for her misguided attempt at freeing me... And a rush of new energy fills me.

Whatever the cost to me, I'll make sure she gets out of this unscathed.

With a roar, I hurl myself at the unsuspecting humans, trying to buy her time. I don't care what happens to me, my existence is already gone. Is that what the consort bond means, what it leads to? Then... so be it.

My hands find grip in a Dacian's shoulders. I use my momentum to slam him against the wall, then yank his head to the side and sink my fangs into him. I manage a few slurps of blood before I see fire—feel it. Ash down my throat.

Coughing, I push off the Dacian, then stagger. Someone hits me from behind. Someone else sends a gust of wind toward me, slamming me into the wall. I slide to the ground, landing on my knees. The crack of bones reverberates through my body. Weakness takes over me again...and again...and again.

It's not long before I feel cuffs on my wrists again. But rather than bring me to the cell, the Dacians yank me up. The one holding me up grips a fistful of my hair, holding my head up. Another—the one I'd drank from, judging by the blood on the collar of his shirt—moves toward me, murder on his features.

His fist hits me in the solar plexus, stealing my breath. And then in the jaw. And again in the stomach. I have no defense, other than to take it.

By the time they leave me alone, I have no doubt a visit from Liviu will follow. I almost welcome it, instead of the nightmares I'm bound to feel. To live through.

Then I think of Silviana. Of her faith in me. Of what she said—me not being a bad man.

Through swollen eyes, I look at the cave. Is there something—anything—I can use to write to her?

Before I can find what I'm looking for, the doors open again, and

Liviu's polished shoes soon show up in my periphery. He's silent for a long moment, presumably taking in the damage his minions did. Not that he seems angry.

"Who released you?" he finally asks.

Ice freezes my blood. *He can't know. He's fishing, is all.* "No one."

"I know all. And I know someone released you. You couldn't have done this on your own."

I let out a dark chuckle, but blood fills my mouth. I spit it out, groaning at the dizziness that hits me.

In a whisper, much less imposing or taunting than I'd meant it, I still deliver my final blow. "Maybe you don't know as much as you think."

The pain, when it comes, is almost welcome. I will gladly die for Silviana—so long as she's safe.

And then Liviu says the words I've been waiting for. "My patience is tested. It is time to end you."

Silviana

Darkness keeps hiding me until I'm back in the woods, and back to my apartment. I pace back and forth, forth and back, trying to figure out how to get to Fane. Eventually, I pick up my phone and call him. It rings and rings…and then I hear its ring outside my door.

Desperate, I rush to it, flinging it open. I throw myself in his arms. "Oh, Fane, I fucked up!"

Too late, I realize his frozen status. When I pull back, I only get a glimpse of his features, of the regret, before I finally register the men behind him. "F-Fane?"

He schools his expression into a neutral mask, and says, "What did you do, sorella? Has the vampire addled your brain?"

"I—I don't—"

My gaze goes from him to the men. Dacians. In dark suits. With the Grand Master's bracelet on their biceps, signaling their status as his personal guard.

"F-Fane?" My voice comes out tiny, weak...afraid.

Did my brother betray me?

He sighs as though he's disappointed in me, then gestures to the men. "You were right, it seems. Take her."

They move as one, and before I know it, each one holds one of my arms. But it's Fane—*my brother*—who puts the cuffs on my wrists. The same ones who'll hold back my magic.

Without a single word, he then turns his back on me and leaves. And as they drag me away from everything I've known, everything I thought I could trust, I can't even be bothered to cry.

Shadows move around my hole in the ground. And that's precisely what my prison cell is—a hole in the ground. They've tossed me into some kind of well, because apparently women who fuck around with my kind don't get the same cells as the men do.

I stare in disgust at the mud surrounding me. It rained yesterday, and apparently I don't even get dry confinements. Not that it matters, since it's now nighttime and the temperature is dropping fast. Oh, well.

My anger isn't so much at my confinement, as it is at Fane's betrayal. How could he? We've had each other's backs for our entire lives. And now he betrays me? Was it all a lie, him accepting my choice while hiding his feelings of repulsion?

Did he play me?

I think back to our last conversations, to the way he'd helped me. What did I miss?

And how can I get out of here?

Snickers from above draw my attention. A Dacian peers down. It takes me a moment to recognize Valeriu. "Darling Silviana, what in all hells did you get yourself into?"

I don't bother answering. He'll only taunt me more.

"Tsk, and you've forgotten your manners? What a little bitch you've turned out to be." Another snicker. "A bitch in heat, that is."

With a flick of his wrist, he removes the bars keeping me locked in. Then he sends a gust of darkness down that lifts me, bringing me up. "The Grand Master wants to see you."

I don't trust Valeriu as far as I can throw him. And sure enough, halfway in the woods, he moves closer to me. His hand goes to my shoulder, then down to my breast, his intent clear. I elbow him in the gut and push away, whirling on him.

"What the fuck do you think you're doing?"

"Come now, Silviana... What, you don't like human men now? Only dead dicks?"

Instead of flaring with anger, I smirk at him. "There wasn't anything *dead* about Vlad's dick, if that's what you mean." I let my gaze trail down. "Unlike yours."

Then I turn my back on him, and keep walking. It takes him only a moment, but his roar of rage clues me in that he's running toward me. And I know what he wants—what they all want.

So I wait until he grabs my shoulder, intending to spin me

around...only instead of letting him slam me into the tree, I duck under his raised arm, and come up behind him. My cuffs may be made of dark magic, but they're still *tangible*. And when the chain holding them together wraps around his neck, he screams...and screams...and screams.

The smell of burned flesh is all that stops me. Valeriu drops to the floor, dead.

"Finally. That's one less witness to worry about."

I whirl—on Fane.

"What are you doing here, traitor?"

He tilts his head to the side, listening to the sounds I make—my panting, my shuffling feet—then he lifts his palms up and walks in my direction. "Lana, listen to me—"

"No! NO! How *could you*!?"

He's on me the next moment, his hand on my mouth, his voice low in my ear. "Stop screaming. You'll send them running here, and I need you in the Grand Master's cabin for a reason. Come with me. Please."

He pulls away, resting his forehead against mine. "Lana, please, please, please, just *please* this once, do as I ask you."

So...I do. Because if my brother's going to kill me, then maybe I can at least leave a clue for Vlad or his siblings to find.

The moment we're in the Grand Master's cabin, Fane turns in my direction. His palm bleeding, he holds my hands and whispers the counter-curse to the cuffs. Once they're gone, he reaches for my cheek.

"Lana, did you really think I'd betray you? I'd rather than die than do that."

"I don't..." I stare at my bare wrists, then back at him. "I don't understand. What's going on?"

He holds his hand out in front of him and moves—slower than normal—to the living room area. "Can you help me, please? He changed the location of the hidden compartment from earlier."

I clock it in a corner, hidden under something, and head toward it slowly. A board creaks under my foot, causing Fane to turn in my direction.

"I know you have your doubts," he says, "but listen to me. The Grand Master came to me, saying someone tampered with his stuff. His safe. He'd put things into place that...I didn't see." His voice drops, as it always does when he feels guilty over his eyesight. "I was too arrogant, I should've asked you for help back then, instead of pretending I know all. Anyway. When they came, I had two choices— to admit we were both in on it, or lie, and give you up."

"To save yourself."

"NO! To save *you*, my idiot sorella. I needed you here so *you* can now break into the safe, and then take this scroll to the Dracul siblings. They will give you asylum. Protect you...like I can't."

Tears hit my eyes. "W-what?"

"You heard me. This is the end of the road, Lana. So...will you trust me, like you have up until now? One more break-in, and I promise I'll have you safely out of here."

"But Vlad—"

"They plan to execute him tonight."

A whimper moves past my lips.

Fane takes another step in my direction. "I'll save him, too. But it needs to look like you operated alone in all this."

"You're taking a huge risk. What if they don't believe you?"

He grins, then pulls out the athame from behind him. And before I can stop him, he stabs his gut.

"Fane!" I run to him, but he waves me away.

"No. Do as I've told you. This won't kill me, but it'll convince them that you syphoned my energy off."

"Syphoned...I don't even know how to do that!"

He nods darkly. "I know. But *I* do. And admitting I taught you something forbidden—no matter how big of a lie that'll be—will provide a nice cover. They'll forgive me. They'll trust me. And then I can get more information, and pass it on to you. But, Lana, there is one more thing. If I fail at any point in this, you must find out where those missing pages from Țepeș's journal are, and how Liviu knew Dad was friends with Țepeș. It's the last missing piece, and we both need it. He owes it to us."

My tears run freely now. "Fane... I never should've doubted you, not for a second."

"Shh," he says, then presses the bloody knife in my palm. "Do it. We don't have much time."

Vlad

Before the moon is high, you'll be dead. As will be your consort.

The words haunt me, leaving me unable to sleep, unable to do anything. They know it was Silviana who helped me, and they're going to punish her. And I can't do anything to stop it.

I'm so lost in my dark ruminations, I don't immediately notice the cloaked figure entering the cave. It's not Silviana—I tense. Maybe it's one of the Dacians, come to finish me for good, before the main event.

But it's not. The man comes under a torch and lights it with his hand. His unseeing eyes land in my direction. "Move away from the door."

In the moment I place his face—Silviana's brother—he's already waving his hand to the lock. I can smell blood, a lot of it, but there's nothing on his face or on his palms.

Silent, he moves into the cell, same as Silviana had. I brace myself for an attack. He must blame me for her capture, want my head on a spike.

Instead, he points his hand to the cuffs around my wrists. "Come here."

My feet move of their own accord. What the hell is this magic?

He places his hands on my wrists, and the lighted chains disintegrate. I'm staring at his expression the entire time—the pain on his features as he does whatever this magic is.

"Why are you—"

A muscle ticks in his jaw. "Shut up."

Once the cuffs are gone, he exits the cell and walks toward a tunnel at the back. "Follow me. And be quiet."

Frowning, I listen. For long moments we walk, Ștefan seemingly knowing exactly where he's going. Hand on the wall, he keeps his footsteps light, and I do the same.

Finally, we reach midway through the tunnel and hit an intersection.

"Who were you hired to kill, when Țepeș found you and turned you?"

"Huh?"

My less-than-intelligent reply seems to infuriate Ștefan. "Don't lie to me, vampir. I've just taken you out of the cage, and I can easily toss you back in."

"I'm not lying, just not understanding your question. Or its relevance."

His tone is ice-cold when he says, "Answer the damned question."

"I don't know her na—" I stop, recalling the memory of that fateful day. Up until the other night, I *didn't* know her name. Because I didn't remember. But now... "Florinela. Her name was Florinela, and she was pregnant. I always thought I was hired to kill her because she was a witch."

Ştefan stumbles back a step, as though stunned. Then clears his throat. "What year was this?"

"1707."

He says nothing for a long time. Then, he takes another step, closer to the center of the intersection. "The path you see to the left is your way out, toward your castle. It fades, but it will lead you out of Kogaionon—you will pass through a barrier, more than likely—and back into the woods you know." He takes a deep breath, drops his head. "The path to the right is where my sister is, waiting for you." He scowls. "You'd best get out of here for a bit, until things cool down. They *will* look for her, make no mistake."

My foggy brain takes a moment to register everything. He's giving me a choice—my home, or his sister. But why?

"I don't understand. Why are you helping me?"

Ştefan's calm expression falters, and he shoves me away with unerring accuracy. I slam into the walls—only, now I can see where the blood scent is coming from. His shirt is completely soaked with it.

As if sensing my gaze, and my stunned silence, he pulls the cloak around himself again. "This isn't for you. It's for her. Now go."

I take a step, two, waiting to see if this is a trick. It's not. The moment I realize that fully, I'm already heading down the path he said leads to Silviana.

Behind me, I hear one last whisper on the wind. "Take care of her."

Darkness, of a different kind. Not in my head, but around me. Walls that were half man carved, half nature carved, are my only way out of here. And though I'm moving faster, I'm nowhere *as* fast as I wish I was.

Where is she? Is she okay? Why's her brother bleeding so bad?

Too many questions, not enough answers.

After too long, I emerge out of the path, onto a road. It's a small bike road, leading to a village in the distance. I can see chimneys spewing smoke, and lights.

"What the—"

I look behind me, expecting to see the dark mouth of a cave, but that's not what greets me. Instead, it's the rest of the road. I hold my hand out, hoping the brother didn't lie—and he didn't.

The wind carries a scent, and I turn toward it. Jasmine.

Without thinking, I run down the path. And run. And run.

I know when I've reached her, because the air is filled with her fragrance. When I see the cloaked figure waiting for me in the shadow of a tree, I hesitate.

Maybe it's still an illusion.

Then she removes the cloak and smiles tentatively. "It's me."

One step. Then another. And then I'm running to her, crashing into her, taking her deeper into the woods, and cupping her cheeks. "How are you here?"

"My brother, he—"

And then, I don't want to know.

All I care for is the taste of her lips, so I stop denying myself. I crush my lips against hers, and Silviana clings to me, kissing me back. Our moans fill the air as we move deeper into the woods still. I stumble over a tree root, and take her down with me.

She falls atop me, straddling me, and her quiet chuckle fills the night. "Is that something in your pocket, or are you just happy to see me?"

A broken laugh escapes me at her line, and then I can't. No more joking. No more waiting. No more interruptions.

I grab a fistful of her hair, gently tugging her head back, baring her neck. And then I'm kissing it, nuzzling it, inhaling her sweet fragrance. I find the sweet spot between her collarbone and her shoulder, and nip at it.

Silviana yelps in the air, then chuckles again, grinding down on me. I groan, grabbing her hips, tugging her more over me.

"Can't you do some magic shit, so we can get naked faster?"

Her chuckle turns into full-blown laughter in my ear. Then she mutters something, and I feel my clothes being pulled from my body. I watch in wonder as piece after piece of her clothing lifts off her, as if pulled by an invisible string...until she's straddling me, naked.

"How's this?"

My eyes roam over her figure. "Fucking perfect."

Chapter 20

Silviana

The blue of Vlad's eyes has darkened, but I'm not afraid of him losing control. Not even when he pulls me closer, baring my throat to him, kissing everywhere he can reach. I can feel the desire emanating off him, like a vibration that soon permeates my skin, my insides, everything. It's a desire for *me*, not my blood.

"I'm burning," I whisper, tilting my head further back.

He chuckles against my skin, then his skilled fingers move to my breasts, tweaking the nipples. The sharp tug is soothed by his mouth, but it only makes me squirm harder on his lap.

Slowly, unbearably slowly, his questing fingers move lower,

down my belly, and lower still. When he finally touches the bundle of nerves between my legs, I nearly jump off him. "Shit!"

Vlad's chuckle turns darker, even as his touch slows, lightens. "How about this?"

The new touch skyrockets my desire, and I spread my thighs, giving him more access. One finger slides inside me, then another, and soon I'm rocking on his fingers, begging—pleading—losing myself.

My cry of ecstasy echoes in the forest, and an owl hoots in the distance. It takes me a moment to come back to, for my breathing to slow down. Vlad's rubbing soothing circles on my back, his hardness a stark reminder against my thigh of just how patient he's being.

I nuzzle his neck, nibbling the same way he'd done with me. Deep inside me, hunger rises once more, this time for more—so much more. Vlad's hands tighten on my hips, but I ignore his unspoken warning. Instead, I rise to my knees, reach for him, and slowly impale myself on his length.

"Ah, beloved..." He groans, then thrusts deeper inside me. His hand cups my cheek, his eyes searching mine. Then he tugs my mouth to his and, as the kiss deepens, so do his thrusts inside me.

I let him choose the rhythm this time, but if I thought he was done with me, I'm sorely mistaken. Soon as his thrusts become shorter, closer to his release, he lets go of one hip and his thumb moves between my legs, finding my clit again. There's no slow building this time—I detonate like a nuclear bomb—and Vlad's groan echoes shortly after mine.

I snuggle into Vlad's chest, enjoying the way he toys with my hair. After a few moments, I prop myself up on my elbow so I can look at him. Now that the intensity of the bond has dimmed, I become aware of smaller things about him.

Like how his eyes don't have the dark circles under them. And how his color seems good. Pale, as could be expected, but not the deathly gray I'd seen before. I know now those were related to Zalmoxis' curse, but why have they gone away?

"Vlad?"

"Hmm?"

"How are you so...okay?"

He chuckles and bends to kiss my forehead, before returning to play with my hair. "I can enjoy myself for a moment, no?"

"It's not what I mean." I wait until he meets my gaze, before rephrasing, "Before, when they were keeping you...and even earlier, at the castle...you had moments of weakness. Because of the curse, right?"

"Da."

"Well, you seem fine now."

He seems to mull my words for a moment, then his expression clears. "Nico was never affected by the curse, because it hit Violeta first. But even so, when Tassa accepted him, it seemed to delay Violeta's weakness somewhat. Then when Violeta accepted Marcus, there was an entire change around her. She's almost back to normal now, except for a few weird cravings."

"So...you think because I chose you, and left with you, that the same applies?"

His eyes meet mine. "It must. Why else would I still be here, alive, and able to make love to you?"

A blush creeps on my cheeks and I lower my mouth to his chest, dropping kisses everywhere I can reach in an effort to distract myself. Vlad groans low, and then his fingers sink in my hair, tugging me up to his lips.

"Kiss me. For a little longer, let's forget about anything but each other."

"I can do that," I whisper against his lips.

When he rolls me over onto our clothes, I sink my heels in his backside and moan when he slides back inside me. Soon, I'm lost to the ecstasy of his touch, and moving is the last thing on my mind.

I don't know what wakes me up. Something in the air? A sixth sense? Whatever it is, the minute I'm up, I know we're in trouble.

"Vlad!" I nudge him, and he grunts behind me, then comes up awake.

I can feel it when he notices what I have—the web of light being spun above us in hexagonal shapes. It's what had woken me up, because of the brightness it radiates.

"The Dacians?" he whispers, right in my ear.

I shiver. "They found us."

They were merciful the first time, not killing us. Now? There will be no such mercy. Not when they were ready to kill him—and me, for helping him.

"Let's go."

I get up in a flash, gathering my few things. I quickly cut my palm with the athame, then do the spell I'd done earlier, only instead of unclothing us, I'm dressing us. Then I turn to Vlad—but he hasn't moved.

"What's wrong?"

"I...can't move."

Vlad

They've done some magic again. I'm rooted to the spot, unable to move. All my elation at the last hour, at having her in my arms, disappears with the realization I'm stuck—powerless—once again.

But...maybe not quite.

When Silviana comes toward me, I know I have only one choice left. She'll hate me for it, but I can't go back on my promise to myself, or her brother. I will keep her safe, at any cost.

"Leave," I tell her, though my heart aches even as the words leave my lips. "Go get my siblings, if there's time. If not, just leave and be safe."

"I'm not—"

I turn the full force of my glamour on her. "*Leave.* I'm not letting you take any chances."

She jerks against my mental hold, tries to fight it, but it's no use. I feel it slip on, and her eyes glaze over. A moment later, she's walking away, her steps wooden.

And then, I wait.

It doesn't take them long. Moments after Silviana is gone, a twig snaps behind me. I still can't move, so I wait until the person walks around me, just out of reach of the circle of light.

Liviu sneers at me. "Well, well, well. Look what the net dragged in."

Silviana

No!

I rebel against the mental hold with all my strength. It's no use—Vlad's hold on me is impenetrable.

I've never been glamoured before, and I don't understand why he can do it. Unless that's another lie we were told? But Liza glamoured me, or at least she tried...

Nothing makes sense anymore.

Step by step, I'm getting farther and farther from him. Yet the more distance that comes between us, the more I feel his unbreakable hold waver. Is it that he's tired, or that the Dacians have found him already?

Please don't let it be that. Please, please, please. Not now. We've barely had any time together.

All because of me. If I'd seen through it faster, realized earlier that I was being played, I could have sought help while I was at the castle. From the Dracul siblings themselves. But now, we're far, and there's no way I can get to them in time.

Not when my coven is right around the corner, ready sacrifice him as they'd promised.

I know the Grand Master well enough to realize there won't be any hesitation this time around. No stopping him. Not unless I fight him full front. But to do that, I have to *stop fucking moving!*

Nothing works. No amount of me pushing against the mental control helps.

What if it's not the vampir glamouring, but more a combination of it and our bond...which would explain why Vlad doing it worked, and not Liza? And if I can't push it away...what if I allow it in?

Instead of shoving against the mental hold, I blank my mind out, and let it in. It felt like an external push against my cranium, but the moment I say a mental "okay," the pressure seeps into me. I allow it to control all recesses of me—my muscles become less wooden, more natural, but still pushed by the need to move forward.

Only, even as the hold seems to tighten around me, something else happens. An awareness of otherness—of someone else in my mind.

Vlad.

I don't know how I know it's him, but I feel him. The darkness in him, the guilt, the remorse, his love for me. All of it fills me—as well as his desire to send me away. I was right, his ability to enter my mind had to do with the bond, and not just his vampir abilities. Vampiri *weren't* able to glamour us...and most probably still can't. Unless they're linked to us by a cursed bond, like Vlad and I are.

It takes me a moment to realize what's happened—that I've stopped moving. But when I blink, it's gone. The consort bond helped me break the glamour, and I can move again, in *any* direction I see fit.

Hesitation courses through me. Then a bird chirps in the distance and an idea comes to my mind. I move toward it, slicing the athame into my palm, then holding it out. When the bird flutters to me, I gently caress its feathers, running bits of magic through it. Telling it where to go. Then I dig out a piece of paper from my pocket and write a short message in blood to the only people who can help us—his siblings.

I can only hope they'll get here on time.

Once the bird takes off, my message secured to its scrawny leg, I turn back in Vlad's direction.

I know my people. And because we'd escaped, they won't take chances again. Not this time. They'll kill him then and there, which means my approach must be stealthy.

Voices. I hear them as I approach. I'd hoped we'd have time, that I'd be able to get Vlad and run, but that time is long gone. Through the trees, I can see magic lighting up the meadow where we'd made love. The Grand Master is there, with four of his guardsmen. And Vlad still isn't moving.

Magic leaves me in rivulets, hiding in the earth, and crackling along the tree line. They may be more, but I am a woman on a mission. And there's no way my love for him isn't amplifying my powers...

Vlad sees me when I emerge, his eyes widening. Blood streams down his wrists now. His eyes speak of the horror at seeing me here. At knowing I'm in danger.

Then the Grand Master turns to me. His eyes flash in anger. "You will go against us, to save this monster?"

"Da. Because he isn't the monster—you are."

I lash out with my magic, letting it hit him full force. Then I run to Vlad.

He pulls away from me, and I don't understand why at first. Then he meets my gaze, and his eyes are no longer blue, but completely dark. I know this, I've seen it before—whatever this spell is, whatever they did, I need to pull him back.

"Get away," he says, as if guessing my words.

It's reassuring. At least he's still himself.

The Grand Master moves, I see him out of the corner of my eye. He lifts his hand in the air and Vlad bends over. Then his back cracks. Followed by his wrist. He shrieks in agony, and I feel the same pain, as if a fire's burning a pathway through me.

"Vlad!"

He snarls my way. "Stay away!"

If we're meant to be together, if he's mine for all eternity, then my blood should break this. Whatever blood magic they've done, my connection with him should overdo it all. Same as his connection with me helped me break the glamour.

Without thinking, I pull a small knife from my belt and cut my wrist. Blood gushes out. Vlad turns toward me, his nostrils flaring. He's holding himself in check, trying to. Then he moves closer, one step at a time, as if afraid of his own power. As am I. But I can't let it show, not now. He needs me to have faith, for both of us.

"Come to me."

He inches some more, and again. Then he drops to his knees, and more bones break.

I shove a blast of magic at the Grand Master, enough so he goes on the defensive. I keep my other hand angled toward Vlad. He keeps coming closer, and closer... And then he's on me, and we roll to the ground, and he's trying to hold himself away from my wrist.

"Drink from me," I whisper. "I give myself willingly."

An agonized groan escapes him, and then his mouth descends on my wrist. His fangs pierce my skin even more, and then he's drinking, and drinking, and drinking. The sky above me blurs.

I'd hoped he would snap out of it with a taste, but that's not the case. And if I don't stop him, he'll keep drinking. And if he keeps drinking, I'll weaken, and I won't be able to get us out of this mess.

"Vlad..."

He stills, but before he can move off me, something slams into him. Vlad falls to the ground, a black wolf atop him. Panting, I try to stand, only to find myself completely weakened. The Grand Master advances on me, now that Vlad isn't there.

I don't know who the wolf is. All I know is I need to muster the energy to fight the man running my coven. And judging by the way he's smirking, he's about to school me.

Liviu lifts his hand, pointing it at me. "You are a disgrace to the Dacian legacy."

"I...am not... You are."

Without giving him a chance to strike first, I push the athame blade into my palms, slicing one, and then the other. The blade is covered by blood by the time I'm done, and it drips in rivulets all around me, soaking the grass.

Dark tendrils of magic rise like smoke, lapping at my feet, at the blood, at my intentions. And innocent, they are not.

I focus all my hate on the Grand Master. "You lied to me. You lied to Fane. All this time, you played us like puppets."

"Puppets?" He scoffs. "You were well fed and taken care of, for puppets, were you not?"

"That doesn't take away from the fact you *lied to us*! Our dad wasn't killed by vampiri—Țepeș himself was his friend."

A flicker of surprise on his features tells me he didn't expect me to work it out. "And Ștefan knows this?"

I school my expression in time. "No, he doesn't. I read the journal, when I had it."

"And then you snuck into my cabin and read some more."

I lift my chin in the air. "You always thought me useless, but your wards aren't strong enough to keep me out."

He shakes his head. "As meddling as your father was."

This time, I'm not quick enough to hide my stunned expression. A satisfied smirk covers his features. "Ah, so you don't know *everything*, then. Pity."

I clench my fists. "Tell me." I won't beg, but I will damn well do everything I can to get him to speak the truth. Fane asked me to figure it out...this is my chance. "Is that what was written in the missing pages?"

Liviu sneers at me. "Those pages were torn way before I got my hands on the journal. But I suppose, there's no harm in telling you a little story...for a price."

I feel the slash in my back, and arch against the pain. A cry escapes my lips, but I bite down on it. My gaze flickers to Vlad, still intertwined with the black wolf. He didn't hear me, thankfully.

I glare at Liviu, twirling my wrist and using darkness as a shield, like Fane taught me. I've never been very good at it, but maybe, just maybe, it'll be enough for a moment. "*You* killed my father."

He shrugs, as though the admission is of no consequence. "I was simply a soldier at the hand of the Grand Master before me, child. I followed orders, unlike you, you impudent chit. But, da, I was the one who killed your father."

"And lied to us about how he died." Liviu's bored expression only fuels my rage. "Why?"

"Because he betrayed us!" His flash of anger is quickly followed by a mocking laugh, then another sneer. "Țepeș had been in the wind for too long when we finally caught sight of him again. He'd heard of a prophecy tied with your grandmother." He snorts at my expression. "Oh, don't worry. It was complete bullshit, but the oracle I paid was worth it. Convincing enough to get Țepeș out of the shadows. Incidentally, he chose that night to create his last heir, and thus give us plenty of leads to follow, to keep tabs on him."

He flicks his wrist again, but this time darkness doesn't sink into my shield. Not yet, anyway.

Liviu steps to the side, circling me. "Of course, Țepeș then had to kill himself right under our noses. This was around the time I took over as Grand Master. I never figured out how he eluded us for those last few decades, and how no trap of ours was good enough to ensnare him. But then...a year to the day after he was buried, we had someone stake his grave. And who should show up, but your father? Carrying a leather-bound journal, which he soon buried in the grave itself." He scowls. "No efforts of ours could unearth it. And when we tried to, shall we say, convince your dear daddy, he refused to speak about it." Another shrug. "So, naturally, he had to be dealt with."

"You fucker!" I yell, and open my palms, trying to send a wave of darkness toward him. But instead of touching him, my magic fizzles into thin air.

New darkness slithers at my feet, refusing to let go now that it's been summoned. So, I don't hold it back. I fling my wrists at the Grand Master and, like dark icicles, the magic strikes toward him. He flings his hand up, and a barrier dissolves almost all of them—except one. It cuts through his suit, and his shoulder, dissipating afterward.

Droplets of blood soon soak the material, and he levels a scowling gaze on me.

Magic builds and builds in his hand. He's going to incinerate me, the way he wanted to incinerate Vlad not that long ago. And I won't be able to even try to defend myself.

He releases the magic. It comes toward me, its intent clear.

And then a blast of lightning descends from the sky, cutting it into flaming pieces that drop only a few feet away from me.

The Grand Master turns around, trying to see the source of the power. I move slower, but I still turn in time to see a redhead step out of the woods. Her blue eyes reflect the same light of lightning. I try to position myself in front of Vlad—he's now fully being restrained by the black wolf.

But the redhead seems to have no business with us. Instead, her entire focus is on the Grand Master.

"This is not your fight," Liviu says.

"I beg to differ. What right do you have to play judge, jury and executioner?"

He scowls. "We are cleansing the area of this scum. The vampir deserves it."

"No one deserves to be called scum. Least of all an heir to the voivode Dracul himself. Back. Off." She lifts her hand, and the clouds above rumble. She does something to the air, almost like a rune she draws, and it sizzles, reflecting the same tones of the storm brewing.

I don't know who she is, but I could kiss her right now.

The Grand Master scoffs, but doesn't back off. His gaze moves to Vlad, then me, still bleeding. He smirks. "Have it your way."

He lifts both hands to the clouds now, pulling on everything he can. I know he's about to try and eradicate us—all of us.

"We need to leave!" I shout at the redhead.

She spares me a glance, then the wolf. Her cool expression slips for a tiny second, and I discern concern. The same concern I feel for Vlad, who's on his hands and knees right now, trying to regain hold of himself.

The redhead meets my gaze. "Get your mate and go. We'll take care of this."

I hesitate.

"Do as I say, or we all die here."

That's enough to spur the remainder of the adrenaline in me. I stumble to Vlad, and help him up. He's mumbling something, and it's only as we step away—under the watchful blue gaze of the wolf—that I realize what it is.

"I'm sorry, so sorry. So sorry..."

He's mumbling it over and over again, and it breaks my heart.

I squeeze him tighter around the waist, and push him toward the woods. "It's okay. Vlad, we need to get out of here. Can you carry me? I don't have the strength."

I manage to get us both near the tree line, enough to lean against it. The redhead and the wolf have stopped anyone from following—for now.

As I lean against a tree, I squeeze Vlad's hand in mind. "Please. Vlad. We need to get out of here."

It seems to work, as he blinks, and blinks again. His eyes fall on my bleeding wrist and he picks it up gently, licking the wounds until they stop oozing blood. His sorrow-filled gaze meets mine. "I'm—"

"I know," I whisper. "I forgive you. Please, take me out of here."

He glances around, probably hearing noises I don't. For a moment, I fear he'll go back as some kind of sick punishment to himself. But the moment after, he picks me up and we take off.

Chapter 21

Vlad

I try to shove away the guilt as I'm making my way away from the Dacians, and through the trees. There will be plenty of time for me later to wallow in self-pity and feel bad for what I did. For taking Silviana's blood—again. Especially after sleeping together.

Rivers of shame overpower me, causing me to stumble. I want to prostrate myself at her feet and beg for forgiveness, for absolution, for everything she'll give me. But that time is not now.

Not when we're running for our lives.

"How did they find us?" I throw over my shoulder.

Silviana's hold on me tightens. Her heartbeat is—thankfully—

strong. Whether fueled by adrenaline or something else, at least it's beating. "They must have followed your essence, or mine. Blood magic is powerful. They'll find us anywhere."

"Do they have your blood?"

"Yes."

Shit. I'd hoped to send her away, at least. To keep her out of their clutches, regardless of what happened to me. I'd then be able to keep the promise I made to her brother, and also to myself. But it doesn't look like that'll be happening anytime soon.

"What's the plan?" she whispers in my ear.

My eyes scan everything as I move, zigzagging through the trees. Dominic and Lucrezia saved us, that much I know. Without the wolf and his mate, I'd be dead, and so would Silviana. By my hand.

I shove the guilt away again.

"Going home," I toss back to her. "Only place we can regroup, if my siblings—"

My attention is taken by movement in the trees—someone as fast as I am.

I whirl on my heels and crouch low, gently moving Silviana off me.

"Stay behind me," I mutter as I try to see what kind of foe we're facing now. Whatever—whoever—it is, I'll make sure to rip their throats out before they can touch a hair on her head.

"Vlad, I have to tell you—"

"Shh!"

My muscles tense, fangs bared, my fists clenched.

But what comes out of the tree is not a foe.

"Nico?" My eyes sweep over the others. "Alex, Liza. What are you doing here?"

"We got Silviana's message," Nico says. He glances between me and Silviana, then back at me. His sharp gaze takes in all the scrapes and bruises on my body, the ones that haven't yet healed. "What happened?"

"More like *who* happened," Liza snarls at Silviana.

"Liza—"

"No. She's right." Silviana comes up behind me, straightening her shoulders. Her hand trembles when it intertwines with mine, but she tries to hold herself together when facing my siblings. "I was at fault for Vlad's imprisonment. And I could've helped him a lot sooner if I had accepted our consort bond earlier. But I didn't. And I deeply and truly apologize for that."

She looks at me, and I use our connected hands to tug her into my arms. I don't care that my clothes are ripped and the way she lands only hurts my wounds more. I need to have her in my arms, where she belongs.

I level my gaze on Liza. "We can talk about this later. Right now, we'd best get out of here."

"Where's the fire, though?" Nico says. "The message seemed urgent."

"We were saved," I mutter. "By the vârcolaci, if I'm not mistaken. Dominic and his mate, Lucrezia."

"Convenient," Alex says. "Or does no one else find it so?"

"We're not all as jaded as you are, Alex." Nico sighs. "Do they need help, the wolves?"

I shake my head. "They seemed to have it handled."

"Then let's head back home, and you can tell us exactly how you came to be imprisoned by a group of witches that are meant to be obsolete."

An hour or so later, we're all seated in the castle's library. Nico has Violeta and Marcus on the phone, and I haven't let go of Silviana—only to free one hand so I can chug down some red wine. Not that it does much, quite the opposite. Rather than the smoothness of rich wine, all I taste is ash on my tongue.

At least sitting, they won't see the extent of my weakness. That'll send them in a frenzy.

It's a good thing Mirabela's still away hunting for castles, else she'd be able to see past everything I'm trying to hide.

Liza is seated opposite the fire, but Alex can't seem to stop pacing. His nervous energy rattles me. His issue with the wolves is deep-rooted, but sooner or later it'll bite us in the ass.

The only question is, how badly?

Silviana

Part of the castle is completely burned. Perched on Vlad's lap, I can see out the window, and my gaze keeps going there. *So my vision didn't lie.*

Vlad catches my eye and asks Nico, "What's with the humans? Don't tell me you compelled them."

He snorts. "As if I'd bother. It seems Tassa's managed to win over some villagers. They came to help after seeing the fire, and we haven't been able to get rid of them. Luckily, we'd already disposed of our attackers' vampir bodies by the time they showed up, else I doubt they'd have been as helpful."

As if conjured by her spoken name alone, Tassa bursts in the room—and immediately engulfs me in a warm embrace. While awkward because of where I'm sitting, it's nonetheless the first token of care and favor I've received since returning, and it warms my heart.

"I'm so glad you're okay!"

Vlad coughs by my side and she turns to him, embracing him until Nico pulls her off him. "He gets the point, iubito."

"How droll. The humans sticking together."

I cringe. Alex's glare incinerates me.

"And how do you explain the hell you put my brother through?"

"This isn't—"

Vlad gets interrupted by Liza. "I asked the same thing and got shit-all for my efforts."

"Now, listen—"

I place a hand on his shoulder and gently push off him, standing. But I don't let go of his hand. Head high, holding their gazes, I step in front of Vlad and lift my chin, baring my neck. "I have nothing to hide anymore. I came here with deception in mind and you have every reason to hate me. But it worked against me because I fell for your brother. Hard."

"Yeah, hard enough to get him captured."

"Oh, shush for once, Liza, and give the woman a chance to explain herself."

Liza's scowl deepens at Tassa's command, but surprisingly, she listens.

"Our time away—by my fault, yes, I betrayed you all—only served to show me how deep these feelings run. Deep enough that I've just walked away from the only family I know. And I come bearing information. You can toss me out all you like after"—I ignore Vlad's growl at my suggestion—"but first, would you like to hear the information I have? No strings attached."

It's too big a bait. When only silence answers me, I begin.

"You were all correct." My gaze lingers on Liza and Alex. "I was sent here on a mission to steal Țepeș's journal and bring it to my coven. My Grand Master—the man in charge of the Dacian coven—ran the mission, and I saw it as a chance to climb the ladder in our ranks."

"And get some vampir notches in your belt, no doubt," Alex mutters.

Vlad shifts behind me, and I sense his anger—why am I sensing it so strongly, when before it was just an odd feeling? That's a question for later.

With effort, I push his emotions out of my head and focus on mine. I inhale deeply. "When I came here, I thought you all were monsters. Ștefan—my brother—and I, we were told our family was killed by vampiri under the sigil of the House of Dracul."

"So, you harbored resentment," Violeta says on the phone.

I nod, then, realizing she can't see me, say, "Da, I did. My heart was nowhere where it should've been, focused only on the mission. But then..." I trail off, unsure what words to choose. What will not set off Alex and Liza?

"The bond happened," Violeta supplies.

So much for not setting them off.

"Bullshit!" they cry together.

Liza then takes a step closer, but stops at a look from Nico. "Vlad, did you seriously fall for this shit? She's *playing* you, like she has all along!"

Behind her, same as before, I can see the man from days ago. It feels like so long ago, much more than a few days. The ghost shrugs when he notices my gaze, then leans against the wall, as if to wait it out.

I focus my attention back on Liza. "Believe what you will, but let me finish the story." When she's silent, I continue, "I found the journal. I gave the signal to my coven, but…I wasn't extracted as per the plan, at least not at first. I didn't realize why, but I learned the truth once I was back home."

Nico frowns. "And that was?"

"The Grand Master knows about the bond. He…made sure Vlad and I would be tied together." I chance a glance over my shoulder to my consort, and he smiles reassuringly. It's insane what a simple squeeze of his hand does to my confidence.

Taking another deep breath, I reveal everything else. The imprisonment, some of what was done to Vlad—I'll leave the rest for him to tell—and how I roped Fane into helping me out. What we found out. What we read from Țepeș's journal—that gets a lot of growls and nasty looks from Liza and Alex.

When I finally wrap up with the escape, the role my brother played—and skip over our sex life—I'm greeted by a shocked silence.

Liza's the first to gather her thoughts. "So, tell me why we shouldn't kick you to the curb right now? You're bringing these maniacs to our door, by your own admittance."

Vlad clears his throat behind me. "I have a good reason."

"Vlad—"

He shakes his head at me, and meets his sister's gaze. "I thought you were all for vengeance against the people behind your imprisonment, from ages ago?"

Liza stills. Like a predator waiting for its prey, she tilts her head to the side. Her scar seems starker against the whiteness of her cheek. "Go on, you have my attention."

"The Grand Master Silviana keeps mentioning? That's Liviu."

Tassa gasps. Nico growls. Alex stills, similar to Liza. And on the phone, there's a long silence.

"Say that again," Nico demands, his tone icy cold.

"Liviu. The man we all thought was a vampir hunter, in the caves. Who helped Victor kidnap Tassa. Who had a hand in her father's death." Vlad sighs. "Maybe he is a hunter, for all we know. But he's also the Dacian leader. That, my dear siblings, is not a co-incidence. Father would have said as much."

Another silence lengthens. Then, on the phone, Violeta says, "He's right. Father would tell us to give Silviana asylum."

The ring of another cell interrupts us. Nico pulls the phone out of his pocket and hits a button. Mirabela's voice rings loud and clear.

"I found a home I think we can all coexist in."

"Great. We have Vlad back."

"How is he? Is he hurt?"

"I'm fine, Mira. Got loads to fill you in on. When are you coming back?"

There's an odd noise on the phone, like a baby cat roaring. I frown, and share a puzzled look with Vlad. Mira doesn't even miss a beat.

"Not just yet. I'm getting the last of the paperwork done. But, Nico, there's something else. One of the Ardelean vampiri—one of the ones we glamoured—found me. Seems I can't shake her. She's some kind of guard, or at least she proclaims to be. Anyway, she said there are rumors there's another attack coming against us. A bigger one."

Nico looks at everyone. "When?"

"Shortly. You need to get out of there."

"No. We're not running. If they want to come, they can come. And when we're done ripping their heads off for treason, *then* we'll leave."

Silence on the other end. "As you wish." There's a click as she hangs up.

Nico meets my gaze. "Go on."

Vlad

It's hard, sitting by and letting them all give Silviana a hard time. I know they do it because they've been worried, and in a way, it soothes my own insecurities. But there's only so much I'll be able to stand.

Cool and collected, Silviana answers Nico's plea, and says, "I think you have bigger things to worry about than the Dacians coming after me." She points to the phone. "What Mirabela said, about another attack? It might not be only vampiri."

Alex moves, and this time, I stand next to Silviana and glare at him. He notices my look, and I see him make a conscious effort to keep his tone level. "What do you mean?"

"The journal," Silviana says. "Did any of you actually read it, front to back?"

Nico glances around, then shrugs. "I—I started, but it was hard. Father's death hit us all hard, and for me, it was a reminder of how I failed my siblings in the coming centuries. Mira read more of it—half, I think—but we didn't compare notes. She only said a lot of it was about us, and Father's expectations of us. Then I got distracted once the vampiri came on the scene."

Silviana nods, as if having expected that much. I squeeze her hand again, to tell her without words that she's doing okay. I can tell she's nervous, on the borderline, talking to them like this. And I don't blame her.

"I figured as much." She reaches into a backpack and pulls out some sheets of paper. "These will confirm what I said, but I'll summarize them for you." As she hands them to Nico, she adds, "Your father says he discovered proof of the curse being set by Zalmoxis. He was going to offer himself as sacrifice, so you could all be safe."

Alex snarls. "Bull*shit*! You expect to believe this load of crock? That our father, the most feared fucking vampir and voivode in this region, took himself to the slaughter?"

Help comes from the most unexpected of places.

"It's true," Liza whispers.

Tears shine in her eyes, and she looks at Silviana as if both hating her and admiring her. With shaky hands, she pulls the sheets out of her hands, rifles through them, then hands them to Alex.

"Father... I couldn't sleep, after the attacks. He and I used to talk into the night. He...I didn't realize it at the time, but he was saying goodbye." She wipes at her eyes furiously, then jabs a finger in our direction. "You better keep your damned mouth shut. Last thing we need is the rest of the vampiri hearing of this."

Silviana shakes her head. "I don't think you understand. The reason Țepeș did this is *because* of the vampiri. All those attacks? The clans weren't pulling the strings. Zalmoxis was, whispering in their ears. And then in the Dacians' ears... And the hunters'."

Nico stands then, his arm protectively drawn around Tassa. "You're saying... they're all working together?"

I clear my throat, speaking for the first time. "No. She's saying someone is pulling *all* their strings."

Nico meets my gaze. "Zalmoxis."

My only answer is a nod.

After a beat, his gaze goes to the phone, to Violeta on the line. "Vi?"

"Da, frate?"

"Reach out to Mira. Find the new location. You and Marcus need to join us."

"Is that wise?"

"We don't have a choice. This is a full-frontal attack, and us being separated means more chances they'll pick us off one by one." He runs a hand over his face, then looks at me. "Take Silviana and get some rest. We'll review these pages, and figure out a way to protect ourselves."

I walk Silviana back to her room, more out of habit than anything else. I certainly don't expect her to face me when she gets to the door, an inviting look in her eyes. "Want to come in?"

"I, ah..." I do. More than anything else. What I don't want is to accidentally drink from her again. The wine hasn't given me the energy it usually does, and I don't want to risk it. "Not tonight."

I move to pass her and head into my bedroom, shutting the door softly behind me. I lean against the worn wood, sighing deeply. She will kill me, with those big eyes staring and hoping for so much more than I can give her. So much less than she deserves.

Chapter 22

Silviana

I step into the room, and it's like I never left. The bed is unmade, the windows shut. I open one of them, letting in the fresh breeze.

I wonder if Fane's all right... My biggest worry is they'll figure out that he helped me. They were clearly ready to kill Vlad, and myself, and I have no doubt the same would apply to Fane. I just hope he gets out soon and finds me. I hate thinking of what punishment he'd go through just for helping us escape, if they figure it out.

Part of me hopes they never will.

Then I remember the fight, the craziness, and I shiver.

The Grand Master was never someone I'd ever thought I'd be

pitted against. The memory of how easily he'd tossed the spells my way, and how much I was scrambling to even cover myself and Vlad... It's almost laughable that Alex ever thought I'd be of use to them as a witch. Clearly, he overestimated my skills.

Which begs the question, what the hell will I do when I face off against the Grand Master again?

Unable to sleep, I leave the room and tiptoe to Vlad's. An inkling drives me to him, a need stronger than my own will. He'd declined my invitation, and the only reason he did it is because he feels guilty over drinking my blood again. I'm not stupid, it's clear as day. And I need to nip his guilt in the bud while I can.

The room is quiet when I push the door open. Dark. Faint wisps of moonlight push through the curtains. The only noise is from the en suite bathroom. Through the opened doorway, I can hear a shower running.

Without hesitation, I move toward the door, and push it open. Steam heats my cooled skin. I take off my clothes and enter the bathroom. Then the shower stall.

Vlad's bent over, water ramming his forehead—probably why he didn't hear me come in.

I reach for his shoulder and he jerks, whirling around. His eyes widen, then darken as they take in my naked form. "What are you doing here, Silviana?"

"You know what."

"You shouldn't. I—"

"You're afraid you'll bite me again."

He frowns.

"You're not that hard to figure out, you know."

I take a step closer, and my foot slips on some soapy water. His arm comes around me reflexively, and he tugs me against his chest.

I tilt my head back and grin at him. "Was that so hard?"

"You pretended to slip on purpose?"

I intertwine my fingers around his neck. "Well, when you're acting like touching me will disintegrate you to dust... What's a girl to do?"

"It's not—"

I stop him with a kiss. Vlad groans against my mouth, and I feel him harden against me. When he tries to stop the kiss, I only tighten my grip on him, pressing myself closer, enjoying the friction of his hard body against my softer one.

I wiggle in his arms and pull back for a moment. "Let's get one thing straight. I'm glad you fed from me, and I gave you my blessing to do so. I'd do it again in a heartbeat."

He says nothing, but I can see the guilt behind his eyes, haunting him. Eventually, he whispers, "I could've killed you."

"But you didn't."

"I was close."

"No, you weren't. I'm more resilient than you give me credit."

He shakes his head, but I grab a fistful of his hair to stop his movements. "Just kiss me, Vlad. Kiss me and let's forget all this for a night. Please."

When that same resolution shows on his face, I let go and reach for a soap bar instead. His gulp is loud, even with the shower still running.

"What are you doing?"

"What's it look like? Washing myself."

Vlad

My body stills. I can't—there's a need in me, consuming me. The heat from the shower permeates the air, as does Silviana's scent—the jasmine, and her blood, thump-thump-thumping in my ears.

Water trickles down her back, the curve of her waist, that heart-shaped ass. With graceful movements, she uses my soap bar to wash herself...making every movement as painfully sensual as she can.

She turns, wiping shampoo from her eyes, hands roaming her body as she rinses off. One hand moves between her breasts, then lower, teasing herself with soft touches.

I inhale sharply and her eyes fly open. She sees me watching her. A smile tugs at her lips and she closes her eyes again, depriving me of that soulful gaze. Tilts her head back. Moans. The hand between her legs moves, sliding a finger inside—and I can't hold off anymore.

I'm picking her up, pulling her against me, swallowing her moan with a kiss. She grips my neck, nails digging in, and arches against me. She's wet, so fucking—

I groan, dropping my head on her shoulder as I thrust inside her.

"Deeper."

I go deeper.

"Harder."

I go harder.

My hand sinks into the wall. I want to mark her. Bite into her.

But if I'd thought I was burning before, she utterly shatters me when she says it—"Yours. I...am...yours."

Something burns through me. Building and building. A sensation unlike anything I've ever felt before, equal parts fire, equal parts absolution. And then...I lose myself and thrust as deep as I can. Silviana bites my shoulder as her walls clamp tightly all around me.

I remain still for long moments, just letting the water run over my back until it's cold. Only then do I let her feet touch the floor again, help her out of the shower, and gently dry her off. Silviana enjoys my ministrations in silence, a contented smile on her lips.

When I tug her after me into my room, and on the bed, she still doesn't seek distance. Instead, she curls into me, one leg over mine, her head on my chest.

"Wow." Silviana's breath on my skin has me laughing.

"You didn't say that the first time around."

"That's because you keep on improving."

She looks at me, kisses me, but as she pulls back I catch a shadow in her eyes.

"What's wrong?"

"Nothing, I... Just thinking about Fane." Her gaze shifts to the window. "I hope he's okay."

"There's no way they can figure out he helped us, so he will be fine. Trust in him."

A few hours later, I leave Silviana to sleep and head back downstairs. Alex is awake, by the window, watching the area outside.

"What's going on?"

He gestures to the outside. "Why don't you see for yourself?"

When I look, all I see is darkness and mist.

"Look closer."

After a moment, I see movement. Dark shapes—*furry* shapes.

"The wolves?"

Alex nods.

"Why haven't you woken up anyone else?"

"Because I'm tired of being the warning voice against these ones."

Rolling my eyes, I run back upstairs. First I wake Nico, then Liza, and then I head back to my room and gently shake Silviana awake. "You'd best come with me. The wolves are here."

We head back downstairs, where everyone's gathered around the fireplace. Liza's now by Alex's side near the window, frowning at the outside.

Nico stands. "I'll go talk to them."

"No, let me," I say. "It's me they saved, and... Let me try."

I head outside, Silviana trailing behind me. Out of the mist comes the redhead—Lucrezia—soon followed by her mate, Dominic, in human form. His expression is thunderous.

Without as much as a hello, he starts off. "Explain to me how I move here expecting a quiet life, and yet I'm dragged into your vampir drama before I can even unpack."

I run a hand over my face, exhaustion settling onto my shoulders. "We didn't know. All of this has become more than—"

"More than it should be, yeah." Dom's gaze moves behind me, then back to me. "You've got that damn right."

"What happened with the Grand Master and his cronies?" Silviana asks Lucrezia.

"They fled."

"Because you're a... what, exactly, are you? I've never seen a witch do what you did."

Lucrezia's blue eyes search my gaze, then move to Silviana. She smiles. "I'm a Solomonar."

Silviana frowns, while I gape in shock. "They were extinct! As were the zmei they served." *Just like the Dacians were supposed to be extinct...*

A wry smile twists Lucrezia's lips. "All except two. And I happen to call one of them my friend."

No amount of trying to wrap my mind around that works. I shake my head. "Would you like to come in for a drink? A regular drink, mind. It sounds like we have a lot to discuss."

Dominic looks like he'd protest, but Lucrezia silences him by sliding her palm into his. Fingers intertwined, she nods. "Lead the way."

I do the same with Silviana, and head back inside the castle. Liza and Alex have chosen to maintain their stand by the window, while Nico's presiding from an armchair. He gestures to the couch opposite him.

Lucrezia sits, but Dominic simply arches an eyebrow. "Did you misplace more family than this one?"

Nico pointedly ignores his pointed thumb in my direction. "Please, take a seat. I'm afraid Mirabela's out of town, and Violeta is otherwise occupied with Marcus."

"You mean one's out securing you new housing, and the other's putting out feelers for the vampir clans."

Nico's silence is telling. Dominic's no fool, I'll give him that. Problem is, his comment doesn't appease Alex.

"You're keeping tabs on us, now?" He snarls.

"Why would I waste resources doing that, when everyone already knows your business, fool?"

"Call me fool one more time—"

"Alex, enough." Nico lifts a hand, as if willing him to stay in place. "I'm sure Dominic didn't mean it as an insult. We have bigger things to focus on." He takes a deep breath, then says, "You'll have my eternal gratitude for helping save my brother."

"Yeah, how *did* you know about that, hmm?" Liza's sweet tone doesn't fool me, and I sense Silviana tensing by my side.

Lucrezia doesn't give a sign of being ticked off, at least not visibly. But when she tilts her head in Liza's direction, I could've sworn I saw lightning in her eyes. And judging by Silviana's sharp intake of breath, I'm not the only one.

"We knew about the Dacians from a mutually interested party. When it was clear they planned to eliminate one of you, we couldn't just sit by and not intervene. It took our wolves a few days to track down their whereabouts, hence the delay..." Lucrezia spares me a glance and a smile. "I'm glad we were there in time."

I incline my head. "Thank you, truly. I wouldn't be here without your help."

"This mutually interested party," Nico says, "would he happen to have a bone to pick with a certain god who wishes us harm?"

Lucrezia's smile turns blinding. "However did you guess?"

I think back to the conversation from earlier, outside the castle. And something dawns on me, followed by a dread thicker than I've ever felt.

"Earlier, when you said, 'all except two,' you meant the zmei. Not more Solomonari. The warlocks who used to ride the zmei are well and truly extinct, aren't they?"

Lucrezia simply inclines her head.

"So, the one you call a friend...is a zmeu."

Alex snorts. "What fairytale is this, brother? Zmei were extinct ages ago. You know that, Father schooled us in all manner of supernaturals."

I glare at him. "And doesn't it seem weird he mentioned all supernaturals *except* for gods and immortals?"

Alex says nothing, but I can tell the wheels are turning behind his eyes. Liza glances in the corner, but without me looking there, I know there's nothing to be found. Nothing visible to my eyes, at least.

Nico clears his throat. "Well, I dare say us and your *interested party* have something in common. As, it seems, we do with you. So, what brings you to our door?"

Dominic turns from the display he'd been intently starting at. "An alliance, unwelcome as it might be, it seems. When we moved here, we didn't realize to what extent your vampir drama would affect us."

"So, move out," Liza says.

Dominic throws her a bored look. To Nico, he says, "Needless to say, finding the perfect conditions for my pack to live in are not easy to come by. My blood is in this soil, and I'd prefer to stay here. Which is where helping you comes in."

"You may want to know the full facts," I say.

"Vlad—"

"No, Nico. They have a right to know." After a silent stare, he nods, and I continue, "It's not just the Dacians after us. Silviana is my consort, though they sent her here as bait for me. They intended to kill one of us, so the curse can never be undone."

"We figured as much," Lucrezia says. "The question is, why did they keep you for three days and not kill you?"

I stare at the ground. "Believe me, it wasn't for lack of torturing me. They wanted to use me as bait for my siblings. Seems they got greedy."

She nods, but doesn't seem convinced.

I turn to Dominic. "Vampir hunters and the clans are also after us. You could say we're not Transylvania's favorite people now."

Dominic sighs. "So it seems. What's the plan, then?"

Nico glances at his watch. "Well, Mirabela warned us she heard rumblings of an attack. The plan is to stay here, fight it off and send a message, and then head out to the new location she's prepared for us."

"And from there?"

Nico's cool expression tightens. "We don't need management."

Lucrezia sets a hand on Dominic's arm. No amount of her diplomacy can hide the way his muscles tense, as though ready to attack. "I think what my mate is trying to say is, where can we help?"

Liza snorts in her glass, but at least she doesn't try to dispute anything.

"You can help us make our stand," Nico says. "When they attack, we'll need to be protected from all sides. We can take on vampiri and even hunters, but the Dacians—if they come, we're nowhere prepared for them."

Dominic and Lucrezia share a look, then nod in tandem. Dominic says, "Bine. Tell us where to be, and we'll be there."

Chapter 23

Vlad

When we go up the stairs this time, after Lucrezia and Dominic have left, I follow Silviana back to her room. I can sense the tension and pensiveness around her, but I give her a moment. After all, my own thoughts are reeling.

Zmei. Solomonari. Out of all the creatures...

I sit on Silviana's bed while she goes for a shower, lost in my thoughts. Memories of Father schooling us on the supernatural world, on everything we'd face as royals, assail me. Why wouldn't he mention the zmei? Unless he didn't know that two had survived?

"What are the chances?" Silviana asks as she re-enters from the bathroom.

I glance up, my eyes taking in the towel she's got wrapped around her body, and the one around her wet hair. A corner of my mouth quirks. "Fashionable."

She rolls her eyes, then towel-dries her hair. I watch the smooth action of her hands, recalling other actions they'd performed. Her hands on me. Replaced by her mouth.

My sharp inhale draws her attention. With a grin and a look in her eyes just for me, she drops the towel for her hair and walks over to me. I'm hypnotized by the sway of her hips, even more so when she straddles my lap.

The towel around her body is close to unraveling, held together only by divine intervention. Or perhaps devilish, given how the swell of her breasts teases me.

"Vlad?"

"Hmm?"

She chuckles, then runs her hands through my hair. "I said, what are the chances? Of your father hiding the zmei from you, my coven hiding the truth from us... It just seems weird, is all."

I shake my head, trying to get it away from sex, and back to the present. "I'm not sure."

She bites her lip, then settles her forehead against mine. Her towel-dried strawberry-blonde locks fall all around us. "I had a dream, when I was under. Remember when I was in that cocoon of light?"

"Yeah...?"

"I think, I mean, I'm not sure, but the guy from the bar, Tytus? He showed up in my dream. He warned me against the Dacians and used the exact same words Lucrezia just did. *Interested party.*"

I pull back enough to search her eyes. "You think he's the zmeu?"

Silviana shrugs. The towel comes even closer to unwrapping her body to my gaze. "Not sure. Not like I know much about zmei, period."

"It definitely feels like we have a piece of the puzzle missing."

"You think Lucrezia and Dominic are hiding something?"

"No... Well, I don't know. It just seems odd, that they're willing to risk so many of their people to help us save ourselves."

"Maybe it's not about saving you, and more about fighting off Zalmoxis."

Her words spark something in my mind. An old tale Father told us, about zmei and... What was it?

I look up at Silviana, the dark gray of her eyes clouded by desire, and I forget myself. It won't be long until the attack, and the last thing I want is to spend our last quiet hours theorizing.

I reach up to cup the back of her neck, and pull her mouth to mine. With a groan, we tumble back on the bed, and forget the rest of the world.

The smell burns my nostrils first. Then, downstairs, Alex roars. "They're here! Get your asses up!"

It takes a second for my brain to sluggishly get back on track. And when it does, my entire body tenses.

I shake Silviana awake. "It's time."

We talked about this, in between lovemaking and theorizing. But even as she yanks herself out of sleep, I can tell she's distracted.

"What is it?"

"There's...something odd in the air." She stops, pulling on one of my sweatshirts. "Pass me the knife."

I glance at her athame blade, on the dresser by my side of the bed. "No, don't—"

"Please."

Grunting, I toss it her way. Silviana cuts into her palm, closes her eyes. I see a few red drops drip to the floor, and look away. She might trust me, but I still don't trust myself.

Her gasp soon has me pushing against my own impulses and looking at her. "What is it?"

She opens her eyes. "It's not just vampiri. There's a group of Dacians heading this way."

"Fuck!"

We'd known there was a chance for it, but we'd hoped otherwise. Nico's worried that using the wolves mean we're bound to owe them, something that makes Alex and Liza decidedly unhappy. Well, looks like we won't have much of a choice.

I open the door and we rush out. By the time we make it downstairs, fire reflects off the windows.

"Did you hear?" I ask Nico.

"Da, your voices carried. It's not good."

"Where are the wolves?"

"They'll be here. They promised."

"You're a fool for trusting them," Alex mutters.

Silviana

I know Alex and Liza don't want me here, their glares over their shoulders are enough to tell me so. But I'll be damned if I let Vlad face off against the Dacians without me.

"What's the plan?" I ask Nico. He, at least, will see fit to put me to good use.

He stares at his watch, making a face. Then he brings Tassa's hand to his mouth and drops a kiss. "Time to go, iubirea mea."

It makes sense he'll send her away. She could be collateral, and then all this will have been for nothing.

To me, he says, "You're coming with me and Tassa. Violeta and Marcus are waiting on the edge of the mountains, near Oradea. They'll keep her safe for a while, and you can help watch my back as we go."

I nod.

"Vlad, Liza and Alex—you go ahead and intercept the vampiri. The wolves will show up when the Dacians do."

"Three against a couple dozens," Alex mutters. "Gotta love the odds, brother."

Nico spares him a rare grin. "Not for long." Then he gestures at me, and takes Tassa to head outside.

Vlad grabs my wrist before I can leave. His gaze meets mine—fearful, for my safety. I force a smile, and raise my hand to his cheek. "I'll be okay. *You* be careful."

He lets me go, mindful of his siblings watching us like hawks. I'm almost glad to exit the castle.

Tassa breaks out of Nico's arms at my approach, wiping away her tears. She gives me a wobbly smile. "Hell of a night."

"I know." I want to tell her I'll help keep him safe, but I'm not sure if I can. So I keep my mouth shut and wait for his signal again.

Nico soon picks up Tassa in his arms, then glances at me. "Can you hang onto my neck?"

"Uhh..."

"Unless you'd rather walk?"

I shake my head. "I have a better idea." Using the athame, I slice into the cut already on my palm and let it bleed a little more. With a little incantation, the shadows around the castle converge at my feet, forming a fog that soon lifts me.

Nico arches an eyebrow. "That'll keep you going?"

"Until we reach our destination, yes. And I can still cast other spells."

He seems satisfied, at least enough to turn to the woods. "Time to go, then."

It feels like the run through the woods only lasts half an hour, maybe less—instead of the nearly three hours of a drive it would've been. Nico zigzags between the trees faster than lightning, and while I'm slower, I still manage to keep him in my sights.

We arrive at the rendezvous point on time. Violeta and Marcus step out of the trees. Unlike last time I'd seen her, Violeta's dark circles are lessened, and her color seems healthier—for a vampir. I take it as a good sign that me and Vlad being together has improved things for her, too, at least temporarily.

Nico lets Tassa back on the ground and buries his head in her neck. A moment later, almost abruptly, he hands her to Violeta. His voice is gruff as he says, "Protect her."

"With my life, brother," she says and takes Tassa's hand.

Marcus looks at him, then me. "You sure you don't need another hand?"

Nico shakes his head. "No. I know the military man in you wants to join in on the action. But the best thing you can do is keep my sister and my consort safe."

Marcus touches his fist to his chest, which I take it to mean his agreement.

Nico turns to me and points to his back. "Hop on, Silviana. This time, I'm driving."

The moment we're away from them, something tells me to be on high alert. At first, nothing sparks. But then I sense something in the woods and—

"Watch out!" I tap Nico's shoulder in time, and he crouches, avoiding by mere millimeters the two arrows headed for our heads.

He rolls and drops me to the ground, then gets back on his feet. Fangs extended, muscles tense, his ferocity is enough to send shivers up my spine. The four attackers coming out of the woods are, unfortunately, even worse-for-wear. Red eyes, human-looking otherwise, they seem to be out of their minds. Which isn't very reassuring, given their black-leather clothing and the crossbows in their hands.

Hunters. Just what we needed.

"Fuck," Nico mutters. "They're high on muroni blood. Watch your back."

"High on—"

I don't get a chance to ask questions. Nico lunges on the first one, ripping his throat out. He ducks the second's arrow, narrowly again, then a third jumps him from behind. I call upon my dark magic and cast a spell on the fourth attacker, binding him to a tree until its branches snap his spine. His lifeless body falls to the ground.

Nico's still fighting the third one, so I focus on the second. It's a woman, with wild eyes. She moves closer to me and something about her aura—her energy—sends me moving backward.

Her lips curl—she senses easy prey. But then her eyes widen, and she glances at the darkness sucking on her. It's my turn to grin. Her body drops to the ground, lifeless.

A panting Nico turns to face me, relief etched on his features at finding me alive.

"What was that about being high on muroni blood?"

He shakes his head. "Long story. I'll tell you on the way. If they found us, there must be more heading to the others. We should hurry."

I climb back on his back, and we're off once more.

Vlad

Engaging a gang of vampiri is nothing new. Alex, Liza and I spread into a triangle formation, same as we've done when hunting muroni clusters. We make quick work of the first ten, then wait and watch.

"Something's wrong," I mutter. "This is too easy."

Liza snorts. "You have a death wish or—"

Her words trail off on a cry of pain. I whirl on her, only to find an arrow embedded in her shoulder.

"Liza!" Alex moves to her, already positioning himself to protect her body from another attack. He catches the next arrow with his bare hands, and tosses it back to the attacker hidden in the woods. A gurgling sound lets us know it found its target.

With a groan, Liza yanks the arrow out. She frowns at the blood-tinged tip. "Silver. Cleansed with holy water, judging by the stink." She tosses it aside, scowling. "Boys, get ready. We've got some hunters on our tail."

Given her murdering urges when it comes to them, I know we're in for a bloodbath.

I think what neither of us are prepared for is a group of vampiri *and* hunters emerging from the trees. Instead of fighting each other, the dozen of them are split into pairs. One hunter watching each vampir's back.

"What the fuck?" Alex snarls.

My thoughts exactly.

Then, muscle memory takes over. "This changes nothing," I yell. "We go!"

As one, we attack, zigzagging. At first, we're successful, because they can't pin us down fast enough to use their crossbows. But, soon, their arrows find more marks than misses.

Liza limps to me after killing one. "Vlad, I can't believe I'm saying this, but we might have to retreat."

I stare at the meadow we're in—more vampiri seem to emerge from the trees. The last thing I want to do is retreat, but we're no good to anyone dead.

Just as I'm about to give the signal to retreat, a whistle resounds from the trees. And then another set of vampiri pop out.

"We're so fucked!" Alex yells.

But instead of coming for us, the vampiri are attacking the others. My eyes widen.

"No, Alex. They're here to help us. Look at the emblems on their cloaks!"

"I've been a little too busy surviving to check out their fashion sense—"

"Just look, dammit!"

He finally does as I ask, and I know what he's seeing. An M for the Munteanu clan.

It must be what Nico meant. Someone sent word to them to

come and help us.

It's with relish that we jump back into the fray, this time energized, and knowing we're not alone.

I'm halfway through ripping out another vampir's throat, followed by his hunter, when I sense her presence in the meadow. I stop mid-strike, looking around—

"Vlad!"

Alex barrels into me, sending me flying. I rise in a crouch, snarling and ready to tear into him—but bite my words. He's taking a stake out of his side, grimacing.

He tosses me a glare. "This isn't the time for a distraction! Get your human out of here!"

I go to Silviana, but she's tossing spells. Problem is, I know I won't be able to pull her back. Not when she's this focused. She has something to prove.

But she has no choice. I won't give her one, because I won't lose her.

So I rush at her instead, grabbing her by the waist, and take her back to the castle. When I deposit her on the ground, moments later, I'm met by her shocked gaze, soon followed by realization.

"Don't you dare leave me behind!"

I cup her cheeks. "Do you think I wish to? I never want to be parted from you. But I cannot allow you to put yourself in danger again."

"I can help. I have magic."

"And they know all your tricks."

"Vlad—"

I press my mouth to hers, stealing the objections on her lips, until she's clinging to me. Then I leave at vampire speed, before her pleas get to me.

On my way to the clearing, I notice more vampiri laying out traps. The moment I catch Nico and Liza's attention, I wave them over. "We need to move. The Munteanu clan have this, we need to pick off the ones in the woods."

Liza nods. "I'll let Alex know to watch his back here."

When Violeta had to fight off vampiri to save Marcus, I thought I understood her pain. But it's nothing like what I now feel leaving Silviana behind. The only thing that keeps me focused is that I'm the first line of defense and this is my chance to keep the promise I made to her brother.

The vampiri who clash with us are strong—some old, some young. And they've come prepared, with everything from swords to stakes. Only problem is, they were never trained by Vlad Dracul the Third. And we were.

Without even consulting, we split again in a triangle formation that allows us to take on everyone while at the same time keeping an eye out on each other's backs. We don't bother with weapons. Our hands and bodies are it.

Liza, despite her small stature, easily takes on five bigger than her. Nico, in complete contradiction, moves slowly—until they strike. His quick jabs and hooks are enough to dizzy his opponents and leave them fucked. He's ruthless—taking their weapons and beheading everything in sight. It would be concerning, but his performance only enhances my own bloodlust.

It takes me until the third kill to realize what's going on—I'm salivating for vampir blood. And once that realization hits me, nothing else matters. I want to sink my fangs into my next victim with an intensity that shouldn't be possible.

The next idiot is mine—and once I partake of his blood, nothing else matters. Only the next one. And the next. And with each feed, I'm moving faster, with more accuracy than I've ever had. Feeling stronger. Invincible.

Vaguely, I register the vampiri's looks of horror, and confusion. It's not until I face off against Liza that something hits me as being wrong. I stop...and take in the carnage. Blood drips off my clothes, my hair, my face, my hands.

"What—who—"

Liza gulps. "You did this."

And then pain shoots up my spine. Fire. I drop to the ground. Liza comes to protect me, but my gaze is on another. Ştefan, Silviana's brother, emerging from behind a tree.

My eyes scan the woods—are more Dacians here?

As he advances toward me, there's a warning in Ştefan's eyes, but Liza attacks. I want to scream at her to stop, but it's too late. She slams into him, and they fall to the ground. It takes Ştefan a moment to get his bearings—long enough for Liza to punch him, hard. Then she reaches for a rock to her side, and my eyes widen.

"Liza, *no!*"

Only, to my surprise, instead of bashing his head in, she drops the rock and stumbles off him, as though in shock. Ştefan reaches for her and catches air, but Liza's already gone, disappearing into the trees.

What the hell?

The other Dacians, however, aren't playing. And it's the intensity of their attacks that tells me something else about Ştefan —his attack on me wasn't as real as it could've been.

Without waiting for another vampir to take him on, I do. The force of me tumbling into him sends us flying backward. Ştefan gives an *oompf* of pain as his back hits the tree. I pretend to punch him in the stomach, but stop short of actually hitting him.

"Bend over!" I hiss.

Ştefan's expression gives away his recognition of my voice, and then, a half second later, he bends over. I lean over him, as if to grab his neck, and drop my voice to a whisper. "Silviana's fine."

Relief's on his face. Then he lunges up, his head smacking mine. He follows it by a few punches—I make an easy target, stunned as I am. Moments later, magic surrounds us—a faint fog.

Ştefan wrestles me to the ground. "I don't have much time. You need to get Silviana away."

"Where?"

His hand finds my forehead and he presses—hard. Images hit me—a map. And then he lets go.

"In two days, I'll meet you there. Be safe until then."

Chapter 24

Silviana

Vlad may not want me to go with him, but it doesn't mean I can't do something to help him and his siblings. Their strength comes from the same blood as Dacian magic. Which means if I can strengthen them and weaken the Dacians... it'll be worth it.

I may not be as strong as Fane, but I'm not useless. Still got a couple of tricks up my sleeve.

I run inside the castle, stopping by the kitchen and picking up salt, sage and lavender. My second pit stop is by the library, where the Dracul siblings left the scroll I'd nicked from the Grand Master. Time to put it to good use.

Once I'm inside my room, I push away the faded carpet until the hardwood floor is all I see. In my palm, I roughly mix the sage, lavender and salt, then sprinkle it in a circle. Hopefully, the positive energy in the elements will keep the spell contained.

But if it worked to get the Grand Master to make a deal with Zalmoxis, then maybe it'll work to gain me access to enough power to cast a shield of protection on all of them...and syphon off the Dacians' energy. *Hopefully it'll be as easy as Fane made it sound.*

I take a deep breath, focus on the images again, and squeeze my palm until blood starts flowing freely from the cut. Step by step, I use the hardwood floor as my canvas, until I've drawn everything as it should be.

When I'm done, I take a step back, toss the scroll in the middle, and call upon fire. Flames the color of ice ignite the paper in a whoosh. As they burn, they take the essence of the Grand Master with them.

Then, and only then, do I start intoning the spell. I close my eyes, keeping my intention focused on what I need—power. More power, to do good. Good, good, good, always good.

Images of Dad's smiling face cluster in my mind. His warnings about magic, about consequences. My gut clenches in a painful reminder that what I'm doing is risky.

Vlad needs this. I need this.

As I focus more and more, I feel the blood keep dripping by my side. The windows burst open, and a strong gust of wind follows. My hair flies all around my face, but still I don't stop, repeating the incantation, focusing on my magic.

But something...something's wrong. I feel it in the air, in the electricity tinging everything around me. When I open my eyes, darkness is all around me, like a fog. My heartbeat picks up.

This isn't supposed to happen.

I try to slow down, to focus back on my intentions, but it's as if the darkness has a mind of its own now. It twirls and twirls, forming random patterns in the air.

The wind stops whipping at my cheeks. But the darkness doesn't stop moving. Instead, it meshes together, forming a shape…

I take a step backward. "W-who are you?"

The creature in its depths moves forward, as if wanting to step out of the shadows. But they hold him back. I can see it's a man now, with a long beard.

"I am who you called upon…."

The voice makes me shudder—deep, rough, a voice of the Otherworld.

"Zalmoxis."

A dark chuckle escapes him. "You called upon me. Why fear me now?"

Because I was stupid. Because I didn't realize how dangerous this could be. Because…

This might not be what I'd intended, but there's no reason I can't use it. Time to get some answers the Dracul siblings can use.

"I do not." I lift my chin up, forcing myself to portray a strength I'm nowhere close to feeling. "I need answers."

"I have all the time to give the answers you seek, human. What is it you wish to know?"

"Why are the remaining Dacians trying to call upon you? Why do they hunt the heirs?"

"They hunt the heirs at my command."

"What?"

The chuckle grows darker. And then he's in my head, drawing

into my memories. I lash back—only to be catapulted into his pain, his raw anger... The floor moves underneath me, undulating, and when I glance down, I see a pit of darkness. And a face, terrible in its wrath, opening its mouth—

"NO!"

But it's too late. Darkness climbs all over me, and with it, the presence. Past my calves, my knees, my thighs, my torso, up my throat, into my nostrils... I simultaneously choke on something and am unable to draw air through my nose. My mouth opens in a silent scream, even as I claw at my throat in desperation.

There's no escaping this. No escaping the slithering entity in my mind, pushing past my boundaries, pulling at my memories. Mom, Dad, Fane...and then everything goes black.

I open my eyes, but I'm not my usual height. Instead, I'm tiny. To my side, Fane waves, his eyes bright and...*seeing*. We're outside in a field—playing it seems. It feels as though I woke up from a terrible nightmare, but my brother's there to make it all better.

"Come, Lana! Food is ready!"

Giggling, I follow him over the hill, and back home. Except...it's not the home I remember. Not the one I have pictures of, at my apartment. The village looks a few hundred years older, for one. And our house, painted in white with dark window frames, is olde worlde—purposefully made to seem old—like I've seen in those live museums around the countryside.

Fane crosses the threshold and into the house without a care, but I find myself slowing down. Taking it all in. If I look down the street, I can see horse-drawn carriages; women carrying buckets of water; men returning, sweaty, from the fields.

What's going on?

More giggles from inside the house pull me in. I walk inside, my wide eyes taking everything in—the lack of a stove; the cold ground, with a handsewn rug covering it; a wooden table, with wooden bowls and spoons. In a corner, on the fire pit, a large bucket's boiling, hanging from the ceiling. A stew aroma comes from it.

"Davide!"

I turn, no longer interested in the food. My mom and dad are embracing by the window. Foreheads resting against each other, noses touching, they're the picture of love. Fane stares at them, munching on a loaf of bread.

Mom turns to me, handing me a loaf as well. "To keep you going until the food is ready."

"Did someone say food?"

I turn, and an elderly woman walks in. I shouldn't know her—I don't have any pictures of her. But her white hair, pulled in a braid, and slightly stooped posture are immediately familiar.

The young me opens her mouth and says, "Buni!"

But then, behind her, a black hole opens. Dark laughter echoes, and the image around me disappears, fading away, until I'm all alone. And still he's laughing, and laughing, and laughing.

You're mine now, Zalmoxis whispers in my head.

And no matter how loud I scream, all he does is laugh.

Vlad

The magic is too strong. Even with a few of the vampiri dead, it's clear they have more control over what they're doing. A leg up on us. At least until the wolves come. The minute their furry bodies step into the meadow, the tide changes.

Lucrezia follows in their wake, surrounded by lightning. It sizzles and crackles around her, as though it's protecting her. When a sorcerer tries to stop her, she zaps him back—he doesn't get up again.

Another, younger one, tries to attack her. "What the hell are you?"

"I'm something older than you can understand." She smiles. "Best not to try."

Fire surrounds her and takes him apart. She's just as ruthless as we are—but then again, she has a mate and a son to protect.

By the time she takes control of the scene, I'm thankful. At least until her gaze turns to the castle. Fire fills the air, smoke and ash. And a sense of foreboding fills me, clogging my throat.

I stop dead in my tracks. Nico turns. "What is it?"

My chest feels like I can't breathe. My mind is filled with—nothingness. I had Silviana there, before. But now it's blank.

I turn, in the distance seeing the outline of our castle. And something like a dark cloud above it.

"I have to go back."

"What?" Lucrezia asks. "Why?"

"Because—No! Silviana!"

I'm moving before anyone can stop me. She can't be harmed—she *can't*! I haven't gone through all this shit to lose her now. I refuse, dammit. I can't be losing her, not now, not ever.

But it's like my feet won't bring me as fast as they usually do. By the time I get to the castle, it's for a window to explode. And another.

"SILVIANA!"

Ash clogs my throat. Some lonely vampir tries to come at me, and I eliminate him like a mosquito. And then I burst into the castle. Heat upon my skin, blazing ashes everywhere—but I keep going. I have to find her.

I burst into her room. Take in the drawings on the ground—runes?—and the dark fog she's in.

She's on the floor, a shape taking hold of her. I remember what she did last time, and cut my hand. The darkness takes over, drinks the blood, and the shape disappears.

"Silviana!" I pick her up in my arms, holding her to my chest. Something like sorrow rises inside me. "Please. Please be all right."

She stirs in my arms, and I look at her—but it's not gray eyes that look back. It's cold obsidian ones, with a hint of malice in them. And then she blinks, the gray is back, and her eyes roll in the back of her head as she faints.

All I can do is hold her, rocking back and forth, hoping I haven't lost her.

It takes the better part of half a day for Silviana to wake up. Only to fall right back asleep. Nico, Alex and Liza come back, reporting the Dacians are gone, no traces left. None of Ștefan, either. The wolves returned to their area, and we're without answers once again.

So I return to Silviana's chamber, and climb in her bed, holding her against me. She feels colder, like the events—whatever they were—drained her.

An hour later, she moves against me, her eyelashes flutter, and she opens her eyes.

"You're awake!"

"I... what happened?"

"I was hoping you could tell me."

She tries to think, crunches her face, as if she's in pain. "Sorry, I'm drawing a blank. I know.... I know I was trying to help you. To find out why the Dacians were invoking such dark magic, and..." She shakes her head. "I'm sorry, it hurts so much when I try to remember."

"It's okay, it's okay." I hold her closer to my chest. "You're okay."

But she's not okay. She's trembling in my arms, and it feels like nothing will ever be right again. Whatever that was, whatever attacked her, it was in here. In her room, in this castle.

In. Her. Mind.

Silviana

It's the middle of the night. I'm aware of the darkness even in my sleep, even with Vlad's arms around me. He's constantly whispering, coaxing me into doing his bidding. When I'm not thinking, he's there. When I'm not moving, or keeping my mind occupied, he's there. Incessantly whispering.

Every hour that I'm not awake, it feels like he takes over me more. Even in my sleep, at first all I felt was a caress. Like someone touching me. Then I realized it wasn't from outside, but from the inside of my body. It was coaxing my muscles into moving. And then my mind into staying asleep.

And then he's...my hand is moving... and I—

"NO!"

I jump out of bed, magic seeping out of my hands, unbidden, uncalled. I'm not bleeding anywhere, so how can it be ready to answer my call?

"Silviana, it's me," Vlad whispers, somewhere close by.

But I can't see him. *Why can't I see him!?*

"She won't hear you."

I blink at the darkness. At the cloaked figure emerging out of the shadows. Him, I see. His presence seems to be almost glowing, radiating an inner light. "F-Fane?"

"I'm here, sorella. I've got you."

I run into his arms, hoping he'll chase the dark monsters away, same as he did when we were children. Nothing else will help. No one else can get through. Only Fane.

Behind me, I hear a door closing, and know Vlad has left. Part of me feels guilty, but the other part is too relieved to see Fane here.

I pull a little out of his arms and glance up at him. "How did you know I needed you?"

He reaches for my face, his fingers tracing my features. "Because I always feel your pain, Lana. Even from far away." His hand drops. "Can we sit, and you can tell me what happened? I don't have long until I have to return."

I nod, and lead him to a small couch by the window. "How did you even get here?"

Fane makes a face. "I took a page out of the Grand Master's book and created a portal."

"I'm sorry, *what?* How is that even possible? Our magic—"

Fane shakes his head. "There is so much we were told that were lies. But it doesn't matter. Point is, I'm here, and we have limited time. Tell me everything."

"I don't even know how much of it is real and how much…"

"Just try, Lana. Please."

After a beat of hesitation, I acquiesce. The darkness in my head is too strong to keep it all to myself. "I was trying to help the vampiri. Thought that I could reach into the darkness, somehow drain the Dacians who were attacking. But…I opened the way to something much darker."

"Zalmoxis."

Tears fill my eyes, spilling on my cheeks. "I feel like I have no control over myself, Fane. I woke up with magic at the ready, nearly attacking Vlad!"

"Shh." Fane squeezes my hand in his, then urges, "Keep going, Lana. What else?"

"I… Zalmoxis, he entered me. My mind. I don't know how to explain it. But when he did, I started seeing things. With…you and me. As kids. With Dad, and Mom…and Buni. We were so happy, Fane. But they weren't…the memories didn't make sense."

His hand on mine squeezes harder, almost to the point of pain. "Why not? What didn't make sense?"

"Well. The pictures we have, at the compound, of our old home all show a modern one. What I saw, in the images, was an olde worlde home. Like those types made out of mud with reinforced cement. White outside, dark window frames. Dark roof. And in the kitchen, when Mama was making food, it was…it was old. I mean, pre-1900 old. There was no stove. No heating. No modern appliances."

Fane's hold on my hand releases, and he leans against the couch. A loud sigh escapes him. "Da, I thought as much. Zalmoxis entering your mind, it undid whatever block was put in there by the Grand Master. The same block I've had, which after you left, I found a way to undo."

I gape at him, though he can't see me. "*How*?"

"Using the counter-spell to the Grand Master's. It wasn't easy, and it needed a helluva lot of blood. But it was worth it, once I knew the truth."

I gulp. "So you're saying he, what, altered our memories?"

"That's exactly what I'm saying. I reread all the journal entries we copied from Țepeș's journal, too. And I went through more of Liviu's forbidden books. As far as I can tell, Dacians were always able to live longer lifetimes, two to three times the length of regular human lifetimes."

"So...up to what, one hundred and fifty years old?"

"Or two hundred, sometimes. We see it less now because of the curse that affected the vampiri. Zalmoxis was, according to the information I found, pissed off at the Grand Master for not finding Țepeș and hurting him before he killed himself. As a result, the Dacians' magic started wavering. Lifetimes became less lengthy. And the price we pay for our magic has become...much steeper."

I take in his pale skin tone, paler than normal, and bite my lip. "How much blood did you have to use for the portal, and the counter-spell?"

"A lot. But it doesn't matter." He takes a deep breath, then says, "As far as I've been able to gather, Dad was around twenty-something when he met Țepeș in 1769." He pauses. "You know your vampir's history?"

I frown at him. "Da, I was given a file on him before my mission. It covered the basics. That he made a living as a mercenary, but became a teddy bear after being turned. Or, so it was thought."

Fane nods. "Right. I didn't want to shock you, is all. So Vlad—your vampir, I mean—told me when I released him that in 1707 he was sent to kill a pregnant woman. He didn't, because Țepeș intervened. That's when he turned him. But the woman...her name was Florinela."

My jaw drops. "Florinela?! That was *Buni*'s name!"

"Yep. Believe me, it shocked the hell out of me, too. So Țepeș saved our grandma from near death. The child she carried was our dad. Who then met Țepeș when he was older, and became friends with him. Whether Dad ever knew that Țepeș saved Grandma or not, I don't know. But then Țepeș sent his heirs into hiding, a few decades after he met Dad, so in the 1790s. And shortly after, he killed himself. Dad paid for their friendship, because he was found out."

Tears fall down my cheeks now, recalling what the Grand Master sneered at when I'd battled him. "Liviu told me why. He said when Țepeș turned Vlad, it was the first time they'd caught sight of him in ages. His appearance gave them a new chance to follow him, to keep tabs on him. But then he killed himself, right under their noses. And... After he was buried, Dad went to the grave. To return the journal, that Țepeș had left him to keep." I wipe at my cheeks. "If he hadn't gone, they never would've known. He'd be alive, not killed by his own kin!"

Fane opens his arms, and I bury myself in them again, in his familiar embrace. Sobs wreck my body, but even while I cry, I'm aware of the darkness in my mind. Of Zalmoxis, patiently waiting for the moment when I'm unaware once more, before he strikes.

Eventually, I quiet down. It takes everything in me not to give in to the sleepiness and fall asleep.

"Fane..."

"Mm?"

"You know this means we're practically, what, over a hundred years old?"

"One hundred and twenty-three, by my calculations."

"Wow." And to think I'd thought Vlad was ancient.

I burrow in Fane's arms once more. "Will you stay, please?"

"As long as I can, sorella. As long as I can."

Vlad

I give them a moment. Exiting the room, but not leaving the area. I'm glad Silviana thinks it's okay, but I've got questions for her brother. Starting with how he knew something was wrong.

Liza waltzes down the hallway, wiping at her mouth. "Jeez. When's the last time you ate something?"

"A while."

She stops in her tracks, tilting her head. "Is that why you're so grumpy?" She sniffs the air, inching closer. "Wait, no. There's another human. A *male* one." Her gaze meets mine, frowning. "What's going on? I know that scent."

The door opens before I can say anything, and out comes Ştefan. Now that I'm out of the caves, back to my regular self, I don't see him as a threat anymore. His blind gaze looks around, and settles on Liza with uncanny accuracy.

"Who brought this stray in?" she asks. "And can you tell it not to stare at me?"

Hmm. Why is she acting like she didn't just fight him off in a meadow, and ran off like a cat scared of water?

"*He* can hear you," Ştefan says. "I'm blind, not deaf."

"My bad," she mutters, and waves at me, taking off. "Later, Vlad. Enjoy. Or...not."

I scowl at her, then turn my attention to Ştefan. I'll have to figure out Liza's weird mood later. "Sorry about that. How did you know Silviana was in danger?"

He touches his fist to his chest, rubbing as though it hurts him. His voice is barely above a whisper when he speaks. "I felt it. We've always had a connection, but I *felt* the darkness enter her, as though it was entering me. I knew I couldn't wait until the deadline I'd given you, not if she was in danger." He shifts toward me a little more, dropping his fist. "I was hoping you could tell me more. What happened, exactly?"

I run a hand through my hair, then lean against the wall. I'm unwilling to leave her side, despite the answers he seeks. "After you did that thing...in the forest. I was fighting, and sensed something was wrong. I came here and found her, on the floor. There were runes all around. Nico sent pictures to Lucrezia, she said she doesn't recognize them. I don't know what to think."

I glance inside the room, at Silviana's sleepy form. Whatever Ştefan did, at least it got her to rest.

"There was something else. Her eyes...they were dark. Unlike her. But then she blinked and it disappeared. But I feel..."

"More?"

I nod, unsure what else to say. "Something like that. In the bond, there's a faint presence, like it comes and goes."

Ştefan scowls. "It's Zalmoxis. At least, it's what Lana said."

A shiver runs up my spine. I don't get scared easily. But the way he says that name...

"I can't stay," he says. "If my people find me gone, they'll come after me, too. And it'll serve a bigger purpose if I stay behind, for now."

I shake my head. "Silviana wants you safe. We can protect you, same as we will her."

His mocking smile hits me hard. "Protect me? You misunderstand, vampir. No one can protect me, not after what I've learned." He waits a beat, then adds, "Did you know? About our age?"

"Know what, exactly?"

"Liviu. He said nothing, while he kept you?"

"I would tell you if he had."

Ștefan lets out a sigh. "The Grand Master wanted you for your essence. He admitted that much, correct?" At my whisper of assent, he adds, "Up until recently, I thought—as did Silviana—that we were normal. Aged like mortals, except for our magic. But that's not the case."

The scent of blood hits my nostrils first, then Ștefan mutters an incantation, and a small orb of light glows. When it's gone, two sheets of paper float in his outstretched hand. He shoves them in my direction.

"Show this to your siblings, before leaving. It might come in handy, or at the very least buy Silviana more favor with them."

I glance at the papers, written in old Romanian, then back at him. "I don't understand. How did you even read these?"

Ștefan waves his hand in an impatient gesture. "I can use magic to turn any written text into Braille. After Lana left, Liviu and most of the Dacians took off after her. I used their absence to make copies in Braille of every piece of paper I could find in his study. Anything useful, I re-spelled to its original form. Which is how I brought you this. Liviu will never know it's missing from his papers, because the original is still there."

"I've never known witches to be so…"

"Yes, well, Dacians are special. Our magic can do anything, for a price."

I frown as something else he'd said sinks in. "Hang on a second. What did you mean when you said, 'before leaving'?"

"I'll explain in a second. The papers—show your siblings. They'll prove what I'm about to tell you." He clears his throat, then continues, "Dacians used to be able to live for a long time. Not as long as vampiri did, but we could easily live for two, sometimes three, human lifetimes. After your father killed himself, shortly after the last entry in his journal in 1796, our Grand Master received a dream from Zalmoxis."

"Liviu?"

"No, not him. The guy before him. His name matters not, but the rest of this will."

Something about the tension in his body tells me as much.

"When Țepeș killed himself, Zalmoxis said the Dacians didn't live up to their purpose. That for centuries, they were unable to get Țepeș, to make him hurt, and that Zalmoxis himself would have to do the job they had failed to do now. *But* he was so infuriated, and he wanted to make sure they had enough of an incentive to hunt down the rest of the House of Dracul...that he gave them the perfect reason to."

It dawns on me then, like a missing puzzle piece. "My essence. A vampir's essence is pure darkness, and if absorbed would mean, what, a longer life?"

Ștefan nods. "The papers I gave you are copies of records Liviu keeps under lock and key. But, in short, you are correct. Without the essence of a vampir, the Dacians were to slowly lose their magic. Little by little. To give you an idea of our longevity, our father met yours back in 1769."

My jaw drops. "Wait. You're saying you and Silviana are..."

"No, we're not *that* old. Father didn't have us until much later, in the 1890s. Records of our birth in old Dacian archives also support this fact."

I do the math quickly in my head. "So you're a little over 120 years old."

"That sounds about right."

I glance at the door, sensing Silviana's sleepy presence beyond it. "But why... How did neither you, nor Silviana know about this?"

He gives me another rueful smile. "Because after your father sent you into hiding, *our* father paid for his friendship to a vampire with his life. And when he died, Liviu, who'd been Grand Master for the last half a century by then, altered our memories." He takes a deep breath, dropping his head. "I thought something was weird. I've never felt like I belonged in this century...but I put it off to my blindness. And then, when Zalmoxis entered Silviana's mind, it broke the lie. The spell disintegrated, and images from the past—our real past—unfurled in Silviana's mind. I have no doubt they're the truth."

"I... Don't know what to say."

He raises his head, blinking slowly. "There's nothing to be said. I mention all of this not to commiserate, but to give you information to share with your siblings. Enough so they understand Silviana isn't a threat, and they don't try to split you apart."

Something about his tone raises my doubts. "What are you planning to do? You speak as if you won't be around to protect her."

Ștefan says nothing for a long beat. Then, "You can't deal with what's happening to her here. Not when there are so many of you, and darkness feeds on it."

His words have the desired effect, and distract me. "What do you mean?"

"Your siblings embrace darkness. Especially the one who was here. Zalmoxis wants to fuck with you all. Do you honestly think he won't try?"

"You're saying…"

"I'm saying you need to bring Silviana away from here. Remember the coordinates I left in your mind?"

"Da."

"Go there. Don't delay."

Needless to say, my siblings aren't too happy about me taking orders from a Dacian.

"You're fucking crazy," Alex says.

On the phone, Mirabela and Violeta are quiet. Unsurprising, because they probably agree. Liza settles for just glaring at me. Nico, Tassa by his side once again, looks at the papers I gave him—the ones from Ștefan —and nods.

"I get it," he says. "You have to protect her, and you also have to protect us. Go do what you have to do."

I leave as soon as the words are out of his mouth.

"Vlad, wait!"

I shake Liza off. "No. No. And *no*. I'm not going to let some deity take away something I've waited my entire life for. Just because of an issue he had with our father."

"She's just a human. There must be—"

I'm in her face the moment after. "You think I waited this entire time for *just a human*? You know what I lived through, Liza. And I pray you never have to live through as much as I have. Immortal or not, I don't think your heart could survive it."

"I don't have a heart," she mutters behind me.

I let it go and keep walking.

When I enter the room, Silviana turns away from the window. I've got her in my hands, cupping her cheeks, kissing her like this alone will take away his imprint on her.

I pull back for just a moment. "I will not let anything happen to you. If Zalmoxis wants to hurt us, he'll have to take me first, because I'm not letting him own you."

And then I'm kissing her again, and she's melting against me, and I push away her clothes, removing mine in turn, all in a mindless desire, a raging urge to be inside her, to feel her heat around me, to...

I lift her up, perch her butt on the dresser and then I'm between her legs, thrusting inside her. She arches, offering me her breasts, bare from clothing, and I feast on them. Nicking the skin just enough to draw blood, just enough to have a drop.

Silviana moans, clenching her inner walls around me, wrapping her legs around my waist and pulling me closer. The door opens behind us and I snarl over my shoulder, "Get out!"

Whoever it is, they're gone, but neither of us cares, because we're lost in the haze of desire. The one thing that's sure enough, the one thing that's strong enough to wipe away everything else from our minds.

After she's come around me, and I've emptied myself in her, I pick her up and bring her to the bathroom. Turning on the shower, without ever letting her go, I bring us inside it. And as the water beats on her skin and mine, mingling with our tears, I reiterate my promise. "He won't have you. I swear it."

Silviana's sleepy against me when I pick her up in the middle of the night. "Where are we going?"

"Somewhere safe."

"But Fane can't find me?"

"He's coming, darling. I promise. It was his idea."

I don't know if it's the best move. But my siblings need to deal with finding us a new home and I can't afford to be distracted. Nico gave his blessing, so the best I can hope for is that it'll be enough for the rest to eventually stop being pissed at me.

Soon as I'm away, I follow the images Ștefan left in my mind. Oddly enough, it doesn't take much effort. Soon, the surroundings fade away. And then I'm in front of a cabin. From the outside, it looks deserted. I step inside and settle Silviana on a comfy bed, covering her with a blanket.

And then the waiting begins. I try to stay by her side in case she wakes with another nightmare, but she sleeps soundly.

With the sun rising, she keeps sleeping. But outside, the world wakes—and three shapes emerge from the woods. Ștefan, Lucrezia and Dominic.

I step outside. "Is this safe?"

"Yes." Ștefan nods. "And if we want to have a chance, we'll need help. I brought the only two people who know more than we do."

"About Zalmoxis?" I stare at the wolf. He shrugs.

Dominic shrugs. "Not me." He jerks his thumb out to Lucrezia. "Her."

Ștefan must pick up on the annoyance in his tone, as he adds, "This is my sister we're talking about. We exhaust all possibilities. It's non-negotiable."

After a beat, I nod, and they follow me inside the cabin. Dominic stays outside, presumably to keep an eye out. The moment we're inside, Lucrezia walks to the bed.

Silviana stirs awake, and her eyes settle on Lucrezia, then on her brother. "Fane!"

He moves toward the sound of her voice and perches on the bed, reaching for her hand. "I'm here, sorella. I'm here."

Lucrezia gently touches Silviana's forehead. She tries to move away from her hand, but Lucrezia shakes her head. "Let me."

"What exactly are you doing?"

"Trying to feel—" She frowns and removes her hand as if burned.

The door opens, and Dominic pokes his head in, as if he'd felt whatever she did.

Lucrezia's gaze goes to him. "You were right. We need Tytus for this."

Tytus. I know that name. Silviana was right, the guy from the bar is the zmeu that's been right under our noses. I guess this explains why I felt he was something much larger than any of us...

Dominic grinds his teeth, then nods. "Ileana will know where he is. I'll be back within the day." He looks at us, then walks to his mate and gives her a lingering kiss. I catch the whispered, "Watch yourself."

"Is Tytus the zmeu, then?" I ask the moment he's gone, needing confirmation.

Lucrezia sighs. "Da. One of the last of his kind."

Silviana swallows hard. "But they're—"

"Your only hope. They were created to protect gods. They can also show you how to fight them." She meets my gaze. "Unless you have a better idea of getting rid of the one in your mate's head?"

Silviana buries herself in my chest. And I have no better answer.

Chapter 25

Vlad

Lucrezia goes outside with Fane, leaving me and Silviana alone again. That desire to obliterate everything and everyone runs through me once more, but I try to hold it in check.

At least until she looks at me, a silent pleading in her eyes. A pleading to make her forget.

I push off the wall I'd been leaning against and move to the bed, kneeling in front of her. "It will be all right."

"A zmeu, though? Vlad—"

"It's not that unlikely. And if he can help, then that's all I care about." I cup her cheeks, nuzzling her nose with mine. "I don't recognize myself with you, Silviana. My demons disappear, and all I want is for yours to be gone, too. So you don't have to worry about this craziness. And if it means I have to learn how to take on a god, then I will do it. For you. To have you free."

Tears fill her eyes and she throws her arms around my neck, burying her nose in my chest. Her soft body presses against mine, driving my mind to other places.

As if feeling it, she pulls back. Her breathing changes. Her lips are within an inch of mine.

"We'll have to be quiet," she whispers.

I'm already reaching for her long skirt, pushing through the material to find her underwear—she's so ready for me already.

"Very quiet," I agree in her ear.

And then steal the moan that leaves her when my hand finds that spot she loves.

A strong wind outside wakes me. Then the ground shakes as something incredibly heavy lands. I tense, rising from the makeshift bed. Silviana rises with me. A slight shudder goes through her.

"Wait here," I whisper and rush outside.

Lucrezia and Ștefan are speaking with a dark-haired man, Dominic nowhere to be seen. He's taller than Ștefan by a head, and large without being overly bulky. In jeans and a long-sleeved shirt, he could be someone casual—until his gray gaze collides with mine. A gaze I'd definitely seen, once before...in a pub, talking to Silviana.

His lips move, and I hear him from afar, "Is that him?"

Lucrezia glances over her shoulder and nods. "That's Vlad, the mate."

"And where's the girl?"

I move closer, no longer intending to stay away. "You don't get to see her just yet. Not until you explain to me what you were doing sniffing around her, mere days ago."

Lucrezia's eyes widen. I guess she doesn't know everything, after all.

Tytus' gaze never leaves mine as he says, "Perhaps I was simply an interested party."

A snort leaves my lips. "Nice try. Lucrezia already used that line."

They share an amused look, then she says, "He can be trusted. He's one of the cool-minded ones."

If she's referring to me and my siblings, she clearly doesn't know about my history. Not that I'm about to enlighten her.

"Cool-minded or not," Tytus says, "it's not him I'm interested in. It's his girl."

Everything about his words sends my primal senses into overdrive. But all that comes out is, "What do you plan to do?"

Lucrezia sighs. "Vlad, we discussed this. No one else can help your mate. Tytus alone has the knowledge for what the gods are like. So unless you want Zalmoxis to strengthen his hold on Silviana…"

"What she's trying to say is, you'll have to damn well trust me." Tytus moves forward, staring at me from his six-feet-plus frame. "So?"

I glance at Lucrezia, then Ștefan. He's uncharacteristically quiet. "Fine. But I'll bring her out here."

A few moments later, I'm back outside, Silviana under my arm. Tytus glances at her, then me. "I'll need you to remove your arm off her so I can read her aura properly."

I scowl, but do as he asks, even if everything inside of me screams at the action.

"I thought zmei only have access to elemental magic," Ștefan says.

Tytus grunts. "Among other things. We also have access to primordial magic—spirit, too. Now shush."

"We're not children," I mutter. "I, for one, have lived hundreds of years."

Tytus glares at me. "And I have lived millennia. We can keep comparing dick sizes, or you can let me help your mate. Which will it be, vampir?"

I look away, silently giving my consent.

Silviana

I feel like I'm living in a fog. If Vlad touches me, or speaks to me, his touch and voice grounds me. Anyone else? It comes and goes. Even Fane. I'm dimly aware of his presence, of his concern. I wish I could tell him why I did what I did—and ask him why he's able to be here, without the Dacians on his ass?

But I can't.

I can't do much else other than try to make it through the fog.

Because...he's there.

Zalmoxis.

I feel his presence like a leech. Sucking on my energy, my magic, everything he can reach. Our stories said he was imprisoned, but he doesn't feel imprisoned in my mind. He feels free, and like he's enjoying this all too much.

A chance to hurt the Dracul lineage? Why would I not enjoy it, beautiful Lana?

I shudder at his voice in my head. *Stop, stop, STOP! Just leave me alone!*

Dark laughter is his only answer. At first. And then he whispers, *I will never let you go.*

More shivers rack my spine. I've tried everything, shoving against him, thinking spells, but no amount of any magic I do will keep him away. He's a god. And what gods want, they get. Unfortunately for me, it seems Zalmoxis wants my mind.

I was stupid to try to reach the darkness, to try to outdo the Dacians. I didn't know what I was inviting, and as a result, I fucked myself over—and Vlad. And our bond.

The result is I live in a state of almost suspended animation. Vlad's touch brings me back to life, like when he comes inside the cabin we're in and says help is here. I follow him blindly outside, into the cool weather. His arm is around me, keeping me steady and rooted...protected.

But the moment Vlad's arm falls from my shoulders, darkness lingers at the edges of my consciousness. It's demanding, aggressive, wanting more. Zalmoxis reels in anger, and that anger bursts through me.

I see a hand reach out for me—try to swat it away. It grips my wrist.

Zalmoxis roars in my head, speaking a language I cannot understand. Each word feels like a flogging of my mind. A moan escapes me, a tortured cry.

"You're hurting her," someone says.

I know that voice. But...

"I'm not. Let me do this."

Something touches my forehead, and I catch the sizzle of magic. And then it's everywhere—on my skin, in my mind. Darkness rebels, trying to dig into me. Zalmoxis roars louder. His desperation claws at me, tears into me. I feel like my insides are being torn apart. Like I'm becoming nothing, untethered.

Am I falling? I must be falling. No one can sustain this much pain. And live.

In the distance, I think I hear my brother calling out. Then another voice... Vlad.

But darkness is more compelling, eating at me, demanding more—and then light. Light bursts through every edge of my consciousness, razor sharp. I cry out in pain, but also in deliverance.

And when I open my eyes again, there is no darkness. Just Vlad's arms wrapped around me, Fane's hand on my shoulder, and a familiar man facing me with a bemused gray gaze.

Even as I try to put a name to the face, I'm being pulled into a sweet, normal, slumber.

Vlad

When Silviana drops into my arms, I want nothing more than to strangle Tytus. Ştefan rushes to me, helping me with her, though he shouldn't have bothered. I know he just wants to make sure she's okay—but is she really?

Together, we bring Silviana back inside the cabin. Ştefan pushes away the hair on her forehead, and drops his forehead to her hand. I know this is a sibling moment, and I leave them to it. They have a much healthier relationship than I do with my siblings, and on some level, it hurts seeing it.

The moment I'm outside, I notice we've lost another person— Lucrezia.

I arch an eyebrow toward Tytus. "Did you eat her, or something?"

"Funny," he says sardonically. "The zmei legends are rooted in *some* truth, I suppose, but it's been a while since I've eaten a young maiden."

"Good to know."

We stare at each other. After a beat, he looks at the cabin. "How is she?"

"I should think that *I'd* be the one asking you this."

"Fair point."

He moves to a few feet away from the cabin, and draws a rune in the air. A moment later, a fire starts in the pile of wood. I stare at it for a beat, recalling a time, long ago, when Father had mastered dark magic.

"Tell me it worked?"

"It did, in so far as it *can* work." Before I can ask what he means, Tytus asks, "How well do you know the history of your name?"

I arch an eyebrow. "If you're trying to get to the fact that my name—Vlad—is like my father's name.... Been there. It's why I always figured he chose me."

"That isn't what I meant," Tytus says.

Huh? My blank expression must communicate the same, because he flashes a tired smile. "Your family name, little vampir. Dracul."

"Da, it means the devil. Everyone knows that."

"It also has a different meaning." When I don't supply it, he adds, "Dragon."

My jaw works and I find my mind sluggish. "What are you getting at, exactly?"

"Vlad Țepeș's lineage doesn't only have influence on vampiri and wolves. It also has ties to dragons. To zmei. To...my kind."

"Impossible! He was born well after your time."

"He was. But the fire of the dragon coursed through him. It's why Zalmoxis thought he'd be perfect to protect his daughter."

"But he wasn't—he—"

Tytus simply watches me as I try to make sense of this new twist. Is that true? Was Father targeted because of his lineage? And if so, what about us? What made him choose us...? Did he do it knowing that it would come to this, or are we an unfortunate collateral, too?

Tytus stands, running a hand through his hair. "I must return home. In answer to your question, Silviana is not all right. She will not be, until Zalmoxis is defeated. But due to her link to him, she may be your way into his mind."

I close my eyes, not wanting to think of ever having to use her that way.

"For the moment, she will be all right. I've put barriers in her mind designed to keep Zalmoxis out, which should work. Temporarily, at least. Keep her away from your siblings, and Zalmoxis might lose interest." His expression darkens.

"You don't think he will though, do you?"

"No. I think we've stepped into a war far above our heads, and we'll need all the help we can get."

"More help than from zmei who've been extinct?"

"A hell of a lot more."

An hour later, Tytus is gone—his zmeu transformation is something I'll never get out of my mind. One moment I was facing the man, and the next, I was facing the dragon beast ready to take my head off. I'd never been so aware of my mortality as I was in that moment.

Still shaken, I'm contemplating our conversation, when Ştefan exits the cabin and joins me by the fire.

"I don't understand how he was able to do what none of us could."

Ştefan turns in the direction of my voice. "You would if you had our knowledge."

"What, about zmei? I know about as much as you do. Probably less. They're creatures of myths."

Ştefan snorts. "As are you, technically."

"I'm right here, in flesh and blood."

"And so is he."

I shake my head. "But zmei were destroyed."

"Or so the legend goes. That they became too arrogant, that the gods turned against them, used immortals to kill them off. Or, to sway the fates. But reality is, it's not true. The Cavaleri Serafim tried." At my blank expression, he adds, "You do know about them, no?"

I shake my head.

Ştefan says, "They were a branch of zealot knights, given magical powers to specifically kill zmei. Their order—the Order of the Cavaleri Serafim—has been around for as long as zmei. They hunted them for that long, too, with magic. They always have a dark mage, a necromancer with them, who uses zmei bones from previous victims to attack living zmei."

A shudder runs through me. "That's disgusting."

"It is, but it worked for a long time. The Serafim used to track zmei by drinking the blood of one, cementing their connection to them, and thus allowing them to follow wherever—through portals, even."

"I don't understand. How do you know all this, if Silviana didn't?"

It might be a trick of the flames, but Ștefan seems annoyed. Then his words clue me in as to why. "The Dacian philosophy is that the men should be taught everything, and the women only what is necessary. They're kept away on purpose." After a beat, he adds, "When I went back, I was able to dive into more information on the zmei, and thus found this bit about the Serafim. I guess you could say these knights are about as devoted as the hunters who tried to get you."

I frown. "Are you implying they're related?"

Ștefan shakes his head and moves with unerring accuracy to sit on a boulder. "Not implying. It's the truth."

I glance at the cabin, where Silviana is resting now. And then I move toward her brother, drawn in despite myself by the story he's so eager to tell.

"Once upon a time, the Serafim were proper knights. Until they became warped, demanding to kill anything supernatural."

"And they went after the zmei?"

"Da...and nu." He picks up a stick and draws a circle, then a line in the middle.

"It amazes me the things you do when you're blind. I'm assuming you lost your sight young?"

Ștefan stares toward the flames—he must sense the heat—for a long moment, before saying, "I lost my sight the same night we lost our parents. The attack was brutal, not that I remember much of it, even now. All I know is when I came to, darkness became my friend, in more ways than one."

"You mean, because of the magic?"

"Da…and nu. Since I lost my sight, my magic seems to have become enhanced, for lack of a better word. Liviu himself told me I'm more powerful than most Dacians under his command." He gives a one-shouldered shrug. "It makes me different from them—being both blind and powerful. And Liviu has had to invest in certain technologies to make life easier for me. But despite it all, none of my so-called power stops my peers from underestimating me. I've gotten used to it."

"Underestimate you?" I let out a short, stunned laugh. "You were able to find your way in a battle, in the middle of unfamiliar woods, with various attackers nearby."

There's another beat of hesitation, then, "It's because I saw you."

I frown, though he can't see it, and wait for an explanation.

"People I'm connected to, whether by choice or not, they emit a glow. It's not seeing, nowhere close to it. More like a fog of light in the midst of a sea of darkness. But when I focus on it, I've noticed I'm able to pinpoint their location better. It comes in handy during battles like the one I was part of. Not that I get to practice much since, most of the time, Liviu keeps me away."

And yet he hadn't this time, knowing he needed his strongest weapon to get Silviana back—and eradicate me. My palms sting, and it takes me a moment to realize I've been clenching my fists so hard that the nails have dug into and broken the skin.

Ştefan chuckles at my silence. "I've learned not to let my limitations define me, vampir. As have you, in a way. As has my sister, even in a coven where women are easily dismissed. Every barrier can be broken, it only takes the will to do so." He taps the stick in the circle, then cuts it in half. "Now, back to what I was saying. Half of the Serafim went after zmei. And they grew and grew. The other half continued to be soldiers, until they ran into vampiri." He looks in my direction. "By the time your father's time came, they were well versed in the art of killing you."

"But that's not possible. The hunters we've met, they've always been isolated."

"Da, isolated. Because they believe themselves to be isolated. But a big part of why they're able to transfer knowledge from generation to generation, is because of their invisible masters."

"And who are those?"

Ștefan shrugs. "That is where my knowledge ends. Based on your father's journal, Silviana and I theorized it might be the Dacians themselves."

"So you're saying it's not just the clans coming after us, but these hunters... Like what we saw in the woods. They were pairing up with vampiri, to take us out."

"Unheard of," Ștefan says. "It's abhorrent to think of the two factions working together for one goal."

"And yet, they are."

He inclines his head. "It's my belief that's how the other royals— in other regions, outside of here—ended up eradicated. Not through the joined efforts of clans trying to dethrone them, but through hunters who banded together in one common goal."

I think back to Silva, and Liza, and the shit they lived through— their torture at these monsters' hands. My fists clench on my knees. "I won't let any of them hurt my family. Nor your sister."

Ștefan arches an eyebrow. "And are you prepared to do anything?"

"Yes."

"Even stay away? Let your family deal with their own shit?"

I don't even have to think about it. The choice is simple. "Yes."

"Good. Because Tytus is correct—Silviana can't be around your siblings. There's no telling what Zalmoxis will do now that he got in her head. And until he's defeated…you have to keep her interactions with your siblings very short."

"I understand."

"Do you really? She gave up everything to be with you."

"And I will do the same."

He sighs.

I add, "What about you? What will you do?"

An odd expression crosses his features. "There's an artefact that can help Silviana and your siblings. It's with an oracle my people use. I plan to take it."

"Will it be freely given?"

"I don't care. For my sister, I'll cross whatever lines need to be crossed."

My gaze gets lost in the flames. I get that. I would do the same for my siblings.

The fight is getting harder. The enemies are multiplying. And I'll have to sit out of a few fights, like Violeta. But I'll make damned sure it won't be forever. After all, our fight against Zalmoxis, and our success are now completely intertwined with Silviana's future. And mine. In more ways than one.

Ştefan nods and waves his hand, as if shooing me away. "Go be with her. I'll keep watch."

I listen to him and head back to the cabin. Silviana turns in bed toward me, and opens her arms without a word. I join her in the blankets, enjoying the warmth of her body, the steady thrum of her pulse. This quiet is all we need, for now. I will protect her and the rest of my family with my life if it comes to it.

When I jerk awake what feels like moments later, I know something's wrong. My first thought is for Silviana—but she's asleep against me.

I listen to the outside—all quiet. Not even a crackle from the flames, it's all gone. And when I slip out from her embrace to check, so is her brother.

Chapter 26

Silviana

I wake up, stretching against a hard body. My eyes fly open—the darkness, it's gone!

"Easy..."

My body freezes. I wait for the whispers, the coaxing, the laughing. But there's...nothing. I reach into my mind, waiting for Zalmoxis to pounce—still nothing. No dread in my stomach. No shudders racking my spine.

I turn in Vlad's embrace, feeling a smile stretch my lips for the first time in what feels like forever. "Vlad, it worked! Whatever the zmeu did, I... I don't feel Zalmoxis anymore!"

It takes me a second to realize he's not quite as happy as I'd expected. And a different kind of dread fills me.

"What happened?"

He hesitates, then says, "It's Ștefan. He's gone."

I shake my head, refusing to believe the words. Stubbornly, I toss the blankets off me and run outside, yelling for him. But Vlad's right... Fane's gone.

When I turn to Vlad, I can't hold back my tears. "He wouldn't just leave me. He wouldn't!"

He pulls me against his chest, ignoring my fists flying against him, and holds me close. "I know. But he said he's got to find something, something that can help you. And, for now, we have to figure out a way to protect ourselves, too."

His tone has me pull back. "What do you mean?"

He tucks a strand of hair behind my ear. "Tytus' tricks may have worked for now, but they won't last forever."

I gulp, staring at him for answers. My earlier happiness evaporates.

As if sensing it, Vlad moves closer, cupping my cheek. "Iubito, I'm sorry. I wish it was that simple, but it's not. Tytus warned we'll have to keep you away from my siblings, for the time being. Zalmoxis still has a way in."

Tears fill my eyes. "First Fane, and now I have to lose you?"

"No!" He moves closer, cupping both my cheeks now as he forces my gaze onto his. "I will *never* leave you, Silviana. Not unless you ask me to, and even then... I still won't. "

"I don't understand."

He kisses my forehead, then my eyelids, then my lips. "I'm here, with you. We'll stay away from my siblings—and, in a way, it might be better." At my confused expression, he adds, "For too long, we've held back. Hidden in the shadows. I think it's time we take back our throne, and teach the vampiri that they cannot fuck with the House of Dracul. But when my siblings go do that, it'll cause...ripples. Perhaps it's best we stay away, for our own sake—and theirs."

My heart thuds harder against my chest. It was bound to happen. The Draculs have been pushed too far, and even the nicer ones like Vlad have had enough. I remember Liza's words, and Alex's behavior. They've been held back like hounds bound with leashes, and now, they'll be allowed to do their worst.

Dacians, my own people, were among those who stood against them. And they will be punished. But does this mean it'll force the vampiri to come out of the shadows? All I can hope is that it won't. Because I don't want to lose Vlad, and, oddly, any of them.

I glance over at the forest, at wherever Fane disappeared. My brother wouldn't leave me alone, I know it in the bottom of my heart. But I also know he was conflicted. If he left—and that's a small if—of his own accord, he'll come back. And if he doesn't, I'll make sure to find him. But in the meantime, helping Vlad is where my energy needs to be redirected to. Because if the House of Dracul falls, we fall with it. All of us.

I think back to the darkness, to everything Tytus shoved away. I survived it all for a reason. And it's not so I can cower in fear. It's not so that I can simmer in indecision.

"That'll be dangerous," I finally whisper.

Vlad still doesn't let go of me. "I know. It will be more dangerous than anything else we've undertaken. And it will test the boundaries of right and wrong. Will you enter this new world with me, iubito? Because I swear to you, I will do everything in my power to protect you, and find Ștefan and bring him back to you. But I can't do this without you."

I gulp past my fear and cup his cheek. "I'm with you, always. I swear it."

A faint light escapes my palm, soon diffusing into his skin. Vlad's eyes shine a bright blue for a moment, then his smile is as blinding as the sun.

He leans over and kisses me—a promise. To forget the deceit, to embrace the future, and to always protect one another.

A promise I think we'll need.

Epilogue

Far away from the vampiri, in his little wolf village, Dominic leaned in an armchair. Lucrezia was on his lap, nuzzling his neck, and they were both enjoying a well-deserved quiet moment.

"Quite a fight we pulled," Dominic whispered. "I hope the vampiri don't make a habit of bringing us into their drama."

Lucrezia's chuckle resounded in the quiet room. "Would we ever deny them, dragul meu?"

It took all his skill not to roll his eyes. And then a knock sounded on the door, and he tensed.

"It's fine," Lucrezia whispered.

A moment later, the door swung open of its own and Tytus walked in.

Dominic snorted. "You actually grace us with your presence this time, not just messages?"

"The time for messages is over. A bigger fight is coming. I'd hoped with sending you here it might mitigate it, but it seems I've only made things worse."

"How, Tytus?"

"Well, for one, the gods are at odds. And for another, they now walk among us."

Lucrezia shared a look with her mate. "What's so dreadful about that?"

Tytus sighed and took a seat at the table, facing them. "Let me tell you a story about a god who did something so heinous, he had to be put away... Not killed, but imprisoned, forever living in limbo. And how he dragged a certain vampir king with him out of vengeance..."

The war for the throne begins with book 4, Liza's story! Sinful Salvation will be available in late 2022, but **you can pre-order it now.**

And if you enjoyed Vlad and Silviana's story, please consider leaving a review at your choice of retailer. Even a line or two makes a huge difference to an indie author!

Have you read them all?

ROGUES EXTENDED UNIVERSE – READING ORDER

Moonlight Rogues

Flaming Rogues

Immortal Rogues

Lost Royals of Transylvania

Vârcolac Legacy (coming 2022)

LOVE MY BOOKS?

Want to get your hands on them and review them first, before anyone else?

Sign up for my ARC team now

And you'll get to read and review everything first....

Including the next *Lost Royals of Transylvania* **novel!**

Vampires, sibling rivalries and mysteries continue.

ABOUT THE AUTHOR

Alexa Whitewolf is a fiction writer, newspaper columnist of daily issues and author of the critically acclaimed *Moonlight Rogues* shifter series.

Alexa has been a lifelong writer and first began creating other worlds and characters at the ripe age of 12. Growing up in the Transylvania region surrounded by epic mountains and a never-ending stream of legends and stories was bound to create an overactive imagination. This shines through Ms. Whitewolf's writing by creating worlds filled with unique folklore, life wisdom and plenty of furry creatures.

An avid traveler, Alexa writes under a penname and spends her days between an office job and writing in Canada's capital, when she's not flying somewhere with lush landscapes and plenty of hiking trails.

Her series focus on strong heroines, kind yet sexy men, fights of good and evil and the never-ending learning curve of humanity's strong—and weak—points. Romanian folklore is intertwined with her writing, more notably in her shifter romance series, the Moonlight Rogues. Her other series draw on world mythology, such as the Avalon myth and Arthurian legend (*The Avalon Chronicles*) and Ancient Egypt (*The Sage's Legacy*).

You can follow her blog at www.alexawhitewolf.com/blog or on social media. Her column in Observatorul also tackles various issues, including health, technology, and a writer's life.

If you want up to date releases, make sure you sign up for her newsletter. For new releases notifications, you can also follow her on Amazon and BookBub

Also by the Author

Rogues Extended Universe

Moonlight Rogues series
Moonlight Rogues: Origins
First to Fall
Second to Surrender
Third to Tumble
Last to Love

Flaming Rogues series
Fanning the Flames
Igniting the Ice

Immortal Rogues series
Secret Shadows
Archer's Arrow
Cat's Charms
Trickster's Trap
Fickle Fate

Lost Royals of Transylvania series
Immortal Illusion
Cracked Casualty
Deadly Deceit
Blind Burden
Angry Addiction
Primal Protection

Demoni Sancti Extended Universe

Standalone
Blazing Ashes

Demoni Sancti series
Fallen
Broken
Unshackled
Risen
Ascended

The Avalon Chronicles series
Avalon Dreams
Avalon Wishes
Avalon Nightmares
Atrox

The Sage's Legacy – YA series
The Dragon Medallion
The Dragon Manuscript
Relics of the Underworld

Standalone novels
Blood Ties, Love Binds
Unconditional Love

www.ingramcontent.com/pod-product-compliance
Lightning Source LLC
Chambersburg PA
CBHW060410030726
47495CB00003B/509